The Long-Ai

BOOK 2

THE GOLDEN CORD

JON HOPKINS | THOMAS HOPKINS

The Golden Cord

Copyright © 2019 Jon Hopkins and Thomas Hopkins. All rights reserved. No part of this book may be reproduced or retransmitted in any form or by any means without the written permission of the publisher.

Published by Wheatmark®
2030 East Speedway Boulevard, Suite 106
Tucson, Arizona 85719 USA
www.wheatmark.com

ISBN: 978-1-62787-676-6 (paperback)
ISBN: 978-1-62787-677-3 (hardcover)
ISBN: 978-1-62787-678-0 (ebook)
LCCN: 2019905961

Bulk ordering discounts are available through Wheatmark, Inc. For more information, email orders@wheatmark.com or call 1-888-934-0888.

Dedication

Jon—To my gorgeous second-blessing wife, Valorie. "Her eyes, the color of a puddle reflecting the blue sky after a noon day's passing rain, twinkle when she laughs."

Tom—To my lovely wife, Diana, who brings color to my life. "She stopped and picked a red poppy and placed it playfully on the tip of her nose. She put the flower in her hair, winked at him, and skipped lightly on her way."

Acknowledgments

Heart of America Christian Writer's Network for support and grueling critique: www.hacwn.org.

Diana Hopkins and Aubuchon Photographic for beautiful assistance in cover photography and support: https://www.facebook.com/aubuchonphotographic.

Deane Pennington as our sensational seamstress.

Grael Norton for lending us a hand and putting his heart into our novel.

Signs of Life Bookstore in Lawrence, Kansas, for providing a comfortable place to dream: http://www.signsoflifebooks.com/

Trace Willhite for being our adventurous cover model.

Our many beta readers for excellent feedback. Publishers and editors at Wheatmark Publishing.

The Long-Aimed Blow on Facebook:
https://www.facebook.com/thelongaimedblow/.

Our webpages:
www.jonhopkins.org and www.thelong-aimedblow.com.

You can download the app for the game Latrunculi from Google Play, iPhone, or iTunes.

"It's all part of the adventure."

List of Characters

Alexenah (Ah-LEX-eh-naw): the kind Jewish mother of Jachin and Boaz.

Amminus (Ah-MEE-noos): the brave eldest son of Cunobelinos.

Aulus Plautius (Ah-luss Plow-tee-oos): brutal commander of the Roman forces invading Albion.

Boaz (BOH-az): the identical twin brother of Jachin. Thinks without acting.

Caedmon (KAYD-mon): a tribal leader and friend of Amminus.

Caoimhe (Kay-OH-mee): the loving wife of Togodumnus.

Caradoc (Kah-RAD-uhk): the youngest son of Cunobelinos. Ambitious high king of Albion.

Cartimandua (Kar-ti-man-DOO-ah): queen of the Brigantes. Mother of Raena.

Tiberius Claudius Caesar Augustus Germanicus (Ty-BEER-ee-oos Klaw-DEE-oos KY-sar Ah-GOOS-toos Grr-MAN-ee-coos): disabled fourth emperor of Rome.

Cunobelinos (Koo-noh-bell-EE-noos): the son of Tasciovaunus; father of Amminus, Togodumnus, and Caradoc. He ruled the combined tribes of Albion from AD 10 to AD 40.

List of Characters

Diona Granni (Dy-OH-nah GRAN-nye): Lais's grandmother and baker of pies.

Epaticus (Eh-PAT-ee-koos): the youngest son of Tasciovaunus.

Epos (EP-ahs): large man with a big heart.

Fergus (FUR-goos): "The Strong"; tribal leader of Albion and friend of Amminus.

Fetch (Fetch): the gregarious barkeeper at the Boar's Head Inn.

Gaius Julius Callistus (GUY-uhs YUL-ee-oos Cah-LEES-toos): Greek imperial freedman during the reigns of Roman emperors Gaius and Claudius. Adviser and physician.

Gaius Julius Caesar Augustus Germanicus aka Caligula (Kuh-li-GOO-lah): third emperor of Rome.

Gladys (GLA-diss): daughter of Mara and Caradoc.

Grael (GRAY-el): simple farmer.

Jachin (JAY-kin): the identical twin brother of Boaz. Acts without thinking.

Joseph (JOH-seph): known as Tinman. Merchant who resides in western Albion.

Kendal (KEN-doll): a tribal leader, farmer, poet, and bard.

Kenjar (KEN-Jar): conniving high druid of Albion.

Lais (LAY-ees): Batavii maid. Helps physicians.

Loukas (LU-kahs): the beloved physician in Ephesus.

Mara (MAHR-uh): once a barfly, now wife of Caradoc.

Marcus Marcus Caelus (MAR-koos MAR-koos KY-loos): Trierarchus of the Roman trireme Morta Columbarium.

Narcissus (Nar-SISS-oos): freedman adviser and interpreter to Claudius.

List of Characters

Odedicus (Oh-DEAD-ee-koos): Roman oarsman on the Morta Columbarium.

Paulus (PAH-oo-loos): Christian teacher and scholar in Ephesus.

Phoebe (FEE-bee): Nurse and benefactor.

Primus (PRY-moos): the frolicking first dog of Jachin and Boaz.

Raena (RAY-nah): Cartimandua's perky, spirited daughter.

Rego (RAY-goh): landlord's son. Lives down a hill in a deep furrow in southern Albion.

Rufus of Ephesus (ROO-foos): assistant in Loukas's clinic, aspires to be a physician.

Scribonius Largus (Skry-BONE-ee-oos LAR-goos): a prolific writer of pithy sayings.

Servius Sulpicius Galba (Sir-VEE-oos Sul-PIK-ee-oos GAL-bah): exacting commander and trainer of Roman legionnaires.

Sophronios Demetrios Alkimopoulos (So-FRON-ee-oos De-MEET-ree-oos Al-kee-MOP-ooh-loos): caring Greek physician.

Tasciovaunus (Task-ee-oh-VAH-noos): the high king of Albion; father of Cunobelinos and Epaticus. He ruled the combined tribes of Albion from 20 BC to AD 10.

Teague (Teeg): a roof thatcher and tribal leader. Amminus's friend.

Tiberius Claudius Nero (Ty-BEER-i-oos Klaw-DEE-oos NEE-row): Roman emperor from AD 14 to AD 37.

Toenin (TOW-nin): the short, prideful son of Broc.

Togodumnus (Tog-oh-DOOM-noos): the middle son of Cunobelinos.

Verica (VER-ee-kah): former king of the Atrebates in southern Albion.

1
CHAPTER

Diminished

*That moment when ranked as a mere child,
we become attached to the shrinking of our dreams,
and the theft of our freedom.*

— Scribonius Largus

AD 15—Camulodunon, Albion

"*This will be great!*"

Caradoc urged the purloined pony to a majestic trot. He rode past workers gathered beside a bridge leading to a half-finished grand hall he called Grandfather's Folly.

A man dressed in a farmer's faded brown tunic and plaid *braccae* handed a child to a woman whose curly red hair matched the infant's. "That's my horse! He's taken my horse."

She hugged the child close. "Husband! Isn't he the one we were talking about?"

The Golden Cord

Caradoc circled.

Brushing dust from her blue dress, a gray-haired woman said, "Stubborn, insolent boy." She pulled her shawl tight around her shoulders. "Will we ever be safe from his mischief?"

"Good morrow to you, Grael." Caradoc bowed deeply with a flourish. "And to you, ma'am."

"You stole my horse!"

"Aye, I have." He laughed. "I will continue to harass you and your friends until you—"

Grael grabbed for the ropes. "Why?"

With a smile on his face, Caradoc answered. "Because I can."

"You're scarcely old enough to grow a beard," screamed the old woman.

"I will have this land." He backed his pony and leaned forward. "It will be mine, if I have to steal it from you one pig-eyed horse and bowlegged cow at a time."

"I won't let you do it. Your grandfather Tasciovaunus will not allow it. When he gets ahold of you—"

Caradoc pivoted the pony and galloped down the road. "No one can stop me."

Grael leapt on his horse and pursued at full speed along the narrow road that curved beside the river. The others mounted and joined the race.

As they reached a bend at the base of the hill, Grael dashed up alongside. He stretched.

Caradoc turned to Grael and grinned. He twisted the reins short to the right. Grael shouted in surprise as the thief plunged down the steep bank and into the icy river with a splash. His steed shied and reared high into the air, but Caradoc held on.

The pursuer's horse slid down the hill and collided with the stolen mare. Grael leaped at Caradoc, seized him by his shoulders, and dragged him from his horse. Pulling Caradoc's sword from its sheath, the farmer threw it into the water.

Like two cats hung over a line by their tails tied together, the two men fought.

A quick-fisted backhand from Caradoc broke the man's nose.

The older man tripped Caradoc and shoved him below the current.

Caradoc groped and flailed until his hand chanced upon a rock in the riverbed. Whacking Grael on the side of the head, he knocked him unconscious.

Caradoc coughed. Gagged. He vomited water as he spewed curses. "I acquired this horse. Many others. I'll do as I please. I am Caradoc!" He hacked. "I am the prince of Albion!"

Others watched as Caradoc dragged the dazed Grael up the opposite shore. He lifted Grael by his tunic and placed the man's neck into the crook of the elbow where dangling muscular limbs of a twisted Carpinus tree branched.

Struggling to breathe, Grael held himself up by his arms. The branches tightened around his neck with every writhing move.

"Don't go anywhere," Caradoc snarled. He punched the man in the stomach, then marched against the current to retrieve his weapon and the pony. Once on shore, he shook his blade tauntingly toward the crowd.

No one moved.

Caradoc paced.

Grael sucked in air.

"*Yeaagg Cuno Caradoc!*" The long blade sliced in a broad arc and severed the man's hand at the wrist. He kicked the severed hand into the river.

Gagging among staccato screams, Grael removed his belt and wrapped his arm to stop the gushing blood.

Caradoc leaned in and hissed through his teeth, "I will build my hillfort on *your* property." Squatting low on the sand—sword on his knees—he glared at the assembly on the shore.

A man astride a black war steed cut through the crowd and thrust into the river. He stopped halfway. "Let him down!"

"What are you doing here, Grandfather?"

The man pushed the warhorse forward and touched his sword. "Cut the man down, you dim-witted child!"

The Golden Cord

Caradoc hesitated.

More warriors breached the hill.

Caradoc grunted. Swinging his sword, he sliced through the branch close to Grael's neck.

Grael tumbled to his knees. Holding his mangled arm tight to his chest, he rose and raced to the other bank.

The high king, Tasciovaunus, and his men crossed to where Caradoc stood.

About to be publicly castigated, Caradoc scoffed. He doused his grandfather's hot gaze in the water of his tempered pride as he reluctantly sheathed his sword. It didn't matter. Punishment meant nothing to him anymore.

"How many men have you killed?"

Caradoc glowered.

"I have slaughtered hundreds!" Tasciovaunus said. "They weren't half-senseless drunks or half-drowned farmers. They were strong warriors worthy of the fight. Every life means something, boy. Every soul has a purpose." He paused. "When I was your age, I led men into battle against the Trinovantes. I had a wife, a hillfort, and responsibilities. I cared about my brothers. Because I serve the people, they serve me." With a slap on the rump, he sent the stolen pony galloping across the river. "I didn't find it necessary to kill or bully."

Caradoc sneered.

"If you continue down this course—the road before you will only be paved with the deaths of men who won't follow you. Can't win love through threats, boy. Men follow me because I show purpose. What is your purpose, grandson?"

He'd heard it before. He didn't care. He turned to leave.

Tasciovaunus clutched Caradoc's shoulder and turned him around. "I'm talking to you!"

"I have my own purpose." Caradoc spat.

"Right now your *purpose* is to follow me, and do as I say."

Caradoc opened his mouth to argue as the king's warriors stepped forward.

His grandfather slapped him. "All I want to hear from you is your consent."

Caradoc swallowed hard. "Yes, sir."

Diminished

Walking to his steed, Tasciovaunus raised his hand to halt his men. He retrieved a battle-ax from his pack. "You like to cut off limbs?" He tossed the weapon to his grandson. "How are you with an ax?"

Caradoc caught the implement by the handle and spun it with a flourish.

His grandfather pointed to the tree where Caradoc had suspended Grael. "I have need of the Carpinus."

"The hornbeam?"

"Up the tree—if you can climb—and start shearing the limbs. Start at the crown and proceed down to the crotch. Keep it straight. It will be used for my throne in the new longhouse."

Caradoc nodded and turned toward the tree, grumbling under his breath.

"One you will never sit on," Tasciovaunus added.

Unsheathing his sword, Caradoc laid it against a rock. Biting his tongue, he grasped the limb that had held Grael and climbed the Carpinus tree.

Footholds and handholds were difficult to find. Halfway up, Caradoc reached high for another limb and missed. He plummeted to the ground with a thud. The ax landed near his head.

"You idiot. Can't you do anything?" His grandfather grasped Caradoc by the arm in a twisting grip. "Get back up there, you little runt!"

The warriors laughed.

With the ax stabbed into his belt, Caradoc climbed the tree once more. When he reached the crown, he tied his belt around the trunk.

He swung the ax. Not getting a clean cut on the dense wood, he wrapped his legs to steady himself and swung the ax again. This time the ax found its mark. Three more blows and the branch came free. The severed limb fell next to where the warriors spread out a lunch for the king.

The king spat out his food. "Foolish child. Toss it in the river."

With each successive cut, Caradoc envisioned his grandfather's neck. He tossed the branches into the water. They floated like dead bodies, bobbing down the river toward

The Golden Cord

their final resting places. Some caught on rocks, and a few bunched up together, holding on to each other.

When Caradoc finished cutting all the limbs, he came down and stood sweating before his grandfather. "I'm done."

"Oh, you're not finished yet. Fell the tree. My men will do the bucking. I don't trust you to cut it to the correct size. Next we move to the Andreadsweld. You will join us there when you finish here."

Caradoc growled. He wiped sweat from his thin moustache and set to chopping. Most of the people left. The warriors and Tasciovaunus vacated too. With each stroke, Caradoc cursed his grandfather's name. A few final notches and the tree fell.

"Yaeee-uggh!"

The ax dropped.

Then he remembered the day wasn't over. "Bull's breath!"

Retrieving his sword, he headed toward the ancient forest, ax in hand. He found his grandfather and his men hard at work felling the tall pines.

Tasciovaunus tossed a pair of climbing spikes to Caradoc. "About time you arrived!"

"What are these for?"

"Put them on your ankles, dimwit! You'll top-cut the trees."

Caradoc strapped them on his ankles as others had done.

"Keep cutting, men. We need to finish this before rain arrives—and watch out for that foolish runt in the treetops. He couldn't pee in a bucket without someone's help."

Caradoc seized the ax and followed his grandfather to the tallest pine tree. The climbing spikes stuck in the soil as he walked.

"This time you'll not cut off the limbs. Go to about fifteen feet from the crown and cut it off. That's where its circumference will best match the base. Tie the rope to it so the crown will safely fall without breaking the long trunk we need for the grand hall. We will delimb the portion you cut and fell the tree at the foot," the high king said.

"While I'm still up there?"

Tasciovaunus tossed a long rope to Caradoc. "No, boy."

"What am I to do with this?"

"Use the rope and spikes to help you climb the tree like that man is doing over there." Tasciovaunus pointed to another clansman climbing deftly up a nearby pine. "Then harness yourself and use the rest of the line to drop the crown. Once you've finished your cut, rope the nearest tree and swing over to it. Cut its top off. Keep going to the next, and the next, until it gets dark. Hope the rain stays away. It makes the bark slippery. I wouldn't want to be up there."

Caradoc found the climbing easier with the rope and the spikes once he became used to them. He grudgingly left his sword behind, setting it carefully against a tree stump. It would get in the way. Once he reached the crown, he used the rope to harness himself to the tree and set to work with the ax. Safely lowering the detached section, he used the line to lasso the next tree and swing over. As his skill improved, he began to enjoy himself.

The clouds above darkened.

Atop the fourth tree, a gust of wind struck with such a force that Caradoc could barely hold on. "Great Borrum's beard!" He dropped the ax.

Thunder ripped the murky heavens. Icy rain pelted him unmercifully. He lashed the rope tighter around the trunk and fastened himself as best as he could. The tree swayed and whipped Caradoc around as he held on for dear life. Back and forth and around. His stomach lurched. Branches of other trees slapped his arms and legs. The branches tore his tunic. He ducked his head and held strong.

Crack! An ancient pine broke two-thirds of the way up and crashed to the ground. Other trees began losing limbs as the wind surged through the forest.

Caradoc ducked his head and turned his thoughts inward, where another storm raged. The derision and insults of his grandfather buffeted him. He knew exactly where the wind originated. How it moved his soul to bitterness. Threatening to explode, it desired to vent and release.

"Yeaagg Cuno Caradoc!" he screamed into the furious storm.

The squall stopped as suddenly as it had begun, but

his inner rage lingered. As he swayed, the tempest inside him finally shaped itself to his will. He groaned. He untied the rope and let it fall. It tangled in the detached treetops below. There were no men. They must have seen the storm coming and left long before the downpour. No one warned him.

He eased to the ground and collected his sword and ax. With purpose, he headed toward Camulodunon.

⌘ ⌘ ⌘

Though the new longhouse stood half-finished amid construction, Caradoc entered. Rain bled down his mud-soaked face.

His grandfather stood with his back to him at the end of the hall.

With each stomp into the great room, Caradoc punched holes into the new oak floor with the spikes he still wore. A trail of muck followed.

"Grandfather."

Tasciovaunus crooked around. "What are you doing? Get those things off your feet. Get back out there and finish your work!"

Caradoc glared.

"Are you deaf? I said go—"

The ax flew from Caradoc's hand, cutting deep into the pristine oak at Tasciovaunus's feet.

"Childish!"

Caradoc turned his back to his grandfather and trudged toward the door. The scraping tree spikes sounded like raven's cries. He stopped at the grand doorway. Removing the spikes, he dropped them to the floor. Caradoc roared, "I quit!" and walked out.

2
CHAPTER

Predicament

*Great harm is remembered in marble.
Honor is written in the dust.*

— Scribonius Largus

AD 34—Caradoc's Hillfort, Camulodunon, Albion

The biggest dog in the room was Caradoc. He paid attention to her, told her she made him feel alive, could be himself with her, and said she'd be his wife. To her, it was a game to garner Caradoc's love. It was part of Caradoc's path to the throne and the high kingship to which he now held title. She was going to be his queen.

At Mara's feet lay the body of a dark-haired woman. To the left, a second victim—a young boy, not but twelve summers old. Blood covered the dirt floor of Caradoc's roundhouse.

The Golden Cord

Mara was not innocent. She understood and was complicit in the death of Cunobelinos. She had delivered the poison asp to Caradoc's father herself. He said the snakebite would only enfeeble Cunobelinos—not kill. It was all a pack of lies.

His uncle Epaticus was dead. Caradoc probably orchestrated that as well. Everyone died around that man. His eldest brother, Amminus, was exiled. But . . . she surveyed the room . . . to eliminate his slave wife and children? What did that achieve? He could have exiled the twins and their mother as well.

She bit her lip. "He is good to me."

Finding an old green cloak on the floor, she wrapped the body.

"Caradoc promised me." He assured her of the fulfillment of her desires—different than the other men's pledges of love. Queen? A better title than lover she supposed. He referred to her as "maid"—a title, not a name. Certainly not one of endearment.

The body was difficult to lift. So, best she could, Mara dragged the wrapped form out of the roundhouse. Once over the threshold, the body slipped down in the covering, and the revealed heels plowed lines in the dust. Out of breath, Mara let the body lie and went to the barn to fetch a cart. When she returned, she positioned the form on the handcart and wheeled it down to the cattle barn next to the pigpen.

"Wait here, dear. I must finish the tasks your husband gave me." Mara turned and slipped on barn waste. She reached out to the cart to balance and clutched the body instead. An arm slumped from the cart toward the mess on the barn floor below, pointing.

Mara stared for a long time. Gently reaching down, she positioned the arm back into the cart. Mara clasped the delicate, cold hand—not unlike her own—and gave it a light tap before letting go.

"This brave woman deserves honor. People thought well of her. She never spoke evil of anyone. She was kind, even to me. Surely she knew about her husband's doings." Mara shuddered and put her fingers to her lips to cover an exclamation.

A heavily accented voice called at the gate of the hillfort. "Hello? Anyone at home?"

Wiping her hands on her dress, Mara ran out. Before her stood an elderly man—a merchant by his attire—and another man, presumably his slave, who stood head and shoulders above the tallest man she had ever seen.

The merchant bowed. "Excuse our intrusion, miss. I am Joseph, and this is my friend Epos."

"I am Mara." She gazed at the barn. "Caradoc's wife."

"Ah, I am a seller of metals and used to trade with Cunobelinos, the high king. I heard he was ill."

She wrapped her hands in her dress. "He's dead. Caradoc is king now."

"Hmm . . . and Caradoc's brother? I assumed Amminus was the eldest. Should he not be king?"

"Exiled."

Nodding his head, Joseph turned to leave. He stopped. "What of Alexenah? Is she around?"

Clasping her trembling hands together, Mara forced a grin. "I am the only one here."

"You look troubled. What is it? The king's death?"

"It's been a terrible night. We have been robbed. A thief killed Alexenah." Tears cascaded down her cheeks as she recited Caradoc's instructions. She wiped them with her sleeve.

"*Al ha-panim.*" Joseph shook his head. "And the twins?"

"Taken. Caradoc presumed they were to be held for ransom, or most likely sold to a slaver."

Joseph's eyebrows lowered. His mouth drew down to the side. Epos nodded.

She told them the story exactly as Caradoc made her rehearse it.

"Where is the body?"

Mara froze.

"Alexenah's body. You said she perished in the robbery. What will become of her remains?"

Glancing to the pigpen, she said, "Burial, I presume."

"May I take Alexenah with me?"

Her mouth quivered. She raised her eyebrows.

"It is all right. Alexenah was from my clan. I wish to bury her as is proper according to our custom."

"Very well." Somewhat reluctant, Mara escorted them to the barn. How could Caradoc fault her for letting these men take Alexenah? He told her to get rid of the body. He didn't say how.

Joseph lifted a corner of the old green cloak. "Poor child," he said.

Mara didn't know if he meant Alexenah or her.

Epos gently picked up the cloak-wrapped body.

"This is a kindness you do for us in this time of terror. We thank you. May the One God be as kind to you. Verily, blessing will come from your progeny."

As the two men walked out the gate, Mara ran to the back of the hillfort, where Caradoc kept the horses. "Go. Get out of here. Shoo!" The horses galloped out of the pen and down the back way to the woodlands. "If he asks, I will simply say I disposed of the trash as he demanded."

Out of breath, Mara watched a newborn soay lamb jump and play in a nearby pen. She placed a protective hand over her belly. "He doesn't know."

3
CHAPTER

Damaged

Flashes in the world of pain's memory are like ravens who fly to the dung heap to feed on unmerited torments.

— Scribonius Largus

Boaz woke. His mind jumped from one subject to the other as he lay on the floor of his father's roundhouse. He pushed his hair aside. It felt like dried mud on his forehead and cheek. A bitter taste and a strong earthy fragrance, reminiscent of the first plowed fields after the winter's cold, assuaged his dulled senses. Boaz shivered.

In the past, he and his brother collected stones that the *cas chrom* dug up after each plowed row. A new crop emerged every year.

"They're golden nuggets," Jachin said back then. "Let's see who can find the most."

They stationed the stones around the edge of the field, adding to the ancient stone wall. Exhaustion setting in, they sat against the wall, pleased with their riches.

Boaz's breath fogged that chilly morning, the memory frozen in his mind. As he exhaled, he marveled at how something invisible could turn into a fragile specter—plainly seen, yet not grasped—and then vanish. "Look, Jachin, I'm breathing fire!"

The hearth's warmth burned low with a popping that brought Boaz to the present. He found himself not in a field of golden stones or even a wheat field of sanctuary. Instead, he lay on the floor of the roundhouse—in a pool of blood.

He tried to sit, but he slumped back with a slosh. Wincing in pain, he grabbed his weak and unmovable arm. A boney knot protruded from the front of his shoulder. Why did it hurt so much? He lay there for a few heartbeats, afraid to move, riding the waves of agony. "Aaagh!"

When the pain subsided, he sucked in another deep breath, eliciting daggers of pain to his ribs. His head cleared. Yet, as his thoughts became more lucid, more memories pushed to the surface. Time stood as still as his arm.

"Where's your brother?" his father blasted. The memory seemed distant, but it was as close as the broken table lying next to him. His father had picked him up by his shirt and shoved him against the wall of the roundhouse; then his father swung Boaz around by his arm and slammed him into the table.

Boaz flinched at every word as it replayed in his mind.

Alexenah screamed as she ran into the roundhouse. "What are you doing? Stop!"

Caradoc struck her.

She fell to the floor, blood streaming from her nose. Boaz wished he could stop his father—and help his mother.

Lifting a log, Alexenah faced her husband. "You can beat me, but I will *not* let you hurt my sons anymore."

Caradoc scoffed. His derision hurt Boaz more than his delivered blows as he relived every moment. The sound of the log hitting the wooden door as Caradoc snatched it from her, the screaming, the laughing, and his own groaning.

She looked to Boaz. "We are leaving!"

"You think you are free?"

"My God has delivered me. I am free!"

"You perceive slavery as freedom? Even without me, you are still a slave. You have enslaved yourself. You are a slave to your god. To your philosophy of . . ." he pulled her close, ". . . kindness."

Alexenah met his father's gaze. He appeared sober, yet drunk with power and ambition. What sin had she ever committed that he should treat her so?

"My God has delivered me. I am free!" she said again.

"See if he can deliver you from this!" Caradoc struck her.

She stood firm, pulled her torn gown back over her shoulder, and raised her chin high.

Boaz remembered nothing more. Didn't want to remember.

Groaning, he struggled to bring himself back to the present. Fear flooded his soul. A warm blood-tinged tear dropped from his chin to the blood-pool mirror below.

Before him lay a fragmented drinking cup on the floor. *The Seder Cup*? The broken reddish-brown pieces of the goblet appeared like stepping stones in a frothy red wine lake.

He swooned again. Reflective thinking hurt. Everything hurt.

Whenever his father had been drinking too much, *Matrona* declared, "Your *Tahdah* is in his cups again." The secret signal for them to run away and hide.

He pictured his father staggering home from the Boar's Head Inn like he did so often, and the hair raised on the back of his neck.

Alexenah stole him and his brother away from home to safety many times the last few years. When they couldn't keep up, she picked them up, one in each arm, and ran out the door and around to the back of the thatch-roofed roundhouse. At first these escapes had been a grand adventure, heightened by the ever-present fear that Father might find

The Golden Cord

them. Later it became survival. The family lived in constant dread of Caradoc's outrages.

His mother always calmed the boys with stories of her homeland. Matrona was a skillful storyteller. She was even better at hiding. They spent the night in a barn, wagon, or with a neighbor's livestock until their father passed out or left the hillfort the next day.

Back then, the boys thought it fun to outthink their father.

No one outthought Caradoc. Boaz's muscles tensed. Tightening soon became trembling, and an ardent desire that Matrona would find him, and they would run away and hide. But he didn't hear her secret message to indicate they needed to go. The room was silent, except for the smoldering firepit.

Shuddering, Boaz shoved his left arm back under his body and rose to one elbow. His right shoulder and ribs ached intensely. His reflection in the red wine revealed a bulging goose's egg of a protrusion and a gaping cut across his eyebrow.

Dark-red blood smears splattered the floor of the roundhouse where he lay. Nausea filled him. Pain grew. "Matrona," he said in a panicked whisper.

On his knees, he crawled like a three-legged dog to discover where the blood trail led.

The door to the roundhouse stood open.

Boaz stiffened.

His father stood in the doorway.

4
CHAPTER

Superfluous

*Trauma is the furnace where
futures are forged.*

— Scribonius Largus

"You little piece of mongrel vomit!"

Boaz scooted from the sudden lightning strike of words. Caradoc kicked his son.

A loud crack came from his side. Boaz landed on his tortured shoulder. His life pushed out of his lungs. The pain was excruciating.

"In the name of Bel, why must my sons be so thick-headed?"

"Matrona?"

Caradoc shoved the broken table aside. "Dead. Goat's breath! Where is my cup?"

"Jachin?"

"Dead."

"No, he's not," Boaz muttered.

"Don't sass me, boy!" Caradoc seized him by his armpits and slung him over his shoulder. Ducking under the doorway, he marched out into the gray day straight to the cattle hut. Mara knelt there with a bucket and a broom. Caradoc slammed Boaz onto the floor of a chariot. "What are you doing here?"

"I'm cleaning your mess," Mara said. "I thought the boy died. Which one is this?"

"Don't know. Don't care. I've a meeting in Camulodunon. What did you do with their mother?"

"I disposed of her as demanded."

"Good."

"The boy looks dreadful. Should I look after his wounds?"

"Go clean the roundhouse. Remember to tell the story as I said. Exactly as I told you. Now get to it, woman!"

Caradoc cursed the horses and tightened the hitches. Cursed again.

A raven called in the distance.

As Caradoc worked, the chariot rocked. In the dusky light, Boaz rode the pain to a better place in his mind.

"Whad'ya do, Jachin? How did you escape the blow?" They were in the wheat field. Their sanctuary.

"I ducked and hit the table. Knocked over a jar of *woad*. It broke and cut me."

"That's how you got that blue stain on your arm? It looks like a bow."

As Jachin rolled up his tunic sleeve to show his brother, he said, "Tahdah is good with the bow."

"Yeah, like the time he shot that raven. It had wings this long." Boaz outstretched his arms as far as they could go.

"He tossed the dead bird into the pigpen. The pigs ate it, Boaz, feathers and all!"

Caradoc jumped over the rail of the chariot and thrust Boaz to the side.

The jolt brought his mind to the current trauma. Boaz moaned.

The raven cawed once more.

Scrunched up to protect himself from another blow, Boaz peered through the wicker side railing. The pigpen was not fifty paces from the chariot.

"That's where he is," Boaz whispered.
Caradoc slapped the reins on the horse's back.
Before he fell into thankful unconsciousness, Boaz heard his father's all too familiar farewell: "I need a drink!"

5
CHAPTER

Appointment

*Truth costs little in life's transactions.
But most men prefer to buy exorbitant lies.*

— Scribonius Largus

THE BOAR'S HEAD INN, CAMULODUNON

Sophronios Demetrios Alkimopoulos wiped the moisture from his bald head with a cloth and replaced his petasos. An instructor at the celebrated Herophilean School of Medicine at Men-Karou gifted the straw hat to him before he left on his journey to Britannia. Alexander Philalethes told him that Hermes, a god of transitions and boundaries, wore a hat such as this as he protected travelers. It was truth, to be sure, as Alexander always spoke truth. It was apropos for a physician to wear on his travels to bring him luck—not that he believed in such things.

Appointment

Sophronios positioned the loose-hanging soft hemp cords that threaded through the broad, floppy brim to fall neatly in front of both ears. He lifted his long beard, prematurely whitened, and tied the cords under his chin using a surgeon's knot.

His medical colleagues had told him he was unprofessional. They jested and said he looked like a farmer and should toss his *anóito kapélo* into the sea as soon as his ship left the port of Ephesus.

Throw his "silly hat" away? Like rubbish? Nonsense. Despite its condition, the now weathered and beaten hat held purpose. It had been his consistent friend and only companion on his journeys to the unfamiliar regions across what the local tribes called the Great Green Sea.

He intended to return to Men-Karou with his petasos when his tasks in Albion were completed, and he wasn't about to let the unsavory weather deprive him of that wish. However, today his petasos was little comfort from the pouring rain soaking him from head to heel.

He stepped from his wagon and pulled his gray *chlamys* cape around his shoulders. He shook his head, declaring his final response of "No." Rain drops splattered in all directions.

"Come along, girls. Let's move over here to the grass," Sophronios said.

Leaving the two donkeys hitched to the wagon, he secured the reins to a pole near a patch of grass and weeds on the south side of the building. He did not name his work animals, as it was foolish to do so.

He rubbed the rain from his eyes and squinted at the wooden sign hanging crookedly above the door of the tavern: "Boar's Head Inn." He grasped his hat as a gust of wind blew along the deserted street.

The sign creaked on its hinges. It gave the impression that the pig on the sign oinked, "Greetings, traveler."

Sophronios smiled and entered the tavern.

"A little wine to warm your bones?" shouted a man behind the counter as soon as the heavy door closed. "It is our very best wine in these parts."

He walked farther in, skeptical about the wine being

The Golden Cord

worthy. He pushed his cap back such that it lay on his back, held by the cord around his neck. He removed his *chlamys* and shook it vigorously as he examined the innkeeper. The man wore an unlaundered apron, baggy plaid trousers, and a stained sleeveless shirt. On his worn, dirty face, a mountainous beard and frizzled mustache grew like an unkept garden.

The man smiled a toothless grin and patted his wiry dark hair. He removed the kettle from the fire and poured a dark-red liquid into a thick clay mug.

Sophronios placed the cloak on a nearby table. "That would be nice. Thank you," he replied in the man's own language.

"Name's Fetch. I warmed this with a little spice. I don't want you to catch a chill."

"You are most kind to do me this honor." Sophronios picked up the warm mug and sipped the spicy red drink. Not his best wine, but at least it was warm, and the scent of the spices helped cover up the stench of the tavern. Although the spacious room appeared clean, the odor of stale wine, sweat, and leather was hard to miss. Some men liked the smell. He much preferred the aroma of chamomile and lavender of a city bathhouse. He sipped again. "A pleasure, to be sure."

"I knew you'd like it!" The barkeep pulled a rag tucked in the drawstring on his waist and wiped the wet ring the mug left on his counter. "That will cost you two *sesterces*."

Seemed like a lot. Should only be a few Roman *asses*. Sophronios pulled two coins from his leather purse hanging at his waist. "Of course. A man must make a living." He was careful about thieves on the roads and only kept enough in his purse to satisfy the robbers so they would leave him in peace. He kept the rest of his money hidden in his wagon.

"You seem to be a long way from home, traveler. How is it you know our tongue?"

"I seem to have a knack for picking up languages. I traveled your fens and forests for most of this summer to collect specimens for my medicaments and poultices. I am a physician. I journeyed from Phrygia, seeking rare healing herbs

Appointment

that cannot be found in my own environment. I am afraid I ventured farther north than I intended."

"Well, welcome, friend!" Fetch poured more of the mulled beverage into the man's glass even though it was only half empty. "Two more sesterces for the wine."

Sophronios eyed the innkeeper and smiled. Although he admired the man's entrepreneurial methods, he wasn't fond of parting with more coin.

He drank some more. The flavor improved with the second mug. Perhaps the herbs had infused the liquid more thoroughly. It flowed smooth and comforting going down. "Perhaps I can barter with you, barkeep."

The proprietor leaned forward on the bar. "Please, call me Fetch. I insist."

"I know an excellent recipe for herb butter you might like." The physician walked toward the table where he had laid his cloak. He rummaged through a pocket and removed a small rolled sheaf of papyrus.

"Sure enough, I'm always lookin' for new recipes." Fetch snatched the scroll, opened it, and with a nod placed it in a drawer behind him. "What brings ya to my esteemed establishment on such a dandy day as this?"

"I have a prearranged appointment with a man . . . about a pair of boys. I recently reached the decision that I need a couple of assistants on my travels home, as my eyesight is not as it once was. I need help cataloging my many herbs and plants collected this past season. I will also prentice them as physicians and sponsor their education at medical school in Phrygia—if they show any aptitude."

"A curse 'tis to be troubled by the eyes—not that you deserve such poor luck, I'm sure. I know the man you are needin' to see. As sure as the wind and rain followed you here, I 'spect Caradoc will arrive directly."

6
CHAPTER

Transactions

The sale is not as important as what you do with the purchase when you get home.

— Scribonius Largus

Boaz cowered behind his father in the chariot and absentmindedly rubbed his hurt shoulder. Torrential rain beat him. Water dripped from his long, wet hair into his swollen eyes. The rain washed the blood from his tunic to the chariot floor. Silently, he cried.

Coming to the Boar's Head Inn, Caradoc jumped over the rail and secured the horses. He always tightened the reins around the post more than necessary.

"Come on. I don't have all day!"

Boaz struggled off the chariot. His father seized his tunic

and half-dragged, half-carried him through the door of the *taberna* straight to the bar.

"Bring me some wine, Fetch!"

Fetch held out a mug.

Caradoc snatched it and gulped its contents. Wiping his mustache, he dragged Boaz to his regular table and stopped. "Who the devil are you?"

In Caradoc's chair sat an older man. A white ring of soft curly hair encircled his bald head. What he lacked on the top, he made up for with his beard, as it grew to the middle of his chest like puffy clouds. He wore a loose-fitting bright-yellow tunic, trimmed in red braid around the neck and sleeves. A bronze fibula the size of a man's thumb, in the shape of a serpent on a staff, fastened to his left shoulder. The local tribes' brooches held their capes in place. This brooch held nothing.

The man stood and held his hand in greeting. "I am Sophronios—a physician. I was to meet Caradoc regarding the sale and transfer of some boys into my service. Are you that gentleman?"

The warrior did not grasp the proffered hand, so the stranger stroked his beard with it and broadly smiled. Caradoc shoved his son forward. "Do you have the payment?"

Stumbling to balance, Boaz stood in front of the man like a lifeless hunting trophy. With his head downcast, he grasped his tunic with his left hand and squeezed. Rainwater scattered sawdust below him as it dripped. His right arm dangled at his side.

Sophronios lifted Boaz's head. "Let me look at you, child."

Boaz watched through wet hair strands as the physician made his examination. A straw hat hung by a string on the man's neck. He had never seen a hat like that. Jachin always put his cap on the statue of *Lugh*. Boaz shook the memory away.

For some reason, Boaz wanted to remember this man's face—like it was important. All he could do was to compare him to what he knew. Great Uncle Epaticus's head was bald like this man's—only this man had a ringlet of hair around his head. His uncle shaved and oiled his pate till it shimmered like a stone in the river. Where his uncle's face was stern, this man's face was rounded and flushed around the nose and cheeks as if embarrassed. Not necessarily fat, but neither was he thin. Boaz wasn't sure if he was as old as his white hair made him appear.

This man spoke in the language of Albion. His accent was foreign.

"Tut, tut. What do we have here . . . bruises to the face, a cut above the eye . . . hmmm . . . ecchymosis and edema of recent development. Lift your tunic, lad."

"I can't."

"Do as the man says!" Caradoc boomed with the mug at his lips.

"My arm is dead."

"Let me see. Hmm, yes, indeed." Sophronios smiled, then scowled at Caradoc.

"He fell out of the chariot on the way over here. The roads were slick with rain. It was a wonder I kept the chariot on track at all."

"And the other child? Did he fall out as well?"

"He is no longer with us," Caradoc snarled as he mocked the man's accent.

"I am afraid this is unacceptable."

"We had a deal. Fetch said we had a deal! We had a deal. Didn't we, Fetch?"

"That rascal Broc brokered the deal. I just relayed the messages," the barkeep said.

"Broc is no longer with us either! The deal was made. The die was cast. You must take the boy as is!"

"Hmm, yes, indeed," Sophronios said. He straightened Boaz's shirt. "That was for two boys. I only see one, and he is certainly not a healthy specimen."

Caradoc shoved Boaz toward the man, who caught him in his arms.

Boaz let the man hold him.

"*Quod petimus, non in virtute corporis, pedi. Est animi vis. Fortitudo est ut discere,*" Sophronios said in Latin.

Boaz tried to translate, remembering his studies with

Uncle Amminus. "Strength of body. No, that's not what you seek. You called me 'pedi.' 'My foot'?"

"'My child.'"

"Strength of the mind. Strength. Resolve. To learn. Correct?"

"Do you have that strength?"

"Strength to learn . . ." Boaz straightened and stared into the old man's green eyes. There were flecks—stars of yellow that matched Sophronios's tunic.

"Tut-tut. Yes, my child, I believe you do." He put his arm on Boaz's shoulder and scrutinized Caradoc. "Very well, then. I will take the lad."

"What about payment?"

"Follow me."

Caradoc and Boaz followed Sophronios outside.

The rain had stopped.

Once to the wagon, he opened the back and pointed to several medium-sized amphorae. "For one child, you may take one amphora of wine."

"Two was the deal."

"That was for two boys."

"Roman wine?"

"*Vinum Tempestus.*"

"Goat's tail! Do they think by naming their drink after their gods they own the heavens? Typical tripe of the Romans. They will never leave us alone till they own every square inch of the world. The moon and the sun. The storms. They don't own the sky."

"The wine I offer is their finest."

"Their souls are rotten, yet their wine is respectable."

"So are we agreed on the transaction as I stated?" Sophronios asked.

"Agreed."

Sophronios replaced his cap. "Then it is settled."

Caradoc lifted the amphorae of wine and marched back into the taberna.

Boaz shivered.

"Get in the wagon, Pedi. Time to travel."

CHAPTER 7

Pursuance

At night, the winds chase nothing but darkness.

— Scribonius Largus

THE ROAD FROM CAMULODUNON

Teague drew in a breath. "Please, I have a family."

Caradoc yanked harder on the man's tunic, twisting it in his fist.

"All I know is they were to meet the exiled Amminus before dusk—at the old Nemeton."

"Go on," Caradoc said, his other hand around the man's neck.

"Head south to safety—to the coast. Sail for Rome." Teague forced the words as Caradoc squeezed his throat.

"Is there more?"

Teague pulled up on Caradoc's arms. "Tinman, bring Alexenah . . . and . . . and the twins."

"Borrum's goat! She planned to go with him?" Caradoc tightened his hold until the man gave his last breath.

⌘ ⌘ ⌘

Caradoc rode to a place hidden deep in the Andreadsweld forest. No trails in; no trails out. Only a fragile snake-like trace of smoke rising from the treetops gave any indication of a dwelling this far in the woods. South of the Druid Nemeton and adjacent to a spring fed stream, he found the green sod cottage nestled among the trees in a small clearing.

Caradoc reviewed his plan in his mind. He needed to find the other twin, Jachin. The boy knew the truth about him. The maid Mara knew half-truths and lies. High Druid Kenjar would confirm them.

The recently enthroned king strode to a moss-covered door. He kicked cackling chickens out of his way. Briefly touching the carvings on the frame, he threw the wooden door open, stooped under the lintel, and stepped inside. Several hens sizzled on a spit in the hearth, filling the room with the aroma of an anticipated meal.

"Kenjar! Is the boy here?"

Caradoc pulled a leg from the roasted bird. "Some scoundrel stole my horses and killed my slave."

"W-w-what? Who would d-do such a thing?"

"It was one of Amminus's men. Teague."

"But he is just a th-th-thatcher."

"He recently lost his job."

Kenjar poured Caradoc a drink as he sat at a wobbly old table. "I see."

"The boy helped. I'm sure of it. They seek to destroy me."

"Th-the b-boy? Maybe h-he went to Calleva."

Caradoc stroked his braided moustache. "Ha! Calleva. Yes, that sewer in which Rome's debris collects and rots now belongs to me." Grease ran down his chin. "As king, I will live there."

Something fell in the back room. "C-c-chickens. They're everywhere." Kenjar waved it away as nothing.

"The cur knows too much. Done too much. Seen too much." He ate the last bit of flesh from the chicken leg and tossed the bone. It landed in the fire with a hiss.

"He c-cannot have traveled far. What will you d-do when you find him?"

"Kill him, I suppose."

Kenjar nodded. "Then w-w-what?"

"Even though I am high king, Albion is not yet mine. There is much enemy influence in the south. Verica promised fancy clothes, elevated position, and parcels of land to all who supported Rome. I must offer them more than what they desire."

"Some did not believe you at the c-c-coronation."

"Amminus said I counterfeited, erased, and restamped coins. Well, true enough—but unprovable. Coin is coin, and all men can be bought." He kicked at the fire. "I cannot believe the audacity of that boy. Bold defiance, yet he ran like a coward."

"Y-you will find him."

Caradoc arose. "I must finish what I started. Teague, the horse thief and murderer, has been put to the trial. The old king's funeral is planned. Is it not?" Caradoc put his arm around Kenjar's shoulders. "And you, my grateful servant, I have work for you to do at the hillfort."

"The boy who ran. How will you k-k-kill him?"

"I'll hire an assassin."

8
CHAPTER

Homecoming

The heart of a tyrant is an empty shell of a home.

— Scribonius Largus

THE ROAD TO CARADOC'S HILLFORT

A chill persisted in the morning air, and the donkeys' breath fogged as they protested the whip. "Each awakening is a beginning," Sophronios said.

Boaz leaned next to the old physician, both wrapped in a colorful blanket against the morning chill. Sophronios enjoyed the warmth of the child's body against him as the boy slept, but it made him a little uncomfortable. He was not fond of children, as he had never married and was not a family man. He envied those with lots of youngsters, as their lives were undoubtedly full. But to him, children were noisome and rude. He acquired a protégé only because he needed the help and was hopeful this one might learn his trade.

Sophronios was concerned about the fresh injuries and what this boy must have endured. He glanced at the boy's bruises and frowned. He couldn't imagine living in such an environment permitting such abuse. He knew the difference between ill-treatment and tumbling from a chariot. He vowed to attend to the lad's wounds as soon as they were well enough away from the tavern.

Finding a shaded area near the dirt road, he parked the wagon and climbed from the seat. The rain of the morning had moved on, and the sun played hide-and-seek with the clouds.

He grasped his cape tighter around him as he moved to the back of the wagon and opened the doors. A strong herbal aroma emanated from the neatly packed storage bins. His carriage was not as fancy as the *Carpentum* in which Roman matrons were conveyed in the public festival processions, but it was sturdy and suited to his needs. And if necessary, could comfortably sleep several people.

Sophronios lit an oil lamp with a flint. He opened a small drawer and dispensed a pinch of the contents into a crucible. He ground the leaves into a fine powder with a granite pestle. Satisfied, he poured a little spirits from a bottle into the crucible and mixed it with the powder. He added oats and enough chicken broth to make a porridge. He heated it over the lamp and poured the concoction into a shallow wooden bowl.

"Here, Pedi, come down from there and sit by the side of the road against the wheel. I have some oats for you."

Without a sound, Boaz did as requested.

"Here, eat this." The physician handed him the bowl and a wooden spoon. "Slowly now. No need to hurry nor to worry. Your father is no longer your concern."

Boaz set the bowl in his lap. With his good hand, he held a spoonful to his nose. "It smells like weeds."

"That is because it is made with weeds. Now eat up, Pedi."

"I drank something that smelled like this before, when I was sick."

Homecoming

"Interesting. *Those* weeds are hard to come by. That is one of the reasons I came to your island."

"What kind of weeds?"

"I will teach you in time, Pedi. No more questions for now. Eat. All of it."

Boaz's eyelids drooped. His tongue thick. "Mah harm thurtss."

Sophronios removed the bowl from Boaz before he dropped it. "Tut-tut. You will be well soon enough. Your shoulder needs reminding of where its home is."

When certain of the herb's efficacy, and the boy benumbed, he positioned one hand on the boy's elbow and the other on his injured shoulder. With a slow deliberate movement, he rotated and lifted the arm. The physician sensed the familiar click as the shoulder popped back into its socket. Boaz moaned but did not awaken.

⌘ ⌘ ⌘

When Boaz woke, he was back on the wagon, leaning against the physician.

The donkeys trotted an easy pace as they pulled up to a hillfort—Caradoc's hillfort.

Boaz tried to swallow, but his mouth was too dry. He wiped sweat from his forehead and a creamy substance above his left eye. The wound had been sutured. The ointment stank like pig dung. It was awful! Positioned in a sling and swathe made of bleached muslin, his arm felt better.

"What did you do?"

"I situated the shoulder into the socket. It went home. Does it feel better?"

"Yes, my shoulder and ribs still hurt, but the bandage helps. Thank you."

Sophronios touched the brim of his hat and nodded. He pulled the wagon through the gate and into the fort.

"Which one of these buildings is your home?"

Boaz sat up straight. He pointed to a roundhouse that was not only larger than the others but also well built and sturdy. "How did you know where I live? Why did you bring me here?"

"The innkeeper was so kind to give me directions—after I gave him a few recipes. You need to get your things, Pedi. Although I do not have much room, get what you feel is most important to you. You are accompanying me on a long journey."

"I don't have much—not anymore."

"Each awakening is a beginning."

As they pulled up to the roundhouse, a diminutive man with a glistening bald head and bushy eyebrows glided out of the building. A comely young woman carrying a wooden box of soiled rags followed closely.

"Do you know these people?" asked Sophronios.

"That is Kenjar the Druid, and Mara the . . ." His voice trailed off, and he didn't finish.

"Ah, a druid! Is he the one who gave you the weeds to drink?"

Boaz nodded.

"I must speak with this man while you gather your belongings." Sophronios jumped down from his wagon and took the reins of the donkeys. Leading them, he wrapped the reins loosely to a post. "Good morrow, sir!" Sophronios called. "Are you a healer?"

Boaz slipped down slowly, careful not to use his injured arm, which now fit snuggly to his chest in the sling. He stumbled to his home and entered warily. His breath labored as if he had run a race against Jachin. He nervously surveyed the room while he licked the salty sweat drops forming on his upper lip. No noticeable trace of the battle from the day before, except a pile of wood stacked near the hearth. Someone had cleaned and swept smooth the hard dirt floor. Had his mother been there? What happened to her? Where was his brother?

He grabbed his knapsack and threw his shoes into it. Looking around the bed area, he picked up a cat's skull Jachin had brought home. He set it down. "I'll leave this for Jachin when he comes back." He caressed the multicolored ragged garment they wore at the last Bel-tene festival. He shook his head. No need. Then he spotted the game he and Jachin had played so many times. He checked the pieces to see that all were present before placing it carefully in the

Homecoming

bag. There wasn't much room for anything else. Nothing else mattered to him.

Boaz moved to the entryway. He unlatched the heavy wooden door.

Several torch-bearing warriors rushed throughout the hillfort.

Daylight poured through the open doorway into the sizeable room that had once been his home. He turned to take one last look. Something shiny caught the light. Under his father's chair, near the kitchen area, a glint of gold shimmered. He moved the seat to the side with his hip.

Half-buried in dust was a golden cord. The one wrapped around the pugio his mother had shown them. What was it doing here? Boaz plucked it up and put it in his bag. He searched for the blade, but he only found the empty sheath. He collected that as well.

A smoky fog came from the rafters. The hearth was cold. The door slammed. A flick of flame. Then a cackle. Parts of the thatch roof fell to the floor and ignited the bedding. The hay and herbs hanging from the rafters in the sleeping area burst into flames. The room filled with thick black smoke.

A blazing beam fell before him, blocking the door. Sparks sprang everywhere. The roundhouse was ablaze!

9
CHAPTER

Declarations

Tears down childhood's cheeks never dry.

— Scribonius Largus

Urgent blows and pounding on the walls, accented with yelling, shook the building. Flaming ash dropped all around Boaz. An ax bit through the side of the roundhouse.

"Pedi, are you in there?"
"Yes!"
Sophronios peeked through the gap. "Hurry, Pedi, or you will be roasted!"
Boaz hugged his bag and rushed to the opening in the wall. Sophronios pulled him through.
Boaz coughed. "I'm okay."
"I am sure you think you are, but I must assure myself of your safety."

Declarations

His examination was much more thorough than Boaz wished.

"You'll be safe here by the front gate."

The fires raged as men set each building ablaze. Boaz stayed far away from the ruckus.

The physician took Boaz's bag and threw it in the back of the wagon. "I must get some things out of the wagon and finish with the healer. Stay here, Pedi. We will leave shortly and head south to the coast."

Boaz slumped down by a wheel. Every building blazed now. Warriors made sure of that. They emptied the weapon storehouse, then burned it too. The big heavy doors buckled from the heat.

What about the animals?

Over by the pigsty, Kenjar and Sophronios talked loudly, at times laughing.

Boaz rose and balanced against the cart. What could they possibly find that was funny about the whole fort going up in flames? It didn't make sense. Boaz ambled away from the commotion.

Now, clear of the smoldering hillfort, he breathed the fresh air. He squinted up to see the sun peeking out of the dense, rising smoke clouds. Although the sun warmed his shoulders, his bare feet chilled in the cold mud. His strength returned a bit. He took a few tentative steps.

He straightened his tunic, adjusted the sling, and pulled his braccae up around his waist as best he could with one hand. The thick wool garment, woven by his mother, comforted him. "Every stitch is placed with love," his mother would say. He examined the tear in his braccae that his mother mended. Absentmindedly, he reached up and touched his forehead wound.

Befuddled, Boaz made his way out of the gate of the hillfort, walking haltingly at first, then running toward the river. He paused by the statue of Lugh to get his breath and stretch his legs. The harvested wheat field lay before him, but that wasn't his destination.

He considered the hunting trail, but he turned and headed the other way. When he reached the river, the brisk water was full of debris.

He shivered. *Heavy rains will do that.*

Each step grew heavier as he walked farther to the midden. Uncle Amminus had told them once that it was important to place the garbage pit downriver of the dwellings so as not to contaminate the water supply.

The bank of the river around the mounds of debris was built up with boulders. The swollen river lapped at the edge. A portion of the garbage smoldered in several places. Repugnant odor stung Boaz's nostrils. He found a long, thin stick on the ground nearby and poked the garbage heaped up from years of waste.

Used, broken, and worthless items inhabited the midden. Broken pots that could be used in any way—all metal—and anything wooden were seldom thrown on the heaping mound of rubbish. Wood would be saved, reused to build something else or burned in the hearth for heat. Metal would be melted down and used again. Items thrown into the pile that had no value whatsoever would be burned. Rain, frost, and the trampling of farm animals would destroy even potsherds that were left.

Boaz wasn't sure what he might find here. He needed to know. There was no sign of Matrona or Jachin in the fort, so maybe Caradoc killed them and threw them on the garbage heap. Father always did that—either the garbage heap or the pigsty.

Boaz poked at animal waste, food scraps, and human excrement with his stick. Taking out the refuse was a hated chore. Most food scraps decayed and provided fertilizer for the farmers to spread on the fields and gardens. Dogs might chew and gnaw the animal bones and carry them off toward the woods. None of those details helped him find his mother and brother.

Boaz moved timidly, looking for any sign of his family. As he rummaged, raucous caws came from a group of crows picking at the refuse. They fluttered to the nearby trees, continuing with their mocking cries as Boaz sifted through the remains of his family's life—a bowl, a torn dress, a new belt they once gave to their father.

Boaz searched all around the pit and down by the river's edge. The last thing he remembered was his mother falling to the floor after his father hit her. *They would not leave without me—they wouldn't. They must be dead. Tahdah killed them.*

Two summers ago Boaz had seen his father kill a troublesome raven with an arrow from fifty paces. He lifted the enormous bird, removed the arrow, and threw the body into the pigpen, saying, "Pigs are the scum of the earth! They will devour anything and everything!"

The next morning Boaz and Jachin checked the pen for the bird and were astonished that no trace could be found, not even a single black feather.

They must be there. Somewhere. Their bodies could not have vanished. *Has the river washed them away?* He again thought of what father had done with the raven.

With sudden horror, Boaz thought of Primus. He let out a scream, dredging up the unimaginable pain of having watched his father kill their dog. Boaz fell to his knees and wept.

The pigpen ...

Boaz sprang to his feet and brushed his tunic, shaking off senseless details and memories. He ran as fast as he could back to the hillfort, past the smoldering buildings, and to the livestock pens. Mud-covered hogs squealed, terrified of the smoke and fire. A warrior holding his nose shooed them out of the pen with the butt of a long spear.

Had his mother and brother's bodies been thrown into the pen? How could anyone do that? His father could. His father would.

He explored the pigpen as he rubbed at the wound on his forehead. "Boar's dung! He put boar's dung on me?"

The thought of the hogs fighting for position as they devoured pieces of his loved ones' flesh made Boaz sick. Nothing but rancid black mud and slime. Bending over the rail of the pen, he vomited. Boaz fell to his knees, grabbing and tearing at his tunic with his good arm. He pulled the sling off and threw it. He screamed out for his mother as uncontrollable sobs of horror and grief flooded from deep inside until there were no tears left.

He was utterly isolated and alone for the first time in his life. His only brother had been his best friend. He loved him dearly. He was more than his best friend. Being twins, they belonged together. They were a part of each other and were never apart. What would he do without Jachin by his side?

Did Father ever cry for me or my family? No, Boaz never saw him cry. Never saw him try to make things different or try to make amends for the things he had done to them. Boaz's crying lessened.

Suddenly Boaz became cold inside. He rose from his knees, raised his head high, and made his way to Caradoc's gate, where the physician had told him to wait.

Kenjar and Sophronios loaded two heavy boxes in the back of the wagon, and then the physician handed some bottles to the druid. Hopefully, Sophronios and he would leave soon.

Leaning against the gate, Boaz observed the familiar surroundings of his home—now only charred skeletons: the roundhouse, weapons storehouse, cattle barn, and the healing hut. And lastly, to the trophy skulls hanging from his father's gate, all dark and disfigured.

"Tahdah never cried for his sons, and never again shall I cry for him."

CHAPTER 10

Voyage

*You can't always tell where you're sailing
by the tilt and luff of the sails or
even the point on the horizon ahead.
Sometimes you must look at the wake behind you.*

— Scribonius Largus

AD 34—THE GREAT GREEN SEA

Everything changed. Jachin felt it in his belly. It rose, fell, and rose again. Distant voices floated above him as he swayed in his hammock between dream and reality.

In the darkness, someone whispered his name.
"Jachin."
He grumbled groggily. The hammock swung to and fro in rhythm like a cradle rocking him to sleep.

The Golden Cord

"Jachin!" This time gruffer. "It's time for your watch. Up now, or I'll cut you down!"

He didn't budge.

A shout came from above. "Stand by to go about!" The cacophonous scrambling to turn the merchant transport *Ianus Inceptor* away from the strong wind's path annoyingly jangled his hammock.

"Mains'l haul!" Another command.

Above him—on the deck—men worked hard, pulling the ropes to change the sail's tack in the rough seas. It was a fitful dream.

The room suddenly tilted. Jachin's hammock—a little over a foot beneath the one above him and the same distance to another below—banged against the wooden sidewall of the ship.

"Up or down?" A brief pause. "Now!" A curved knife slashed the rope attaching Jachin's hammock fast to the deck spar. "I guess you prefer down."

Jachin tumbled, barely missing the berth below him. His eyes opened wide with the sudden jolt of the hard deck. He sat up, shaking his head. There, standing above him, loomed the watch commander with a vicious looking knife in one hand and a sizeable oil lamp in the other. The eerie glow illuminated the old sailor's weathered features in a demon-like manner.

Jachin drew his fingers through his long locks, tucked his legs under, and rose to a precarious stance on the swaying underdeck. "Okay, I'm up," he mumbled.

"Humpf. More like down." The watch commander disappeared into the darkness with his lamp to awaken the other hapless sailors who missed the call to change shifts.

Blindly, yet methodically, like ghosts rising from graves, the other seafarers moved about the close cabin confines, grabbing their gear for the next watch.

Stiff and sore, Jachin wobbled in the dark on spindly legs as the vessel drifted back and forth, and up and down.

Another tilt, and a roiling knot grew in his stomach. He gagged and swallowed bile. As his eyes adjusted to the darkness, Jachin willed himself not to heave. The cabin's odor told him that he wouldn't have been the only one to have done so.

Once balanced, Jachin tightened his braccae and staggered to the ladder that led up through a square opening in the deck—a path more remembered than seen.

Jachin climbed half-heartedly into the darkness above. "Some adventure *this* is."

Wind immediately lashed his face with unsympathetic sea spray as the driving rain pelted him. Once on deck, he squared his legs and clutched the wet rail before him. To gain balance, he focused on the white canvas sails flapping in the dark-gray storm.

A gust of wind filled the main sail to its fullest, stretching the fabric taut with a loud snap. Waves pummeled the starboard bow as the merchant ship dug deeply into the dark sea.

"Let go and haul!" A booming voice arose above the roaring sea.

The sailors, only silent shades in the night, pulled and released rope until the vessel rose to an even keel. The white canvas lined up with the starless horizon. For a moment, the craft eased with deep crashing sounds of the sea beating against the bow like a rhythmic *Bel-tene* drum. The mast creaked, and lines buzzed from the squall above the topsail.

A surge of wind shoved him forward. Jachin grabbed one of the sailors nearest him.

"Mind yer struts, sailor!" said the watch commander. He dragged Jachin by his tunic to the side rail. "This be your watch, lad. Standfast."

Jachin gripped the rail tight as a wave hit. Briny seawater retreated through notched gaps below the rail and back out to the deep.

Unaffected by the blasting spray, the watch commander let go of Jachin and patrolled the slippery deck.

Before him swayed another silent sea-soaked sailor in the dark. He thrust the lines for the lee braces upon Jachin's chest.

Jachin grunted.

The sailor pulled his drenched cloak around himself,

The Golden Cord

crossed his arms, and shivered—head down—waiting for the call to change watch.

Another crashing wave slammed the ship, sending water high over the rail. Jachin held the rope and ducked his chin into his chest to avoid the deluge.

When the wave withdrew into the night, Jachin checked the other side of the deck to see who held the opposite brace ropes. He wiped salt water from his face and shook the dream remnants from his mind like residual sea foam on the deck. His stomach lurched again.

"Who matches us on the other side?" Jachin yelled.

"Amminus accords the windward lines."

Since they had boarded the merchant ship, Jachin seldom saw his uncle Amminus. They had met up at the druid grove where Jachin hid from his father. Since Caradoc exiled Amminus, Jachin agreed to travel with him. They were going to ask Rome to help with the chaos Caradoc created. Knowing that he would stand watch together with Amminus strengthened his resolve. A wave of calm came over him.

Jachin cupped his mouth. "Amminus!" The loud din of crashing waves swallowed his voice amid the wind and the snap of the sheets above.

A smaller swell crashed behind. The storm weakened.

"How long has this storm been going on?" he asked the sailor closest to him.

"Most of the night. It is too late in the season to risk these seas."

A horn blew. Without another word, the sailor before him joined the others changing watch. They scampered across the deck and down the square hatch like the sea escaping the notches at the rail.

Before Jachin could establish a slippery foothold at his post, they called to change tack. He let the rope slide through his fingers until it slackened. Gathering the coils, he wrapped the line around the belaying pin as he had been taught—what was it—yesterday? It seemed like years. He led the line under and behind the base of the pin and then around the head in a looping pattern till at least four turns were completed. He twisted the coiled line once more before he slipped it over the top of the belaying pin to sec in place.

The *Ianus Inceptor* settled down on a new ta___, hauled on the starboard, and gathered speed into the night.

Suddenly a massive wave slammed the vessel on the opposite side and tipped it upward. As the ship skewed, Jachin slammed against the rail. The hard wood bit him squarely in the lower back. He turned and grasped the rail, wrapping his arms around the wet wood and waiting for the ship slope to right itself in the wave's trough. If they were not careful, the shift could take a man off balance and toss him over the side into the deep. He glanced to see if Amminus was still there.

"I can't swim," Jachin said as the *Ianus* slapped the water with a loud clap.

The craft leveled.

"Holdfast!"

He grasped the line. It bit into his tender, blistered hands.

"Brace the halyards!"

Jachin readied to pull.

"Let go and fly!"

Jachin strained as he heaved the line toward him. He had to pull twice as fast to reach the same length of line as the sailors. Grabbing length after length of the line attached to the bottom sail boom, he let the line coil behind him like a snake on the deck.

"Belay that line!"

As he tied the line around the pin, he dreaded the probability that they would do this repeatedly until the sun rose.

Between tacks, Jachin reflected on how he had come here. Killing his mother. Running away. Stealing to survive. Hiding in a druid grove. Then being found by Amminus, who his father had exiled from Albion.

He wished they paid more coin so that they wouldn't have to crew the ship. Amminus said they would need the money when they arrived at their destination to pay for bribes and promises. Still, he wanted to only be a passenger. He knew their identity must be kept secret from the crew. If the sailors found out that they carried the rightful

The Golden Cord

ruler of Albion, no telling what would happen. He squeezed the wet strand of thick rope. His hands were raw with pain.

Another tack.

Another rest.

He thought of his father and the last time he had seen him—right before he had run away. Nausea overwhelmed him again. He kept the anger inside as long as he could.

Jachin wrapped his fist around the line and squeezed. "You shoved Matrona in front of me like she was your shield." He touched the pugio in the rabbit-skin sheath tied to his leg. Jachin once again recalled how he held the blade when it entered his mother's delicate belly.

"How could you do that?" Tears mingled with the salty sea and rain as drops ran down his face. "*How* could *I* do that?"

Jachin stared mindless to the stinging sea spray. "Father . . . Tahdah . . . *I hate you!*" He screamed into the night. He coiled the line at his feet, making ready for the next tack. "Boaz . . ." he breathed.

On the horizon the sun's golden rays peeked under dark rain clouds, illuminating the scene before him for the first time. Reflections of the gray swirls danced on the whitecaps of the sea. Bright, glistening oranges and reds interspersed among the deep grays and greens of the troubled deep. The waves appeared ten to twelve feet high to the crest. All night they had been on a hard tack against the wind to sail through the storm.

Amminus had garnered passage across the Great Green Sea to meet Imperator Gaius at the mouth of the Rhenus River in Gaul. That was where they were headed.

The sailors talked of the imperator when they ate their quick meals down below deck. They called him "wild and irrational."

I can deal with that. I will ask the imperator to use his army to kill my father. I'm certain the man would do it. That should appeal to someone who is wild and irrational.

The watch commander called for a long tack and gave the men relief until the watch horn blew again.

Jachin leaned against the pinrail as the seas calmed. His stomach churned and roiled. He wished he would go ahead and vomit. He couldn't remember the last meal that stayed in his gut. He would feel better if he relieved his stomach. How much longer could he go on like this?

After checking his lines, he fell back on his haunches. Exhausted, he turned to a sitting position against the main post. His arms ached. A sharp pain jolted his side as he drew his fingers slowly through his hair.

Jachin lowered his head and prayed to his dead mother's god and cried. "I wish Boaz was still alive."

The watch horn blew.

Jachin didn't look up when his replacement began to check the lines. He drifted into slumber—back to the dreams of golden wheat and laughter.

Suddenly someone slowly lifted Jachin to his feet.

"Come on, son, let's eat breakfast," Amminus's voice assured as he backed down the ladder to the dark room below.

Jachin started to follow, but his stomach lurched, and his head spun. He leaned over the rail and finally vomited.

Without warning, a rogue wave blasted the stern. The Ianus Inceptor pitched high and came down with a hard wallop on the water. The sudden slap unhinged Jachin's grip and hurled him overboard.

CHAPTER 11

Lost

Death's casket is the remedy of every sorrow, except when carried by those left behind.

— Scribonius Largus

A trumpet sounded at the bow of the Ianus Interceptor. "Man overboard! Portside," the tubicen called.

The captain shouted above the prevailing gale winds. "Go to your first-watch workstations. This is more important than anything else. Take count. We don't want to waste time on a *falsum terror*."

Everyone rushed to their mustering stations. They would discover who was present and verify that it was not a false alarm.

"By the god's bones," Fergus grumbled as he joined his close friend and sword brother. "We are here, Amminus. With me is Kendal, the bard, and Caedmon."

Lost

Another trumpet sounded, and attendance was taken, each man counting off in turn.

"Send word to the captain!"

"Everyone to a man is accounted for, sir."

"Save one."

"Down the scuppers like a rat. Right before me eyes, I saw 'em. Lost for good, 'e 'tis."

"The young boy from Albion."

"Jachin!" Amminus cried.

"No lifeboats. Can't risk more loss. Report to me when the soul is found," the captain said.

The search began. All activity focused on finding the boy. To avoid confusion, the men searched down and aft on the portside and up and forward on the starboard. They left nothing unturned. Lines were uncoiled, sheets shaken out. Barrels poked into. Lookouts were sent up mast to search the sea.

The heavy *Ianus Inceptor* circled sluggishly to the left, traveling again along the vessel's track, offset to one side, then traveled back in the opposite direction of that track, offset to the opposite side.

"Clear!" Called the deckhands as they finished each standard search pattern.

"We will remain at sea till success or satisfaction."

"By that, the captain means that we search until a drowning has been confirmed," Fergus said.

When it appeared that they had exhausted all approaches, and the men had turned the ship inside out searching stem to stern, another trumpet signaled. It was the same as the first blast, only it had a different ending key sound. More morbid sounding, like a funeral lament, it announced the end of the search.

Those not on watch milled about or went below deck. Amminus kept vigil. He could not concede that Jachin had drowned.

"He's slipped his moorings, e'has," a sailor told Amminus. "Keep one hand for yourself, I says."

"Aye," said another. "A sailor's safety is his personal 'sponsibility."

"He'll have the devil to pay."

The Golden Cord

Amminus seized the man by his shirt. "Pay the devil?"

"He's talking about the pitch on the keel, Amminus," Fergus said as he pulled the two apart. "It's just a saying."

Amminus pointed at the man. "What does it mean if not about Jachin?"

"You know. The keel!" Fergus thundered.

"Yes, it's under the ship."

"Exactly. The most difficult place to apply dark pitch tar runs along the underside of the V-shaped hull. They call it 'the devil.' The longest seam," Fergus explained. "They think the youngin' went down there and became stuck between the devil and the deep blue sea."

"He sleeps in the arms of Neptune now."

Amminus clasped the offered hand. "I'm sorry. He's my nephew."

"Slog along, ye landlubbers. Third watch, you're up. Ye have work to do!" the captain roared.

Amminus had missed his shift to sleep. He moved as though his body was not a part of him. His thoughts distant, his actions mechanical. Jachin was gone. How effortlessly the captain abandoned the search. How dispassionately he pronounced the boy perished.

Amminus's men were assigned the job of caulking the deck. They always did this after a storm while the boards are softened with seawater. They also washed the surface to remove salt from the grain.

"Jachin has salt in his grain that no amount of scrubbing will eradicate," Fergus said. "They'll find him."

Activities resumed as if nothing had gone on before. Amminus scrubbed with a solemn diligence.

After cleaning the deck, they pushed thick twine into the joints and poured a mixture of pitch tar and vegetable glue to caulk the seams. Others mended torn sheets. Amminus uncoiled the line to dry and coiled it again.

Fergus approached his leader. "The boy's loss is difficult, but we must continue on. A warrior must have a larger life to honor and serve, or he will become a warrior for nothing but his own pleasure. We sail to the mainland to garner support for our cause. Amminus, I must know: Why is it so important to stop Caradoc? Why not just let it go?"

"The land is darkened by my brother's lies," Amminus replied as he uncoiled the line again.

"You have put out fires before, my friend."

"My brother will oppress the clans to his will, and they will serve him. They will end up being his weapon in the destruction of all we hold dear."

"What if you don't succeed in stopping him?"

"Fergus, there are souls who call out to my passions. Those who are oppressed and exploited, I must release those who are enslaved and used. I must free those who don't have a voice. I vowed long ago that with the help of my friends, I would save my people from the flames of duplicity and deceit. I must speak for them." He paused and thought of Jachin. His confidence wavered. His words fell hollow. He fumbled with the rope. "They sent me away. I fear I am perhaps no longer the one for the task."

Kendal took the line from Amminus. "Perhaps it is because you have felt forgotten," he said.

"Not forgotten, Kendal, just lost. Day by day I look at others and long to help. To rescue. To love. And now this. My ambition is more than my ability. I stand impotent," Amminus said. "I stand watch as my loved ones die yet again. Broken inside, I long for the courage to do that which I dream to do."

"You will have the opportunity, my friend," said Kendal.

"Surely this does not please Alexenah's god. To let Jachin die . . . how could he allow this? Where was this god as the storm raged? Where was he when Alexenah and Boaz breathed their last breaths? What wrongdoing did they commit to deserve his punishment?"

"I don't think Alexenah's god manipulates us like the Roman deities control their devotees."

"I should have protected them!"

"*Shoulds* are clubs we strike our own heads with. What could you have done? Like your grandfather, your father, your wife, and your baby before them. They are gone," Fergus said.

"Where do I walk now, Fergus? I'm left with tear stains in the sawdust and desires left unfulfilled. I hold tightly to tomorrows that never were, nor ever will be."

"I've been there too," Kendal said.

Amminus hung his head. "I said I would be there for him and raise him as a father. He was alone. Now where is *my* purpose to live?"

"There is still meaning in your life, Amminus. Make these moments count, and give the dead their due. Cry if you must. Curse if it feels right to do so. You are not at fault. And," Fergus wrapped his huge arms around Amminus, "you are not alone."

Amminus let Fergus give without giving back. It didn't feel right. He received the concern but had nothing left with which to reciprocate. He stepped back and slumped to the deck. "If I cry, I am weak. If I get angry, it only distances me. The fire still smolders, my friends. I don't understand."

"All those things that mark you when you are young, they make you who you are. You can never escape from them," Kendal said. "You must return to the burnt ground of your past and learn to grieve."

"I disagree. Don't go backward. Move beyond it," Fergus huffed.

"For once I agree with Fergus. Let go of this grieving spirit. Quench it, my friend," Caedmon said, joining the group's discourse.

Amminus fingered the blue bead that hung around his neck next to Alexenah's leather treasure pouch. "Some days fear rules my heart."

Kendal pointed. "You wear the Stone of the Brigantes. Does it not stand for hope, courage, and strength of that tribe?"

Amminus shook his head. "It used to. This stone weighs heavy around my neck, Kendal."

"Are you helpless to deal with Caradoc?" Fergus sounded intense. "Will you also lose your homeland? Consider Albion."

"Thank you for giving me focus, my friends. But to let go or continue on, I cannot decide. Sometimes I feel that everything is payment for my past sin. Like the great fire, Caradoc fans the flames. All Albion calls out from the ashes of my soul. I cry for their pain," Amminus said.

"Their fate will be the same as those you have lost as

long as you stay lifeless. Your gaze is down and backward, friend. You must make a choice. You forget your goals." Fergus stood. "This is not a war of your making. Which side are you on, Amminus? Albion's or Caradoc's?"

Amminus picked up a brush and scrubbed. "Or Rome's? What does it even matter? Everyone dies."

Fergus took the brush from Amminus. "Would you want Jachin to see his uncle like this? How quickly you have succumbed to defeat. This is not the Amminus I know and love. Strength and determination define you, like I have seen so many times."

Kendal sat next to him. "Perhaps Fergus speaks true. A wise man still has his past, but he doesn't live in the past. Even when he has lost so much, he keeps going forward."

Fergus helped Amminus to stand. "One step after another. Do good till you cannot do anymore," Fergus said. "You taught us this, my friend."

"I see a boat on the horizon. A light . . ." Caedmon said, barely a whisper.

"I cannot relent to your advice, my friends. I will circumvent my fears for now. Let my labor lead to indifference if I must." Amminus headed astern.

The rest of his men moved along the deck as they continued retarring the boards.

Amminus stood by the rail where he last saw his nephew and stared at the dark rough waters below. He grasped his necklace—both the bead and Alexenah's pouch—and wrenched them from his neck. He held it out over the water. The men had reached out to him in an uncomfortable way, yet their care was comforting at the same time. Kind of like when Alexenah would hug him. *Be brave*, she said. *Be brave.*

Sighing, Amminus wrapped the leather thongs around his fist and held the treasures to his chest. Eventually, he tied them back around his neck and returned to the drudgery of hard work. This time with determination.

He seized a short iron bar with a long wooden handle from a bucket of coals and dipped the red-hot rod into a bucket of cold pitch. The tar softened and congealed around the iron, so it could be applied to the needed area of the deck where they had pushed the twine into the wooden seams.

The Golden Cord

"You are right, my friends," he said, rejoining his men on the deck. "As always, you are right. We try our best to do what is necessary. We trust that our decisions will be honorable and right. In the end, we are accused, rejected, and ostracized by the very ones we saved. But we persist in our deeds. If those we help are not satisfied, we ask, 'What would you have me do?' Other men make the same choices—take the same hard road. We trust that one life matters, and it wasn't our life; then we do the hard things. The hard, hard things we do—whether we grieve or gain—it must be done. Yes, my friends, I will grieve. I am in exile." He took a leather thong from his belt and tied his hair back. "But I will not be idle."

"Why is that boat on the great sea?" Caedmon asked.

This time the men looked where he pointed.

A ship sailed hard-tacked on the horizon in the growing light of the morning. A light shown from atop its mast. A signal?

"Testing its reliability, preparing for war," Fergus said.

At that moment the trumpet sounded.

"Found him, they 'ave!" someone cried.

"He's alive!" yelled another.

Amminus jumped to his feet. "Where's the boy?"

"On the Roman *trireme*!"

"What?" Amminus rushed to the rail. He laughed. Danced for joy. Hugged Fergus.

"Didn't you see the signal? They musta fished 'em out!"

The command to jibe. The *Ianus Inceptor* brought the mainsails into the wind.

"Yes, let's go get Jachin!" Amminus yelled.

The merchant vessel turned sharply away from the Roman trireme.

Amminus gripped a rail to keep balance. "Where are we going?"

The captain approached them. "The trireme has a mission to patrol. They will make short sorties from shore to sea. Seeking pirates, if I know my ships. And that one I know. They are military. The *Ianus Inceptor* is not. That is the *Morta Columbarium*. Their *trierarchus* is Caelus, and he will not give the boy over to us. He is a hard man. It may be two years, five at the most, that they are out at sea. They follow us not. Besides, I have contracts to fulfill. That storm and search set us back half a day."

"What are you saying?"

"We are heading to harbor."

12
CHAPTER

Capture

*Few by death gently slope away
in graceful resignation.*

— Scribonius Largus

Jachin sank into darkness. As soon as the energy of his plunge was spent, he fought toward the surface. He burst through rough waves and clamored for breath. He swallowed salt water, sucked it into his lungs. Coughed. He struggled to find anything to grab on to. Nothing. His clothes clung about him, hampering his movements. Every time he lifted an arm above the surface, it were as though a hand grabbed his ankle and pulled him under.

I'm in the water. Hate water. Cold. Salty. Going to die. Jachin sank once more. *Must live. Kill my father.* He pushed to the surface. Gulped. Icy darkness lashed at him from all sides. He held his breath again. *If I don't breathe, I will die, if I do breathe, I will die.*

He submerged.

The hammock rocked. Floated. *Let me sleep*!

He rose to the surface. Guzzled air. His mouth filled with water, and he sank again. Bitter to his bones. A warmth came over him like a blanket in winter. Boaz and Primus lay next to him on the softest cool green grasses of the wheat field, dreaming the most delightful of dreams. He lightly floated above the waves of wheat on the shoulders of Boaz. There he felt the bolstering boost of his brother. When he moved his arms, he could push himself higher in the sky to just above the treetops. There was a ringing in his ears. He stopped struggling. Let go. No longer pained or chilled, he floated.

A hook snatched him by the back of his tunic.

Slamming Jachin hard on the wet deck like a fresh catch of the day, several men stripped his clothes from him. They turned him on his stomach—head to the side—and pushed water out of his lungs. Others rubbed his arms and legs to warm him. *Voices through a fog.*

"*Flotare* from a wreck. I claim the prize."

"No, fool. He is *Jetare*. Thrown overboard for sure. Look at 'em."

"*Quod autem praecisum fuerit!*"

"*Iudaea. Non est Iudaeus.*"

"Yes, a Jew. He has been cut."

"And this mark on his arm, bluing with a scar. What does that portend?"

"Slave."

"If so, what is attached to this little fish's leg?"

"Little fish! Ha! *paulo piscis*. He's paulo piscis!"

As a man touched his leg, Jachin startled and drew his knife.

"Pugio? He has a pugio!"

Coughing, Jachin scooted back to the rail, where he found sailcloth. He wrapped himself in the tattered material and stood to his feet, swaying, holding the pugio at his side.

"The paulo piscis lives!"

"Quick, hook 'em agin 'fore he dives back into the deep!"

"Let 'em go. He's a paltry catch."

"Jew! Slave!"

As they clambered around him, Jachin brandished the blade.

"Careful now. This little fish has teeth!"

A man sporting a bunched-scarf neck knot, gray drab tunic, and short *braccae*, circled to his left. A legionnaire drew his sword and advanced. Another sailor put a knife between his teeth and gathered rope.

Striking out, Jachin sliced the attacker on the forearm. The marine dropped his weapon. The others rushed, but Jachin was quick with the blade. They could not get close, let alone contain him.

"Don't injure him! Neptune has found him," cried a gruff voice from the crowd.

"If Neptune saved this piscis, then he firstly put him in the *mare*."

"To drown him!"

"One who is rescued from drowning is a *Netunus filius*." It was the gruff voice again. "You all know that," a muscular man in Roman armor with a helm in one hand and a long-hooked staff in the other said. He wore a blue woolen tunic, with roomy sleeves, under his breastplate, and a weighty gold ring on the little finger of his left hand. In soaked *caligulae* boots and felt stockings, the man slosh-stepped toward Jachin. About his shoulders draped a sky-blue fringed *sagum* cloak—the color of Neptune—dripping water to the deck.

It is Neptune himself.

The men saluted with a singular thud as their fists beat their chests. The armored man waved his hand, and they scrambled to their stations.

Jachin scrutinized his new foe—not dropping his weapon or his guard.

"Why did you wrench me from the waves?" Jachin asked in his best Latin.

"Neptune saw your value."

"I should be dead."

"Not much value in a dead man. Where did you get that blade?"

"Who are you?"

"I am Marcus Marcus Caelus. The *trierarchus* of the Roman trireme *Morta Columbarium*. Trierarchus Caelus to the sailors on this vessel."

Jachin trembled. "So you are not Neptune?"

The man squinted and half smiled at the boy. "No, but I am one of his closest friends."

Looking aft and stern for escape, Jachin remained careful not to let Trierarchus Caelus out of his sight, and the pugio was always at the ready. He shivered violently; the pugio quavered in his hand. "Only pirates use t-t-triremes."

"That they do. That they do. Nowadays the leading force sails *quintremes*. Put your blade away, slave."

Jachin replaced the pugio in the rabbit-fur sheath strapped to his leg. "I am not a slave."

"I am not a pirate. Our oarsmen get paid by Rome. Who tossed you overboard? We do not use slaves aboard this vessel."

"I am not a slave."

"So you said." He scowled. "I don't believe you."

"I don't care."

Tightening the sail cloth around him, Jachin shuddered from the cold. He coughed again and vomited seawater. He stumbled forward.

Caelus let him fall. He removed the pugio and sheath from Jachin's leg.

"Get this little fish some warm clothes and some grog," the trierarchus yelled to the crew. "Have him take Vigintus's place at the oars when recovered."

"No pay, sir?"

"Why bother. He'll be dead before we reach land anyway."

13
CHAPTER

Domination

*Difficult is sorrow's transient journey.
Few there be that reach joy's distant shore.*

— Scribonius Largus

THE OCEANUS

Two armed soldiers escorted Jachin below deck, dragging him and slamming him on the third seat from the back next to a wiry, bald oarsman. Once seated on the bench, they placed a shackle on his ankle.

"Afraid I'll run off? Like I have anywhere to go."

The soldier punched him in the mouth. "*Tace, canes!*"

Jachin spit blood. He'd work on his Latin so he could complain with enthusiasm next time.

Another soldier hurled a biscuit at him. He almost put the crusty piece of bread in his mouth, when all the oarsmen began beating on the worn smooth wooden handles of their oars—with their biscuits! They sang a song, keeping time with the beating of the biscuits.

"'Tis ta chase the weevils out," the wiry man said.

Jachin inspected his biscuit and out crawled a little brown bug. He looked closer and saw what looked like a fat white worm wriggling out of a hole in the biscuit. He pounded the roll against his oar, and more bugs came out. He pounded again, a bit too hard, and the dry bread broke in two. Half of his meal crumbled to the wet floor.

"*Odedicus*. Name's Odedicus. Call me Oded."

Jachin nodded to the man sitting next to him on the bench. He bent low and picked up the biscuit half. It smelled of urine.

"Do what I says, kid, and you might live." Oded snatched Jachin's biscuit. "You'll give me a portion of your meal. The best part, mind you."

Jachin stared numbly as the man ate his biscuit—grubs, weevils, and all.

"You'll do my night watch—and your own."

Barely enough skin stretched on this man's thin bones. There was an evil look to his sunken dark eyes and a firmness to his thin white lips.

"Right, boys?"

Jachin flinched.

"Right, Oded!" they replied in unison.

He was used to his father's tirades and belittling abuse, and certainly Toenin had bullied him, but this was different. Though frail looking, this man's demeanor threatened grief. Jachin tightened his muscles. Not to fight, but to protect. How in the name of his mother's god was he going to survive? Comply? Escape? He wanted to jump back into the sea and sink into the deep. He didn't want to deal with any more pain and abuse. They were wise to shackle him.

"Quit your yappin' and start rowin', ya scum!" screamed a man from the deck above.

The oars began to move in harmony to the sound of high-pitched pipes and rhythmic chanting. He grasped the smooth wood and pulled when Oded pulled. Why didn't they use the sails like the merchant ship? The men rowed for an hour—two to an oar. At first Jachin's palms reddened; then they blistered on top of his blisters. At the end of the period, a horn blew, and Jachin's chain was removed. The men scampered aft and down a ladder to their sleeping quarters. As they passed a barrel three-fourths full of a green liquid with small living things swimming in the scum, Jachin's stomach lurched. Scrawled on the barrel was the Latin word for "water."

Oded took a ladle and scooped up a portion of the liquid. He drank it, careful not to spill a drop. He didn't offer any to Jachin. "Water is rationed, it is," he said.

Half-dressed men packed the crew's quarters. Oded took a lower hammock by the door.

Jachin climbed into the hammock above. His stomach growled, but he wanted sleep more than food. Oded, however, kept talking.

"First hour of the day, the trierarchus walks the deck," Oded said. "Do not disturb him. Expects the deck to be sanded before he takes his first step, he does. Trierarchus Caelus likes ta feel wind on his cheek and note the shadow of sail and deviation of the rudder. Only Caelus knows our mission. Youse listenin', Piscis?"

"Yes."

"Rudder man, when rebuked, yells at oarsmen. Got it? And no biscuits."

Jachin wasn't sure that was a bad thing.

"Short on water. Short on stores. Shortage of wood. Meat only brought to a boil and fire put out. Two days it will be gone. And brew? Can't have shortage of that. After days at sea without touching sand, I hears we go ashore on the morrow looking for grub."

Perhaps there would be opportunity to escape. Jachin lay back and closed his eyes.

Creaking, footfalls, hobnailed boots above. Singing wind in rigging. Sailor's snores.

A man woke him. "Time for Oded's watch. And after that, your watch, *Servus*."

Trudging to the upper deck along with others who were on watch, Jachin made his way in the darkness to the bow. Clouds blocked any stars. Below him protruded a bronze battering ram. Each side of the elongated bow displayed exaggerated wide-open eyes. He hoped his own eyes stayed opened and alert—for what, he did not know. At least he didn't have to pull line or oar. He leaned against the railing and briefly thought about jumping. A faint whisper of wind in the ropes and the slap of sea on the brass ram teased Jachin's eyelids. He gripped the rail. The pain of his blistered palms kept him awake until the dim light of morning.

Several sailors scrubbed and sanded the deck until the clouds parted, revealing the violet sunrise. A *cornu* blew the signal for shift change.

Jachin rushed below to his hammock, only to run into Oded.

"What're you doin'?"

"My watch is over," Jachin said.

"Time to row, Paulo Piscis."

That day they pulled into a bay and dropped anchor. Several skiffs ventured out to shore with fully armed legionnaires. It was not long before they returned.

Jachin helped pull rope to raise the anchor, and they sent him to the oars. He took his seat next to Oded. A soldier shackled him again. It was pointless, but Jachin complied. He would get his chance if he stayed vigilant.

"Scuttlebutt is that they found no supplies," Oded growled.

"What does that mean?"

"More rowing. We turn south by southwest."

"Where did we land?"

"What do you care, slave?"

"I just wondered where we were."

"Britannia."

Jachin stopped rowing. "Albion?"

Oded cuffed his ear. "They found a settlement, but all the occupants were dead. A real massacre, they says. No supplies. Water fouled. One hellish site it must have been. Barbarians and butchers, the lot of 'em. The whole village burnt to cinders."

"Caradoc," Jachin said under his breath.

That night was the same. Double watch on the bow. Rowing during the hot day. He rarely saw the sun. To stay

The Golden Cord

awake was his hardest task. To fall asleep on guard duty was a death sentence. Jachin considered it.

During the morning break, the sun appeared through the clouds, and the men could come on deck before sitting on the rowing benches below. Word was they would use sail today.

"Let's have a spittin' contest. Can you spit, Piscis?" Oded asked Jachin.

"If I drink a little first."

Oded laughed. He drew a line in the sawdust left by the morning deck sanding. "Stands here. We both spit on the count of three. Whoever is closest to the line without going over, wins. Winner gets the other's biscuits today. One. Two. Three. Spit!"

Jachin spit as hard as he could. The sputum landed in front of Trierarchus Caelus on his freshly sanded deck.

Oded laughed. He had not spit.

"Who spat on my deck?"

"I did, sir," Jachin said.

"All hands on deck!"

Several men grabbed Jachin. They stretched his arms above his head and tied his wrists to the mainmast. He had no idea what happened. Should he fight back?

With his back to the sailors, two soldiers ripped his tunic off.

A man holding a tattered rope approached him and hit Jachin on his exposed back with the whip.

Jachin sucked in a breath and rode the pain, determined not to scream or cry. His father once accused him of stealing a pastry and beat him. He didn't steal it, and even now he wasn't sure of any personal wrongdoing. Each of the twenty-one stripes directed his anger and hatred to Oded, who had set him up. Jachin slumped, his wrists raw from the rope, his back bleeding. By the way his back and shoulders burned, he guessed that not a bit of his skin lacked abuse.

"Untie the boy and hang him from the standing rigging," the trierarchus ordered.

Barely able to stand, let alone walk, Jachin faced the sun. His arms were now outstretched on ropes supporting the mast. He gritted his teeth as they doused his wounds with vinegar.

That night he did not stand watch but remained tied to the cables. Oded was not happy and glared at him the entire duration of his watch.

The next day they untied him and removed his braccae. They marched him to his post on the bow while others laughed and mocked his nakedness. He wanted a drink of water but did not beg.

⌘ ⌘ ⌘

Several days passed. When not sleeping, sailors tutored him on nautical terms and tying knots. This proved helpful. Fleet soldiers, or *milites classiarii*, like the man with the scarf who first attacked him, worked the sails. Armed soldiers, *nautae*, stood around dressed for battle. Who they were ready to fight, Jachin had no idea. Below were the oarsmen—*remiges*—three tiers of them. And there were 169 hired legionnaire oarsmen who were called *miles*. And one slave. Jachin was the only slave. Dressed in tattered braccae and tunic, he stood barefoot at the rail. Yet he held his head high as workers on the docks watched the trireme sail into a harbor.

"You are forbidden spoil, drink, treasure, or women. Supplies only. We must be seen as friends. Friends who will dock here often," Caelus told the landing party. "We offer them wealth and peace. They will know we are from Rome, and as such we walk a thin line between hatred and acceptance. We'll eat before we go ashore so you won't be tempted to enjoy yourselves. We are here on business."

The men groaned.

"Need full bellies. Never shop when hungry, I says." Oded, for as thin as he was, never missed a chance to eat. The old sailor gave Jachin a mug of greasy, watered-down beer and two biscuits.

Jachin didn't trust the man, but he nodded as he took one of the biscuits, which he had begun to call "worm castles." He crushed it against the rail and mixed the crumbs with the brew. The worms floated to the top. He skimmed them off and threw the weevil larvae overboard.

"Shouldn't waste good food, boy. Here, put these on!"

Oded threw a short tunic, braccae, and sandals to Jachin. The clothes were too big and smelled of urine.

"You is to go ashore with me and secure stores for replenishment. Others will take empty water barrels to fill."

Jachin stepped into a skiff with Oded. His back still sore, his lips dry and cracked.

"I'm going hunting," Oded said.

"Hunting?"

"I needs a woman."

This man was no different than his father. Was every man like this?

"Lie for me," Oded said, slapping Jachin on his battered back. "If'n youse run, I'll hunt *you* and skin ya alive when I catch ya. And I wills catch you, boy. Mark my word."

Jachin did not recognize the harbor; however, the residents' activities and familiar speech led him to ascertain he must be in the south of Albion. Verica's land. Home.

They pulled the skiff on shore, and Oded gave Jachin a stern look and took off toward town.

He couldn't believe his luck. Left alone as the *miles* scattered for their various duties of procuring goods, Jachin eagerly trotted to the first home. He thought of telling them he was a captive but wanted to keep what skin he had left. Wounded as he was, running off was not an option, as he had nowhere to go. Besides, he wouldn't get too far until Oded found and beat him. It didn't fit in his overall plan anyway.

Knowing the language, he asked for anything the villagers could spare. The lady who came to the door gave him a vase of cow's milk. Jachin sniffed the amphora. It was at least a day past sour. At the next home. He traded the milk for eggs. As he progressed down the lane, he traded the basket of eggs for a bridle. He continued door to door, trading up until a farmer gave him a skinny old cow.

Pleased with his fortune, he headed back to the *Morta Columbarium*. He met the inebriated and empty-handed Oded stumbling toward the skiff.

"That is the ugliest woman I ever seen!" Oded said.

"She's a cow."

"No need to call her names."

Once on board, all applauded the cow's arrival. Once brought back to health, this animal would provide milk, cheese, and later, fresh meat for the men.

Jachin beamed.

Trierarchus Caelus approached. "Who's responsible for this animal?"

"That would be the paulo piscis, sir," slurred Oded.

Jachin bowed his head now, thinking this might not have been such a good idea.

The trierarchus took the sickly looking cow from him. "Next time hunt for venison."

CHAPTER 14

Fighting

Many people bypass advice altogether and still find what they're looking for.

— Scribonius Largus

Oded remained a constant nemesis. And to make it worse, Trierarchus Caelus gave Oded the task of physically training Jachin.

The next day Oded began in earnest despite his raging hangover. "A legionnaire's training is done in five stages. Theys have to always have the advantage on the field. But we's stuck on this dung bucket of a vessel!"

The day was already hot, and there was very little breeze. He rubbed his bald head with a wet rag and set Jachin to marching the length of the ship, from bow to aft and then back again.

After about ten trips, Jachin stopped to rub his shins.

Oded waited for this moment. "Your legs have to be

Fighting

strong, Paulo Piscis. You can't just sit at the oars all day. A legionnaire must walk twenty miles in five hours and still move the next day—and in full armor! The ways you is marching, youse won't make it till lunch."

He lashed Jachin on the back with a tattered leather strap. "Get moving, Paulo Piscis!"

The marching continued till dusk.

The next day Jachin could hardly stand. Every day he wasn't rowing, he marched. Just when he believed he'd gotten past the worst, it got worse.

Oded directed Jachin to the aft of the ship and placed a long, thick wooden pole into a hole situated on the deck. Dented and scarred, as if a dog had chewed on it for days, it stood there like a fence post without a fence.

He handed Jachin a wooden sword heavier than the standard practice *rudis*. "Here."

"What am I to do with this?"

"Fight the post."

Jachin swung the sword in a wide arc, striking the post. The jolt jarred his hand.

Several sailors laughed.

"Youse gonna play at it or practice like a Roman? A Roman uses jabs, thrusts, feints, and lunges. Ne'er the edge of the sword. That is what barbarians do."

Oded grabbed the sword from Jachin and showed him the moves. This was different than any training he had in Albion.

"I'll be back fer ya later. If'n I's catch you slackin, you'll be flogged agin."

Striking the post with the wooden sword, Jachin attacked. And attacked. And attacked the post until the sun touched the horizon. When his right arm got tired, he switched to the left. His arms ached, as did his torso. Hardly able to run his fingers through his hair, Jachin ached all over.

The next day Oded placed a large palette behind the post.

"What is that for?"

"It's so youse don't throw the *pilum* into the sea, youse *stultus*!" Oded barked.

The Golden Cord

He showed Jachin how to hold the pilum spear and threw it at the post. It hit dead center.

"Go get it, Paulo Piscis. It's your turn."

Jachin retrieved the pilum. This spear had a nice balance to it. A rounded wooden stick about as tall as Toenin, with a thin iron spike on the end, ending in an arrowhead-like point. He took aim at the practice post. His first fling missed and fell short. It took many tries to get the weight and throw correct. Oded finally gave up yelling at him and left him to practice on his own. By the end of the day, he was hitting his mark consistently.

His teacher showed up as the sun set. Oded fastened a large leather button on the pointed end of the pilum, making the tip spongey soft. Giving it to Jachin, he stepped in front of the post.

"Spear me."

Jachin was glad to comply. He reared back and let the pilum fly. It struck Oded on his shirtless chest. He didn't even blink.

"Now it is my turn. Remove your tunic."

The thrown spear struck Jachin with a painful jab, knocking the air from him. No more damage occurred other than a dark-red mark above his heart. He stood tall as Oded picked up the pilum to throw again.

"You have to learn how to throw and how to receive." Oded let the spear fly, striking Jachin on the forehead, knocking him to the deck. He quickly got up and started toward Oded with his fists clinched. Oded kicked the pilum with his foot, tossing it through the air and into his hand. He swatted Jachin across his ankles, knocking him off his feet. Then he pulled the leather button off and pointed the pilum at Jachin's chest.

Jachin had enough. "How many days must I do this stuff?"

"This is justa start to acquaint youse with your training stages. After this week, youse will alternate days with the trierarchus for navigation training. Tomorrow youse will learn the agility drill. Youse have ta climb an' leap in full armor o'er a vaulting horse. And the last drill is to learn to be a unit. Youse have already learned that at the oar. You

Fighting

know many trumpet commands already. There are many more to be learned."

After several weeks, Jachin was more than bruised. He had been humiliated and derided daily. Exhaustion overwhelmed him. Each day was an uphill climb that ended in a short rest. He slept as if dead.

Now he worked with the trierarchus.

"Training is more than just getting fit," Caelus said. "Learning technical fighting skills teaches discipline."

"Discipline or discouragement?"

"Discipline. The discouraged are executed. The legionnaires will teach you how to fight not only with a sword but with fists. That is good, since you have a proclivity for getting in trouble with the commissioned sailors. I need you to be strong and quick. You have a knack for the fight and seem to learn quickly."

Caelus told him to meet him during the night watch. Besides all his training, Jachin still had his duties. He rarely had any time to himself.

"Tonight I will show you the stars and teach you navigation."

Tired and worn out, Jachin met Caelus at the bow of the ship. The ocean was as still as a glass mirror, and the sky was moonless.

"Right there," Caelus pointed. "Seven stars form the Big Dipper, the well-known bright stars in the constellation Ursa Major (the Bear). It shows us the direction of north. The Big Dipper—the men prefer calling it 'the Drinking Gourd'—and part of Ursa Minor, the Little Dipper, or Little Bear, is over this way." He moved Jachin's hand to indicate the stars position. "The sailors call the Little Dipper 'the Dog's Tail' or the 'Ship Star.' It is always visible. Follow Little Bear to navigate. He will lead you north. The brightest star in that constellation is Polaris—the North Star."

"Got it. That's north, but how do I know where we are?" Jachin asked.

Caelus handed Jachin an interesting wooden instrument. Round and platelike, with writing carved around the edges and a knotted cord attached to the center. It appeared quite old and well worn.

"What's this?"

"Navigators of the ship, by men such as you, are called *gubernatores*. I will teach you how to make use of wind, stars, nautical manuals, and experience to make voyages safely and repetitively. During the day, when visibility is good, we use the sun and watch the shoreline for known landmarks. To navigate at night along a degree of latitude, a sailor needs to find how far—or to what degree—the northern stars are positioned in the sky. This plate is called the *kamal*."

He took the instrument from Jachin and placed the end of the knotted string in his mouth. "It works better if you have teeth to hold it."

Holding up the plate, Caelus moved it closer and farther from his face several times until the northern stars and the horizon below corresponded to the plate's upper and lower edges. The distance the plate lay away from the face—measured by a string tied to the center—determined the latitude.

With the trierarchus's help, Jachin was soon able to match the markings and determine the position of the ship at that precise moment. "Okay, this is fine for navigating at night, but what if we sail in the daytime and cannot see the shore?"

The older man picked up what looked like nothing more than a stick. "This is the *gnomon*. When the sun is out, the *gnomon* casts a shadow. The sun's position differs daily in direction and length." He placed it in a hole in the center of a disk that floated in a large bowl of water. "Following the marks on the disk, one can figure where they are by the length of the sun's shadow made by the central pole. Of course, there is no shadow at night."

"It looks like a sundial!" Jachin said.

"Exactly."

As the days went by, along with astronomy, Jachin also learned the geography of the shore as they traveled back and forth, watching for pirates. He learned to watch the waves and to understand the different winds and their tendencies. With all his new tools, he could determine the direction, position, speed, and distance of the ship. He used what was called a *wind rose*. The wind rose was a drawing

Fighting

with a circular spoked wheel. Similar to a map, the longer the spokes, the more prevalent the wind direction in that area of the Great Green.

Jachin and the trierarchus grew to enjoy their talks in the late evenings, something Jachin ascertained angered Oded, so Jachin made sure to tell him about it at each day's end.

Caelus often illustrated his teaching with stories. "A recurring theme runs through old stories that makes known the kinship of bears and humans. Bears lumber along on all fours, or they will stand on their hind feet like a man. They will gesture with their front paws. Ursa Major, in its travels throughout the heavens, constantly changes positions, seeming to run along on all fours nearest the horizon, and then rising to its hind feet to begin the ascent back into the sky.

"The story goes that one day a beautiful maiden named Callista was hunting in the forest. She grew tired and laid down to rest. The god Jupiter noticed and admired her beauty. Callista later bore a son from this union that she named Arcos. Of course, Jupiter's wife, Juno, became extremely jealous and turned Callista into a bear. To ease their son's grief, Jupiter changed Arcos into a bear as well. Then, grabbing them both by their tails, he swung them into the heavens so they could live among the stars.

"Juno, angrier than ever, went to the gods of the sea and demanded that they forbid the two bears from wading in the water on their long and endless journey around the northern sky."

"So that is why the stars of Ursa Major and Minor never go below the horizon?"

"Exactly!"

The next few months flew by for Jachin. He gained not only in strength but also in skill. Soon he bested many legionnaires in practice fights. He had garnered a little of the hungry *miles'* respect with the offer of the cow he brought on board, but when they saw how serious he was at training, they left him alone. They didn't threaten to use him as fish bait anymore. And he spent less time at the oars.

Little did they know, Jachin trained with the aim to kill his father.

15
CHAPTER

Asklepios's Rod

All health is not found in medicine.

— Scribonius Largus

Several months ago—Regnum, on the south shore of Albion

A young man with a broad-tooth grin like a broken stone wall loomed above Boaz.

"Who are you?"

"I'm Rego. Well, that's not my real name, but that is what everyone calls me. I'm the landlord's son. I live down the hill in a deep furrow, where the ground wrinkles."

Boaz frowned. He wasn't sure if the boy's missing teeth were natural or if they had been knocked out. Boaz turned over in the bed to face the wall. "Go away." He pulled at the linen sling that Sophronios had replaced. The tightly tied swath that circled his chest rubbed his throbbing shoulder. He couldn't move the arm. He couldn't move the bandages. He kicked the woven cover off. After traveling slowly for a fortnight in the physician's wagon to the seaside town of Regnum on the south shore of Albion, he hurt all over. He endured bruises on top of bruises.

Even though a Roman trireme sailed from the town the day before, the boisterous seas usually halted travel this time of year. No other ships were scheduled to depart, so Sophronios procured lodging for them from these friendly tribes in the south. They would winter in this town. That much he recalled. Someone carried him to this room. Rego? More likely Sophronios.

"Your master sent me up here to fetch you. He said it was time for your studies to begin."

"Humph."

The boy shook Boaz's shoulder. "Come on with you now. I have chores to do, and I don't have time for you to go back to sleep. The man was most strict in his demand." Rego shoved him again.

Boaz turned over and groaned.

"Hey, didn't I see you begging door to door yesterday?"

"No. Go away."

Another poke. "And you need a bath. You stink!"

Boaz swung around. "All right!"

"Ouch!" they both cried.

Rego grabbed his nose to stop the bleeding. "What'd you do to me?"

"Nothing."

"I think you broke it!"

Sophronios rushed into the room. "What is all this yelling?"

"Boaz broke my nose!"

"Your nose hit my arm." Boaz rubbed his elbow and gave his best disconsolate look. It wasn't hard to do, as his arm truly hurt.

"Let me see, boy."

Rego removed his hands from his face.

"Demeter's biscuits, I believe you are correct in your

diagnosis." The physician reached up, pinched Rego's nose firmly, and gave it a pugnacious tug.

"Ow!"

"Here, hold this rag against your nose. The bleeding will subside. All bleeding stops."

"Yeah, when I'm dead!"

Boaz chuckled. Glanced at Sophronios, then back to Rego, and smiled.

"Each awakening is a beginning," Sophronios said.

⌘ ⌘ ⌘

Later that day, after his studies, Boaz made his way to the small creek behind the modest home where they stayed. Sophronios removed the sling and swathe so he could take off his tunic and wash both himself and his clothes. He grudgingly agreed with Rego. He stunk. With the old blood, sweat, rain, and muddy road splatter, he was overly ripe.

The town abutted a small wood of evergreens and pin oak. Brown-and-orange leaves bunched together at the bottom of the tree trunks like worn-out leggings fallen to a man's ankles. The fragrant pines, warbling birds, and rippling water of the bubbling creek all encouraged Boaz to feel more at ease. He plodded down the path toward the water.

The trip had been a long three days, and he was physically exhausted from Sophronios's prescribed daily routine of exercises. He had a long way to go—both in recovery and travels.

What awaited him at journey's end excited him. The physician apprenticed him. Boaz was not sure of what that meant. To his thinking it was nothing more than thralldom. He was bought and paid for with wine, and Sophronios had him doing everything for him like a slave. Nevertheless, this was a new beginning and a chance to not only learn new skills but a chance to forget old shames. Laughing with Sophronios and Rego lightened his mood.

Boaz set his bag down and removed his tunic. He picked up a rounded stone from the edge of the creek and weighed it in his hand. He tried to skip it across the water, but his grip was weak, and it splashed with a kerplunk.

He retrieved *sapon* soap from his sack and stepped gingerly into the creek. He scrubbed himself until his skin reddened, trying to erase the stains of the past. Thinking pained him.

His morning assignment from Sophronios consisted of memorizing six Latin nouns and to decline them into their various forms before breakfast. Sophronios also told him he needed to continue moving his arm to gain strength. It felt good to be free of the sling. The cold of the water eased his pain.

After rinsing off, he retrieved his tunic and braccae, smelled them, and threw the rancid rags into the creek. He gazed at his reflection in the water and decided it was best to not go traipsing through the forest in his altogether nakedness, so he recovered his garments. He scrubbed his clothes against a rock with the *sapon*—scrubbing and scrubbing—to remove the stench. Unable to dry them, he wrung them out as best he could and put the trousers and tunic on wet.

As he walked back to the inn, the sounds of the villagers and other travelers swelled as the town awakened. The normality of beginning the morning routines to sell their wares, clean, or converse about the latest scandals of the town soothed him. He wondered what they said about him and Sophronios.

He practiced the Latin nouns in his mind, having only come up with five. He soaked up languages like a sponge in a deep bucket. It was almost a game to him to replace old words with new words.

Suddenly he tripped and fell prone.

Hissss.

A movement only inches away from his face revealed a snake poised to strike.

"Don't move," Sophronios said. He saw Boaz fall and ran to his side. "Don't move a muscle. Don't even breathe."

He didn't. In this frozen moment, he studied the beast. Was this the same kind of snake that Jachin warned Amminus about? That one killed his grandfather.

"That is an asp," Sophronios whispered. "It is very dangerous. One bite and you will die."

The Golden Cord

Suddenly the asp hissed and struck out.

Boaz stayed still.

The asp reared again, but instead of delivering a lethal bite, it turned and scooted into the tall grass like Jachin running into the wheat fields back home.

Boaz exhaled. A whimsical grin came to his face as he turned over to see his teacher looking at him.

"What?" Boaz asked.

Sophronios lifted his robe and hastened to where Boaz lay. He helped him up. "So much for washing." He scraped the mud and leaves from the front of Boaz's tunic. "Weren't you afraid?"

"I guess the asp was curious about how a boy looked up close. Did you hear him? It was like 'hiss.' His tongue kept darting out. Captivating!"

"Apollo has truly chosen you, Boaz." Sophronios chuckled. "Come along, Pedi."

Later that morning, after they broke their fast, teacher and pupil sat close to the fire, warming the shivers, the bloody noses, and snakes from their minds.

"Did you know that the snake is a symbol of medicine?" Sophronios asked. By this time Boaz knew that by the tone of his voice another lecture loomed ahead.

"No, sir."

"You remember me telling you about Asklepios, the god of medicine? He was the son of Apollo and a mortal woman named Koronis. His mother died in labor, but Apollo rescued the child and carried the baby to the centaur Chiron, who raised Asklepios. He instructed him in the art of medicine. It is said that in return for some kindness rendered by Asklepios, a snake licked the boy's ears clean and taught him secret knowledge. To us Greeks, snakes are sacred beings of wisdom, healing, and resurrection."

"Because it sheds its skin?"

"That is part of it. Thus our symbol, the *Rod of Asklepios*—a snake entwined upon a staff." He picked up a snakelike stick. "The duality of life and death. The medicine and the illness. The healing and the hurt."

"Like the brooch you wear?"

"Yes, just like that." He tossed the stick into the fire.

"Your first prescription to learn is *'One should use yew tree juice as a cure for snakebite.'* Now tell me the declensions for today."

"*Putidus, putidi, putido, putidum, putido, putide.*"

"And their meanings?"

"Rotten, decaying, spoiled, infected. Like a festering wound."

"Use it in a sentence."

"*Ego sum puteo*—I don't stink."

"Oh, but you did. You definitely did."

16
CHAPTER

Education

Dream's confusion that lingers before the half-shut eye are born from thoughts unspoken.

— Scribonius Largus

The next few weeks dragged for Boaz. The wheat fields around Regnum appeared bare and empty. The leaves dangled tenuously on the trees. A thick fog scattered frost on the ground most mornings. As the days shortened and the cold of winter settled in, he continued to heal, but the chill intensified the pain in his shoulder. Stiff and sore, he diligently did the exercises Sophronios prescribed.

He rubbed his arm as he sorted and catalogued the various herbs and plants his master collected in Albion. Sophronios kept him busy making jar labels and herb bottle signage. Boaz had no idea there were so many plants,

Education

and he was even more amazed that each one had a different name. He struggled with Latin spelling and writing the letters. Sophronios hid his infirmity, but Boaz noticed how close the physician leaned in to read the fine print on the labels. Because of this, Boaz wrote the letters large enough so that Sophronios could see them.

He added small drawings of the plants to the labels and next to the listing in the catalogue to help him remember what they looked like.

Boaz liked being busy. It pushed away any thoughts about what had happened to him. He didn't have any answers, but it was no use looking for them in his head.

One morning, warmer than usual, the sun shone bright through the open window in the house.

"Let's take a walk. Bring the board game," Sophronios announced.

The two travelers walked for a time, then sat under an old tree. Boaz set up the *Latrunculi* game on the board that Jachin brought to him when he recovered after his father beat him half to death. Maybe more than a half. Three-fifths? Doesn't matter. *Don't think about it.* But somehow the memory remained in his bones. His body experienced a portion of the trauma every time he went back there in his mind. The pain somehow didn't differentiate between then and now. *If I think about it, it makes me feel wicked. It makes me feel a partner in the crime.* He lowered his head and squeezed his eyes shut. He couldn't grieve what his body felt back then. Not now. *Don't think about it.*

Rules were explained as Sophronios studied the board. "It is like one I played in Rome," he said and made his first move.

Boaz moved a stone on the board to counter.

"So quiet, Pedi, these past few days. Does the scar on your head cause you so much pain that it hurts to speak?"

A shake of his head communicated, "No."

"It seems to have healed nicely. Tut-tut. Must have had a proficient physician," Sophronios said.

Another move set his master up to lose a piece no matter how Boaz responded. "It was just some guy along the road," he said.

Sophronios raised an eyebrow. "Tell me what you are thinking."

"Nothing."

"This 'nothing' you are thinking about have anything to do with your mother and brother?"

"It's your move."

"Of course, Pedi." Sophronios made a move, hesitated, took it back, and made another. "It is your turn. Move wisely."

Boaz pushed his game piece forward, not only capturing one of the stones but also setting up another impossible situation for the physician.

After a moment he said, "I had a hog named Julius Caesar."

"A long-dead dictator? How odd."

"He ate a raven."

"A boar hog? Named Julius Caesar? I am sure there is a story there."

"That's what happened to the raven . . . and Primus . . ."

"What's Primus?"

"Our dog. Tahdah killed him and fed his body to Julius Caesar."

"Tahdah?"

"My *pateras*."

"Interesting theory. What evidence do you have of this against your father?"

Boaz shoved the game board away.

"Oh, my dear boy, I do not know what happened. I only know what I have been told. However, this man, Caradoc, strikes me as a man of spurious means. I do not doubt that the dog and raven came to an untimely and nefarious end. It gives me much grief to hear of this. I am of a certainty that Julius Caesar had nothing to do with it."

Glancing away, Boaz bit his lip.

⌘ ⌘ ⌘

That night Boaz tossed and turned in fitful sleep. He dreamed.

"Come on, boys. Keep up!"

Education

"We're coming, Uncle Amminus," hollered Boaz. He wiped dirt and mud from his face as he headed off in the other direction, chasing something in the sparse grass. Suddenly the object of his attention alighted on his bare chest. Boaz smiled broadly and turned toward his uncle and brother. "Look," he whispered pointing to the long-legged grasshopper. "I caught him."

"Don't move. I'll get 'em," Jachin said as he brushed his hair back out of his face.

Amminus shook his head and rolled his eyes. "Not another distraction."

"He tickles!" Boaz laughed.

As Jachin reached toward the insect, the grasshopper jumped. "Where'd it go?"

"It's on your head!" screamed Boaz through fits of laughter.

Jachin batted at his hair.

"Aaghhh! Get it off! Get it off!"

Amminus snatched the grasshopper from Jachin's head. Their uncle handed the green creature to Boaz, who cupped both hands gently around the critter. "Now that you have him, what are you going to do?"

"Let's take him home and show Matrona. We could feed him grass and dirt and keep him in our room," Jachin said.

"Grasshoppers don't eat dirt."

"Yes, they do!"

"Don't be dull-witted, Jachin. I'm gonna let him go." Boaz opened his hands and shook the grasshopper to shoo him off. It jumped directly toward Jachin.

"Stop it, Boaz!" Jachin whacked the grasshopper away with his hands, turned, and slugged Boaz on the shoulder.

"Ow!" Boaz lunged toward his brother, and they began to wrestle, falling to the ground in a cloud of dust, arms, and legs.

The grasshopper grew to the size of a man, and in Caradoc's voice said, "Stop this childishness!" The beast beat the boys with a leather belt.

Boaz awoke in a sweat.

Above him a spider had woven a web. He batted it down. Just a bad dream. He drifted to sleep and dreamed again.

The Golden Cord

Amminus had seen enough. He grasped each of the twins by an arm and pulled them apart. "How are we ever going to get the cow milked if you boys keep fighting?" He directed them to the barn.

Amminus handed a bucket to Jachin. His uncle grabbed some rope hanging from a peg, made a noose, and walked carefully up to the milk cow. While voicing soft reassurances, he placed the rope over the animal's head and around her neck. The twins stood back.

"Won't she buck or kick?" asked Jachin.

"It's a cow," Boaz interjected.

Amminus explained, "Cows don't buck. They only kick if you are trying to hurt them, like when Primus chased that calf the other day, and her mother came to the rescue, kicking and snorting."

"Yeah, Primus let out a yelp that could be heard all the way into Camulodunon."

"Didn't stop him, though. He chased the cows again the next day!"

"Primus is a good Catuvellauni. He doesn't give up, even when he has been kicked in the head." Amminus laughed as he tied the cow to a post on the fence. He took the bucket from Jachin and placed it under the cow. He pulled up a stool and sat down. "Have you boys ever milked a cow?"

"No," they said in unison.

"Here, put your hands around the udder like you are grabbing a sword. Now start from the top and squeeze your index finger and thumb. Then use the rest of your fist like this." Amminus pulled and squirted milk into the bucket. He aimed at one of the gathering cats on the rail and squirted it in the face with milk. The cat lapped it up. Meowed for more. Soon a row of cats and kittens of diverse colors and sizes gathered together to get in on the free refreshment.

Jachin reached for the udder and jumped back as the cow slapped a fly with her tail. Gathering his courage, he reached under the cow with both hands as he looked askance at Boaz. At first nothing happened. He kept tugging. Getting frustrated, he scooted back and ran his fingers through his hair.

His uncle positioned his hands around his nephew's

Education

and showed him how to do it correctly. Milk filled the bottom of the bucket.

"Look, Boaz, I'm milking!" Jachin squirted the cats too.

"Hit the black one, Jachin! No, the one with the white spot on his forehead. Now the long-haired gray one. Uh-oh, look out. I think they want the bucket too!"

Just then, Jachin squirted Boaz with the milk, hitting him in the eye.

"Hey!"

Before long, an all-out war broke out as Amminus sprayed first one boy then the other. Jachin fell backward laughing. Boaz took the opportunity and jumped on top of him, knocking over the milk bucket.

"Your mother expects a full bucket to make cream and butter. We better get busy."

The boys milked again until the bucket overflowed.

A dirt clod suddenly hit Boaz in the back of his head. He turned to see his father, Caradoc, standing there with another clod in his hand poised to throw it.

Boaz woke. He had a bad headache.

Again he found that the spider had spun a web above him.

He turned over. "Primus is a good Catuvellauni. He doesn't give up, even when he has been hit on the head." He fell back to slumber.

He dreamed a third dream. This one more vivid.

"Hey, Uncle, can we take a kitten home?"

"What do you want a cat for?"

"So we can have someone to care for, and they would love us back."

"Yeah, and they could catch mice and spiders."

"Cats don't eat spiders."

"Yes, they do. I saw 'em do it lots of times."

"Now you are gonna say they eat dirt too."

"No, I wasn't!"

Amminus picked up the full milk bucket. "Once you get cats around the house, they start having babies, and they grow up and have babies. Before you know what has happened, it will end up like Rome, where you can hardly take a step without a cat under foot," he said.

"Oh, please, Uncle. Please, please, *please*! We will take care of them."

"And we won't let them have kittens ever!"

"Not ever!"

Amminus chuckled, "Okay, get that gunny sack over there. *If* you can catch one, you can take it home. Only one. Not two. Not three. Just *one*."

Jachin and Boaz morphed into kittens—one black with a white spot on its head, the other looked the same.

Caradoc entered and placed the playful two in a sack. He tied them with a golden cord and hung them from the rafter. They meowed, clawed, and tore at each other until the sack dripped with blood.

Boaz awoke with a start. The dream seemed so real. He lit an oil lamp and swatted the spiderweb down again. He dressed and went down stairs. "Tomorrow night I will not go to sleep."

CHAPTER 17

Alignment

The ears of Loyalty cannot listen to another's loud plea.

— Scribonius Largus

AD 35—Camulodunon, Albion

Queen Cartimandua of the Brigantes and her daughter, Raena, entered the king of Albion's great house. She witnessed Caradoc's contrived coronation in this hall on her previous journey to Camulodunon.

The hall was unrecognizable. The new king added tapestries and rugs to the walls, presumably to give the room warmth. It was reminiscent of the coldness of Caradoc's heart, which he concealed with his snake-before-he-bites-you warm smile. Suspended between the tapestries were broken swords of his enemies. Each one placed as a reminder that he prevailed. Smoke from neglected sconces blackened the once beautiful oaken rafters as snow drifted through thatch holes above. The damp darkness mirrored her mood.

High King Cunobelinos's untimely death lingered fresh in her mind. Amminus, her daughter's weapons trainer, was the rightful heir to the kingship. That did not stop Caradoc from stealing the throne and forcing exile upon his older brother. Amminus's whereabouts remained unknown.

This day Caradoc and his druid toady had called the leaders, kings, and caretakers of all the tribes in Albion to meet. She came to see firsthand the ruination of her people with the hope that at least one man would stand up to this brute. Caradoc coerced them to prepare for the danger of an imminent invasion from Rome. Cartimandua sensed that more transpired than the possibility of peril.

She removed a heavy plaid wool cloak from her daughter's shoulders but kept her own tight around her. "Things are going to get rough, my daughter. The coming conflict is not the atmosphere for fostering a budding queen." She knelt before Raena and searched her blue eyes. "I am sending you west with a contingent of my warriors. There is a man there who will teach you proper demeanor and deportment."

"Who?"

The queen pulled Raena in close to her and whispered, "A friend of a friend."

Raena scowled.

Cartimandua suspected her daughter knew she dealt with some unsavory "friends." This was different. She trusted this teacher.

"Look around, Raena. Learn today who you may trust and who is falsehearted."

The various tribal leaders milled about the expansive room and clamored for attention. The high druid, Kenjar, made his rounds, welcoming the guests. Very few women attended this pomposity. That surprised Cartimandua, considering the strong leadership women brought to the clans.

How difficult it must be to corral a herd like this. Each chieftain wanted things their own way. Sociable on the surface yet disinclined to work together. While men got up and

Alignment

gave speeches, asked for support, or had a grievance with another tribe, Cartimandua introduced Raena to some of the men and women who she believed opposed Caradoc.

"That is Antedios of the Iceni on the right by the table that is nearly as immense as he. The Iceni have not yielded to the new king's proposals," she whispered to her daughter. "Let me introduce you to him."

Cartimandua approached the men, who immediately stopped talking and turned to greet her. "This is my daughter, Raena. She's going to be a princess."

Raena blushed.

"Nice to meet you, Raena. You are a lovely lass. With me are my sons, Aesunos and Saenuvax. Aesunos has yet to choose a wife." Antedios nodded toward his youngest son, who ran the back of his hand across his hairless upper lip and smiled a toothless grin.

"He hasn't chosen because no one would have him!" said Saenuvax.

"At least I don't have your dreadful wife."

"Raena is pledged to—"

"Mom!"

"Well, whoever this prince is, he is a lucky man," said Antedios. "You two go get the ladies a drink." The brothers left, continuing to quarrel as they walked to the other side of the hall.

"Why do your sons argue so?"

"Aesunos and Saenuvax have been arguing with each other since they were old enough to talk. They bicker and barter till they drive their mother crazy. They both resent the preferential treatment that I get from Rome. They minted their own coinage, each trying to outspend the other, trying to buy favors from the foreigners. Not sure if that means they align with Caradoc or not."

"At least I know their father's heart allies with mine."

"The Iceni hold with the Brigantes and will remain neutral to this fight. We have no quarrel with the Romans. Queen Cartimandua, the Iceni are your friends."

"Thank you. You are my friend as well. Come along, Raena, we must greet the others warmly."

"Do we really need to do this?"

"You must be ready to take my place if anything were to happen. These men are leaders. Some equal. Some more accomplished. Making contacts with talented leaders is important. And, my dear, whether you listen, pay attention, or remember these names, when it all comes down—and it will—you must remember that there are more on the side of right than with evil. Remember, Caradoc is not the all-powerful, in-control leader he imagines himself to be."

They moved on to men standing under the broken weapons on the wall. They did not look like they were paying attention to the speaker anyway.

"And this is the former king of the Trinovantes, Addedomaros. He is responsible for incorporating cobblestone streets in Camulodunon," Cartimandua said.

Addedomaros pushed past them toward the drink tables. A group of men followed him.

"He is no friend to the Catuvellauni kingship of Caradoc. Those following Addedomaros are the Parisii. He sold them some cattle that will not breed. They have been after him ever since."

"The Parisii?"

"A Belgic tribe from the north. They have tribal combrogi in Lutetia. My guess is they do not follow Caradoc."

"Is everyone here against the high king?" Raena asked.

"Definitely not. Are you keeping track of those who are not with him? It is important that one knows their allies and opposition when faced with the same enemy."

Several men approached her—Togodumnus, with three of his sons.

"Greetings, Dias, Sego, and Rues!" Raena exclaimed.

"Did you bring something for the king, Cartimandua? You know you should not show up empty-handed," Togodumnus said.

Before she could reply, music began, along with dancing and drums. "Although Caradoc does many things to enliven the crowd, the mood is stifled," she said.

"Yes, the air is heavy. Can we talk?" Togodumnus asked.

"Yes, indeed. Raena, why don't you and the boys go get some food while Togodumnus and I speak." Raena grasped Rues's hand and dragged him and his brothers to the ban-

Alignment

quet table. Cartimandua hollered after her daughter. "Don't eat too many sweets, dear!"

The two stepped farther back into the darkness of the room.

"These speeches are insufferably idealistic," Togodumnus said.

"They are nothing but pandering fools stoking Caradoc's ego. They praise his skills. His talent. His kill counts. They appear confident and composed, yet we know they shake inside. They fear what he will take from them." She covered her mouth "Oh, Togodumnus! I am so sorry. I should not have said that. You have so much to lose. I fault you not."

"Cartimandua, it is okay. I know where I stand. I watch them eat, drink, and laugh. I cannot join with them in that. I find myself imitating their facial expressions, all the while abhorring their lively conversations. I am not enjoying myself."

"That is sad, as you were ever the jovial one. Let me ask you: Who is truly with Caradoc?" Cartimandua asked.

"I will name the tribes, but I do so at great peril."

Raena rejoined them, wiping the crumbs of a pastry from her chin. Togodumnus paced.

"It is all right." She touched his arm, circled her arms around her daughter, and held Raena in front of her. "I want Raena to hear this." They faced the man who bravely risked talking to the queen of the north. "Please, go on, Togodumnus."

"Very well. The Silures in the west hate Rome. The Carvetii from the extreme northeast are not represented, but they have blatantly declared many times they wish Rome would sink into the sea. Of course, the Catuvellauni stand the most to gain from Caradoc. The Dumnonii and the Durotriges sent envoys to this gathering and are tightly knit with the high king. Rome treats them with ruthless disregard, possibly because they helped in the taking of Calleva. They will never capitulate to Rome. The highland Caledonii, who are here as well, are openly in opposition to Rome and will back Caradoc fervently."

"Whoa, slow down. I cannot remember these names, let alone pronounce them all!" Raena said.

"Shhh," Togodumnus and Cartimandua said together.

"That is all who follow Caradoc. I believe only six or seven tribes. Yet he continues to court the others with bribes and threats."

"What about the Corieltauvi?"

"Volisios and two more Corieltauvian nobles, Dumnocoveros and Dubnovellaunos, are in the front, feigning allegiance, but they assure me they are with us. And Volisios has ties with the Parisii in the north. Caradoc deems them as no serious threat to him or the Roman advance. The Conii are also no threat to the high king, although I heard they sent men to Rome often seeking support. Viroco of the Cornovii resists Rome, saying he is willing to die with his followers if need be."

A horn sounded, and Kenjar announced the high king.

"We must hurry. That only leaves the Dobunni, right?"

"King Bodvoc of the northern Dobunni is with us. On the other hand, Corio, leader of the southern Dobunni, joined Caradoc during the attack on Calleva. The minor kings of the southern coast, which Rome called *Regneses*, would most likely allow the Romans into their homes unopposed and give free access through their lands. Verica's son, Cogidumnus, already lives as a Roman."

"Add to that the Atrebates—if Verica is reinstated—the Belgae, Brigantes, and Cantiaci, if Amminus ever returns."

"We must keep together, Togodumnus, and not let Caradoc steal their hearts with promises."

"Quickly now," he whispered. "Kenjar said something about recompense for fealty. How do we oppose his gold?"

The corner of Cartimandua's lip pulled back and slightly upward. "Caradoc seeks to receive, seldom to reward."

18
CHAPTER

Allegiance

Deceitful men display beautiful pictures to the blind.

— Scribonius Largus

The high druid, dressed in his usual white flowing robe and a red mark on his shoulder, called for attention. "Gather around the hearth—the natural life around f-f-fire—a central axis from which all f-fruition f-f-flows."

Kenjar's stuttering always made Cartimandua uncomfortable. She wanted to help him say the words. How he ever ascended to the position of high druid, she didn't know. He was the only man who had escaped the Atrebates's raid and the great fire that followed. Most likely the blaze was a ruse to hide more sinister crimes the druids committed.

While Togodumnus pushed toward the open hearth,

Cartimandua remained in the back near the ornate oak doors with her daughter.

"Each s-spiral of the *triskele* of life radiates from this flame afforded to us by our chief among chiefs, the celebrated Caradoc. His noble acclaim is our f-f-flame," Kenjar sang out.

"Do we have to listen to this?" Raena groaned. "Can we go home now?"

"An oath of allegiance must be given."

"The Brigantes will swear fealty to Caradoc?" Raena asked.

The queen shook her head. "I owe this man nothing, but I must make a show of support."

"I don't understand, Mother. Why must we do this?"

"Feigned fealty has its advantages."

Caradoc entered. He flung off his cape and walked barefoot across the ashes of the hearth. He planned this for effect. The crowd applauded and yelled cries of amazement and appreciation. Cartimandua was not impressed with this trick.

The king quieted the cacophonous crowd and began. "Thank you for coming! I know every man and woman here today has sacrificed their time to heed my call. Let me begin by saying that no one person dominates another." He waved his arm in a swath around the hall to the tribal tapestries of all that he had dominated. "Like the swirl drawings of the clans of Albion, each of you develop independent patterns. The corresponding circular lines and spirals follow and part on parallel tracks. We carve isolated circles, varying in importance and size. Men are the carvers. Men are the creators."

The chieftains all nodded.

"Sounds like bombastic barking to me," Raena whispered to her mother.

"Yes, he states the obvious. Patterns are ingrained into our culture. Even a child like you knows that, Raena."

"I am not a—"

Cartimandua put her hand over Raena's mouth.

"This isolation is acceptable, concerning the progress of our realm in that we each separately advance ourselves the best we can. This diversity encourages growth." He paused.

"Think of our land. We are adept to mold an ungainly and most irregularly shaped surface into a graceful and wholesome plait. How much better would our land be if our lives flowed together as intricate *interwoven* cords? Then let us do so with our clans!"

Cheers and applause filled the airy hall.

Cartimandua wasn't sure they understood what he suggested, except that he spoke with such bravado and fancy words. To her, his words were nothing but the bluster of hollow promises and *flatus* winds. If he speaks his lies boldly enough, they all will believe him.

"I cannot weave the tribes together on my own. A high king does not *control* all; he *rules* all. There is a difference. But when it comes to protection from invading strangers who want to steal our homes, we must come together to forge this cord from golden strands entwined as one piece to stand against our foe." He paused again, brashly stepped to Antedios, and lifted the man's torc.

"We wear open rings around our necks. They are not connected, but open." Caradoc put his fists together and then moved them apart to appear like the torc. Like our homes—circular, but open at only one door. We proclaim loudly all are welcome, yet we will stop all *enemies* who wish to enter."

The assembly nodded and grunted approval.

"On a broader sense, the home we love cannot be left open to harm either." He grasped the man's torc with both hands and bent it so that the two ends met, practically strangling the man. "We must close the gap. We must form a full ring of the clans of Albion that no one can penetrate—a blood brotherhood connected by the cord of common ground. Complete."

A red-faced Antedios turned, gasping for air. It took two men to loosen the torc from his neck.

"This we *must* do in the spirit of kinship. We *must* band together to beat this foe!"

More hails of acclaim and praise for the man who would buy them with lofty promises or destroy them with brutality. Were they all drunk on his power? Cartimandua hid her scowl and grasped Raena's hand.

"From this day forward, I will no longer own property. Neither hillfort or person. Albion doesn't belong to me. I belong to Albion!"

"All hail the king of Albion!" called Kenjar as others joined in chanting Caradoc's name.

"I release all my slaves. What's more, I likewise relinquish my hillfort and go to dwell at the crossroads of our people in Calleva. I will make myself available to all. From that center we will radiate to form an unconquerable force."

"He gives away his hillfort—already scorched and blackened?" Cartimandua said under her breath.

"Mom, you're hurting my hand."

Kenjar stepped to the side as Mara approached Caradoc. Dressed in the plainness of a tribeswoman, with an apron at her waist, she took his arm and smiled.

"To seal my promise, I take Mara—a simple server—as my wife to show the clans my desire to free all from oppression."

Mara beamed. Cartimandua was certain she glowed with more than pride.

"How do you plan to do this?" Caradoc's brother asked from the crowd. Togodumnus breathed deeper and more rapidly than normal. He rubbed his palms on his braccae. He never spoke up in council. Perhaps it was a planted question.

"Unlike some, my brother, we are not weak. We stand here as chosen warriors. We will build upon that foundation by incorporating and equipping your sons to serve and to protect our homes. They will be treated as my personal wards, like sons of the king!"

Antedios called out, "So you begin by taking our sons?"

The first sign of dissent perhaps emboldened by Togodumnus's question. It would not be tolerated, Cartimandua was sure. She searched Caradoc's face for signs of wrath.

"I only do this because the land requires that I do so. I listen and obey its need. Real authority belongs to the land. All I ask of you is what is already owed to the soil—your faith and allegiance." Caradoc smiled. "As the land provides and rewards our valor, I will also give much reward."

There—he said it. Reward. They care not for dust. They

Allegiance

care for riches. They are planted and watered. He now applies the manure and harvests the crop—flesh and fealty.

"For every son you send, I will provide cattle and property to their families. Kenjar assures full druid support. The spiritual men already seek signs of success. He will consecrate our contract with the oak knowers this day."

"But we are not one people. We fight among ourselves like hungry dogs," Antedios cried.

Caradoc's smile turned to solemn sternness. "Have you not been listening?" Did he not understand the torc illustration was meant to intimidate him? "We have rivers, forests, and the sea as boundaries. Bulwarks are built to keep out beasts and others. But there are no barriers to mark the boundaries between each other. We are one people—one land. Let us bind together as a singular barricade against our foe."

Cartimandua scoffed. Why would Caradoc even answer Antedios? This could not end well. What could she do? The people were bought and paid for long ago by this conniving manipulator. She was certain this man spoke his own death sentence. She vowed to not let his death be insignificant. She would find a way to stand against Caradoc.

"You should remember this day, Raena."

"I will not forget."

Caradoc continued to address Antedios's insolence as if talking to all who might resist. "Rome does not live here. They live in their palaces, laying upon their cushioned divans and ingesting food till they vomit. Our life is simple—harsh—a constant struggle against unfriendly elements of life. The sky above, as the dust below our feet, proclaim witness that the sea is a barrier they are afraid to breach. They envision us as vulgar barbarians who eat their young. Ha! They shake and tremble in their sandals. We are robust and strong. We are fitly created to resist these fat, lazy men. I will be victorious over those who despise us."

Caradoc stepped upon the dais. "Give me your sons, and I will give you victory. Give me your sons, and I will give you riches. Join with me, and I will give you land. More than that, I will give you peace!" He jumped down from the dais and moved to the hearth.

The Golden Cord

"Our laws are not written in stone like the spirals of the *triskele*, but in the customs and traditions of the tribes. We come together this day in exquisite symmetry. Our oath is the arm of the law. Our oath calls the gods to witness."

Kenjar stepped forward with a knife.

"I give you my oath and ask yours in exchange. All the *tuath* must give assent and allegiance. Do I have your fidelity?" Caradoc took the knife from the druid. Lacerating his arm, he let his blood drop into the hearth. The coals hissed. "Yeaa-aagh!" Caradoc yelled.

Many of the chieftains stepped up and took the knife from Caradoc. They cut themselves and added drops of their blood to the flame, with the battle cry ringing the rafters of the immense hall. Togodumnus joined them. Cartimandua did not. Antedios did not. No one represented the Atrebates. Small-minded men pushed aside the dissenters. Even those who Cartimandua knew did not follow Caradoc spilled their blood and shouted their support.

"May the land swallow us up and the wind suffocate us. May the sky fall on our heads if we break our solemn vow," they all cried.

Caradoc shouted above the din, "No one can prevail against us. We will be drunk with the blood of the red-robed Romans!"

While the people scampered to the tables to drink proffered wine, Caradoc stepped through the crowd to the back. Kenjar joined him as he waited by the enormous oaken door.

The men stepped outside. Cartimandua strained to listen to what they were saying. She could only hear bits and pieces of the conversation.

Abruptly Kenjar stepped back into the hall, nodded his head, and spoke two words. "*Mors mangone.*"

Death Dealer? A *mortifer*? Cartimandua gasped and clutched Raena close to her. "He plans to hire a *mors mercator*—an assassin!"

Raena looked up to her mother. "For whom?"

CHAPTER 19

Shame

Filling your heart with 'shoulds' is like filling a cup with bitter water. The cup may be full and quench your thirst, but it will leave you wanting something much more pleasant.

— Scribonius Largus

Regnum, southern Albion

Rego handed Sophronios a recently deceased cat that he found in an alley.

"Ah, just what I needed."
"You need a dead cat?" asked Boaz.
"Bring my instrument case, Pedi, and we will commence with today's lesson."
"You gonna look at his guts?" Rego said. Even though he lived down the hill, the tall boy seemed to always be around the house. He was all arms and legs.

The Golden Cord

Sophronios prepared the animal for the dissection by splaying it out on the examination table. "Today we will study comparative anatomy by examining a *felinus*."

"Once I found a toad and threw him up and watched him splat on the cobblestones. His guts poked out!" Rego said.

"Thank you for that visual, Rego," Boaz said.

"And no, we are not going to throw the cat into the air," Sophronios added.

"Cats always land on their feet anyway," Rego said.

"How did it die?" asked Boaz, poking at the carcass.

"It probably starved, or more likely froze to death," answered Sophronios.

"Well, if we aren't going to throw him up, how do we see his guts?" Rego asked.

"First we tie the legs apart on this board; then we skin the cat." Sophronios removed a stone from his pouch at his waist and poured oil on it. He rubbed a scalpel to sharpen it as he talked. "Begin your dissection at the wrists, like this. Be very careful to only remove hair and skin so that we save the muscle underneath."

"My muscles are bigger than Boaz's."

"Shut up, Rego, or I'll punch you in the nose again."

"Rego, I need your help. Could you hunt down some valerian root in the woods for me? I need the complete roots of six plants."

"Is that the plant with the smelly pink flowers?"

"There won't be any flowers this time of year, Rego. Look by the stream near the dry, stony soil of the road. It yields a root much richer in oil than herbs closer to the water."

"I know the place!" Rego said.

"And leave the toads alone!" Sophronios yelled as Rego headed to the door.

The physician peeled the cat's skin back smoothly. "The felinus will not feel a thing, for he has kindly left his body for us to study. It is but a shell—the flesh and bones of a soul that has gone home."

Excitement and interest in learning something new soon replaced Boaz's nausea. He moved in closer. "What is valerian used for?"

Shame

"Sleep. I am unable to rest when you wake up screaming all night. Would do you some good to take some before bedtime as well."

Sophronios made another incision. "Dreams come from a multitude of thoughts. They comport no meaning but what we give them in the light. Best you keep your mind on things at hand and let go of the past."

How did he know what I was dreaming? It is as though he can read my thoughts.

"Hippocratic doctors do not practice human dissection. The body is sacred. Although I follow Herophilus, I honor Hippocrates. Some still practice the art on the corpses of condemned prisoners. Since we have no prisoners awaiting execution, and I doubt if Rego will volunteer to have his skin removed, we will use this ill-fated animal."

"Why a cat?" Boaz asked, glad they quit talking about him. He chuckled to himself, picturing the physician tossing Rego into the air like a toad.

"Because an animal's muscles and organs are very similar to ours." Sophronios pointed with his scalpel. "Take for example the *biceps brachii* of the arm."

Boaz leaned in, then retreated, holding his nose. "That is one smelly old cat!"

"Herophilus was the first to perform a public dissection of a human about four hundred years ago. He said that the brain was the center of the senses. There are *poroi*, or passages, that connect our sense organs to the brain. Like this fiber here." He pointed to a silver thread along a muscle. "Hippocrates believed the brain to be the dwelling place of intelligence and the repository of dreams."

"I thought it was the heart." The dreams of Boaz's heart were sorrowful memories.

"No, that is the center of the circulatory system, as we shall see. Erasistratus initially revealed that central truth. The exalted Hippocrates believed that—"

"Did I ever tell you about the kittens my brother and I caught? They were wild, and we caught them with our bare hands."

"Please pay attention, Pedi, or we will never finish by lunchtime."

Boaz was not very hungry. He wasn't sure why he blurted that out. The more he tried to control his thoughts and emotions, the harder it became. Perhaps it was remnants of his dreaming. He bit his lip and focused on the teaching.

⌘ ⌘ ⌘

That evening Sophronios went out to the wagon and brought back a box of various wooden objects and what appeared to be a couple of flat, round stone wheels. "Here, Pedi. This is your next exercise."

"What is it?"

"It is a rotational device for forming ceramic objects."

"A potter's wheel!" Boaz had seen one before, but it didn't look like this. It was much bigger.

The fire roared in the fireplace, giving off a golden light. Sophronios assembled the wooden boards until they resembled a miniature wooden horse. Boaz moved his stool closer to the contraption.

"The turning platform is connected by the long axle here, to the heavy flywheel at ground level," he said as he placed a metal rod through a hole in the center of the uppermost board. "Next, attach the two wheels—the smaller one to the top of the rod, and the larger one to the bottom. Like so." The heavier wheel was worn, like a cobblestone that had suffered the heels of many travelers over the eons of time.

"This arrangement allows the potter, which will be you, Pedi, to keep the turning wheel rotating by kicking the flywheel with the foot. Others use an actual wheel and spin the spokes with a rod. But this method leaves both of your hands free for manipulating the vessel under construction. It will be excellent exercise for your shoulder. We need more medicine *amphoriskoi*. I will show you how to make the small vases, but we must first gather some clay from the riverbank in the morning when it is light, and the sun has softened the mud."

Over the winter, Boaz made hundreds of vials, cups, and containers of every shape and size—242 to be exact. Sophronios made him catalog each one, size and purpose. His first ones were misshapen and crooked. Sophronios threw all but one massive misshapen amphora away.

Boaz grew bored with making the little *amphoriskoi*. It was tedious and repetitive. One day he threw the clay on the wheel and worked it, adding water, until it was the proper consistency. He added more clay and shaped it. "I'll make a vase!"

It stood half as tall as Boaz. He proudly glazed it and painted it with pictures of the herbs and flowers he had been cataloging. When finished, he stood back to admire his masterpiece.

Rego laughed. "That is hideous!"

"What's wrong with it?" Boaz asked.

"It's all lopsided, and the glaze is all droopy and runny!"

A voice came from behind them. "I believe it is the most beautiful amphora I have ever seen."

Rego jumped.

The boys turned to see Sophronios smiling.

Boaz blushed and lowered his head. What did his master know about art? He could barely see past his own nose.

Sophronios lifted the vase and handed it to Boaz. "We must fire it in the kiln right away."

While they stoked the coals of the kiln to a bright red, he laid a hand on Boaz's shoulder. "We set sail for Phrygia as soon as weather permits. It is there that I will continue your medical training with others such as you. Rego will linger here and toss toads."

Boaz picked up a stylus and wrote in Latin on the bottom of the vase *Abominantur. Made in Disgust*. He added his name in big letters: *BOAZ*. Using a long wooden paddle, he placed his creation into the kiln fire.

"Such as me . . ."

CHAPTER

20

Interloper

Expectation's road often fails when traveled with unfulfilled promises.

— Scribonius Largus

THE ROAD WEST TO GLESTINGA

Raena sat in the back of an uncomfortable and rickety old traveling box carriage on her way to the western shores, where her mother said she must be tutored. She considered it more of a punishment intended to keep her out of the way.

Cartimandua overheard Caradoc and Kenjar talking about hiring an assassin, for whom she did not know, but Raena's mother wasn't going to take any chances with her only child. Her mother wanted to make her journey as inconspicuous as possible. The wagon could be heard for leagues as it creaked and banged over every rock in Albion—so much for inconspicuous.

She brushed iron shavings from her braccae and continued to sharpen her sword. After training with Toenin and the twins, she had become a decent fighter. At least Amminus said so. Why her mother's men protected her, she didn't know. Raena handled a horse and chariot as well as anyone. Besides, she could take care of herself. No more silly games with a wooden *rudis*—she carried a real sword now.

Her mother said, "Maybe you'll find a man in the west to marry."

Yes, ma'am.

"You will learn cross-point stitching."

Yes, ma'am.

"You'll become proficient in Latin and the arts."

Raena tested the sharpness of her sword point with her thumb, drawing a drop of blood. "That should be enough." She sucked the blood from her thumb.

At least Raena's mother let her attire herself comfortably if not a bit plain. Chestnut-brown braccae and matching tunic. Soft buckskin boots rather than sandals. A leather baldric hung over her left shoulder and attached to a simple belt cinched about her waist. Her long dark-auburn hair pulled back in plaits and a braid. Her so-called guards were similarly attired. Nothing to draw attention. The journey west would take two weeks at this rate. She was bored. Sharpening her sword even seemed dreary.

Whoosh! Thunk!

"Ambush!"

Raena flung open the side door of the carriage and leapt outside, holding her sword at the ready.

"Arrows!"

Barbs came from every direction, none hitting their mark—that is, if the mark had been the guards. Either these bandits were terrible archers, or they were purposely trying not to kill the men. Arrows—two or three at a time—never from the same place twice. The guards followed the predictive pattern of flight and rode on ahead to cut the attack from the next assumed volley point. They left the wagon unprotected, save a single sentry.

"Fine, just leave me. I'm going back inside," Raena said

The Golden Cord

to the remaining guard. She yawned and went back into the wagon and shut the door. She wasn't concerned about them leaving her alone, as she could take care of herself, although she decided to pass information about this grave oversight to her mother.

"Your guards are easily spooked."

She twisted and pointed her sword under a young man's chin. He sat casually inside the wagon, drinking from a well-oiled leather flask embossed with intricate designs of entwined horses. The top and stopper were gold.

"Is that Cunobelinos's old flask?"

"Maybe."

Raena lowered her sword and ardently hugged him.

"How'd you—"

"That spindly guard was easy to circumvent."

"Are you coming with me to the west?" she asked.

"Is there any money in it?"

She regarded him dubiously. "Toenin," she clicked her tongue, "always looking for the reward."

"Is that so wrong?"

"Well, no. Not if it is honorable work."

"I'm on a mission."

"Where? To the coming conflict with Rome?"

"As far away from that as I can get. With nothing in my hand. Only dreams in my pockets. Oh, and this," he said as he stoppered the flask and put it in a leather bag on his belt.

"You shouldn't run from confrontation," Raena said.

"Yeah? Isn't that what you are doing?"

"Yes, but—"

"Uh-huh."

"Come on, Toenin. It's not my idea. It's my mother's. If it were up to me, I would be helping to not only defend our people but also to lead the attack."

"Never been one to wait on the sidelines, have you, Raena?"

"I'm not stupid. I know what is going on. Verica has left the South leaderless, with no support from Rome. His son is a joke. We should take those lands as soon as possible and set up our defenses."

"What do you mean *we*? I thought the Brigantes were staying out of this."

"With the Brigantes and the Iceni defending the northern limits of the land, our flank would be protected."

"So Cartimandua is joining Caradoc?"

"Are you a spy for the king?"

Toenin winked.

"Right, and I'm a Bel-tene bull. Let's say that if Rome reaches our shore, we'd be ready for them. Personally, I think we should cross the Great Green and attack them while they prepare their armies. They would never expect it. Catch them with their braccae down. That's how I would do it."

"Roman legionnaires don't wear braccae."

"Yes, they do. How would you know?" She punched him in the chest. "If you are so smart, how do *you* think the clans should proceed?"

Toenin looked to the ceiling of the wagon and remained uncharacteristically quiet.

"Well . . ."

"They couldn't win without your sword, Raena. You were the best of us. Except for maybe Jachin."

"Hey now." Raena slugged him again.

Toenin grinned.

"If Amminus were here, or Fergus the Strong, things would be different. They are both grand leaders. Even Teague could do better than Caradoc—if he were still alive."

An awkward silence filled the wagon's small room.

"Sorry, Toenin, I get carried away on that subject. I know Teague was friends with your father."

"My father didn't have any friends." Toenin twisted and squeezed his fingers together. "Sad about that man, Teague. Taking advantage of Caradoc to steal from him when the king had eyes elsewhere."

"I can't imagine that is true about Teague, Toenin. He had a family."

"Yeah, didn't we all. Lots of deaths lately."

Talking about death bothered her. "Where have you been, Toenin?"

"Avoiding stuff. You got any food?"

"Sure." She got him some smoked meat from her basket. "Sorry, it's cold."

Toenin ate greedily. He must have been starving.

"Togodumnus said he'd take me in." He wiped his hands on his tunic. "But really, how many kids does that guy have already? His wife is always pregnant. That's not for me. I'm better off on my own. Yep, I have no friends, no father, and no family. I'm a ragamuffin. Even when my father was alive, I was on my own. I do as I please. And you?"

"I don't know exactly where I'm going. Mom was kind of secretive."

"That's probably a good thing. You never know these days whose side someone is on."

"I know what you mean. Which side are you on, Toenin?"

"I'm on Toenin's side. I'm too short to fight." He looked in her eyes. "You fight well, but you're not mean. You love showing everyone that you can best any man or woman. I think you *are* the best." He smiled. "The king could use your sword."

"Mom feels I need culture rather than conflict."

"You could fight and be cultured at the same time!"

She looked at her thumb. "To me, it's a competition. I've drawn blood."

"But never taken a life?"

She picked up her sword and scraped the stone down its edge again. Sparks flew. "Not yet."

"Got any more food?"

Raena tossed him an apple.

Toenin took a big bite.

"I'd rather fight the Romans, Toenin. Or at least fight Caradoc."

"Caradoc is going to fight the Romans. You can't fight both."

"He stole everything good from me, Toenin."

"Not everything. I'm still here." He beamed. Apple juice ran down his chin.

She eyed Toenin and smiled. Then she frowned and looked away.

Toenin finished the apple and put the core in a pocket. "Don't you owe Jachin a kiss?"

Normally she would hit him for saying that. What did it matter? She sheathed her half-sharpened sword. Jachin was gone. Boaz too.

"Raena, why don't you ask those guards where you're going?"

"Their lips are as tight as—"

"Ha! She's sending you to the druids on the Island of Mona!"

"Not likely."

Toenin stared at her. "Then where?"

"Why are you even here?"

"To say goodbye." He opened the wagon door. "Your sentry is relieving himself. Gotta go." He chuckled. "Nice chatting with you. Have fun in the west." Toenin jumped off the wagon and picked something up out of the bushes on the side of the road. As he lifted a bow and a quiver half-full of arrows over his shoulder, he stared at Raena standing at the door of the wagon.

She doubted she would ever see him again.

Toenin waved and threw her a kiss. He hollered back as he ran like a rabbit down the road. "By the way—Jachin is still alive."

CHAPTER 21

Struggle

Not all battlefields are located in soft meadows.

— Scribonius Largus

OCEANUS

After leaving the harbor, the Morta Columbarium finally entered easterly winds.

"Set sail!" came the order on the deck above Jachin. He was glad, as that meant he could stop rowing. The calm winds of the last two days made for slow going on such a large trireme, despite three levels of rowers.

"Why are we still rowing?" Jachin asked.

It had been long enough to have the sheets up and to be under way, but the orders to "lay on your oars, spoons up" had not come down. The piper suddenly stopped his rhythmic tune. Jachin looked at Oded.

"Pirates."

"How do you know?" Jachin said.

Struggle

"Tis the time of year pirates threaten Rome's grain imports."

Horns signaled men to their stations.

A thunderous rumble rocked the ship as the first oars shattered, pulling the handles from the rower's grip. Oars snapped one at a time coming toward Jachin. He ducked. The handle of his oar dipped under his seat and sliced up, breaking the bench. Jachin and Oded went flying. The oars behind him continued to break, sending splinters and rowers tumbling throughout the galley.

Oded, brandishing a short-barbed spear, pushed past Jachin and headed to the upper deck. The scrawny man moved with purpose and resolve. It was as if he had been transformed into a hardened soldier at the sound of the horns. The other rowers, some cut and bleeding, grabbed broken oar handles, or whatever they could find, and followed Oded to face the attackers.

Chained to what remained of the bench leg, Jachin scooted close to the oar window to glimpse anything happening. He lifted the leather patch that served as a seal against water.

A lightning fast *liberna* had sailed directly toward them at full sail on a reach with the wind. Jachin ascertained that the opposing boat was about eighty feet in length. Its forward-raking mast flew a single square sail with the visage of Medusa on the center of the cloth. Jachin counted thirty oars on either side furiously paddling.

Sailing straight toward the portside, the pirate ship staged for ramming again. The sizeable bronze-plated ram's head, called a *rostra*, headed straight toward Jachin. Without the oars on one side, and the sails yet to be deployed, the vessel sat crippled and vulnerable. He scrambled to release his bonds.

At the last minute, the liberna changed tack and rudder to maneuver toward the bow.

The *Morta Columbarium* pitched to the starboard as a wave rolled the warship. The ruthless pirate vessel struck the ship an unforgiving blow on the portside. Jachin slammed to the middle of the room, his shackles broken free from the bench.

The Golden Cord

Wasting no time, he raced up to the deck, with his leg chain trailing behind.

"We're heeled to leeward. Our bottom's exposed!"

"They've hulled us between wind and water."

The liberna shifted sail and back rowed to free the ram from the *Morta Columbarium*. If the larger ship settled in the water, it could lock itself on the ram and either break the rostra or pull the pirate vessel down with the damaged vessel as it sank.

"Raise the main!" Trierarchus Caelus called as soon as the liberna was free. "Sharp jibe to port!"

The ship turned toward the retreating vessel so that the ship would face the attackers head-on and bring the exposed keel back below the water. The legionnaires took their places, weapons in hand.

Instead of fleeing, the liberna turned and confronted the trireme broadside. *Ballistae* launched flaming pots of pitch and charcoal from the pirate ship. Jachin dodged the projectiles as the crew quenched the fires with water.

"If these flames spread, we've no choice but to jump overboard. Be burned alive or drown."

Fire or water. Neither option sat well with Jachin.

They could not chance another ramming. To counter, Caelus commanded catapults to launch grappling irons. The Roman *harpax* latched on to the enemy vessel with its metal claws so the sailors could reel them in like a monstrous fish. The men pulled the pirates toward them. The liberna commanded the wind but could not escape now.

When the vessel drew within reach, the pirates lowered a wooden boarding ramp with railings on either side. A long steely spike, like a crow's beak, extended from the plank's underside. Mounted on a turntable, they swung it by a system of pulleys over the deck of the Roman ship.

"They've got a *corvus*!"

The ramp dropped, impaling the deck.

The pirates raced across with swords raised.

Legionnaires met them with shields braced, scattering the enemy to the flanks, where they attacked them with their gladius and spears. Sailors with clubs, billhooks, and gully knives joined the fray.

Struggle

Jachin ran the opposite direction toward the trierarchus's quarters. Once inside, he found his pugio and his makeshift sheath where the trierarchus kept it safe for him. Jachin suspected he meant to keep it. He attached it to his leg and sprinted to the deck. Jachin entered the fray, slashing at every man he didn't know. He hoped he targeted the right ones. The pugio pierced the pirate's stomach like a shriek amid silence. Jachin twisted the blade as he withdrew it. The man slumped to the deck, bleeding profusely.

It soon became every man for himself. The sailors prevailed, and it wasn't long before the pirates knew they were not only outnumbered but had attacked a vessel full of Roman legionnaires. The soldiers chased the pirates back to their ship, shoving those who tried to block them into the water below. The pirates raised their sail and turned it from the wind to no avail. Attempts to cut the corvus loose failed. The attached ship could not go anywhere. The legionnaires scrambled to the pirate ship and put every attacker to the sword.

"Roma Victor!" the men yelled.

Jachin joined in, although it felt odd to celebrate with these men when so many had died.

"Water's coming in!"

Men hurried down the hold and soon returned with report.

"We are taking in water. The ship is sinking!"

"Is there any hope of repair?"

"The damage is below the waterline and too severe."

"Abandon ship!"

They would use the attacking vessel as their own, leaving the *Morta Columbarium* to sink.

Oded pushed past Jachin to the other boat, shoving him back. "You'sa slave. You stay."

Grappling ropes were cut, and the corvus was raised.

Rigging and the remains of the battle scooted across the deck to the rails when the *Morta Columbarium* listed.

Jachin stumbled and grabbed the railing.

He stood alone on the tilting bow among the bodies of the slaughtered pirates and a few sailors.

Conceding defeat after being put up against the fence

The Golden Cord

by the bully once more, Jachin slumped against the rail. He had no humor left to confront this affair. No strength to stand.

Before the liberna disappeared over the horizon, his anger flared. "No. Not again. I am done letting others control me! How dare they leave me to sink with the ship!" Without thinking, he moved to action. He grabbed mantles and smothered the fires. What he could not squelch, he discharged to the sea.

Determined to survive, he sought to stop the leak if he could. The vessel listed so much to starboard that it brought the damage into view. A gash the size of his head breached the bow below the waterline on the portside. If the hole was not repaired, and the waves roughened, this ship would certainly sink

"That's all?" The damage was under the left eye of the trireme like a big bruise. "I can fix this."

He set the sail and turned into the wind and let the sheets luff.

"Eyes to the wind," he said.

He sewed pieces of rope fibers and twine through a spare sail, giving it the look of a quilt, like his mother would make. She called it "fothering" the material to make it strong. Tying rope to the four corners, he took his creation to the bow and shimmied out along the bowsprit and down onto the ship's rostra. He lowered the sheet and maneuvered it to cover the hole. He knew it would not be watertight, but it might slow the leak and allow repairs to be made. He pulled the ropes taut until he heard a sucking sound as the sail covered the busted area where water flooded in.

Down in the galley, he waded to the front. The fothered sail worked. For the most part the hole did not leak. Only a trickle of seawater seeped in. Taking a rounded block of wood used as a table pedestal, he shaped it to roughly the same size as the hole with a hand ax. Then he took a mallet and hammered the wooden plug into the breach. To be sure, he gave the plug one more blow with the mallet.

Jachin gathered two wooden buckets and tied a line to the handles. He threw them in to the flooded galley and filled them with the water. He put the line over his shoulders and carried them to the deck, dumping the water over the rail. His effort to save himself and the ship continued until the sun sank below the horizon, and the injured vessel no longer listed to the side. He freed the chain from his ankle with a mallet and an iron rod. Pointing the prow in the direction the others had sailed, he manned the rudder and navigated into the dark.

CHAPTER 22

Reparation

*He who beats oppression's passion
overcomes but half his foe.*

— Scribonius Largus

Port Gesoraicum, northern Gaul

The next morning Jachin milked the cow, who somehow survived the battle.

"I guess they left you behind too, old girl."

He drank the warm sweet liquid and ate all the biscuits he wanted. After his breakfast, he searched the deck for anything he would need to survive.

Lying on the deck was a man with eyes wide open. This man's face and twisted, lifeless body would forever be etched in his memory. The first man he killed. Never did Jachin consider his path would lead to killing another man. He only wanted to kill his father. He didn't hate this man, nor did he avenge himself in this butchery. Was this murder?

Reparation

Was this right? Was this good? They attacked. He reacted—that's all. Before him lay a man whose life was ended by him. Did this man have a brother? Will they seek him for revenge? All the pirates were put to the sword. None survived. No one would know what he had done—except him.

Then the thought struck him: This was not the first death by his hand. Caradoc was to blame. It was by his father's hand when Caradoc used his mother as a shield. But she died by *his* hand. Jachin never accepted any of the blame until now.

He ran his hand through his hair.

"What makes you any different than me?" he said to the body lying before him. "How does a man reconcile murdering his own mother? Is it any different to kill in battle?" He tried to shake off his feelings of guilt. He shoved the swollen body into the sea, along with the others. As each corpse splashed into the brine, he pictured his father. "No, it was him. Wasn't my fault."

It was good to be alone—more time to gather his thoughts and his resolve. Constantly checking the plug, he assured himself there was no leakage. He took residence in the trierarchus's cabin. A dimly lit room with a mediocre desk strewn with maps tacked to the board and an unmade bed. A dresser and a small table that still held an unfinished meal. For a man who wouldn't walk on deck without it being sanded and polished, this fastidious man was a slob in his private life.

Jachin rummaged through the dresser drawers. One was locked. He found dry clothing and changed into more comfortable clothes. The cabin was in shambles. Jachin cleaned it and straightened the papers, the maps, and the books.

Caelus had a collection of weapons: sabers, falchions, several *spathae*, a gladius, and an assortment of pugios. Jachin's pugio was destined to be a part of this hoard of plundered points.

Jachin smiled as he pried open the locked drawer with his pugio. This is obviously where Caelus kept his most valuable possessions. On top was a parchment. He unrolled it and thumbed through the pages. "The ship's orders—

worthless." He replaced them and picked up another rolled parchment. This proved to be a map. He could use that, so he set it aside. Underneath the map was a beautifully carved clay pipe and a sock of what looked like dried leaves. "Now this is something!"

Out on the deck, Jachin made sure he roped the rudder securely in a position to navigate to the southeast. He sat on the bench by the rudder, filled the pipe with the leaves, as he had seen Caelus do, and lit it with a flint he found in the pocket of his new clothes. He sucked the smoke into his lungs and coughed. Perhaps this was not a good thing. He emptied the pipe and placed it in the pocket with the flint. A soft bed and fruit. That sounded much better. Jachin was glad to manage his own life for once.

Fair skies, calm seas, and a steady light breeze encouraged him as he navigated toward the mouth of the Rhenus River, where he and Amminus initially headed before he fell overboard. Jachin once hoped he would find his uncle waiting there for him. But now it didn't much matter. At first he had secretly sent letters but had never received a reply, so he stopped writing to the man who had initially taught him how to read and write.

He often dreamed of the prospect of finding the Roman imperator and convincing him to attack Albion. He would accompany them and find his father. Whether Rome conquered his homeland or not, it was not his concern.

On the third day he spotted white birds with long pointed wings and black markings on them. They circled the ship, squawking their greetings. Where there were birds, land was not far away. He untied the rudder and maneuvered the boat in the direction the birds originated.

Running short sail, he manned the helm until he sighted land. He checked his map. Not the Rhenus, but instead he sailed into the harbor of the premier provincial naval fleet of the Roman navy at Gesoraicum, which served as the headquarters for *Classis Britannica*. Not the river base he expected, but it would suffice. He gladdened at the sight, knowing he would soon be free of not only this ship and the sea but of all the pain he endured under the hand of Oded and Trierarchus Caelus.

Reparation

As Jachin steered the trireme through the harbor, men gathered on the docks.

"The *Morta Columbarium!*"

"It's empty."

"A ghost ship!"

Jachin appeared on the bow and tossed lines to the men waiting for answers on the dock. As soon as their shock subsided, they secured the ship. Jachin leaped to the wharf and walked past the astonished onlookers into the harbor town. Now wearing clothing fit for a legionnaire—blue tunic, leather leggings, and his pugio strapped to his side—he proudly stepped into a tavern to barter for a meal. Much to his dismay, the room was full of sailors—men from the *Morta Columbarium*! Would they congratulate him or arrest him? Before he could run, they surrounded him.

Men scattered as Oded came forward. "The paulo piscis can swim!" He slapped Jachin upside his head and laughed.

Jachin rushed Oded and knocked his tormenter to the floor. In an instant he had his knees on Oded's shoulders and battered him in the face with his fists. He didn't care. They could flog him again, but he was going to let Oded know he was done putting up with his abuse. About to land another blow, soldiers pulled him off the scraggy old sailor.

One of the townsfolk rushed in. "The *Morta Columbarium* is in dock!"

Rushing outside, the crew joined a parade of townsfolk heading toward the harbor.

"It's a miracle."

"A cursed apparition of death," another said.

Jachin joined the throng to the dock.

Standing proudly on the wharf, Jachin expected to be welcomed as a hero. Instead, he was confronted by the crew.

"Thief!"

"Brigand!"

"Pirate offal!"

"What?" Jachin said.

Vigiles Urbani burst through the crowd and placed shackles on Jachin's wrists. Through his screams of resistance, the city watchmen dragged him to the town lockup.

The Golden Cord

Another stripe on his back. Another dirt clod to the head. Another fence.

Trierarchus Caelus reclaimed the pugio.

Jachin endured the prison while the guards taunted him about needing 140 men to pull rope in order to bring the ship to dry dock for repairs. They reported that over 100 woodcutters, carpenters, and metalworkers worked to get the vessel back to straights. Jachin didn't care. Ironically, the food was better in prison.

After the ship was seaworthy, they escorted Jachin in chains back onboard the renovated *Morta Columbarium*. Although he had spent time in a Roman jail, he felt stronger. Healthier. More confident.

"This slave is not strong enough to pull oars all day. Strike his chains. Put him to measuring," Caelus said to the crew. He never mentioned anything about his clean cabin.

Once out to sea again, Jachin spent easier days determining swiftness and depth of the sea. He plotted the ship's position, the wind speed, and direction of travel. He tested tide and flow of every current in the Great Green, keeping a lunar observation log. The opportunity to study maps made by Julius Caesar afforded him information seldom shared. Food fare was more commiserate with his new standing as navigator.

Jachin kept busy, and he avoided the firm-lipped Oded. At times Jachin hunted for his sandals, only to find them in the latrine. Dead rats hidden in his braccae led to guffaws from his shipmates. He continued to find himself in fights with the crew, but he no longer did Oded's nightly watch.

Oded never discovered the drawing of a stick man being swallowed by a fish that Jachin put on the bottom of the old man's water mug.

23
CHAPTER

Collection

If a man cannot hear his enemy's dreams, he cannot reach their hearts.

— Scribonius Largus

SOUTHERN ALBION NEAR CANTIACUM

Caradoc paced the hard dirt floor of the roundhouse. Hides hung haphazardly around the walls. Meat dried from the rafters. He stood in the home of one of the chieftains of the south, known simply as Regini. They were more hunters and traders than farmers in that they lived in and around the area between the Andreadsweld forest and the southern coast of Albion.

For the past month, Caradoc traveled with a small band of warriors and Kenjar, the high druid, who came in handy when it came time to pressure the tribal leaders. Together they drummed up support for the fight against Rome. Caradoc was certain Rome's invasion was imminent. He wanted everyone to be ready.

They had gathered food, artillery for slings, horses, coin to pay warriors, and hay for animals. Warriors fletched so many arrows that Caradoc wondered if there were any ravens left in Albion with feathers. Today, while his small troop of warriors gathered men and supplies, Caradoc and his druid were to meet with the leaders to garner help building earthworks in Camulodunon in preparation for where—according to his spies—the Roman army would most likely beach their warships.

Caradoc put his feet up on a table and leaned back, hands clasped behind his head. He traveled all day, and soon the sun would set. No one defended the hillfort, and filth lay scattered everywhere in the yard. The place was empty. He had sent word of his coming, but now he waited. Why weren't the chieftains here? He did not like that at all. This was the last hillfort to visit on his mission to garner support. But this one may prove to be more difficult.

Grael lived in this hillfort alone. His wife, children, and friends had kicked him out of Camulodunon long ago. Only a fool would stay with a one-handed farmer. Why the Regini took him in, he couldn't grasp. Yet Caradoc needed his support. Not that he was important, but his land was of strategic significance. And he needed laborers.

The southwestern tribal leaders, Tincomarus and Dubnovellaunos, ran to Rome like whipped puppies with their tails between their legs. This produced much unrest among the other tribes. Caradoc dealt with that. Like Calleva, he took over their homes by force or coercion. The cowardly kings jumped ship, and the fight hadn't even begun. They did not love Albion as he did.

Trinkets, gold, and empty promises seduced weak men. Hopefully Grael would arrive soon with the remaining chieftains to hear his plan. He would show these doubters how weak they were without his warriors to protect them.

The late king Cunobelinos tolerated balance between those for and those against Rome. Caradoc removed the old man and his timeworn methods. Balance was a vision seen from the corner of the eye, and Caradoc saw much.

Cunobelinos planned the friendly invasion for years, of that Caradoc was certain. His father sent Amminus to rule Cantiacum with the idea to place a friend of Rome in a position to ensure the enemy's safe landing. But with Amminus gone, and since the kings of Cantii minted no coin of their own, the people of Cantiacum followed him.

"Where is Grael Shorthand?" Caradoc bellowed to an empty room. The hearth fire crackled but gave off little light. Caradoc paced. "I have more important matters to attend to!"

Was this man even important to his cause? Caradoc placed people in positions for *his* purposes. He gave Togodumnus his father's land to rule while he invaded south of the Tamesa. He gained pledges of support from the Durotriges in the west. He'd conquered the southern section of the Dobunni without much effort.

Kenjar was instrumental in assuring the druid aid. Druids spread his fame in the midlands and northwest so that most of Albion yoked themselves to Caradoc's cause. He achieved more than his father or grandfather had ever imagined by maneuvering the tribes of Albion to agree to fight as one people. No small task. It all came at a cost.

Men saw him as either a headfirst thinker or an uncontrollable child. Ha! He was the greatest freedom fighter to ever walk the grasses and woods of this land. He vowed to keep Albion pure, to keep their families and friends from the evils of Rome. How he did that didn't matter. The end justified the means. The people wanted—needed—stability. He understood the danger. No change. No integration. No adapting to the Roman way of life, especially if he couldn't control it. Caradoc knew people wanted things to stay the same. He prepared for this all his life. Caradoc was satisfied he would win.

Yes there were a few Roman troops stationed in Albion, such as the man he killed on the road to the Boar's Head Inn long ago. Probably Roman guards of nobles and merchants. Like fleas safeguarding a rat.

But all it boiled down to was a king collecting his debts.

Kenjar stuck his nose in the door. "They c-c-come!"

"Finally!"

The tribal leaders of the Regini entered the grand hall slowly. Those few who carried swords had hands on their hilts. Caradoc noted their unease. He did his best to look pleased, despite his distaste for their garments. Two leaders wore Roman togas. Others wore dung-covered hides. How dare they show up in such blatant disrespect.

After introductions, a few platitudes, and pouring of drinks, the chieftains were eager to get down to business.

Grael began in earnest. "You promised if you became king, you would protect us. Now you take our sons from their homes, leaving us defenseless. You reserve our provisions and food supplies for your own while we starve."

Caradoc leaned in to listen. He wasn't sure why they chose this cripple to be their spokesman. An old farmer among hunters. He had taken from this man before. That was true. This might be easier than he imagined.

"The Romans desire Albion. Of this there is no doubt. The rich black soil of the lowlands. The beautiful hills and woods that cover the south. The many caves there. The silver ore in the Mendip Hills. The iron of the Cantii, and limestone, like a belt crossing the land, is tempting to any merchant. And don't forget, they seek your animal hides to cover their dainty divans. Does it follow that for Albion to prosper, we must *give* it away?" Caradoc said.

"If we want wine and oil, we must deal directly with Rome," Grael said.

Ah, this was probably their real quarrel with change. Caradoc had put a stop to those imports, except for his own supply of wine.

"What more do you need?" Caradoc asked.

"Will not Rome provide for our needs?"

"What do you *need*?" Caradoc sneered.

"We need for our families to be safe and to prosper."

"Rome provides for their *own* needs—at *your* expense. If dirt is not important, why does Rome want ours? Rome seeks its own advantage—not yours. They will rape you. Unlike dung, favor from Rome does not roll downhill. Not everyone can benefit from trade, but all can benefit from my leadership. Together we must defend our land. You've enclosed hillforts with banks and ditches. You use them to protect yourselves from each other. But they won't protect against Rome. You must do more. I need warriors!"

"We do well. Our trade is our defense against Rome," Grael said.

The chieftains grumbled in assent to that. They appeared restless and unconvinced as they looked to each other for rescue.

Caradoc sought a way to pull them back. To make them understand. He couldn't believe anyone would not choose him over Rome. What could he say to convince these simpletons of his need and their path to ruin? "Rome will rope in your authority—your defense—and herd your power out of the cattle crib to another's pasture."

"The kings of the South sought shelter in Rome," Grael said. "They feared you would take them by force."

"They are cowards," said Caradoc, clenching his teeth.

"And what about your brother, Amminus?" This was the first time any of the other chieftains spoke. Caradoc didn't even know this man's name.

Caradoc knew that would come up. He glared at the leader in the toga. "Cunobelinos exiled my brother for treason." It was a lie, but one he propagated ever since he banished his brother.

The man stepped back as though Caradoc had struck him. He would not speak up again.

"We have the right to do things as we please," said Grael. "We don't wish to wall off our forts."

Caradoc lifted a small statue of Apollo from a nearby shelf and held it out to them.

Grael gasped.

"I know exactly why you don't want walls. You desire Roman temples with marble columns, elaborate baths, and exquisite flower gardens instead. You actively seek Rome's pleasure even to the point of offering to their little gods."

"Rome's soldiers are embedded within our land to protect the trade interests. That is all."

Caradoc smiled his best smile and rested his hand on

The Golden Cord

the hilt of his sword. *Why were these men so thickheaded? Couldn't they see the danger?* "They *will* invade."

"Why would they do that when we want to trade with them? We can fulfill their desires, and we will be paid well for it," Grael said.

"Control. They want control." Caradoc moved closer, waving the statue in his face. "What of their exorbitant taxes and long years of required military service?"

"Many of us want the *Romanitas*—the Roman ways—fashion and money."

"You're already rich."

"Roman trade is our livelihood. In the south, our friends trade with Rome daily. They tell us we will become rich men."

"Well, Grael, you cannot find freedom in words and trade deals. We must deal with the invaders by the sword, by revenge."

"Revenge for what? What harm have they perpetrated toward us? You don't rule over the Regini. You overlord and exact more from us than we can deliver. We are Roman. Why would we go back to our old ways? Why would we fight for what we already have?" He showed Caradoc a handful of Roman coins.

Caradoc knocked the coins out of Grael's hand. "You are pretenders; they take your identity and enslave you with propaganda coins."

"They spend just as easily as your coin."

Caradoc's head jerked up. He let the marble idol fall to the floor. Apollo's head broke off. "I should've cut off *your* head when I had the chance. You want people not of Albion to be our rulers? People who do not understand our ways? Our life, our language, our laws? Think of the blow to your children when Romans overrun your homes. Rome is as subtle as an assassin. They expect us to hand over our land with diplomacy—without fuss. Verica and the traitor Amminus are in Rome as we speak, pouring poisonous lies in the imperator's ear. I sent letters to Rome, asking for them to return our fugitives. They failed to do so."

This seemed to be news to them, as they struggled to somehow stand their ground. Caradoc was tired of playing games. He went to the heart of the matter. "Are you aligned with me or with Rome?"

Grael folded his arms. "We don't care who is in charge as long as we have food and a roof over our heads." He turned his back on Caradoc. "And as long as it is anyone but you!"

"Kenjar, hand me a spear." Caradoc turned slowly to face the crowd with a short spear. "You cannot kill with the butt of the instrument." He struck Grael in the back with the blunt end.

Grael turned and held his ground.

"You cannot dampen the blow by cowering to their ways. You will fail, Grael. Rome is our enemy." Caradoc twirled the weapon around. "See how the tip points to the enemy? You put it close to them and push." He targeted the point to Grael's chest and thrust it into his heart.

A collective gasp arose from the others as Grael slumped to his knees.

Caradoc put his foot on Grael's lifeless chest and yanked the spear out as he kicked him backward. He pointed the bloody tip of the spear to the crowd. "Cunobelinos is not here to negotiate trade deals anymore. You have grown fat and lazy. Do. I. Not. Prove. My. Point?" he said as he pointed at each one.

"This is how we will win against Rome. To face them with force. Straight away you must throw off these dresses you call togas. Let your mustaches grow again and become men. You are nothing but clientele of the Catuvellauni. I paid for your skins. Debt obligates clients to return favors. Do you desire Caradoc as patron, or would you have Rome as your slave master?"

Only a few gave assent and remained. Others fled.

Caradoc dismissed them with a wave of the spear.

CHAPTER 24

Influence

When you please the fancies of men, they avoid what they dislike and seek gifts elsewhere.

— Scribonius Largus

Caradoc had come up against opposition before, but this was the first time he could not convince the leaders to join him. Only a couple remained to give allegiance. "This trip was worthless."

He lowered the spear and squatted next to Grael. "Listen to me." He lifted Grael's head. "You'd like for Rome to invade, wouldn't you?" He shook the lifeless head of Grael as if the man nodded in agreement. "Here's my plan. Since you asked how I will protect you. Rome's legions will arrive at Rutipiae and move toward the Tamesa River; however, this is our home turf. We know the territory. They don't.

"Okay, I acknowledge that the South is affable to Rome. Some believe they will land there, thinking that they will be welcomed with open arms. If they do, then by the time they make it to Camulodunon, we will get wind of it. No?" He shook the man's head back and forth. "Oh, Grael Shorthand, they will come. Like Caesar, they will come. They will flood the land with sewage. This time we will not hide." He let go of the dead man's head and stood.

Watching the doorway while he addressed the waiting kings, Caradoc continued. "We will not flee. We will be ready for them. We will exploit the two rivers as barriers. We will build up walls at Camulodunon. They prefer to fight on open terrain. We will close them off, taking them apart piece by piece. They cannot win."

"The water is s-sacred. It will p-p-protect us," Kenjar said.

"Togodumnus will command the troops on the front." Then leaning down, he whispered in Grael's ear. "You can't use Roman wine and oil as battle tactics." Caradoc thumped Grael's head with his knuckle. "Mark my words: Rome is a rapist. She lures you in with her jewels and fine linens. Her soft words spoken in a treaty. But I assure you that all she wants is what you have. She will chase you into the alley of servitude and leave you naked in the dung gutter of despair and desolation."

He stood. "Draw the enemy into the swamps and forests. Wear them out. That is what I'll do. Draw them in and trap them. First use spears, arrows, and slings. Not face them in open fields. That is what we will do. This is how I will protect you and save the land." He pulled the dead body to a kneeling position. Holding Grael by the shoulders, he beheld his vacant staring eyes. "What did you say, Grael? Will our slingshots overcome Rome?"

He let the body fall just as he did the Roman idol of Apollo. "We can't win by steel alone. We will use words. I have spread rumors for years about the druids' magic. The Romans fear us. They see us as monsters who eat our enemies' flesh. They are repulsed by their imaginings." Caradoc approached the druid. "And we perform human sacrifices, do we not, Kenjar?"

"Or s-so we t-told them as much. They are a fearful s-superstitious lot."

The Golden Cord

"Fools," Caradoc agreed.

"All will follow, C-C-Caradoc!"

Those still in the roundhouse nodded.

"Where else do you have to go? Protect the homeland with me. Don't become a Roman slave wife!"

The words echoed in the room as Kenjar ushered the lingering leaders out the door.

Caradoc sat alone at the table and poured a cup of Grael's cheap mead. The fire hissed.

After a while Kenjar returned. Caradoc was on his third glass.

The druid quenched the lamps around the room. "You have not g-g-gained much tonight. S-s-support on your side is f-fragile." He snuffed another flame. "Some would say you have lost m-m-much."

Caradoc took a long draw on the cup. "What do you mean?"

"Alexenah." Another light. "The twins. Your grandfather. Father. Uncle. B-b-brother." He placed a lid on a particularly huge sputtering smoky oil lamp. "Mara and your d-d-daughter." Smothering the last remaining light, Kenjar quenched a torch in the pot over the fire. "And today's losses s-s-hows that you may lose all s-s-support. P-perhaps you should y-y-yield to the invaders." He added a few more logs and stoked the meager fire. Kenjar had become bolder of late in his advice.

Caradoc filled his cup again. "Sit, Druid."

Kenjar sat opposite his king at the table. "What if you lose what is m-m-most important to you. What if you l-l-lose Albion?"

Caradoc stared into his mug as if the answer was in the mead.

After an awkward silence, Kenjar said, "I'll take my l-l-leave now." He got up and headed to the door. He stopped and turned back. "But before I g-g-go, let me ask you a question: Have you ever b-b-been afraid?"

"My heart rages for peace, Kenjar. I must have complete control to assure accord. I never lose. Nothing stands in my way . . . except Jachin."

"The young man knows m-much but has lost everything. He will not be b-b-back."

"I believe he will return. When you have nothing to lose, you are capable of anything."

"Anything? Even fear?"

Caradoc waved him off without answering.

"What does Jachin love?" Kenjar asked.

"How do I know?"

"Y-Y-You t-took all he loves except one t-t-thing. I guarantee if you hurt the princess Raena, he will c-c-come."

"Cartimandua's daughter? I believe the queen's husband, Benutius, conspires against me in the north. You may be right. Their daughter, Raena, might indeed prove a nuisance. I will take what you say in consideration." Caradoc nodded and waved him on again.

Kenjar turned and glided out of the roundhouse.

Alone, Caradoc drank straight from the jug. He rubbed his forehead and leaned his chin on the ball of his fist. "I've done this, and I've done that." Another swig. "I've won many battles. Conquered many men. I've put my knife to men's throats. I cut off their heads. Displayed their surrender on my gate." He moved his chair closer to the sputtering hearth. He imagined his grandfather's visage in the fire. Caradoc lifted the jug and talked to the flames. "You scoff at me? I have been threatened. Captured. Escaped. I've murdered on the streets of Rome itself. I've been beaten . . ." another long drink. "But I never lost."

A log fell, sending sparks into the darkness.

"I've busted my head open. Broke my nose. Twice."

The hearth fire sputtered and dwindled. Caradoc stoked it once again, adding more fuel. He then sat and fumed awhile. When the mead ran dry, he searched the house for more. Tearing things aside, he broke the place apart until he found a hidden wineskin. It was half full.

He stood and stumbled over to the wall, grabbing a hide to steady himself. He tore it from the wall and covered his shoulders like an old man. He stared into the fire as if staring into his own soul.

"I survived it all. What have I to fear? I did it all on my

own. I need no help. What do I fear? What does it matter to me?" He sat back at the table and downed another mouthful, slobbering the beverage over his chin. He wiped his moustache and belched.

"Fear is an emotion. Most emotions are fake. They just go along with whatever lie you happen to be telling yourself. Whatever lie you believe at the moment."

He crossed his arms. "Who is against me other than Rome? Who opposes me and gets away with it?"

He pulled his feet up under him.

"I don't care."

His words slurred. Another swig. Another look into the fire, as if seeing Tasciovaunus again in the flames. "Fear? I enjoy taking risks that'd terrify the strongest warrior. What they call fear gives me a charge—a focus. Gives me the competence to fix whatever the problems I face. Once two fighting dogs raced up to me, growling and barking. I put my hand out. They lay at my feet." He shivered and pulled the hide closer around him. "I don't care what others think of me. Fear was taken from me long ago. My father never thought I was good enough. And *you*, Grandfather, always pushed me one more rung up the ladder. Kept pushing. I pushed back. I am not a little incompetent child." He turned the wineskin up to get the last dregs. He examined his cup. There was no reflection. It was empty too. He tossed it into the coals. "This is the only thing that controls me. The only thing I cannot control."

Caradoc unfastened his baldric and unsheathed his sword. Holding it up, he beheld his image. His reflection seemed different than he remembered—he was not the same. He set the sword aside.

He slumped back. Rubbed his head again. The flames faltered. "I have enough men. I do not question if I have done enough. I will beat Rome."

Dismayed by the dwindling fire, he closed his eyes.

"Feelings? I don't suffer them. They do not exist."

25
CHAPTER

Return

It is easier to yank someone down from a stump than it is to pull them up.

— Scribonius Largus

AD 37—Lugdunum, northern Gaul

Amminus stood on the pier, chewing on a piece of dried beef as the trireme Morta Columbarium docked at the Roman naval base on the estuary of the Rhenus River. Known as Lugdunum Batavorium, the thriving shipyard was abustle with traffic. He couldn't believe it had been two years since he had traveled from Albion to the mainland.

Lugdunum lay situated west of the convergence of the rivers Rhenus and Sona on the heights overlooking the Great Green Sea. Locals called this body of water *Oceanus*. This fortress of *Lugh*—the raven god—possessed four aqueducts that supplied water to the city. A plentiful water supply, combined with a temple and an amphitheater standing at the junction of four major roads, made this city the cultural center of Gaul.

Confident in his plans, Amminus spent the last few years gathering intelligence and sending correspondence to Rome as Imperator Gaius prepared for an invasion of Albion. He was less concerned about assuming his rightful place on the throne of Albion than he was in stopping Caradoc from taking control of the whole island. The imperator had his own agenda.

Knowing that Jachin was aboard the *Morta Columbarium*, Amminus checked the scuttlebutt at the docks regularly for its return. He received no word until today. Meanwhile, he had secured a job helping a blacksmith. It seemed menial labor, but he would shovel horse manure if he had to so that he could work without attracting too much attention. And he could wait as long as he needed. The blacksmith expressed effusive gratitude daily for the assistance with his forge as he heated and formed ore into tools and weapons.

Amminus prayed daily that Alexenah's god would keep Jachin safe and that the boy would use this time on the Roman trireme to show his worth. Amminus liked to think that his nephew's service on the ship was as if a hammer pounded beauty into the blade that was Jachin.

Jachin would be nearly grown by now. Amminus yearned for his swift return so they could work on his adoption. The imminent arrival of the trireme buoyed his hopes.

He lamented his own ruminations as he spent countless hours contemplating his own losses. He couldn't bear one more. Jachin was his chance to do the right thing. When left alone, he tried to bolster himself up—to relax and not worry. But fear for Jachin filled his thoughts. *What will he do without me?*

He had talked once again to his friends. They determined it unwise to stay in the north, where Caradoc's spies could easily find them. Each man would separate southward to seek a livelihood in this new land, perhaps seek out wives and property. They planned to meet up again at the next Bel-tene celebration in Noviomagnus.

"To spend so much time on a stranger's ship is sometimes worse than drowning," Amminus had told his friends.

"Do you not trust Jachin to stay alive? The boy is determined and skilled," Fergus said.

"What will you do when he returns?" Kendal asked.

"I will give Jachin his true freedom; then we will travel together to entreat the imperator of Albion's need. I have already informed Gaius of the grave situation in our homeland and Caradoc's threat. We will seek his assistance. I sent letters requesting support and explaining our affairs."

"It will be good, my friend. You always seem to know how to do the right thing," Kendal said. The poet raised his chin and sang:

"Because we have lived life,
We shall have no sorrowful goodbye,
But gladness of heart that'll never be lost.
We laughed and fought and fled and dreamed
And rode into the fray knowing the cost.
Our cheeks flooded with rain from the sky.
Our beards frozen with frost.
Because we have lived life,
We shall have no sorrowful goodbye."

Today the song's memory filled his mind with anticipation and hope. He strained to see the trireme as the military vessel docked.

Sailors tossed lines to the landing, jumped across, and secured the ship to the moorings. They hauled it the rest of the way to the dock. It would take a while before anyone could disembark, as the crew had much to do such as belaying lines, coiling rope, and weighing anchor.

As Amminus waited, he recalled the last full conversation Jachin and he had together on the beach of Albion, awaiting the merchant ship to be stocked for their journey into exile. It seemed ages ago. That night had been cold and dark.

"I am not ready," Jachin said, pulling his cloak tighter against the wind on the beach.

"Failures begin with doubts. The moment you doubt, you surrender to the enemy before the battle even begins."

"I'm not strong enough."

"Yet."

"What?"

"Finish the sentence. I am not strong enough—yet."

Jachin bowed his head.

Amminus was unsure how to encourage him. So much loss. So much pain. "Face your goal and about-face your discouraging thoughts. You must have a determined heart, even if you have struggles. It is necessary, and it will be difficult. I can promise you that."

"How do *you* do it?"

Amminus thought a while before he spoke. He was not always sure himself. It was easier for him to encourage others.

"Uncle, if I can't stand with confidence, the opponent will say I am less than a man and dispose of me like an injured pony."

"You must look them in the eye. Your stance shows them you are someone to be reckoned with, and do what you are about to do with cheerfulness."

Jachin stood legs apart, shoulders back. "Like this?"

"Yes, but look as though you are about to laugh at them."

"What if I make a mistake?"

"Remember when you stood against the boys on the fence? You told me you made them laugh. That is what I am talking about."

"To be jovial?"

"Not just that. To be confident."

Jachin sat. "I should wait until I'm better prepared."

"Are you incompetent?"

"No."

"Here, take this lantern in your hand. Stand up. Take a step. How far can you see? Take another stride. How far now?"

Jachin took another step.

"That is all you must do. Take the next step. Your lantern is your confidence."

Jachin shook his head slowly as if he did not understand. He had no humor now. *I wonder which was worse for him. The fence or the father? Is Jachin strong enough for a test such as this?*

"My son, if every man thought higher of themselves, they could accomplish more than imagined. We put the inferiority in ourselves. No one can *make* you feel inferior. With each step forward, we see things clearer. We feel more confident knowing where we are going."

"I see what you are saying." They both laughed at Jachin's pun.

Strong, encouraging words seemed hollow when said by a doubtful man who lived with his own shame. Perhaps he could place courage in this young one's heart—more than he possessed in his own.

"How did you do it at the great fire?" Jachin had asked.

He spoke of the great fire, where Amminus had led the people to conquer the blaze to save their homes.

"Something happened that day on the hill for me. Something changed. I did good when I didn't consider myself virtuous."

"Is that what confidence is, then? Being stupid but looking good?"

"One man may walk the streets looking as though he expected everyone to know him and believe that they should all bow to him, and thus he appears confident. My son, confidence is not outward appearance. It is feeling bad but still doing good, because it is good. Not because you are good, but because you feel that if you don't do this one thing at this one time, then all is lost."

Amminus took the lantern from Jachin. "You must not doubt that good is good. Even if you were the worst man on the earth, had done terrible deeds, to do good is still noble and right." Then he added, "and to help others do good is respectable as well."

He blew out the lamp. "Now, Jachin, take another step."

"But I can't see."

"Do you remember what the light showed you?"

"I think so."

"Take one more step, two, perhaps three. Remember what is ahead of you."

"I did not see that far. I don't remember."

"Take another step."

"What if I mess up?"

The Golden Cord

"What if you don't?"

Jachin stepped once more. There was no purchase for his foot, only air, and he tumbled down the sand dune to the beach below.

Amminus raced down to where Jachin lay. Pulling him to his feet, he looked him in the eye, though it was too dark to make out what face Jachin made. "That is courage, my son. In the battle, you will not see ahead of you. But you must still take the next step whether you win or whether you fail. You do it because it is worthy to do."

Jachin coughed and brushed sand out of his hair.

"I will teach you skill. You have learned so much; however, the courage is yours to grasp." He stopped for a moment. "And faith. Yes, faith. That is something I have yet to grasp myself. Your mother had it. I believe Tinman did as well."

"Who?"

"The friend of your mother from Arimathea. I could see it in his eyes. Faith will lead you in the dark more than courage, I suppose. Perhaps one day you will understand that better than I do."

"I could have been hurt. Why did you do this to me?"

"You needed to see beyond your limits. There are no bounds to what you may achieve. I believe in you." For some reason, his words spoke to his own heart as well. Amminus needed to take his own advice. "You will face the unknown, both the difficult and the easy things that lie before you, Jachin. We're part of all our struggles," he said.

A ramp lowered from the front of the trireme with a loud bang, bringing Amminus back to the present. A group of robust men marched in full armor down the plank.

"Fair winds and following seas!" sailors shouted to each other as they left.

Behind them, another group of soldiers carried horns and drums. A group of nicely clad officers and many sailors trudged off last.

"Jachin!" Amminus yelled.

The group kept walking.

A thin man approached him with a deprecating grin.

"Who are you?"

"I am here to reunite with my nephew."

"And who would that be?" Oded held out his palm for payment.

"Do you understand who I am?" Amminus asked.

"No, sir, I—"

"You obviously don't know who you have on your ship."

"All we has here are legionnaires."

"The one I am looking for was lost at sea two years ago."

"Ah, the slave tossed overboard! You must be the owner of the paulo piscis."

Amminus stepped closer. "He is the eldest son of the high king of Albion."

Oded stood firm. "The little fish?"

"Jachin, son of Caradoc, the rightful heir to all of what you call Britannia," Amminus said, getting up in the man's face.

The soldier took a step back. "Little fish! Front and center!"

A tan, tall, thin, well-muscled young man stepped out of the crowd of men. He wore the blue tunic of a legionnaire sailor. "My pugio," Jachin hoarsely growled.

The trierarchus reached in a bulky canvas bag on the back of one of the other soldiers and pulled out the blade and the rabbit sheath. He handed it to Jachin, who quickly strapped it to his leg.

Amminus smiled and held his arms out to receive him.

Jachin stepped back.

After a silent pause, looking at each other, Amminus said, "How long did you row?"

"Till blisters became calluses," Jachin spat. He turned from Amminus and viewed the coffin shaped *Morta Columbarium* once again. "Why didn't you help me? Why didn't you stop them? Didn't you get my letters?"

"I didn't. I couldn't. I waited . . ."

With legs apart and hands on his hips, Jachin cocked his head and ran his fingers through his hair. He had a look as though he was about to laugh.

"You didn't try."

CHAPTER 26

Skirmish

Emotions cannot conquer the dark storm's decree.

— Scribonius Largus

GERMANIA

Jachin had not said more than two words since they left the wharf several days ago. Amminus rode up next to the young man. He reached out. Touched him on the shoulder. Jachin shrugged him off and urged his mare to a gallop.

Yesterday they passed the *Oppidum Ubiorum*, which housed two legions. One was a Gallic legion recruited from *Gallia Narbonensis* and the other comprised the Twenty-First Legion—all Romans. The travelers spent the night with the native Gallic soldiers. They spoke a similar tongue and were friendly enough, but Amminus was glad to be on the road again. Even with all the activity of the camp, Jachin kept to himself. Amminus worried about his nephew's somber mood. The boy used to always be so high-spirited and cheerful. It would be several more days before they would be at the agreed upon place. There was no hurry. Maybe he would come around.

To avoid running into Roman patrols and bandits, they crossed over the Rhenus at the Oppidum. The Gallic soldiers said it would be safer on the eastern side of the river. Germanic tribes sparsely settled this area because of the thick forest. Despite this, Amminus kept a watchful eye. Traveling along the front was the quickest way, but not necessarily safe.

The morning sun shone a soft light on the narrow road. Amminus and Jachin seemed to be the only travelers that morning. To their left was the dark northernmost slopes of the Black Forest. The Romans called it the *Abnoba Mons* after a local Gallic goddess. Like the Roman goddess Diana, she was the patron of the forest and goddess of the hunt. To their right, a gentle slope of green grasses fronted the muddy river below. The deep and broad Rhenus River was the line of demarcation between *Gallia* and *Germania* and was considered the farthest frontier of the Roman Empire. The Albion foreigners traveled along this border on their way south.

Roman *castra* dotted the countryside all along the waterway on the western shore. The Romans were reported to have kept eight full legions in as many as five posts along the Rhenus in these small fortifications, though the actual number was rumored to be more. Amminus wasn't completely confident in his sources but did not doubt that the Romans had a substantial presence along their most eastern border to guard against Germanic attacks. Correspondence from the imperator himself added credence to the information. One of these fortified military camps occupied the city of *Mongontiacum* at the junction of the Rhenus and the *Moenus* Rivers. It was there that Amminus and Jachin planned to meet the imperator of Rome.

The castrum was described as a complex settlement, with two native villages adjacent to a huge wooden fortress built close to a river port on the Rhenus. Beyond the castrum were rolling hills, the imperator boasted in his letters, where terraced vineyards along the riverbank produced succulent grape clusters. Romans loved their wine.

The shadows from the trees embraced the path like long dark fingers. Amminus trotted up next to his nephew, who had finally slowed his horse to a walk. "Are you well?"

Jachin drew the pugio out of its rabbit-skin scabbard, fingered the sharp tip, and then sheathed it. He heeled his horse and galloped farther down the road ahead of Amminus. There was still much ground to cover. Amminus worried that he would run the mare to exhaustion.

It had been many years since Jachin had ridden a horse. He had only recently gotten his land legs. Holding the reins tighter than necessary, Jachin made the horse uneasy and skittish. Whereas Jachin preferred only a thick wool rug as a seat on his horse, Amminus had purchased one of the new Roman four-horned leather saddles from a soldier the previous night. He liked the way it strapped around the front, across the horse's chest. Similarly, leather straps fastened behind the horse under the tail, allowing a secure rider's seat in most any circumstance. It would not only be advantageous in a battle but also allowed Amminus to ride in comfort; however, Jachin sat stubbornly strong on his steed.

Amminus fumbled with his own reins, finally wrapping them around one of the horns of the saddle. He leaned back and settled in for the long day's ride. Thoughtlessly, he played with the blue stone and the old leather pouch that hung from a leather cord around his neck. Lifting the necklet to his lips, he let the repository of his hope linger in a delicate kiss. He replaced it under his tunic and leaned forward to brush his hand on the horse's mane. Amminus adjusted his weight and caught the reins as they became undone. *Focus. The road ahead. Not the one behind.*

Would the imperator even accept his plan? Would the army be ready? Will they accept him as a proper envoy of Albion, or would they kill him outright as a barbarian? Amminus reported to the imperator all the events that had transpired: Cunobelinos's death, Epaticus's demise, and Caradoc's treachery. He left out the part about Alexenah

Skirmish

and the twins. Or how Caradoc had treated them all shamefully.

He watched his nephew and sighed. What would happen to Jachin? *I should have helped long ago. Saved her and the boys. Boaz is dead. Jachin is turning sour. Every day he grows worse.* He wiped tears from his face with his sleeve and grabbed the reins again. He was glad Jachin rode ahead and had not seen him crying. *Alexenah will not be forgotten. I will build a temple to her.* He paused. The boy had changed. His mood sullen, his demeanor distant. He'd grown taller. Hair longer. Voice deeper. Sea-salt tough and suntanned. Muscles had replaced weak childlike arms. *No, not a young boy anymore. Now he's a man.*

A sound of hoofbeats in the distance behind them caused the travelers to both halt. Soldiers? Rovers? Drifters? Only dust in the air. The wind arose. Amminus paid it no mind, as they were on this side of the river, where they were assured safety.

They urged their mounts ahead, cautiously moving along the path again. As they came up to a narrow pass on the east bank of the Rhenus River, hooves pounded louder on the road behind them. Amminus put his hand on his sword.

"Jachin, hold up!"

From over the rise of the road behind them galloped seven dark horses, with a strong-spirited white horse with cream-colored mane in the lead. Roman cavalry. A soldier in a gleaming yellow masked helm raced his white steed straight toward Amminus. The charging cavalry and their leader rode past him as if he wasn't even there. *Were they after Jachin?*

Twang. Hiss. Thunk. Arrows from the trees above bounced off the Roman's *lorica segmentata*. One arrow found a vulnerable spot, and a soldier fell. His horse continued with the others as the mounted soldiers passed Jachin.

Before anyone could draw a sword or spear, men dressed in the colors of the local tribes appeared from the woods and encircled the Roman troop, bringing them all to a sudden stop, their horses rearing and striking out at their opponents with their front legs.

Jachin jumped from his horse, pugio in hand.

Amminus pulled his sword and galloped toward the assembly. "Jachin! No!"

Seizing the fallen Roman's gladius, Jachin attacked the local assailants from the rear. His unexpected confrontation confused the aggressors, allowing the Roman cavalry to join the fight. The golden-masked soldier remained resolute, with his sword drawn in the center of the fray, but he did not engage the enemy.

Before Amminus could race in to save him, Jachin cut a warrior's Achilles' tendon with the gladius. As the man stumbled, he pierced his chest with the pugio. Then the boy moved to the next closest assailant. He killed two more before they knew what happened. Amminus couldn't believe what he saw. Jachin was in the heat of the battle, fighting for the Romans. He did not like the look on his nephew's face as he continued his melee.

Amminus joined the fight to Jachin's right, his horse blocking the enemy from getting to Jachin, his sword finding its mark. The enemy attackers, if that is what they were, turned on him and Jachin. Caught between them, the Romans cut the assailants from behind.

Dressed in rough hides and metal helms that were not much different than those from his own homeland, Amminus counted at least twenty. They fought ferociously. Amminus dodged a swing. Undercut it. Laid a blow on the arm of the attacker and raised his sword to finish him.

Jachin stabbed the man from behind. The pugio penetrated the man's throat and lingered in time's eye as Amminus viewed the scene from his saddle. The point glared red and gold in the sunlight as if a torch had been lit in the dark.

Swoosh! An arrow sliced Amminus's shoulder from behind as it flew by. Another glanced off his upraised sword and hit the white horse in the flank. The horse reared, and the masked man tumbled to the ground. The Romans formed a quick wall around their comrade with their dark chargers.

Lunge. Jab. Twist. *Did Jachin use that special move he revealed in his training back in Albion?* Jachin downed another. They drove the warriors toward the Roman wall of might, where many met their deaths.

A tall attacker turned and faced Amminus with his spear poised to attack. His light-blue eyes were wild with fury. His nostrils flared on his long-crooked nose.

A horn blasted from the trees.

The attacker smiled. He lowered his weapon and ran the opposite direction into the trees. The remaining attackers scattered for the forest.

Jachin broke the arrow shaft from the thick flank leather strap of the white horse and jumped into the saddle. He reached for the masked man and hauled him up behind him. The Roman troop assembled the horses around them. Jachin and the masked man, along with the cavalry, raced down the road. At first Amminus thought they gave chase, but instead they headed toward the major thoroughfare where they had originally been traveling. The soldiers were right to do so. It was better to escape now before the attackers regrouped.

Yes, Jachin had changed. Grew up. What happened to him on that ship? How could he fight with such self-possession and skill? Amminus shook his head. He could do nothing but follow.

CHAPTER 27

Introduction

You remain unchanged except by the people you encounter on your path to victory.

— Scribonius Largus

The troop escaped, not slowing until they came upon a confluence where another river emptied into the Rhenus. As Jachin turned a corner, he came upon a massive stone bridge crowded with local villagers and merchants. The crowd parted to make way for the soldiers, who rode in single file, with Jachin and his rider on the white horse in the lead. He counted twenty-one supporting piers as the horses passed the cheering crowd on the bridge.

Once across, they entered the *castellum* through a massive wooden gate. The log walls of the fort were the height of three grown men. Sentries in full Roman regalia guarded the ramparts.

The travelers dismounted to water their horses at a fountain in front of the enormous stone columns of what appeared to be a temple. Men and women occupied in various activities of the day filled the courtyard.

"Which god is that dedicated to?" Jachin asked the masked man balanced behind him.

"The locals pray to Cybele—a goddess of earth, fertility, and wild animals. Many of the soldiers worship her. Romans rarely meet a god they don't like. Personally, I prefer the supreme god, Jupiter."

"Do you pray to him?"

"Why should I? One day, in the eyes of the Senate in Rome, I will surpass him in greatness. People will pray to *me*."

Jachin ran his fingers through his long dark hair. Either this man thought more highly of himself, or he joked.

After they dismounted, a soldier approached them. His beard stubble was a mixture of gray with strips of dark-black hair on either side of his chin. Stocky like a tree stump, his arms were massive. His helmet had an alternating black and white plum, looking a lot like the man's beard. Jachin surmised he must be a man of importance.

"How long have you been a legionnaire? Where did you learn to fight like that?" the soldier asked in a gruff, gravelly voice.

"Since today."

"You are just a child." The man squeezed Jachin's shoulder and felt his biceps. "It's the transfer of body weight, not the arm strength that gives force to your cuts and dodge." He moved Jachin to the left and then the right. "Most of the time retreat should be sideways, not straight backward." Then forward and back. "Don't increase distance. Keep close."

Jachin shook the man off and looked at him as if saying, "Who are you?"

The man continued. "You don't need fancy sword moves. All moves that can be made are known. What you need is discipline." He stepped closer and eyeballed Jachin.

The Golden Cord

Jachin did not shy from the examination.

"You have anger in you. But not toward these men. Let's use that."

The masked man removed his helm. He shook his head and wiped the sweat from his eyes. "Training already?" He motioned to the squat man. "Let me introduce Servious Sulpicius Galba, commanding officer of the Upper Germania Legions. The *germani cisrhenani* live on the left bank—to the east—of the Rhenus River, where we were traveling."

All the soldiers turned, saluted, and called out in unison. "*Disce miles militare Galba est non Gaetulicus.*"

"My Latin is not good," Jachin lied. "What did they say?"

"Learn to be a soldier, child!" Galba barked. "Soldiers don't complain and only ask questions when given permission to do so."

"They said, 'Galba is here, not Gaetulicus,'" Amminus answered as he approached the group.

The masked man handed his golden helmet to Galba. "I shall tell you the story of Gaetulicus while the men remove their saddles and prepare us a place for the night." He motioned for Jachin to follow him.

"Jachin, we should move on. We are to meet with the imperator at sunup two days from today at Mongontiacum," Amminus said.

Jachin glared at Amminus and sat down on the fountain with the masked man.

Not that much older than himself, he seemed to be barely a man. Probably in his twenties, with a soft face, no beard, and only fine hairs above his upper lip. His ears stuck out like oversized seashells from his short dark hair, which he combed forward with his fingers. He wore the uniform of a regular soldier. Yet the white horse and distinctive yellow-masked helm seemed a little much. Perhaps he was their bard.

"What did they mean about Galba and Gaetulicus?"

Galba gave Jachin a stone-melting look.

"Losses from the Germanii discourage the men. Their random attacks of our soldiers required suppression to maintain the border. *Apronius* couldn't continue control, so he called for reinforcements."

"Gaetulicus?"

The man took a cloth from his neck and dipped it in the fountain. He washed his face. What Jachin thought were fine hairs turned out to be only smudges of dirt.

"Gaetulicus traveled north and quickly became a problem. He refused to impose discipline. He wanted to be popular. You can't have both. Galba has—how do you say—taken his place."

Jachin listened intently as the man continued. He loved stories. Whether sailors or soldiers, everyone had a tale. And most of them were factual, if not embellished for effect. This report rang true. Real people. Galba was a harsh man who demanded discipline. Jachin could see it in his demeaner and his insistence on instructing a stranger. He must have been sent north to properly train the legions. Jachin had tasted that soup. *A soldier doesn't complain.*

As it grew dark, the men retired to barracks. A whole legion was positioned there, and another detachment was stationed on the other side of the river. In front of their tents the soldiers stacked their gear, leaning wooden poles against each other like the rafters of a roundhouse. A firepit was constructed, but nothing was lit. The legionnaires gathered around the pit and ate from small bags and drank from canteens they all carried. Amminus joined them.

The masked man—Jachin did not know what else to call him—directed Galba to set a wooden case before the gathering. "My brothers, these are for you."

Galba opened the case and gave each legionnaire who had accompanied him on the road a decorative crown. "*Coronae Exploratoriae*," he called them.

"Scouting crowns," Amminus said. "A noble honor." He stood and addressed the man. "Pardon me, I ride with the one who fought so bravely. Let me introduce myself."

The men grew quiet. The masked man motioned for Amminus to continue.

"I am *Amminus sum Cunobelinos filium, qui est filius Tasciovaunus de tribu Catuvellaunii.*"

The masked man and Amminus clasped hands, each grabbing up the forearm in the formal greeting to show they were not enemies. "Welcome to you, and my gratitude for your help on the road this day," the man said.

Jachin's anger burned. Why was his uncle telling them who they were? The Romans would kill them, knowing they were from Albion. Everything was going fine until now.

"Amminus? I perceive you go by another name."

"That is the name I am known by."

"What is the name you sign on communications with the Romans?"

Jachin stood. He started to sit, then rose again. He reached for his pugio and readied to defend his uncle if necessary.

Amminus straightened his shoulders. He chuckled. "On papyrus, I am known as the 'one who is on the road to victory.'"

"*Viatorvictori*! Of course. You were to meet with the imperator in Lugdunum, were you not?"

"Mongontiacum. Another two days ride."

The soldiers laughed. Too much information. Jachin did not trust them, even though he hoped these Romans were to be aides to his intentions.

Galba moved forward, raised his hand, and announced, "This calls for another introduction." He lowered his hand and bent forward. "This *is* the castrum Mongontiacum."

Jachin and Amminus considered each other in surprise.

"Therefore," Galba continued, "I present before you the majestic and mighty Gaius Julius Caesar Augustus Germanicus, known to those who follow him without fear as Caligula."

28
CHAPTER

Movement

Change and circumstance alter our illusion of control.

— Scribonius Largus

AD 37—Carura in Phrygia, Asia Minor

The medical team from the temple Men-Karou made the journey to the city of Carura twice a month for as long as Boaz could remember, and probably for as long as the Herophilean school of medicine had existed. Instead of staying at the caravanserai with the many travelers, Boaz—along with the other students and medical workers—stayed in the gymnasium on thin straw pallets set out each night and taken up each morning so as not to interfere with the young athletes' activities.

Boaz pulled his tunic over his head and fastened his leather belt around his thin waist. Shaking sleep from his head, he slipped on his *solea*, lacing the sandals around his ankles. He rolled up his pallet and stepped over another student. He rushed to meet his mentor at the gymnasium entrance.

Boaz blinked until his eyes adjusted to the predawn light over the mountains in the east. Fluffy clouds lingered above like lost sheep. The brisk morning air felt pleasant on his cheeks. "A good day," Boaz said. He stroked his scraggly beard as he searched the crowd for Sophronios.

A lengthy line of patients and their families gathered on the cold stones in front of the granite pillars of the enormous building used as a clinic. Some stood while loved ones carried others on liters. Many of them walked all night just to be there. Travelers and merchants, stopping briefly in the town for one reason or another, showed up and paced nervously in line. They probably would leave before the medical team saw them, Boaz deduced, as rovers had little patience for waiting.

Different clothing customs made for quite a colorful spectacle while they waited for the physician and his apprentices to attend to their various ailments. A few sheep and half a dozen goats packed into the boulevard with them, perhaps to be used as payment or for sacrifice.

Sophronios stood among the throng, gesticulating with his straw hat to several red-turbaned men in long dusty black coats. Boaz was amazed at how many different languages his mentor spoke and even more amazed when he realized he had easily learned various tongues in his own studies.

The men exclaimed in awe as the old physician told them how far the hat on his head had traveled. They laughed at a joke Boaz didn't understand.

Sophronios winked.

Boaz folded his hands behind his back to wait on his mentor. He winced. His shoulder still gave him pain in the mornings, even after two years since his injuries.

Sophronios said his farewells, promising to tell them more jests when they saw him later in the surgeries.

Movement

Matching his mentor's steps, Boaz and Sophronios headed down the boulevard together in search of an early breakfast.

A scrawny dog ran past them, his nose to the ground in search of food. When it approached them, Sophronios shooed it away with a feigned kick.

"Each awakening is a beginning. How is your appetite, Pedi?"

"I am starved!"

"You're always hungry."

"No, I'm not."

"Precisely. Sometimes you sleep," Sophronios murmured.

After an uncomfortable pause, Boaz said, "I was here on time this morning."

"I arrived before you."

"You instruct that proper sleep and nutrition is beneficial for the body."

"True. Your body is well fed. You have nearly tripled in height since we left Albion. Would that you would feed your mind as much."

Boaz stroked his beard. "I'm a growing young man."

"Then let's eat a hearty breakfast before the clinic session begins."

"What of the others?"

"Those who slept in will bemoan their choice come noon, when there will be little time to partake in any nourishment."

Sophronios put his hand on Boaz's shoulder. Was he going to say something kind? Instead, the old physician pulled at the boy's new growth of facial hair. "Tut-tut. You call that a beard?"

Boaz brushed his hand away. "I realize it is not as magnificent as yours, but I have only just begun, while you have had half a century or more to advance your growth!"

Boaz ran ahead on the steep stone street and paused at the top of the hill. He waited for Sophronios to catch up. He waved at his mentor. Did a slight smile form on the lips of the man who had purchased him as a slave boy in Albion and nourished him with the hopes of becoming a physi-

The Golden Cord

cian? At this distance, he couldn't be sure. Boaz tried his best to please Sophronios, but the man he admired never noticed. Boaz sighed.

He was happy they had come here. Carura was a city of abundant beauty situated in the valley north of the *Kadmos* mountains along the great winding road from Ephesus, which followed the *Meander* River.

The sun's golden crown peeked over the mountains in the east; its rays made the morning clouds appear violet and red. The marble buildings of the city appeared pink.

Not only was the landscape more beautiful than he'd ever seen but it also flourished with interesting folk. Below him wound the busy trade route conveying people from faraway to stay at the various inns and visit the many brothels and temples of Carura. Merchants transported goods along this thoroughfare to Ephesus on the coast to meet seaside merchants bringing wares to the east. With them, they brought their ailments and injuries.

Sophronios lumbered up the hill.

Boaz rested his hands on his chest and breathed in the cool air as if to hold this moment inside forever. This is what it must be like to be loved. To be appreciated. To be noticed. Sophronios's attention to detail fed his own passion for learning, and his master loved to teach. It was easy to overlook his mentor's constant criticism and teasing. It was not so with the other students. It made Boaz feel special and unique. Sophronios—in his own way—showed he cared about those he attended. Boaz wanted to be like his teacher. He wanted to care.

There were so many things to learn. At times Boaz would get away from his patients and his studies to enjoy the many fountains and hot springs in this area. These thermal springs were not only on the banks of the Meander but also flowed within the river itself.

On one sweltering summer day, after working the surgeries, he sought relief by swimming in the river. He found the water cold and refreshing. However, as he came to certain areas, the water was like stew cooking over the fire. This had discomforted him, while others seemed to enjoy the warmth.

Movement

Bubbles showed on the surface of the water where the springs emptied into the river from underground. A jet of hot water from one of the pools on the bank spewed out water and steam several inches from the ground. It came at such regular intervals that the citizens tallied the hours of the day with the number of times the water sprang from its subterranean home.

Many travelers would stop and relax in the pools for its famous healing properties. The more well-to-do in the city did not frequent the river waters. They could afford to pipe the steamy water to their homes and to the numerous bathhouses in the city.

Boaz closed his eyes. He reviewed the details in his mind as if memorizing a dream—a roughly hewn upland region, for the most part. It provided both a home and a highway for a bewildering variety of peoples for as long as there have been humans. The river was deep but not very wide.

An ornate marble bridge—broad enough for ten horses to gallop shoulder to shoulder—spanned the water. Beside the bridge, built at vast expense, stood a magnificent quay made of locally harvested marble that shown like a rainbow in the sun. The boats anchored there crammed together so closely that Boaz could walk a *mille passus* going from boat to boat if he wanted.

Looking east toward Laodicea stood the Temple of Men-Karou, though it was too far to see from there. The celebrated school of medicine flourished under the leadership of *Alexander Philalethes*, who Sophronios called *Amator Veri* because, according to Boaz's mentor, "He always spoke the truth." Herophilus, who was trained in Alexandria, Egypt, established the school. Because of him, the students were called *Herophilii*. Boaz was proud to take on the title. This is where Sophronios brought Boaz to learn the art of medicine, and it was the best thing that had ever happened to him. He put aside the past and thoroughly enjoyed the present. His eyes watered when he thought of his prospects in medicine—something he'd never imagined experiencing.

A persistent rooster crowed among the interjecting sounds of a few barking dogs. "I used to think roosters only crowed at sunrise." Boaz laughed. "Roosters in this town

The Golden Cord

crow all day and all night long!" Because of this, he stuck wool in his ears at bedtime along with taking a mixture of herbs to curtail dreaming.

"That rooster is going through puberty," said Sophronios, out of breath.

Boaz reached for his instructor's arm to assist him up the final steps of the steep hill. "What do you mean *senex*?"

"He sounds like you when your voice started changing. Ha! All squeak and honk!" The physician laughed as they walked together.

After a few minutes of silence, Boaz said, "That was a long time ago."

"Last week, if I remember correctly. And do not call me an old man. Although my vision and my hearing are not as good as they used to be, my memory is very much intact, Pedi."

"It is, Master Sophronios. Forgive me for questioning it." Boaz smiled. His master was indeed the smartest man he had ever met. He liked the way his mentor joked as if they were friends.

Walking down into the city proper, they passed the same emaciated dog, now devouring garbage someone had thrown to the gutter. Boaz scowled. He rubbed the back of his neck.

"The people here treat the strays worse than they treat their slaves," Boaz said.

"The only thing a dog is good for is a swift boot to the ribs," Sophronios grumbled.

They passed so many buildings that Boaz thought Carura was the biggest city in Phrygia. There were about as many inns in Carura as there were temples. When they arrived at the end of the street, they stood in front of the Caravanserai. The Traveler's Inn, an unadorned gray stone building with rectangular walls, stood near the principal road from Laodicea to Ephesus at the entrance to Carura. This is where they would eat a fine breakfast.

They entered through a spacious portal big enough to permit heavily laden camels and other beasts to the markets inside. The courtyard opened to the sky and the rising sun shone on the inside walls, crammed with stalls kept by sleepyheaded merchants and their servants. Each identical compartment was packed brimful with boarded animals belonging to the travelers, together with their abundant merchandise to sell. Popular among guests was the black wool brought from Laodicea, famous for its delicate touch on the skin.

The inn provided water for consumption and washing—a rare privilege. On one side, a lavish entrance opened to an elaborate bathhouse. Fodder for animals, supply shops for travelers, and countless craftsmen filled out the Inn's massive area. Despite all the various smells of the caravanserai, the best was the pleasant aroma of fresh-baked bread that wafted from the kitchen. They sat down to a breakfast of warm bread with dates and honey. Sophronios drank some watered wine. Boaz pushed his glass to the side.

"What a glorious day!"

"Looks like it is going to be another sweltering day seeing patients, Pedi. Always the same. Backaches and bellyaches."

"Are you talking about yourself, or the patients?"

Sophronios laughed.

"They bring their votives to offer up for cures. Anything from clay feet to whittled wooden eyes. I marvel at their creativity in fashioning them to appear lifelike. I suppose the more realistic, the easier it is for the gods to recognize them." Sophronios paused. "After clinic today, I plan to go to the bathhouse next to the brothel."

"There are so many in this city!"

"Both brothels and bathhouses."

"Seriously, which one—in case I need to find you."

"The one with footprints on the stone walkway leading into the place. Do not feign innocence."

Boaz's face warmed as he blushed. "I have never been inside. What is it like?"

"It is adjacent to the bathhouse. Many don't know that there are two entrances—one from the Marble Road and one from *Curetes* Street. There is a dining hall on the first floor. On the second floor, there are a number of small apartments, whether for rooming or for pleasure, I cannot accord. On the west side of the house, there is a reception area with brightly colored mosaics on the floor, symbolizing the four seasons. You would like them. The chamber beyond that accommodates an elliptical cooling pool. On the floor of the pool, there is another mosaic depicting three women eating and drinking, a waitress standing, and a mouse and a cat nibbling crumbs from her hand. Very imaginative."

"I hear their seafood is excellent. Comes from Ephesus," Boaz said.

"I have been to the diner once or twice, and indeed the fare is excellent."

"I do like the baths at Men-Karou, but the water is not always warm."

"In addition to the cooling pool, this bathhouse has a circular room with twenty-five bathtubs filled with steaming water piped straight from the hot springs, so it is always the same temperature. The adjoining circular sweating room is the grandest I have ever seen, and I have beheld plenty in my travels."

Boaz reveled in the amazing architecture and beauty of this place. And the description—so exact—from his mentor of a place he would never go. Very different than the huts and hillforts of Albion.

"Is that why we always come to Carura, Master? The bathhouses?"

"The reason we come here is because there are not very many physicians for a town of this size. And it is good for your training."

They finished their meal and headed back to the gymnasium for the start of clinic. Boaz felt full and happy. Life was good.

Boaz pointed down the street, where all the townspeople wandered and worked. "I know what you mean about the lack of good medical care in Carura. I've seen the Judean, that drunk doctor *Didymus*, driving his chariot around town like a maniac."

"The city is not entirely devoid of care. The *pater familias* provides most of the medical care. The heads of each household treat most illnesses and minor wounds themselves. There are a few midwives, and the soldiers have the *medicus*. Many of the soldiers learn to provide first aid to

Movement

their comrade's wounds in the field. Others go to the temples to entreat the gods for a cure. Didymus serves his purpose, but he cannot keep up with the demands of the people. Wasn't your mother Judean?"

"I'd rather not think about that."

"You will talk about it when it is time for you to do so."

The two came to the top of the next hill just as the red sun peaked its head from behind a blushing cloud.

Young boys rushed naked from the gymnasium and into the streets. Their naked bodies, covered in oil, glimmered in the morning sun.

Sophronios pointed. "What in the world are those boys doing?"

"Chasing a hare!"

"That is the funniest sight these old eyes have ever seen!" Sophronios laughed so hard his shoulders shook. Boaz joined in.

A loud boom, followed by a rumbling sound, suddenly shook the ground.

Boaz supported his master to keep him from falling. It seemed like the earth under them rolled. They fell together to the cobblestone street. The rows of apartments and shops shook violently. Marble columns collapsed in huge chunks like a child's building blocks. The roar of destruction echoed from the hills.

Boaz coughed and gagged.

The earth, constant and unmovable, became fluid. It rocked and rolled like a ship on the Great Green—only much more unnerving.

Finally, the low rumbling stopped. Dust lingered in the air like pink clouds, covering the debris of the city. As the dust settled before him, Boaz gasped. The marvelous architecture and grandeur of the city vanished in a cloud of dust. Carura lay in ruins.

CHAPTER 29

Destruction

Never fret when the puzzle pieces fall to the ground. They can still be reassembled.

— Scribonius Largus

Boaz wiped grit from his eyes and helped Sophronios to his feet.

Without hesitation, Sophronios headed down the hill toward the gymnasium. "We must gather what supplies and instruments we can find. The people need our help," his mentor said.

Women, crying in despair, clung to their children. Bloody men stumbled in a daze. Mud-covered boys from the gymnasium cowered together, surrounded by the vast rubble. Other medical students and helpers crawled from the wreckage. What was left of homes blazed with ravaging flames. The stench of sulfur from long cracks in the ground overwhelmed Boaz amid the destruction.

Destruction

Boaz faltered. Almost stumbled. His legs shook. He wanted to help, but there was so much. How would he even start? Emotions numbed, he felt more like the dead than the living.

At the bottom of the hill knelt a man sobbing into his hands. "Poseidon punishes us with his trident. Poseidon punishes us! Poseidon. Poseidon. Poseidon's trident sends thunderbolts through the earth to punish our souls!"

Sophronios gripped the man by his shoulders. "Poseidon must be in a foul mood indeed for sending this earthquake storm, but, dear sir, we need your assistance." He helped the man to his feet. "Steady yourself."

The man sobbed and shook, but the teacher's calmness strengthened him.

"I need you to find as many tables that are whole and bring them to the gymnasium—or whatever is left standing of the school building. Bring sheets and rags. Cloth of any sort for bandages. Enlist others to assist you. We must set up a surgery right away."

The clear morning revealed the full impact of the quake. Buildings collapsed upon each other like sheets of papyrus tossed to the floor. Bodies lay everywhere, many crushed under the granite stones and heaps of rubble—barely recognizable as human. An arm here, a leg there, protruding from under the chaos of marble. An older man was impaled by a jutting timber that perched precariously from the pile of what used to be his home. The outcries of those seeking their wives, their children, and their relatives echoed off the hills.

"Everyone be still, silent, so we can hear for calls of help," Sophronios said.

He directed the students to setting up a makeshift triage and surgery center where the wounded could be assessed and treated. Others secured supplies—water to wash wounds and cloth for bandages. They used their hands, shovels, anything they could find to uncover the living and the dead. Those milling about pitched in to help. The old dog who Sophronios had shooed away barked, signaling those alive under the rubble.

Boaz found Sophronios's rolled leather case of surgical

instruments, and they salvaged as many ointments and unguents as they could find.

Aftershocks rattled Boaz's nerves along with the remaining standing structures. Rescue workers struggled to hold back anxious parents from the rubble. Some questioned the quality of the school's construction. "The shed I built didn't collapse, but the school did," said a potter.

Boaz and the others worked all day and through the night as victims with cuts, crush injuries, broken bones, burns, and the like came to them. Makeshift beds and tents lay up and down the street.

A young yellow-haired girl about Boaz's age carried a basket from one bed to the next. She touched each patient as she bent low to speak to them and offer water or wine, bread, and honey. She brushed her hair out of her face and placed a strand behind her ear, which appeared bruised. She caught Boaz's eye and smiled.

His cheeks warmed. He gazed at the patient before him, lost in thought.

An older man pushed Boaz aside and pulled a long-curved knife from the red leather girdle around his corpulent waist.

The interloper wore a wool tunic that fit tight against his body and a black linen turban on his head. Boaz turned up his nose—the man stunk of wine.

"What are you doing?" the man said.

"I am trying to save this man's leg," Boaz replied, taken aback that someone would question his skills. The best had trained him. "What are *you* doing?"

"I'm trying to save this man's life!"

The wounded patient wept as the man removed a leather flask from his girdle, gave the victim a drink, then poured some on the wound and the leg. "If you are unwilling to prescribe wine liberally to your patient, then you should take it yourself." He took a long draught.

"I've heard of you. You're that Jewish physician, Didymus."

"I am. Now hold his leg."

To Boaz's surprise, after applying a tourniquet, the local doctor skillfully sliced through the man's thigh, cutting to

Destruction

the bone in an instant. Taking a saw from his girdle, and with a few strokes, the leg came free.

Boaz held the leg in his arms and tossed it into a pile with other disembodied limbs.

"Close the wound, while I hold the ends together." The surgeon's cut angled allowing him to bring the edges together to form a stump.

Boaz seized his needle holder and sewed.

"You call that a stitch? Give me that!" Didymus grabbed the instrument and finished suturing.

Boaz struggled to hold the skin together without letting his arms shake. "What do you call that stitch?"

"Mattress stitch. Holds the wound together better than what you were doing."

"I see."

"Do you? With all that hair in your face, I am surprised you ever know where you are going! Hand me some more of that suture."

Boaz assisted him blotting the blood, so the surgeon could do his work, throwing the bloodied rags into a pail at their feet.

All around them others attended to the fallen and crushed humanity. Children separated from their families wandered the streets aimlessly. Some cried. Others stared numbly into the rubble. Roman soldiers from nearby *Hierapolis* soon arrived. They assisted in finding survivors and removed the dead. The magnitude of the chaos was beyond anything Boaz had ever seen. Yet in that chaos, a certain order remained.

"There have been many quakes before," Didymus said. "*Euseistos* is what they call the countryside around Carura. No city is more prone to earthquakes—unless it is Laodicea."

"You saw the earth shaken this severe before?"

"Oh yes. I remember the *Izmit* earthquake and wondered why so many people had to die. Not one structure stood."

"This is my first."

"We haven't had one this destructive in a long time. We will recover."

"Why do people continue to rebuild?"

"It's a crossroads, says some. The climate is mild, and the soil is rich, say others."

"Won't it all fall down again? It seems so futile. Are all our labors futile?"

"No, Herophilii. All is not wasted. The Almighty One is good."

"It would have been good if this never happened."

"If not earthquakes, it would be invasions. Jews like you and me live with risk all the time."

An aftershock nearly knocked Boaz off his feet. He imagined Poseidon's breath battered him from beneath the ground. How did this doctor know he was half-Jewish?

"Hold tight, Herophilii!" Didymus barked.

Boaz felt small and powerless in the face of all the forces the earth shaker represented. "I'm exhausted."

"Don't be so easily shaken. Learn from Sophronios. Nothing moves him. Be of sound mind."

Someone reached from behind Boaz to take the bucket of bloodied rags and replace it with an empty clay vessel. Again the ground shuddered stronger than the other aftershocks. Boaz stumbled. The girl he noticed earlier stood behind him.

She screamed. Dropped the pail.

Boaz caught her in his arms.

⌘ ⌘ ⌘

Lais, caught off guard, peered up from the boy's arms. From that brief instant, she considered the young man's eyes. They were the color of ashes. Underneath, she could sense a fire burning in his gaze. She was skilled at reading men and their desires. This boy's eyes showed real concern. She didn't quite know what to make of that.

He lifted her, and they stood face-to-face. She steadied herself and lowered her head. Her long-sleeved tunic appeared torn and soiled with dust and blood. She felt ashamed that she was barefoot.

"Are you well?" Boaz asked.

"Yes, considering what has happened. I think I'll be

fine," Lais said and added in her native language, "but I don't think I'll ever be the same."

"I doubt that any of us will leave here unscarred," Boaz said in the same language. A simple Celtic dialect.

"You speak my language! Although the accent is different—softer—I can understand everything you said. Where are you from?" It'd been forever since she had spoken to anyone in her own language.

Boaz picked up the pail and replaced the bloody rags. "I am from Albion, and you?"

She helped fill the pail. "I am from what the Romans call *Batavia*."

"I know of it. Northern Gaul. I've never been there. How is it you came to be here in Carura?"

"That is a long story, best left for telling when the need is not so pressing. I believe your master needs your assistance."

"Oh, he is not my master—"

Didymus seized Boaz by the arm and dragged him away from her. "Quick, Herophilii, I need you over here!"

"I'm Boaz. What is your name?" he called.

She looked back and smiled. "I will tell you next time we meet."

CHAPTER 30

Injuries

Cruelly sweet are the echoes of early years.

— Scribonius Largus

Sophronios leaned on the dock's skeleton. Death's odor lay heavy in the air. They performed seventy-five surgeries in nine days. The Caravanserai and adjoining brothel's collapse killed many workers and their patrons. Those passing through ended their travels in a common pyre.

An angler said the river emptied and then flowed backward, carrying boats with it during the quake. Bodies floated, some face up, some face down, swollen, and unrecognizable. The physician's vision steadily worsened, so he had to take the man's word on it. He secured his petasos, tying the strings under his beard. He turned away and headed back toward the center of town.

After the earthquake the people lived in their open

Injuries

gardens and farms. There were only a few shops—pieced together from unburnt stone and boards—that were able to sell supplies in the town. An abundance of children wandered the streets, separated from their families. Soldiers hunted for the lost. Anyone alive now would truly be a miracle. Looting ensued. Punishment was brisk and assured.

No aftershocks, though Sophronios was told there were many in the aftermath of this battle. Along with his eyesight and hearing, his sense of touch was afflicted. His feet tingled like pins and needles. Maybe he just didn't feel any tremors. He needed treatment himself, but there was too much to be done that caring for his own needs seemed trite. He hid his afflictions by letting the students take on more tasks. They were thankful for it, and the experience benefited both Herophilii and their patients. As it was, he had to basically get right on top of a wound to see and sew it.

So many had perished during the quake, or soon after, that instead of graves they burned the bodies in fires outside the city. Clouds of smoke during the day and the glow of the blaze at night could be seen for miles. Burning flesh nauseated Sophronios. Some died for want of assistance—too much to do. Many were never identified. They'd sort that out later, he guessed.

The town's people refused to go home in fear that any building standing would fall because of the aftershocks. At night they slept in tents or slumbered in the streets and overhangs. They burned wood from collapsed buildings, huddled together for warmth. The flames that ravaged the cheaper homes and shops still lit the nights. Diarrhea sickness snared those still alive.

The Temple of Athena fell, so the devoted had nowhere to make offerings. Treated with herbs and opiates, patients brought votive offerings for the doctors instead.

Boaz worked a lot with a certain girl. Sophronios noticed their interactions. Interaction? More like flirtation. The two had even been seen walking down to the hot springs together and at times when he needed them, they both were missing. He let it happen. It was nice to know that during destruction there was happiness . . . and perhaps love.

He was young and in love once. Met her in an herbal

shop at a market in Laodicea, where he worked part time while still a student at Men-Karou. She ran in from a sudden downpour, soaked to the skin. Her hair dripped rain on her stola, which clung against her body. Rain drenched her from head to heel. He couldn't help but laugh. At first she seemed angry; then she joined in and giggled so sweetly. He offered her a towel as they talked and laughed together. There would be no business that day.

Her name was Kalliope. Sophronios had seen her before. She worked in a local pottery shop owned by her parents. He asked her to dinner and for months they saw each other often. Sophronios was smitten. He was sure this girl would be his wife. He imagined his life with none other than her. No one had ever shown thoughtfulness like she did. She could talk for hours about the littlest thing while at the same time show him the utmost attention to his pontifications and meanderings. Kalliope had brought color to his life. He felt alive when with her. He felt whole. He was in love.

One sunny day while traveling together in his cart, Kalliope told him she loved Demosthenes Philalethes, a fellow medical student. She did not love Sophronios. They parted ways only to run into each other many years later. Strange, it rained that day as well. They shared a meal at a local tavern.

A musician played the *Cerbesian*, a Phrygian melody on a *tibia*—a woodwind pipe—which shared its name with a bone in the lower leg. Kalliope sang along. She had a beautiful voice. Sophronios could still recall the lyrics as transcribed by Strabo:

I sow the furrows of the Berecynthian fields,
Extending twelve days journey.
Where the seat of Adrasteia and Ida resound
With the lowing of herds and the bleating of sheep;
All the plain reechoes with their cries.

Sophronios thought the song about *Tantalus*, the king of Sipylus, and his eternal punishment by Zeus illustrated the rich but wicked man's temptation without satisfaction. It was appropriate, although he didn't realize it then.

His hopes raised and his spirits lifted until she asked

Injuries

about Demosthenes, now the current head of the Herophilean school of medicine at Men-Karou. She told Sophronios she married another man who owned several local silver mines. Her unfortunate husband died in a mining accident. Kalliope had a son. She named him Demosthenes. Sophronios was crestfallen. He never saw her again. He never loved again. Instead, he devoted himself to Mistress Medicine and to his students.

Boaz and Lais worked together, laughed together. Sophronios scrutinized the couple like a doting father. He had reason to. Boaz stopped asking for sleeping herbs. He knew Boaz blocked out his past abuse, but he worried that a wounded heart would devastate him. The couple sat with each other at all meals. They touched often. Held hands. They reminded him of his lost love and the lofty dreams he gave up by becoming a doctor. It was worth it. He loved teaching and the prospects of improving the lives of those he cared for. He was satisfied.

"So many wounds," Sophronios said as he walked up to the makeshift *valetudinarian* where they treated the patients.

"*Khaire*! Didymus!"

"*Khaire pollá*! to you as well, good master."

"How's it going with the young lady, Pedi?" Sophronios asked.

Boaz handed a small jar of pungent cream to an elderly woman and ignored the comment from his mentor. "Make sure you apply this twice a day, and keep the wound covered with a clean cloth," he told the woman.

"I saw you two together. Oh, the way she looks at you," Didymus added as he applied fresh bandages to another patient.

"I'm too busy for such nonsense," Boaz blushed. He ushered in the next patient, who had a painful swelling to his thigh. "This is going to hurt," he told the man.

Boaz retrieved a scalpel out of his pack and, without warning, opened the abscess on the leg with a swift cut. A profusion of pus and cuss words burst from his patient.

"Nicely done," Sophronios said. "You are becoming an accomplished physician. Not there yet, but maybe one day."

The Golden Cord

Boaz packed and wrapped the wound with bleached linen and told the patient he could leave, which he did with much haste. "Next!" hollered Boaz. "I can't believe how many people we see every day! Some come for the simplest problems. Illnesses that their house slave could have cared for with home remedies."

"But their house slaves are not the famous earthquake doctors. They come to see us because they know we care," said Sophronios.

"I do care. It's just that some days I wish someone else would care for them."

Sophronios sat down on a stool near the physicians. "You seem to be in a hurry. Do you have some place you need to be, Pedi?"

Boaz shook his head.

Sophronios fanned himself with his straw petasos. "Thank you for helping us in the clinics, Didymus. There has been so much to do since the earthquake, and your assistance has saved many lives."

"What else would I do?" The old village physician straightened his turban, drank from his flask, and began the work of setting a broken arm. "My building is but ruble, and you have all the best helpers." Didymus nodded to Boaz as he twisted his patient's arm to set the bone. The sustained screaming didn't seem to bother him.

A small troop of Roman soldiers marched in full armor, headed who knows where to do who knows what. Although an immense help with the clean up after the earthquake, their rowdy evenings were now troublesome. Uncouth and uneducated brutes.

Construction began on a new state-of-the-art bath building to replace the collapsed one, taking up a whole city block. Sophronios had his doubts that the soldiers would use it.

"Are there any more patients waiting?" Boaz asked.

He seemed eager to be on his way. Sophronios was right—he *did* have somewhere to be.

"Looks like a group of them coming down the road," Didymus said.

Injuries

Boaz washed his hands and pulled off his apron. "That was the soldiers."

Sophronios smiled. "Maybe they all have gouty toes and need your attention, Pedi."

Boaz gave Sophronios his best hang-dog look.

"Oh, all right. You may go."

Boaz rushed out without a word.

Sophronios sighed. "So many wounds."

CHAPTER 31

One Furtive Teardrop

❦

*Love's nurturing spark blossoms
in the fireplace of need.*

— Scribonius Largus

AD 38—Carura

Boaz carried an old tattered blanket and a small basket on the path to the woodland. The air seemed alive, crisp, with a hint of fresh apple blossoms in the air.

Lais ran ahead through the purple and yellow wildflowers toward the ancient stone fence. She stopped and picked a red poppy and placed it playfully on the tip of her nose.

One Furtive Teardrop

Boaz laughed.

She put the flower in her hair, winked at him, and skipped lightly on her way. She sang a familiar Celtic song:
*"It would be good to have a bear for a friend,
to be able to walk silent in the forest with him."*

Her accent was thick, but the words he understood. She wore a clean light-blue shift that hung loosely at her shoulders. Where she had found such a dress after the earthquake, Boaz had no idea.

Walking to the woods, he memorized every bit of this beautiful young woman. Her blonde hair shone golden in the late morning sun. Her eyes, the color of a puddle reflecting the blue sky after a noon day's passing rain, twinkled when she laughed. Her cheeks dimpled when she smiled. She spoke with a slight lisp combined with her accent from her native tongue. The softness of her words melted him. He loved the way she would pronounce the word "kiss" or "lips." She was small of build, petite, not boyish, and not overly rounded like a tavern girl. She had a blue tattoo on her left ear. When he first saw it, he thought it was a bruise. Boaz never knew its significance, and she never volunteered an explanation.

She helped the physicians care for the survivors of the earthquake in Carura, and Boaz found himself seeking her assistance just to be near and feel her energy. Sometimes their hands would touch as she would hand him a surgical instrument or bandage. The gentle way she would hug her patients, and the uncomplicated way she talked to them, showed she cared.

She loved to dance and would often pull others at random from the lingering crowd to join her. She enjoyed doing this with older men as a jest. The befuddled old man's face would suddenly light up in laughter and gaiety because of the gift of her presence that she so freely gave them. It was a welcome bit of brightness in an ugly situation.

Boaz picked up his pace and finally caught up with her at the stone fence in front of the copse of trees. "This is the place I told you about. We are almost there. Just beyond this fence. Wait till you see it!"

He set the basket down and the blanket on top of it. The fence was only knee high.

She put her hands on both his shoulders.

He grabbed her waist and lifted her over the fence. After she straightened her dress, he handed her the blanket and the basket.

She ran on into the trees singing another song.

Boaz leapt over the fence and followed her. He only ran a short distance through the tall oaks when he came into a clearing free of any trees, bushes, or rocks.

Lush grass covered the ground where Lais laid the blanket. She removed bread from the basket. "This place is wonderful, Boaz! It is just as beautiful as you described it." She waved the bread, as she was constantly talking with her hands.

Boaz fell on the blanket with a not too elegant flop. "I am glad you are pleased."

"You are so graceful," Lais observed. She twirled her hair between her fingers.

He rose to his feet and brushed himself off. "I planned it that way, just so you would notice me." He embraced her and gave her a gentle hug. "Be careful with the wine. I pilfered it from Sophronios's private collection. You know how he prizes his wine."

"Is this amphora one of your creations, Boaz? I can tell by the wonderful lifelike drawings of herbs and flowers around the top. It must be one of yours. You are such a talented artist!"

They rested on the blanket. Boaz lay down, leaning against one elbow beside her. "I am not that good. I just draw it as I see it. You should see some of my earlier works of pottery and drawings. They were atrocious to the point of comical!"

She poured the wine for them both and handed Boaz a cup.

Her eyes sparkled as she sipped.

He regarded the cup, swirled the wine around, and eventually set it down without taking a drink. "I really don't drink," Boaz said, "but thought you might enjoy it."

Lais leaned over and kissed him on the lips. "Tastes wonderful," she whispered and kissed him again—longer this time.

One Furtive Teardrop

Breathlessly, Boaz smiled.

Lais giggled as she touched Boaz's scraggly beard. "It still looks like puppy hair."

"Such demeaning talk from such a beautiful lady."

"You really think I am beautiful?"

"Yes."

She kissed him again. A tear fell from her eye, and she furtively wiped it away. "This is the first time I actually believe someone who has told me that I am beautiful. Thank you."

Boaz and Lais lay on their backs, enjoying the warmth of the spring day. She nestled in the crook of his arm. His hand fell asleep, but Boaz didn't want to move it and spoil the moment.

The sun sparkled as it shown through the leaves of the trees above them like sparks of light.

"Did I ever tell you that I am Batavii? My father's name was *Chariovalda*."

Lais never talked of her past. Neither did he.

"Was?" Boaz shifted and moved his arm from under Lais. He sat up and studied her face.

Her hands moved as she spoke as if she was placing her words in the air before her. "He was a chieftain of the Batavii, killed when fighting for the Romans."

"Why did he fight for the Romans?"

"I was very young, but I remember the stories. It was a campaign of Germanicus to retaliate across the Rhenus River against the Germanic tribes that massacred three legions in the Teutonburg Forest. When we learned he was slain in the bogs, my mother feared for my safety and gave me to her brother *Avgoulinos*, the owner of the brothel. She knew the feuding Chiefs wouldn't support her. Avgoulinos took good care of me, as he was fond of my mother and did it as a favor. He took me with him on his travels to find new courtesans. That is how I ended up in Carura."

"So you are a princess?"

"I was."

"Me too. Well, not a princess. A prince."

She hit him on the chest. "No, you weren't!"

"I was. In Albion."

The Golden Cord

After a long silence, Lais touched his face with her fingertips. It soothed his spirit. "Do you miss your homeland, Boaz?"

Boaz visualized the wheat field. He smiled.

"I miss my cousins and my mother," she said. "Especially my father. I just adored him. He always called me his little blue-eyed flower."

"I miss my mother. I do not miss my father."

"I thought all boys worshiped their fathers as gods or heroes."

Lais made him feel safe. But was it safe enough to talk about what he had pushed aside for so long? "My father was neither. Caradoc. Caracticus to the Greeks and the Romans."

"What is he like?"

Boaz did not answer.

"Do you have any brothers or sisters?"

"I had a brother—Jachin. He is dead."

"Oh, I am so sorry to hear that. Were you close?"

"Twins."

She hit him again. "Now you are telling untruths!"

"Yes, we were exactly alike, only different. I grew tired of being called by his name all the time. Sometimes I just let it go. I know it bothered him too. Mother used to say we were two peas in a pod, and my uncle would say we were two leaves from the same tree."

"Jachin. Jachin and Boaz. Those are strange names for someone from Britannia."

"My mother was Jewish. She named us after the twin pillars of Solomon's Temple."

"Solomon?"

"A man of prodigious strength from my mother's homeland. He built a temple with two massive columns in front of it holding up its enormous roof. He named the twin pillars Jachin and Boaz."

"This Solomon must have been a celebrated hero to have a temple so big that he named the columns on it. Was he her god? Where was this temple?"

"Jerusalem. That is where my mother's people came

from. Soloman was not a god. My mother told us stories from her homeland. Sometimes I would see a tear come from the corner of her eye, when she thought no one watched. I often thought she remembered her home and family at that time." He lay back on the blanket. Lais joined him. His voice cracked. "She is dead too."

Lais turned on her side, reached her arm across his chest, and lay her head on his shoulder. "You must miss your mother and brother very much."

"I cried enough. I always wanted my father to change—to be different. To be more like my uncle, Amminus, who was more of a father to me and my brother than my father ever was. No, my father never tried to change. He never tried to make amends. I vowed to never be like him. I am a healer. I care about others."

Lais lay her fingers to his lips as if to soothe the words coming from his mouth. They both lay there for a while. Boaz's breathing slowed. His pounding heart was tranquil. They dozed in each other's arms.

A rustling of the leaves at their feet awakened the nappers. A spectacular mahogany stag with magnificent branched antlers came into the clearing and stood before them. A light-brown hind stood to his side. The doe was the color of rust and the bark on the trees, with a pale cream-colored rump patch under her tail.

The hart stomped his front hoof three times and snorted. It seemed to Boaz that the stag stared right at him as if to say, *"This is my forest. This is my doe. You are welcome here, but remember, I am in charge."*

Boaz and Lais did not move. Their breath caught in their open mouths.

Suddenly the stag turned and ran out of the grove. He jumped over the stone fence and raced through the open field of flowers into the trees beyond. The doe followed close behind.

An owl hooted and took flight from the trees above them.

Boaz and Lais gawked at each other in awe.

After a while, they gathered their belongings.

"I have something to tell you," Lais said.

Boaz picked up the blanket, handed one end to Lais, and together they folded it.

As their hands touched, she met his eyes.

"I am in love with you."

Boaz dropped the blanket.

32
CHAPTER

Hunting

Be cautious of finding what you seek on the road to ruin.

— Scribonius Largus

FOREST OUTSIDE MONGONTIACUM

Imperator Gaius asked Jachin to meet him early in the morning to go hunting. Jachin could hardly wait. He had not hunted since the sailors stalked deer when the Morta Columbarium docked at a secluded bay for a week of resupply and refilling of water barrels. That jaunt with Oded and his friends was not pleasant. The time he and Boaz chased imaginary beasts in the forests of Albion had been a much more pleasurable and memorable adventure, even though they never actually killed anything but shrubs and bushes.

He liked Gaius. He had an energetic, enthusiastic quality about him that Jachin couldn't help but admire. It was so different than the soldiers and sailors who always seemed mad about something. Jachin constantly kept his guard up. With Gaius, he felt safe. He was only a few years older than Jachin. It was like having a brother again.

Wearing a new red Roman tunic and soldier's boots, he strapped on his pugio and picked up a cluster of arrows and a bow to his liking. A legionnaire gave him a look but didn't stop him. He knew who accompanied Jachin that morning.

Jachin hastened down the road until he saw a red rag tied to a tree. He turned left into the woods.

Stepping from behind an old oak, Gaius asked, "What's with the bow and arrows?"

"You said we were hunting."

"Can you shoot that?"

"Sure."

"Hit that tree with an arrow."

Jachin notched the bow and loosed it. The arrow jumped and fell to the ground. The string grazed Jachin's arm. "Ouch!"

"You must nock the arrow on the string, *fatuus*."

"Do I *look* like a fool?"

"As a matter of fact, yes"

Jachin huffed. Another attempt sent the arrow flying. It missed its mark and hit another tree.

"Missed," Gaius said, pointing to the tree again.

"Oh, *that* tree." Jachin let another arrow go. This time falling short of either tree.

"You are terrible with a bow. You couldn't hit the side of a mountain if you tried."

"You may be correct. Back in Albion, I'm famous for being exceptionally good at shooting into ponds and losing arrows. I'm more accomplished with a pilum."

Gaius laughed. He removed two long leather strings out of his pack. "Leave the bow and arrows. Instead, we will use these."

"Slingshots?"

"Have you used one before?"

Hunting

"Yes, when I was young. These won't kill a boar or a deer. My grandfather Cunobelinos said they were for distance and harassing the enemy."

"Yes, it's a distance weapon, but your grandfather is mistaken. It is a formidable weapon and could cause as much damage as an arrow if thrown properly," Gaius assured him. "At a hundred paces, a Roman slinger can kill a man."

Jachin accepted the long thin strap of leather and weighed the sling in his hand. It was widened in the middle to hold stones of varying sizes like a pouch. He placed a spherical stone in the center pouch. While holding both ends of the leather straps in his hand, he whirled it around over his head until enough speed was created, and then he abruptly let go of one end of the strap, releasing the stone to the target. Surprising both Jachin and Gaius, it hit the tree with a thud, sinking into the bark.

"So are we hunting Germanii?"

"Not today. We will be targeting the dreadful squirrel."

"What?"

"Today we attack the formidable squirrel army hiding in the trees."

Gaius handed Jachin a cloth sack with a leather drawstring.

He untied it and lifted the flap. Inside, Jachin found a white crystalline substance. Dipping his finger in the powder, he tasted it. "Salt?" They had salt on the ship, but the trierarchus guarded it closely. "That's expensive stuff."

"It is great for preserving meat until eaten."

Jachin knew this. Sometimes the imperator talked down to him like he was stupid. Other times he spoke as if they were longtime friends.

"Do you know what to look for?"

"Yes, we have squirrels in Albion. Squirrels forage during the day and are not night animals because that is when predators are about. When they are not foraging for acorns and seeds, they sleep in the trees in nests made of sticks and leaves."

"Well, maybe you are a hunter after all. Come, I saw a bunch of nests down by the river."

Jachin squelched a slow boil. Was Gaius somehow making fun of him? He needed to understand how this man worked if he was to use him to get back to Albion. He could play dumb if that was what the man needed of him, but he didn't like it. He allowed Boaz to rattle him and pick on him—it was tit for tat and all in fun. They stopped when real anger ensued, but he didn't like to hear it from another.

They walked through tall oaks, scrub brush, and berry vines with tiny thorns grabbing at their legs.

Ahead of them, the Rhenus rapidly flowed on its journey toward the sea. It widened at this point such that Jachin doubted a soldier could sling a rock across to the other side, despite Gaius's bragging.

No boats on the river today. This was not a reliable place to cross to the other side. Besides, the Germanic army might be lying in wait for the imperator.

At the river's edge, Gaius knelt and picked up small stones, weighing each in his hand, keeping some, tossing others. "You must choose your ammunition carefully, Jachin. There are many stones that look useful but have flaws that cause them to fly indirectly or to break under the pressure of the snapped sling."

Jachin chose his stones and placed them in his belt pack as did Gaius. He considered what the imperator said and thought it applied to choosing men as well. He wondered if he meant it as a caution. As they walked back through the trees, Jachin kept his thoughts to himself. That was how men hunted. Quietly. Apparently, Gaius did not know that rule.

"My father's name was Germanicus, commander of legions on the Rhenus. My mum was Agrippina. Caesar Augustus was in power when I was born. I was the favorite of the Roman legion's camp. Mum dressed me as a little soldier. I was quite adorable. That's where I was given the name 'Little Boots.' Caligula is not my given name."

Jachin kept up pace, searching the trees for the squirrel army.

"There was an uprising among the Germanic tribes, and the soldiers wanted my father as imperator. He received honor and a triumph when he returned to Rome, but no

Hunting

position. I was the only one in father's chariot at that parade into the great city. I was five years old."

Gaius pointed at a ball of leaves in the nook of the topmost branch of a tall oak tree—a suitable nest. Believing a squirrel slept in the nest, Gaius set a stone in the leather pouch in the center of the long cord. He checked its weight in the sling. Unsatisfied, he flicked it out and chose another more to his liking. Swinging it around over his head, he released one string and let the stone fly. He reset another stone before the first one hit the tree limb, just below the nest.

Leaves scattered as a red-tailed squirrel exited and scampered along the limb.

Gaius fired shot number two and hit the squirrel square on the side of its head. It fell to the ground stunned. It lay on its back, legs up in the air, striking out to an invisible opponent. Gaius finished the kill with his knife.

Jachin was caught up in the excitement of the kill. "Woohooo! That's one!"

Gaius gutted and skinned the creature and stuffed the bloody body in Jachin's salt sack.

"Nice kill." Much different than killing pirates—at least there was purpose in this murder.

"Yes, but where there is one, there are more. Let's keep going."

"Have you ever seen a lizard?" Jachin asked.

"Of course. I saw lizards in many different lands. I traveled with my father when he reorganized governmental affairs in the eastern empire. We visited Actium, Euboea—"

"I have an idea about lizards and squirrels," Jachin interrupted.

"Great. Would love to hear it. Then we voyaged to . . ." He continued to list all the places he had traveled.

Jachin yawned.

". . . Alexandria, up the Nile to see Memphis and the Great Pyramids. Then back to Syria, where Father died. Poisoned they say. Maybe by Imperator Tiberius himself. I have my own ideas about that. I was only seven years old."

"I have always wondered how when you grab a lizard's tail . . ." Jachin continued with a smirk.

"Yes, yes. It comes off."

"Yes, but then it grows back!"

"Very well. How interesting."

"Okay. Well, in my land—"

"Much of my father's popularity was always shown to me as well. It was the best days of my life." He stepped over a fallen tree and looked back at Jachin. They seemed to be stepping over their own conversation as well.

Jachin relished changing the subject and goading Gaius. It was a game he liked to play called '*auribus teneo lupum.*' When holding a wolf by the ears he liked to see how far he could go before the wolf either bit, fought back, or left him alone. Either way, it was a win for him.

"I never told anyone this. Jachin, you seem smarter than you let on, and you are undemanding. I told the Senate that I didn't care if they *liked* me as long as they *feared* me. You don't seem to fear me. That makes me comfortable enough to converse. But for Jupiter's sake, where are you going with this lizard story?" Gaius asked.

"Well, in my land, we use squirrel tails for clothing accents and for fashioning fishing lures," Jachin said. "I think if you could mate a lizard with a squirrel, then you'd only need one squirrel for its tail. 'Cause the tails would grow back!"

Jachin had him now.

"True. But how would they mate?"

"I don't know. Get them together and play soft music on a pipe?"

"Ha! That would be funny!" Gaius laughed heartedly.

"And we could make a fortune in the empire. We can call them *squizzards*!"

Gaius slapped him on the back. "That's fantastic!"

"Look, another nest. A big one," Jachin said.

Wasting no time, Gaius loaded his sling and fired.

Jachin did the same and let his stone fly as well.

The nest burst with leaves falling every which way as the stones hit their mark. Gaius waited with another stone for the squirrel to run out. Nothing.

"Huh." He fired again. Nothing.

Hunting

Jachin and the imperator both sent a volley of stones into the nest high in the tree. Still nothing.

"No one's home," Gaius said, and turned to go.

Jachin shrugged his shoulders.

As they walked away, a sudden thud echoed behind them.

Both turned.

Jachin drew his pugio.

33
CHAPTER

Bravery

Bold is the man who fights no one.

— Scribonius Largus

On the ground lay a fat squirrel. Bushy red tail. Healthy coat. Beady eyes glinted in the light. No signs of trauma.

"There was one up there after all! Looks like it just lay down and died. Must've scared it to death!" Gaius said.
"He must have been reluctant to die."
"Most are."
Gaius raced over to retrieve it, and another squirrel fell from the nest, hitting him on the head.
Jachin laughed.
One. Two. Three more slowly fell from the nest above.
"Five squirrels!"
Gaius grinned. "That is more than enough."

Bravery

They sat down on the ground and skinned the animals. Gaius with his knife, and Jachin with the pugio.

"In my life, Jachin, I lived under constant conspiracies." Gaius touched him on the arm. "Never trust."

"Surely."

"Murders and executions happened every day. I stayed low and watched. When I was seventeen, my mum was suspected of being thirsty for power."

"What happened?"

"Uncle Tiberius exiled her to the island of *Pandateria*. She starved to death."

Jachin gutted another squirrel. "This political drama is similar to what I experienced growing up."

"I eventually boarded with the very man who exiled my mum and imprisoned my brother. He later gave me the *toga virilis*—the symbol of manhood."

"What did you do?"

"I acted like it didn't bother me, but it did. I played my part and learned my studies. That year, when I turned twenty, I was made *quaestor*."

"Investigator?"

"I thought you said your Latin wasn't that good."

"I know what a quaestor is."

"I conducted audits. Very boring. They just wanted to give me something to do so that I would stay out of the way.

"I bided my time. I wanted more. A couple of years ago. Tiberius drew up a will. My second cousin *Gemellus* and I received equal shares and were named joint heirs. It was confusing. I don't think Gemellus was happy. Hand me another squirrel."

Jachin thought there was more to the story, but he didn't say anything. He placed his squirrel into the salt bag and retrieved another animal for Gaius.

"Gemellus was a nickname. It meant "twin." He had a brother that died as an infant."

Jachin shook his head in unease.

"Oh yes. Then there was this girl I liked—she was married. She set me up. Everyone was out to get me. They made up things to make me look crazy. They thought I was paranoid. I had reason to be. Every day I lived in fear of assassination. Uncle Tiberius died, and some senators pointed fingers at me, claiming that I had poisoned him. Ha! That very day the Praetorian Guard proclaimed me as imperator. Go figure. The Senate accepted the declaration."

"That's good, right?"

"They thought I would be an easy man to manipulate with their praise. I was only twenty-four. Traveled ten days to get to Rome. People stood beside the road and called me charming names that one would give to a lover."

"Sounds like an advantageous position."

"It has its perks. How about you? Do you have a nickname? What are you called?"

"Back home I was called *Comghan*."

"What is its meaning?"

"Twin."

"Interesting."

"I had a twin brother. My father killed him. And my mom. And . . . my dog."

"Who then is Viatorvictori?"

"Amminus—he's my father's brother."

"Interesting. Give me that last squirrel. I want to skin him in a different manner. Watch out for Amminus. Don't trust him. Don't trust anyone. Not even me. Stay with me, and you'll be a distinguished general one day."

"You are like a brother," Jachin said. "A sword . . . err . . . sling brother!"

"Brother? No, not family. A *contubernalis*," Gaius said.

"You really test my Latin. What is a con . . ."

"Break it down. 'Con.' You know that?"

"'With.'"

"And you know the next part—'tuberna.'"

"Oh, a taberna. A tavern?"

"No. 'Tuberna' is a Roman tent used in wartime. A *contuberinis* is one of eight soldiers who share a tent. It is the maximum number of men who can fit in a standard tent."

"I understand. The soldiers sleep in the same place. Probably fight together. Watch each other's backs."

"There were eight of us on the road, remember? We were

contubernales. You came to our rescue. One died. You are now to take his place."

"One of the *contubernalis*?"

"You got it. Ten *contuberinis* equals a century. Five centuries make a cohort, and one hundred cohorts make up a legion."

Gaius cut around the hands and feet of the squirrel, made a slit down the middle of the thorax. He kept the head attached to the fur. "What is that blade you carry, Contuberinis?"

"A pugio"

"Not a pugio. It is longer by half, yet not quite a gladius. And the coloring is unique. Where did it come from?"

"I am not exactly sure," he lied.

"My uncle Claudius would know it. He studies that stuff—that is, when he is not drooling on himself. I watched you skin the squirrels. It must be very sharp."

"The pugio keeps a keen edge. It has never been honed as far as I know."

At that, Gaius stood. He took the squirrel skin and stretched it over his hand, putting two fingers into the head and his thumb and little finger into the front legs. He turned it around to show Jachin. "I bow to you, mighty squirrel killer," he said in a tiny high voice.

"Ha! A puppet!"

"We are all puppets."

Jachin pictured Gaius skinning men and making puppets of their hide.

"Let's go scare Galba."

34
CHAPTER

Plans

Many hoofbeats enter the cave of deception, but few come out.

— Scribonius Largus

MONGONTIACUM

Weeks passed. Amminus saw little of his nephew. Jachin either walked with Gaius or trained with Galba. Amminus continued to ask for an audience with the imperator, with no response until today. Gaius summoned Jachin and him.

"I really like Gaius," Jachin said.
"His ego is too big for his *galea*," said Amminus.
"I think his helmet fits just fine."
Amminus sighed.
The imperator's tent was massive, and the vast interior was highly decorated with richly woven tapestries and marble statues of dead Romans and various gods. A water foun-

Plans

tain surrounded by green leafy plants stood in the corner. Fancy woven rugs covered a wooden floor rather than the ubiquitous dust. Instead of a hearth in the center, a lamp in the shape of a massive dog heated the room with brightly glowing coals in the hound's stomach.

The imperator warmed himself at the lamp. He positioned his scarlet *paludamentum* over his arm and turned to greet his guests with a broad smile on his young face. He wore a dazzling embossed golden breast plate over a scarlet tunic. Golden *baltea* hung from the *balteus* that circled his waist. The paludamentum fastened at one shoulder, and a wreath of pure gold sat upon his head. In his hand, he held his galea. The spectacle brought to mind the image of a statue of the Roman god *Mars Ultor* that stood by the tent entrance. Off to the side, an elderly man sketched the imperator's visage on papyrus. Gaius shooed him away.

"Do not speak until spoken to," Amminus whispered.

Jachin scowled at his uncle.

"Thank you for coming," Gaius said. He seemed much more official in his demeanor than the childish young man who hunted with Jachin and chased soldiers with a squirrel puppet.

"I sought to meet with you for some time. I am glad you agreed to see me," Amminus said.

Gaius sat on a divan and raised his hand. A servant took his galea as another brought him a golden cup filled with red wine. "Please, sit down. Rest yourselves. May I offer you a drink?"

Amminus remained at attention and gripped Jachin's arm so that he would do the same. "No, thank you, Your Eminence. We will make this brief. I will get straight to the point. I want to adopt Jachin as my son so that not only is he the son of the current, though spurious, high king of Albion, but he would be a freed son of the proper high king."

"Which would be you, Viatorvictori?"

"Yes, my claim to the throne is assured, but was stolen by lies."

"And Caracticus, Jachin's father, is this man who took the title?"

"You are correct, sir. If my request is granted, there

The Golden Cord

would be no question as to who would be next in succession. I plan to do a *manumission* in Rome; therefore, if it pleases you, I request a letter of endorsement for Jachin."

"Manumission?" Jachin asked.

This is the first time Amminus mentioned this. He hoped the young man was not too surprised.

"Granting freedom from slavery," Gaius declared.

Jachin turned toward his uncle and clenched his teeth. "Yes, I know what it means. I didn't know it was possible. Why hadn't you told me about this?"

Gaius pursed his lips in thought and smiled. He clapped his hands together. "Fortune walks with you, Contuberinis. We can do it right now. Bring me the book!"

"Wait, I did not bring an offering of gold," Amminus said.

"*Pro gratis*. Your gratitude will be sufficient," Gaius said.

A servant shuffled in carrying an oversized book. Ornamental hinged attachments and engravings in the thick leather made it look wholly official, if not pretentious.

A servant removed a bust of Augustus from a platform, and Gaius placed the book there. He opened the cover reverently and turned to an empty page. Another servant offered him a golden inkwell and a feathered quill.

Gaius put the pen to his lips. "Jachin will need a new name." He dipped the pen into the ink well. "*Sallustius Amminus Lucullus.*" He wrote in the book. "I give this name to you because *Salus* means 'safety.' *Salutaris littera* is the 'saving letter.' Written as the letter *A* in papers, meaning *absolvo*. To set free. Absolution. *Lucculus* was the creator of satire. My favorite form of humor. You can keep your old name, but this is for the records. Like a new birth." He slammed the book closed with a bang. "I have written you into existence!"

Gaius laid his hand on Jachin's head, giving him the new name. "I declare this day, Jachin, filius Amminus, a free Roman citizen. And as son of the true high king of Britannia, the veritable heir to the throne proper."

"I'm not sure what to think. Should I feel different?"

"Probably no more than you did this morning when you brushed your teeth with a willow branch," Amminus said.

Plans

"I've got to let this sink in. What should I do?"

"Go. Walk in your new name. Repeat it to yourself so that you do not forget it. I need to talk to Viatorvictori alone. Can you give us space?" said Gaius.

Jachin nodded. "Okay . . . gotta clear my thoughts on this. Hey, Gaius, perhaps we can play the game Latrunculi later."

"Yes, perhaps I will let you win this time."

Jachin grinned. "I always win."

Gaius patted him on the back. "Ha! We shall see about that, Freedman Sallustius Amminus Lucullus."

Jachin bowed and then glared at Amminus. He brushed the hair from his face and stomped out.

"Do sit down, Viatorvictori. If you are the rightful king, and Jachin is now your son, by my decree, then he is in line for the kingship."

"He should know the things we discuss, but you have sent him away," Amminus said, somewhat concerned.

At that moment Galba entered the room, accompanied by a wealthy looking man.

"This is my freedman, Gaius Julius Callistus. He is not only my physician but also an important adviser on policy and strategy for handling the many conspiracies against me. I trust his judgement," Gaius said.

"If I may put my two *assari* in, Jachin is not to know our plans. He is a naïve young man. Thinks more of himself than he displays. This façade does not bode well. One day, with years of training, he will be a minimal soldier. That is all," Galba said.

Amminus raised his eyebrows, but he did not counter. The boy needed to participate, since any plan for regaining control of Albion would involve him. He would tell Jachin later—if he would listen. In the meantime, he was curious to hear what the imperator would say.

Galba stood behind Gaius, legs shoulder width apart and his hands clasped behind his back. Callistus stood silently beside him.

Servants brought warm towels.

Galba refused.

They offered more wine, nut meats, and fruit.

Amminus chose a camp chair and took a sip of the wine. "A decent wine," he said.

Gaius leaned back on the divan. "Galba trains the legions well. He informs us how the soldiers' preparation is progressing."

In a gruff, Galba-like voice Gaius said, "This morning he reported that, 'Recruits are used to privilege. Not accustomed to hard drills. Reward them; they will underperform when we need them. If you punish them, they do better next time. These legions need additional punishment.'"

"Will they be enough?" Amminus asked.

"We cannot take Britannia without taking full advantage of our reserve," Gaius said.

"True. However, if I may speak freely, I am sad to report my belief that the training is not enough, as I implied this morning," Galba said. "We have not the aptitude to attack across the sea."

Gaius leaned forward. He played with the wine in his cup with his fingers, put them to his lips, and sucked the wine from the tips. He leaned back as if it was not a concern.

"Galba believes—and I think there is merit in this—if we train the men beyond their skills, then the fighting becomes easier. They will undoubtedly outperform," Callistus said.

Amminus bit the inside of his cheek. "How can I be sure you can win this fight? Caesar could not do so with his armies."

"That is up to interpretation. Caesar overstated his predicament," Gaius said.

"The objective is to remove my brother, Caradoc, from power. Not kill him."

"Yes, yes. Place you—the rightful heir—on the throne. I understand. If I get the glory, it matters not to me who rules. The people of Britannia must become subjects of Rome."

"The glory shall be yours, Gaius. But I must also be certain. Galba voices doubts. I ask again: Are the legions ready for battle? Can Rome win this war?"

Gaius took another sip from his cup. "I assure you, Viatorvictori, I come from an extensive line of military com-

Plans

manders. It was on Rome's northern frontier where these legions won their laurels. I will take Rome further than any other commander. I'll be the first to personally lead the soldiers in battle since Augustus."

Amminus stood. "I am confident that is your goal." What he had to say took all his nerve. "Your Eminence, I have overheard talk from soldiers who say you are here to gather riches to fund the army. Some suggest that you are gambling with the lives of the wealthy merchants and clans of Gaul and Germania. I have also heard you come to Gaul to recruit bodyguards for yourself and have no intention to invade Albion."

"Bodyguards?" He smirked and looked to Galba. "Ha! What you say rings true, considering the recent circulated conspiracies. However, do not believe all you hear on the ever-present wind."

"But what about the attack on the road to Mongontiacum? I suspect you staged a mock battle to make yourself look experienced. I have seen one of those so-called enemies from that skirmish here in *this* camp, looking more like friend than foe."

"I do not need protection, Amminus, and I assure you all my battles are real. Those are just rumors."

Amminus started to object, but Gaius continued.

"Others try to destroy me from within before I prove myself. And I don't need anyone's money. If there is a chance of loss, I never gamble. Men of wealth give me riches of their own free will. They do it to get something from me. *Quid pro quo.* I go on campaign and am exposed to inordinate danger while certain rich Romans enjoy the pleasures of the circus or the joys of the theater. Then they return to their exceedingly fine villas. No, I don't desire their gold. As far as the army's readiness? Galba, do you have any more concerns?"

"We have amassed more than two hundred thousand troops—twice the strength of legions deployed by Caesar. We've added to our numbers as new legions have been formed, the Fifteenth and the Twenty-Second *Primagena*. I will train them as hard as I have trained others since I arrived north. But I must be honest, they are not ready to go to war. Therefore, in my opinion—if I may be so bold to say so—regarding the new legions, the first one should be stationed in lower Gaul. The other in the upper Rhenus to fill the gap when we leave for Britannia. They will secure the eastern flank against Germanic incursions that would cut our supply lines and impede our return home. They can continue to train there until ready for battle."

"We have legionary stationed on the west bank of the Rhenus—one mile south of Mongontiacum and north at *Neuss Novaesium*, on the east side of the Rhenus, do we not?"

"Yes, Gaius, but they are not enough."

"It is never enough for you, Galba." Then to Amminus, "That is why I like him—always preparing for the worst."

"But—with all due respect—are *you* ready to conquer Albion?" Amminus asked again.

"Alas, Galba is correct. It is also my opinion that we are *not* prepared."

Galba and Callistus both nodded their heads in agreement.

Amminus paced. "Caradoc is relentless. He has an insatiable hunger for power. All southern Albion will soon be under his rule. We have allowed too much time for *him* to prepare. You must attack now!"

"We cannot divide our legions and conquer Germania and Britannia at the same time. We must postpone," Gaius said.

"You told me that you go north, not to fight the Germanii, but to secretly plan to go to Albion. Now you vacilate. You say you must conquer the Germanii first? Which is it? You cannot accomplish both." Amminus sat back down.

"We communicated this, Viatorvictori. We came to prepare the troops for conquest. Now, as Galba has stated, the troops are not ready to defend the flank. I will not lead a troop that cannot protect its backside."

"I came here to petition your service in the fight. Without your legions, I am afraid all is lost."

"I wouldn't worry. Britannia is nothing but a fly on Rome's behind. We will still get our victory. You must trust us, Viatorvictori. We know what we are doing. We also know what the enemy plans. Send the spy in."

Plans

Through an opening in the back of the tent came a diminutive man who Amminus immediately recognized.

"Toenin!"

Toenin bowed to Gaius and then to Amminus. He still looked young, but his hair on the top of his head thinned and receded like an old man's. "I bring word from our homeland and greetings from your brother Togodumnus, who stands with Caradoc—at his own displeasure."

Toenin gave his report with grave sincerity. "Caradoc has secured a vast and powerful army. He has promised remarkable things to those who will join him. They amass north of the Tamesa River. Caradoc believes the only landing Rome would attempt is at Rutupiae on the east coast of the land of the Cantii. Anticipating Rome to strike on this beach, they expect to devastate and humiliate the legions as they disembark their ships. Victory is assured to Caradoc if this is to take place," he said to Amminus. "Caradoc's wife has birthed a daughter since you were in Albion."

"His wife?"

"Mara."

"Are they safe?" Amminus said.

"Everyone close to Caradoc is in peril," Toenin answered. Then back to Gaius, "Togodumnus has fallen under Caradoc's spell. Kenjar and the druids stand by Caradoc's side. Many Roman *castra* in the South have all been leveled, razed, and left in rubble. Remember, I am just the messenger. They defy you to come and get them." He took two steps back and bowed again, making to leave.

Amminus stood abruptly and grabbed Toenin's arm. "Wait! Do you know about Jachin? Do you know that he is here?"

"Yes, I know. I'll catch up with him another time."

Toenin left as quickly as he came in, but not without taking a covertly proffered bag of coin from Callistus as they left together.

Amminus overheard two whispered words—*non venenum . . . pugio*.

Not poison, pugio? Amminus wondered who they were talking about.

"The planning has come to a standstill," Gaius said. "I

have made up my mind. The legions are not going to Albion at this time."

Would he even go at all? The possibility that Rome would not support him had always been an option that Amminus considered. Not a good option, but an option nonetheless. He knew he'd have to figure out how to stop Caradoc by himself if Gaius would not help. He wouldn't fail.

"Listen carefully to me, Gaius. These announcements are no blow to me. I prepared for this exact turn of events," Amminus said. "My imperator, I have a plan."

"Then out with it. Tell me your plan," Gaius said.

⌘ ⌘ ⌘

Jachin stormed into Amminus's tent. "Do you believe that buying my freedom with your allegiance to Rome makes us friends? Makes us father and son?" He shoved the Writ of Manumission onto Amminus's chest.

"Where did you get that idea?"

"How else would he do it *gratis* if you hadn't sold your soul to his purpose?"

"Jachin, wait—"

"I don't need your lies!"

"What has happened to you?"

"You made plans without me. This is *my* battle."

"To kill Caradoc?'

"You know that."

"There is more to this war than killing one man. If Rome invades, many will die. I cannot condone your desires."

Jachin paced. "You were supposed to be the one who took us away from our pain—to defeat Caradoc. You have been against me since before we left Albion. I felt your treachery when you gave me a lantern and pushed me down a hill. You left me on that trireme for two years. You wish to destroy me. You failed. You failed my mother, you failed Boaz, you failed me, and you failed Albion!"

These were words Amminus said to himself many times. To hear them from this young man hurt deeply. The nephew he loved and swore to protect had turned against him. Amminus attempted to redirect Jachin's anger. "I am commanded to travel to the capital city of Rome and present our cause to the Senate. You cannot come with me."

"I am *not* with you."

"Jachin, I am concerned about you. I—care for you." Amminus reached to touch Jachin on his shoulder, but his hand was brushed away by Jachin's rage.

"All you care about is yourself. If you didn't, then you would have dealt with my father years ago. You would have made my mother your wife. And you would rule all of Albion. All would have been perfect. But no. You have become Gaius's little squirrel puppet."

"I am no one's puppet."

"I don't trust you anymore. Go to Rome. Kiss their feet." Jachin started for the door and turned. "You are not the man I thought you were. I never want to see you again. If I do," he touched his pugio, "you will regret it." And he walked out.

The next day, with a heavy heart, Amminus and several legionnaire left the camp at sunrise, headed south toward Rome. Jachin didn't see them off. Amminus prayed his plan would work.

35
CHAPTER

Departure

≈

There are losses that are only surface wounds which sting more than most. Others are deep injuries that never completely heal.

— Scribonius Largus

AD 39—Men-Karou near Carura, Phrygia

Boaz spent most of his nights ruminating over Lais and his waking hours hoping she would show up at the clinic. Even after all this time, he didn't know where she lived or where she ate when not with him. She guarded this mystery, and Boaz let her keep her secrets. Oftentimes they would talk about their family and the past. Other times she seemed distant and inaccessible.

Whereas Boaz remained closed off at first, he found himself talking more to her than he ever spoke to anyone.

Departure

She laughed at his corny jests. She always brightened his day and made seeing patients in the clinic go faster. Boaz smiled just thinking about her blue eyes. He sometimes went looking for her. *Why do I let myself be obsessed? It must be some sort of magic.*

He jumped out of bed—optimistic about the day. He did a little dance, pretending he was holding Lais. He dressed for breakfast but had other things he had to do before the students all arrived. The morning sun shone through the window, making sunbeams in the dust kicked up from his actions. The wooden Latrunculi board lay opened on his desk. The game pieces scattered. Ordinarily, he would not have allowed the disarray, but today he left them where they lay. He left his bed unmade.

How things had changed for him since the first time he and his brother Jachin had played the game at the Boar's Head Inn in Albion. As he danced out of his room, he hummed a song and shook his head. His dark hair was now cut short in the local fashion. His beard was finally taking form.

He went through the enormous medical school entry, down the steps, and into the huge common area. It was still early, and the room was empty. Marble columns lined the walls on either side. In the back, a series of cubicles were used for teaching, and beyond that, the surgeries and clinics for seeing patients. Boaz raised his hands to his mouth to hoot, just to hear it echo, then thought better of it. How this building escaped earthquake damage, he didn't know.

Boaz passed the sculptured relief of *Men*. The figure, with its Phrygian cap and belted tunic, piously leaned on a staff. The local god stood with his foot resting on a submissive bull. People called on *Men* for healing, safety, and prosperity. To capitalize on his reputation, the medical school was built next to the Men-Karou Temple on the road between Laodicea and Carura. He touched the deity's foot with his fingers, as was customary, and continued to his reading room.

Boaz entered the cubicle, lit oil lamps, and began his studies. Today he translated the early works of Hippocrates from Greek to Latin.

The Golden Cord

He dipped his stylus into the ink when Sophronios dashed into the room, bumping a table and nearly knocking over a bust of Asklepios.

Sophronios rubbed his hip. "Have you seen my clyster?"

"If you would let Demosthenes Philalethes couch your cataracts, you might be able to see that the thing you are searching for is right in front of you on the table you nearly knocked over."

"Ah, so it is." Sophronios picked up the instrument and turned to leave.

Boaz called after him. "What do you need that thing for?"

"We have some new Herophilii, and I need to train them in the proper technique for the eradication of intestinal worms and fevers."

"Enemas?"

"They will practice on each other."

Boaz set his pen down. "Oh, I am sure they'll enjoy *that*."

Sophronios laughed. "I know I will!"

"You seem to be in a good mood this morning, Master."

"Each awakening is a beginning. New Herophilii always energize me. The greener the better. They are always so afraid, yet so eager to learn."

"They will most certainly be afraid of you after today's lesson!"

"You always write in such large letters, Pedi. What is it today? More prescriptions for toothpaste?"

"I am translating the *Hippocrates Corpus*, 'Places in Man.' And as for writing, I became accustomed to inscribing oversized letters so you'd be able to read the herb-bottle labels." It amused Boaz how much he sounded like his master, taking on his traits, and even his mannerisms. Before long, he would probably wear a petasos hat as well.

"You work on your writing and drawings most diligently, Pedi. What do you intend to do with them?"

"I hope to continue your work with the herbs. I intend to write an illustrated treatise full of prescription recipes, remedies, and treatments so that other physicians may learn from the vast knowledge I gathered at your tutelage. Who knows, maybe one day I may even travel back home to Albion to find the plants you could not."

Departure

"How do you feel about that?"

"Gathering herbs?"

"No, going back home."

Boaz peered up from his parchment. "I'm not sure how I *feel* about it. I just thought it would be good to do."

"I hope you find the thing you are searching for," said Sophronios.

Boaz nodded and smiled. He wasn't sure what Sophronios meant.

"I was in hopes that you would stay and join me in teaching at the medical school. One day even taking over my position."

"Really? I hadn't even considered that."

"Tut-tut. I am of the opinion that you would make an outstanding teacher," Sophronios said.

Boaz opened his mouth to say something, but Sophronios turned to leave. "By the way, my eyesight is adequate. Besides, Demosthenes is a buffoon." With clyster in hand, he marched headfirst into the doorframe. He stumbled backward.

"Sophronios!" Boaz raced to his staggering mentor and caught him as he fell. "Are you all right?"

Blood streamed down Sophronios's face from a cut on his forehead. It soaked his white beard and dripped to his toga. "Yes, yes, I am quite all right."

Boaz selected a clean rag that was on his desk and placed it on the wound to stanch the bleeding. "That is a nasty cut. Let me suture it."

Boaz guided the protesting Sophronios to the surgery and laid him on the table. He prepared the suture and threaded the curved needle. "I am worried about you," Boaz said.

"I am quite all right."

"You said that before. I am not so sure. You had several falls lately, and I noticed you having difficulty with balance and walking. I think you have been working too hard. You need to take some time off."

"Look who's giving the master direction."

"I mean it, Sophronios. You need to rest."

"I will, I will. Right after today's lessons."

"You promise?"

"Yes, yes, I promise. Are you finished?"

"Almost. One more stitch."

"Did you hear the *facetus* about the old doctor?"

"Which one, Master? There are more jests about old doctors than there are old doctors."

"Until recently Demosthenes was an ophthalmologist. He is now a gladiator. Demosthenes did the same thing as a doctor that he does now as a gladiator."

"That is an old one!" Boaz laughed, but inside his worry grew. His mentor was not one for repeating old jokes but saved them for new students or visitors.

"I'm an old facetus myself. You are doing a fine job, Pedi. I enjoy watching you grow into such a responsible young man . . . and a fine physician."

Sophronios sat up, and Boaz applied a bandage to the sutured wound.

"Well done, son." His speech slurred. Getting up from the table, his legs wobbled.

Suddenly Sophronios collapsed and convulsed. His arms and legs drew up. His head tilted back in spasms.

Boaz dropped to his knees and cradled his mentor's head. "Someone help me! Come quick!"

As two of the new students came into the surgery, the shaking subsided. Boaz checked his mentor's pupils. One was bigger than the other.

"Help me get him to the table."

The students lifted him carefully to the surgery table. "What happened?" one of them asked.

"*Morbus comitialis.* Seizure. From head injury. Most likely he is hemorrhaging around his brain. Stay with him! I need to get the *modiolus* to trephine his *kranion*." Boaz rehearsed the procedure and the indications in his head as he ran. *In the case of a head injury and possible skull fracture, trepanning may be beneficial to relieve the pressure as blood collects on the cerebral membrane but has no means of exit.* Boaz was certain of his diagnosis and what needed to be done.

Boaz returned with the metal cylinder to find the students dabbing at the vomit that covered their short tunics.

"He heaved all over us!"
"Then he convulsed again."
"*Non spiritus.*"
Boaz shoved the boys aside. "What?!"
Sophronios Demetrios Alkimopoulos lay as if asleep, yet his eyes were open. Spittle at the edge of his mouth. His breathing stopped.

Boaz pounded on his teacher's chest. "Wake up! Wake up, Sophronios! You can't die." Boaz fell to his knees and wailed. "No!"

Thoughts pushed against his brain, begging for release. Keeping them at bay took all his strength. *I must be strong for the Herophilii.* Boaz stood and gently closed his master's eyes.

"You were a father to me, Sophronios." Boaz kissed his forehead. "Rest well, my friend."

He turned to the Herophilii, who stood with bowed heads. "Take care of him for me, for I have not the strength."

Boaz could no longer hold back his feelings. He had not the fortitude to dam the flood pouring from his heart. Despite his promise to never cry again, he wept uncontrollably. He soon found himself on the road to Carura. He desperately needed Lais.

Thunder roared as a summer storm pelted Boaz with rain. He searched to no avail in countless buildings still under construction and repair. He checked the tavern where they often took a break from the clinic to eat a meal and talk. He sat awhile, sipping on a glass of cool water, hoping she'd come dancing through the door. The rowdy regulars made fools of themselves as always, drinking till they fell from their stools. No one had seen the blond-headed girl.

After a while Boaz suspended his vigil and withdrew to the clinic near the gymnasium, thankful that the persistent rain concealed his tears. No patients today, as it was *dies Solis*. Even the physicians had a day of rest.

Boaz sought her among the wards where the worst patients convalesced on makeshift cots. Nothing. No one knew anything. Those who claimed knowledge of her whereabouts were spurious at best, due to the delirious thinking from their feverish injuries. One old man even said she rode a white horse on the ceiling above. Boaz suspected it was the rain he heard.

About to give up, he happened upon dilapidated Didymus. His clothes were disheveled and probably hadn't been washed since the earthquake. Now that things had slowed down from the disaster, the old physician drank liberally.

The physician stumbled. "Let me know if I'm in your way," he said from the floor.

Boaz helped the old physician to his feet. "Oh, I'm so sorry, Didymus."

"In a hurry?"

Boaz attempted to get past the old man.

"You've been crying."

Boaz wiped the tears from his face. "Only rain."

Didymus held his palm up and regarded the rafters above as if expecting it to start raining in the wards.

"I need to find Lais."

"Lais? The blond *Hetaerae* I saw you with?"

"She's not a *Hetaerae*."

"Remember the brothel next to the Caravanserai that was swallowed up by the earthquake?" Didymus brushed his smock with his hands.

"Yes . . ."

Didymus took a flask from a pocket. "The brothel keeper and all the ladies died, save one."

"What are you saying?"

"Your lady friend was the sole survivor. I can't believe you didn't know that."

"That can't be true. She would have told me."

"Doesn't matter. She's gone." He uncorked the bottle and took a long drink; then he replaced the cork.

Boaz got in his face. "Gone? Where?"

Didymus started to uncork the flask again and instead, after several attempts, he returned it to his pocket. "She came here looking for you, what was it? Uh, two days ago . . . or was it three? Said wildfires raged in her Batavii homeland. She seemed very upset. Worried about her family, I postulate. She found a Jewish trader headed north and joined his caravan. Very nice man. Lots of Jewish folks in

Departure

these parts. He traded for the black fleece we are so famous for in neighboring Laodecia."

Boaz sat on one of the empty cots. "She's going home?"

The man fished out the flask from his pocket. Pointed it at Boaz. "Of that I am certain. Guess she wasn't lady friendly enough to tell you farewell."

Boaz put his head in his hands. "I can't believe this is happening. What am I to do now?"

"Anyway," he uncorked the flask. "She told me to tell you something."

"What? What did she say?"

Didymus took another drink. "'Come find me.'"

⌘ ⌘ ⌘

Preparations were under way for the funeral of Sophronios. Demosthenes asked Boaz to address the Herophilii. He said, "No."

Entering his bedroom, he seized the Latrunculi board and stuffed the game and its playing pieces into a leather satchel. He took his traveling clothes and writing utensils. He didn't know if he would ever write again, but he couldn't leave without the parchments. He didn't have much. It was like when Sophronios told him to gather his things when he left Albion. "A beginning," he had said. This felt like an ending.

Boaz kept a cedarwood chest under his bed. He hauled it out and opened it. Boaz took out the two things that meant the most to him—the sheath to the pugio and the golden cord. He added them to the bag. If it came to it, he could sell them.

Boaz stopped by his master's study, where his mentor kept scrolls. He hadn't been there in a long time. In the corner on a stand stood the old vase he made when first learning to make pottery. Why did Sophronios keep it all these years?

Boaz shoved the vase off its stand. "Ugly and twisted trash!" Crashing into shattered shards, the vase spilled out hundreds of gold coins with images of the prominent local doctors Zeuxis and Alexander Philalethes on them. A rolled parchment was among the countless coinage and pottery shards. Boaz fell to his knees. Breaking the wax seal, he unrolled the papyrus sheet.

A letter, written in extralarge characters, addressed to him, read:

Boaz, this is for you.

Congratulations on completing your training as a physician.

Use this money to buy your freedom and start your practice.

I am very proud of you. Well done, my son. Well done.

Sophronios's last words to Boaz were "Well done." And he called him "son"—not "Pedi." Boaz's eyes welled up.

He rolled the letter and stuffed it in his satchel. He found a leather sack and gathered the coins and the pottery shards into it. A disk-shaped broken fragment of the vase lay among the coins. Perfectly round. He lifted it and turned it over to reveal the inscription in distinctly large letters; "*Made in Disgust.*" It shattered in two when he dropped it to the floor. As an afterthought, he bent and picked up the fractured pieces.

Sophronios's medical instruments sat on the desk, neatly wrapped in their leather pouch. He stuck the packet in his belt. "Master won't need these now. Don't want anyone else to have them." Boaz snatched his mentor's straw hat from a peg on the wall. "He forgot his hat."

Placing the petasos on his head, he tied the hanging thongs and left the medical school and Carura behind.

CHAPTER 36

Abasement

*The transient aroma of baking bread
remains long after we are fed.*

— Scribonius Largus

Laodicea

"Get along, girls!" Boaz called as he guided his master's wagon down the narrow way. A herd of exceedingly black sheep crossed before him on the road. The skittish donkeys in front of the wagon were different than the beasts Sophronios devoted so much care to when he visited Albion. They had died long ago. These donkeys were relatively young, well trained to pull the cart, but clearly suspicious of black sheep.

After traveling through an expansive plain, the hills came near the river and then opened gradually, with higher mountains on the northeast. Either smoke or steam arose from the red-and-yellow rocks on the hills. Probably stained due to earth vapors and iron ore in the area.

He followed the road along the river Meander to where it joined the *Lycus* at Laodicea. He met a few travelers on the way, but he did not look at them and definitely did not want to talk to anyone. He kept his head down and the petasos firmly tied to his chin. Drizzle from low clouds made him even more miserable, if that was possible.

The country near the town spread out to the plains where farmers lived and tended the sheep. Vineyards covered the hills. The students often ate raisins made from the grapes grown in this region, and a sort of syrup they called *treacle*, which they combined with other ingredients and used as an antidote for poisons, snakebites, and as a treatment for various other ailments. *Yew tree juice is the proper cure for snakebite. Treacle is best used as a sweetener on pastries.*

He crossed over a deep, but narrow portion of the river on a wooden bridge held up by gigantic piers of hewn stone covered with indecipherable carvings. Laodicea set on a low uneven hill. High mountains covered with snow rose behind the town and included the ancient mount of *Cadmus*, named after the great slayer of monsters—before the days of Heracles. It is said that Cadmus was born there. One story tells how his father sent him on a journey to find his sister Europa after Zeus carried her off—and not to return until he had found her. Boaz thought this was apropos to his current hunt for his beloved Lais.

The eastern part of the hill was lower than the rest, and toward the northeast corner lay the entrance to the city. That is where he pointed the donkeys' noses.

After such a long day, his mind was tired. He needed to find a place to forget. He drove past beggars and merchants hawking their wares as he entered the city. By the looks of the rusty hinges on the heavy iron gate at the entrance, Boaz suspected they never closed it. Tall watch towers stood on either side of the postern to defend the entrance. He noted that and stopped to put all but a few coins into a chest hidden under the floor of the wagon.

He eased the cart through the mob, past the gate, and

Abasement

three impressive white marbled buildings with classic Greek Ionic columns topped by paired spiral scrolls. Boaz wasn't interested in temples. He drove on.

Drizzle turned to unsympathetic rain.

Soon he found what he looked for and secured the donkeys to the post in front of the taberna. He did not think he would find Lais there, but for some reason he wanted a drink. He had never liked alcohol and avoided it because of his father's indulgence, but this day he needed to be numb. To forget. He needed medicine that would ease his pain of loss.

He stepped into the dark smelly room. Removing his petasos, he shook water from its brim, replaced it on his head, and found a secluded seat in the back.

An old barmaid made a vain attempt at wiping the table in front of him and took his order.

"Whatcha looking for?"

"A girl."

"Well, you're in the wrong place for that, honey. Girls can be had across the way."

"I'm looking for a friend of mine that might have come this way. Girl named Lais—blond hair, blue eyes, about this tall." Boaz held his hand up where the top of her head reached his chin.

"Nope, tain't seen anyone like that. Where's she headed?"

"She traveled with a caravan of Jewish merchants. Headed home to Batavia in Gaul."

"Well, honey, if you are going to Gaul, you are needing to go to Ephesus and then north. Where you coming from?"

"Carura."

"Well, you're headed in the wrong direction, young man! Easterly when you need to point west, if you're going to go to Ephesus."

"I can't do anything right."

"Cheer up, lad. Have a pint of mead."

Boaz pulled a gold coin from his leather bag on his belt. He held it up to the light. It had the likeness of Zeuxis on it. He placed the coin on the table. "Keep 'em coming until this runs out."

"Honey, this will buy you the whole barrel!"

He bought several other patrons' drinks too. Seemed like the thing to do to keep them from bothering him. His father always did that. However, two soldiers came to sit next to him.

"Leave me be," Boaz said looking into his glass.

"Got's a foreign accent." The man grabbed Boaz's chin and shook his head. "Ha! Look at his little beard."

Boaz wrenched his head away.

"Crying in your mead, is ya?" The soldier removed Boaz's petasos. "Look, his hat is full of little boy's tears." He put it on his head.

Boaz stood, snatched his hat back from the man, and swung a left hooking blow to the man's chin. His jaw cracked, and the man fell against his companion. They both tumbled to the floor.

The taberna came alive with hoots and hollers as the two men got to their feet swinging.

Boaz held his ground at first but soon became overwhelmed. The men beat him and took what money he had in his pocket.

He scooted back to the chair, righted it, and slowly pulled himself up. He put the hat in his lap and just stared at the table lying on its side.

The barmaid restored the table and left another drink in front of him. "You all right, honey?"

He thanked her and said, "When I drink, I don't think."

"What's that, honey?"

"You know, the mead fills me like a glass full of vomit. When it keeps pouring, it overflows." Boaz took a drink. Blood from his lip mixed with the yellow mead.

"Bad stuff, huh?" She poured him some more. Perhaps she had heard it all from the reprobates in this place. The tears. The losses. The regrets and shame of the lonely men who came here for solace.

"I don't want your pity." He held out his glass. "Pour me." He shooed her off.

She left the pitcher.

Unable to endure the noise of people laughing, he brought the pitcher with him to the wagon outside. Lying on the driver's bench, he dropped the carafe and passed out.

Abasement

Sometime in the night, the donkeys were loosened, and they pulled the wagon to the poor side of town.

The next morning the sun's heat on his face awakened Boaz. He wiped the vomit off his beard and reached behind him for a tonic to sooth his earthquake of a headache. Leaning over the side of the wagon, he vomited again.

"Yuck," said a child below him.

There in front of the wagon, for as far as he could see down the road, stood a line of souls seeking his services as physician.

"I'm not him," he said and washed his mouth with water from a flask.

"Wagon says you are," said a woman with the child.

Wiping his hands, he tended to what Sophronios would have deemed 'Opportunities-To-Do-Good.' A girl with the palsy, a tattered old man with maggots in his wounds, another with troubled breathing who smelled of blacksmith dust. They kept coming.

He spent several days there until he treated the last one. Someone brought him food. He slept on the wagon bench. One morning, when he awoke, someone had covered him with a ragged old blanket.

For the next few weeks every town he passed through sought him for treatment. And in every town—a taberna. He kept moving. Not sure if it was toward or away. Even in his stupor, he helped others. The days ran together, and he began to not even remember what he had done the day before.

He chanced upon a wagon wreck where the overturned wagon crushed a thin man's leg. Boaz amputated the leg. Other victims included a young child and a pregnant woman. The wagon wheel had run over the head of the small boy. He and his mother were dead. He could do nothing for the child but performed what was deemed a *Caesarean* surgery to remove the dead baby from the dead mother. According to local law, the child must be buried separately. To his surprise, the baby lived! He handed it to an old woman in the crowd who had gathered to watch.

He removed more ticks than he thought numerically possible from a demon-possessed child—or so her father claimed. He clipped the tongue of a man who couldn't pronounce his own name; who was married to a woman with only one eye. He applied an unguent to her eyes made from a Phrygian Powder ground from a certain mineral rock from the area and mixed with water. She gave him a votive of an eyeball with a blue iris that her husband had carved in wood and painted. As bizarre as it looked, it made Boaz think of Lais. Each evening he visited the inns and traded what patients gave him for the wonderful mead of forgetfulness.

CHAPTER 37

Disentanglement

Silent screams are heard only by the one held captive.

— Scribonius Largus

AD—39 Calleva, Albion

"Caoimhe, could you help me place these pots in front of the door?"

"Of course, Mara. But why on earth would you do this?"
"Peace of mind. It lets me know when Caradoc comes home. That way he doesn't surprise me. He is oftentimes so drunk, he doesn't notice the clang of the bottles and pots."

They stacked the pots in a way that they would easily fall, laughing about how silly it seemed. Mara knew deep down the necessity of this serious task. The laughter thrust her fear aside. When finished, they sat down to spin wool. Mara had never had the opportunity to learn how to spin as most women do as children. At one time she thought it

The Golden Cord

meaningless busywork. "We must keep our voices down. Gladys sleeps."

Caoimhe set the last pot on the pile. "Of course, my dear."

"Once he couldn't get in. He passed out and slept outside all night. The next morning I found him there laying in his vomit."

"That's awful."

"His drinking has become dreadfully out of control."

"You must live in a constant state of dread."

"I live in constant fear. Your visits allay my alarm."

Mara appreciated the company and easy friendship of Caoimhe. Very different than the clientele she was used to at the Boar's Head Inn. She always seemed so happy, so calm, and free of worry. Caoimhe travelled far from the land that once belonged to the Trinovantes to see her. Her friend cared for others and was excellent at spinning wool. They often spun wool together. At times Caoimhe just came over when Caradoc left on one of his campaigns, asking if there were tasks around the house she could help with. It was a great comfort to have a friend.

For a while they worked in silence. Mara rehearsed Caoimhe's comment in her mind. Yes, it was constant dread, never knowing what Caradoc would do. Always expecting the next backhand or insult. She now understood how it must have been for Alexenah.

Mara picked up a straight wooden rod, eight inches long. Attached to it was a whorl-stone made of ornately carved bone. The rod fit through the middle like an axle in a chariot wheel. This was the drop spindle. They would use it to not only twist the wool but to wind the yarn around after twisting. It was tedious work when done alone. By herself, Mara would hold the spindle in her left hand and draw out the fibers with her other hand. Caoimhe would be her right hand today.

Caoimhe drew out several inches of the rough sheep's wool from a basket and rolled it along her thigh until a thread began to form. She attached it to the drop spindle and handed the wool to Mara who wrapped it over her hand. "Pardon me for saying so, but that man is fearsome.

Disentanglement

I said that very thing to my husband, Togodumnus, just the other night. Caradoc's wife died. Sad thing that was . . . and most untimely."

"How so?" Mara asked.

"She was a gift intended to assure fealty in addition to sending her sons to be educated in Rome, like Amminus did as a boy."

"Amminus's first wife died, didn't she?"

"Yes, the prospect of him remarrying was suspect, so they chose Caradoc to sire the sons. As Romans they would come back home and rule, thereby conquering a kingdom without war. Very clever. Cunobelinos brokered a deal with Rome regarding taxes so the twins wouldn't have to go to Rome. Then again, Caradoc's sons are no longer available, and you have a daughter. So much for promises."

"How is it you know these things?"

"Togodumnus confides in me." Caoimhe spun the spindle as she teased the wool fibers out and they twisted into a thick thread. "Caradoc stopped sending tribute money to Rome. He now encourages all the other clans to do the same. He bullies them and threatens them until they submit. I've never trusted him. He scares me."

Mara nodded. After a length of yarn was made, she unfastened Caoimhe's fibers from the top of the spindle and wound the yarn around the rod. She secured the fibers again and handed it back to Caoimhe who gave it a whirl.

The yarn broke.

Caoimhe drew more wool out and connected it to the other fibers by rolling them together on her leg. She spun her yarn as before and continued her assessment of Caradoc. Caoimhe leaned forward and whispered, "Caradoc keeps everyone in a state of fear. My husband as well."

Mara was amazed that she was this outspoken about her husband, especially when Caradoc kept his brother so tightly under his thumb.

"Togodumnus used to be a fun-loving man, full of joy and playfulness with our children. I loved the way he would tease Amminus in such a lighthearted way. Now, his moustache covers a frown. Your thread is loose, my dear."

Mara tightened her finger around the threads and

The Golden Cord

reflected on what her friend said. A tear formed. She wiped it away.

"Let's change roles. You do the spinning now, and I will hold the wool," Caoimhe said.

"He rids the realms of instigators and enemies of Albion," Mara said. She couldn't believe she was sticking up for him.

"Or more to the point—the friends of Rome," Caoimhe said.

Mara gave the spinner a twist allowing it to slowly lower as it spun. She inspected the basket of wool to determine how much longer she had to endure this uncomfortable conversation.

Mara stopped spinning. She stared into the distance as if gazing into the past with regret. Caoimhe's brash comments deepened her fears of Caradoc. Taken prisoner gradually through courtship, Caradoc's possessive attention equaled love to her. It wasn't always this way.

Caoimhe started to hum a children's tune, perhaps to change the mood. But Mara needed more than that. The spindle and wool tumbled to the floor as she pulled her stool closer to Caoimhe. Mara clasped her friend's hands. She earnestly squeezed them and gazed into her eyes. "Once I thought I loved him, Caoimhe. 'Stay calm and love him. All will work out,' I kept saying to myself. There were times of quiet, usually after times of passion. I used to lay my head on his chest just to listen to his heartbeat. I tried to figure out what it was that made this man the firebrand that he was." Mara took a deep breath. "There are no more quiet times. He's abandoned all tender touch. I fear he seeks it elsewhere." Mara was unsure how much to tell her friend. "I found a lady's brooch in his chariot."

"A fibula? Doesn't surprise me."

Mara looked to the next room where her daughter slept. "I fear he doesn't love me. I fear for my life and the life of our child, Gladys."

"He is an unkind man," Caoimhe said.

"Caradoc is mean. I used to think it was only an act, a way of intimidating others. His anger and outbursts were in contrast to the times he was charming—calculated so that I would appreciate those nice times more. That's what he

Disentanglement

told me. That he is not really that way." She sat back letting go of Caoimhe's hands. "I believed him."

"Does he strike you?"

"He says that violence is his last resort. But my body bears the proof against his lies. He threatens. Makes rules. Demands. He tells me when to eat and sleep, when to relieve myself, and what to wear. I'm so afraid at times that he will kill me if I don't comply. He thrives on knowing that I am thankful to be alive."

"My husband has never raised his voice, let alone his hand to me or our children. He gives me much freedom and takes joy in my decisions and ideas. I think it is the drink that controls Caradoc."

"I've asked him to cut down on the wine and the mead, but that only makes him mad. I care about him and wish I could fix him. I fear his soul cannot be mended. But when I suggest anything, Caradoc takes another drink and beats me." She gathered up the full spindle and bowed her head. "It was always like this. I couldn't see it. Caradoc hasn't changed. I have. I recognize the abuse now."

"That man is incapable of love. Let me ask you something: What benefits have you gained in this marriage? Position, power, prestige?"

"I made a bad choice. He convinces me he is going to kill me through his actions and what he has done before to others, although he doesn't say so."

"What do you mean?"

"He will choke me only to spare me before my last breath; then he laughs. When he first did this, I began to see him as a protector. For some reason, he made me believe that he would always stop. In doing so, he rescued me from the trauma I brought upon myself. After a brutal beating he would leave me alone for a few days. Sometimes I wished that his beating would be more severe just to gain a reprieve. I began to wish he would not stop. That I would die. But I don't want to die, Caoimhe. Please tell me there is another reality."

"He does the same to Albion," Caoimhe said. "There is no kindness in him."

"At first there was. He gave me trinkets little by little. He said I was too much for any man. Made me feel beautiful and wanted. He had me fooled. When we first met, I dressed seductively for men. I was always in charge of things. I used to be in control of men's desires. But not him. I was no more than just a toy to him. Nothing more."

"When he yells at you, what do you think?"

"I thought it was because he loved me. Wanted me to be better. I always felt that I failed him. He told me it was my fault. I was the one who triggered his anger."

"Do you still feel that way?"

Mara paced. "I stayed, Caoimhe. Why did I stay?"

"You thought he would change."

Mara faced her friend. "Besides you, he was my only link to the outside world. At first I loved the gifts. But now, I refuse them."

"Why?"

"To gain some sense of the independence I lost when I married him. Is this how he was with his former wife?"

"Alexenah was different. She saw life differently than we do. She showed kindness despite his unkindness to her. She was strong. She served, yet she never lost control. She gave control to her god. She trusted her god—even in the worst of times. She garnered strength from that and was not afraid of her husband. I'd like to think that in the end, she stood up to him."

Mara knew Alexenah. Appreciated her kind character as she observed Caradoc's slave-wife, the whole time pretending to be their maid. "She was a better woman than I am."

"Do you think Caradoc killed her?"

Mara gathered the baskets of finished yarn and put them away. She believed he did kill her even though she did not see him do it. She knew. "Caoimhe, I wish my life was like yours."

Caoimhe gathered the loose strands of wool that had fallen to the floor. "My dear Mara, my life was not always happy and filled with the joy of children. I was once like you. Abused and used. I was a moth that fluttered from flame to flame. When I reached rock bottom and considered ending my life over a man, my mother, a wise woman, gave

Disentanglement

me some advice. It was actually at a time when we were spinning wool just like this."

"What did she say?"

She handed the wool to Mara. "She told me to take all the tangled threads of my life and unravel them. Then weave them again into a tapestry of beauty. I listened and followed her advice. I started the disentanglement."

"What changed?"

"Togodumnus. I did not chase him; he pursued me. He was my weaver. He helped me to heal. I love him so."

Mara placed the wool in the basket to be used next time they spun together. She liked Caoimhe's story. Mara tried to find humanity in her husband too. But the reality was, he was uncaring. "He is a coldhearted monster."

Clang, clunk, thwack. Pots scattered across the floor of the house.

Caoimhe flinched.

Caradoc pushed through the open door. "What is this on the floor?" He pushed Caoimhe aside and sat at the table. "Get me my supper!"

Mara served him some wine, spilling a drop on his hand.

He wiped the spill on her dress. "Can't you do anything right?"

She ladled some smoked ham and boiled potatoes from a pot on the hearth and set the plate in front of him.

He downed the glass of wine and hollered for more.

"You shouldn't treat the woman you love like that," Caoimhe said.

With a mouthful, Caradoc said, "Money is a roundhouse. It promptly falls to position and fear."

Mara wasn't sure what he implied. It didn't make sense. She glanced over at Caoimhe, who hugged the wall by the door.

He continued, "Power is a longhouse." He shoved more ham into his mouth. "It is strong. It lasts till it rots, or another rebuilds. Love? Love *her*?" He belched. "Love is a barrow grave. It may stand for hundreds of years, but it's full of rotten bones. All valuable contents have been stolen long ago." He pointed at Caoimhe like he had seen her for the first time. "Why are you here? Don't you have a home of your own? Get out."

Caoimhe raised her hands as if to say, "I wish I could help, but I can't." Shaking her head, she left.

When the door closed, Mara said, "Alexenah said her god is love."

"She was an idiot. And you are dumber than she was."

Mara winced. He shamed her constantly. He guzzled his wine and filled his belly, as deep inside her a calm resolve grew. He had made her give up her work at the Boar's Head Inn. "If you love me . . ." he would say. He used physical intimacy as a reward. That was the only love he knew, and he did that with little feeling. Once, she risked her life for an item of her past. She had brought a petite bottle of her favorite perfume and hid it among her few possessions. When he found what she had done, he made her pour the perfume into the pigsty while he watched. She threw out all reminders of old lovers. He allowed no personal things displayed. Made her feel guilty if she thought about her past life, and she didn't dare mention it.

Caradoc would beat her, abuse her verbally, threaten her, and after he sobered up, he apologized, promised to change, and several times gave her expressions of love in the form of gifts. He bought her loyalty. "I'm only like this because I desperately need you," he would say. "You can end the violence by showing more love," he added. What he meant by that was that he wanted her to do something wicked for him—like she did before. He always said the pain he caused was her fault. "If I hadn't done this, he wouldn't be mad now." She would try to say and do anything to get him to come down from his drunken rage. But it only made things worse. The memories boiled her anger to the surface. Now, she watched him getting drunk again, fearing he would hurt her once more. Her anger rose into a kind of courage. Like dross from a pot of heated gold, she skimmed it off.

"She was my friend," she finally said.

"You have no friends. You never had any friends. How many men did you have before me? Were they friends?"

Disentanglement

Gladys stood at the door to the bedroom, rubbing sleep from her eyes and cried.

"Shut the kid up."

"She wants milk."

Caradoc backhanded Mara on her behind as she walked behind him. "Get her some."

Mara stepped into the bedroom to get her daughter's cup. When she returned, Gladys sat on Caradoc's lap.

He gave the child wine. "She's thirsty."

Mara grabbed Gladys. Put her on her hip. Sobs welled up from deep within, so much that she could barely breathe the words, "You will not be alone with my child ever again."

"I never wanted her anyway," he said. "Get outta my house."

Mara had enough. She hugged Gladys close to her breast. Not knowing where she would go, where she would stay, she left. This time she would not come back after he calmed down. This time she escaped.

CHAPTER 38

Blizzard

There are things said, things unsaid . . . and things that cannot be spoken.

— Scribonius Largus

AD 40—Ephesus

Boaz inclined into the wind at the rim of a deep scar in the ground. The fine leather cloak he stole from a dying patient flapped around his legs, giving little comfort or warmth. "If only I could make sense of my life."

He closed his eyes and edged closer to the precipice. He was not afraid, but the thought of the sudden stop if he should fling himself into the canyon below made him hesitate. In his mind, he could see the damage to his body. Fractured bloody limbs—characteristic of his life of loss. Death and destruction seemed to follow him.

Some would stay the next step because of what their

death would mean to others, considering how they might suffer. This did not concern Boaz. He would not be around to care, and besides, no one cared about him. Everyone he ever loved was gone. No family, unless he counted his father, which he did not. His mother and brother dead. Sophronios died. Lais had taken off without saying goodbye. No friends. No one.

He opened his eyes. He was alone.

In the distance, heaping mountains of white billowy clouds dovetailed shades of dark gray the closer they were to the ground. Snowfall veiled the opposite rim of the canyon like a flimsy curtain over a windowed night. The muffled sound of thunder shook his bones.

He shivered and rubbed his shoulder.

The snow line approached him, flurries at first, then white flakes the size of a gold aureus fell in earnest such that the canyon disappeared. The harsh wind pushed at him as he held his hands in front of him to catch the snow, but they remained empty. He turned his palms over. As the wind gusted against the side of the cliff, *the snow fell up*!

He briefly felt the awe of nature that once overtook him with such intensity—back before his life fell apart. Surely this was an omen of the strongest magic—if—he believed in such things. He didn't place confidence in gods, or demons, or anything he couldn't understand. Humans were the hardest to figure out. Souls held no substance. Man was devoid of meaning. Sophronios said that there was a method to understanding, a way to make sense of everything in nature. Accept the ambiguity. This is what Boaz wanted to believe but found it harder and harder to do so. Even his doubts had doubts. He moistened his lips. The taste of cheap wine still on his tongue.

A frigid gust pressed him. He stumbled over his baggage and fell backward, landing lopsided and awkwardly against a long-dead tree.

He grabbed his belongings and checked the contents. Everything he valued was there. He scooted against the trunk and checked his belt. The medical instrument case was still there.

Two new tree shoots grew at the root of the tree beside

him. A few green leaves struggled to hold to the branches in the sudden blizzard. A beginning or an ending? The autumnal equinox occurred two weeks past. Another omen? Boaz shook his head and pulled the cloak closer around him.

His thoughts gushed like a cut artery. His mind crowded with the pearls of wisdom Sophronios imparted to him the last few years of his medical apprenticeship. Some of which the old physician said to him made no sense:

You are complex and unfinished, Pedi.
You hurt, but there is no visible bruising.
A man must face what wounds him and heal.
Must attend to the wound, doesn't matter what you do, just doing it makes it better.
Patior, Pedi, patior.

To suffer . . . patience? Patience implies waiting for relief. Tolerance is all I can afford. I packed the wound—the abyss of my heart—with work, worry, and wallowing," Boaz said. He had pushed the pain down for so long. He didn't want to heal. He wanted to forget. That is why he drank. To forget. To sleep. To not be responsible for anything.

He had traveled aimlessly from town to town, seeking work as a physician to feed his empty belly and wine to dull his senses. He barely stayed one step ahead of his failures. From Laodicea to every small village along the Meander River, he began with good intentions, but soon his patients were complaining that he slept in too late, missed appointments, and even blamed him for their sickness. He no longer experienced the joy he once felt for helping people.

"Each awakening is a beginning," Sophronios told him almost every morning when they prepared for the day.

Once he tried to get Boaz to talk. To share some of his inside *trauma*. "To cleanse the wound," he would say. All Boaz could think about when he said the word "trauma" was to equate it to what his mother called "sins."

"What is a sin?" he asked Sophronios.

"It is when you do something—a thought or deed—where the outcome is undesirable."

"What if you never know the outcome? What if the outcome is good for one and not another? What if the outcome results in death of your mother?"

"Did you kill your mother, Boaz?"

He bowed his head. He was unsure how to answer him. He didn't think so, but sometimes he wasn't sure. He had pushed the memory down for so long that it was all a fog.

His thoughts raced. He tried to hold on. Like the few remaining leaves on the bourgeoning trees, he shook. The temptation of the cliff lingered through the biting snow. He could no longer see the edge, but he knew it was there.

He loved Lais, and she must have loved him. She had said as much. How did he not know she was a hetaera? He couldn't understand how she could be with so many different men and act as if she loved them too.

"She has some crazy ideas about people, but she aided all who were injured during the time of the quake. Such a charming girl. The patients all seem to love her," Sophronios said.

"Why couldn't I have seen the other side to her—the life she lived as a *courtesan*?"

Boaz grasped one of the tree sprouts, pulled it from the ground, and flung it toward the cliff. A gust of wind sucked it out of sight over the edge. His head swam. He vomited. "I swear I will never drink again!"

A raven cawed overhead as it sailed with the wind.

He shook his fist at the bird, faltered, and sat back down against the tree. "Stop mocking me!" He lowered his head. "I have not forgotten my sins."

Numbly, he stared off into the distance. The gaping wound of land cut beyond the cliff's edge. It needed suturing. "The snow still falls like an upside-down waterfall, and I swim against a deluge of decisions I have made. It would all be over if I just take that step. No more hurt. No more thoughts. No more sin. Just drown in the deep cavern of despair."

The snow turned to a mixture of sleet and rain. His knuckles whitened as he clutched the thick leather of the cloak. "Where have all my beginnings gone?" he cried into the wind. "What have they become?" He tucked his chin and turned from the wind. "Have I arrived at this point in my life to only see where I went wrong? All my life I tried to not be like my father, and now here I sit. I am just like him—no—worse. I am me."

A voice came from above him, "A Physician of Men-Karou."

Boaz flinched as a hand touched his shoulder.

"Stand up."

Boaz drew the cloak tighter.

"The river of shame you drown yourself in is not as deep as you think."

"Who are you?"

"I have been searching for you."

"How did you know I'd be here?" asked Boaz.

"I prayed."

Boaz coughed. He wiped frozen phlegm and vomit from his moustache and beard. "Well, now you have found me."

"Are you well?"

"No, I'm a drinking man with a *medici* problem."

"You mean you are a *medicus* man with a drinking problem."

Boaz stood. "That's what I said." He turned. Behind him stood a tall dark man who wasn't going to leave him alone. The cliff would have to wait.

The man beckoned Boaz to follow.

They traveled to nearby Ephesus, where Boaz stumbled over the doorframe to a simple building adjacent to what appeared to be the man's dwelling. Individual empty cots scattered throughout the spacious, dark, unadorned room. Boaz's petasos and baggage lay on one of the cots.

"That one in the corner is yours."

"My wagon?"

"It is safe in the stable with your *equus africanus asini*."

Boaz nodded a thank-you and staggered to the cot. He batted aside a spiderweb in the corner and pushed his belongings to the floor. He collapsed on to the bed and fell into a fitful slumber.

⌘ ⌘ ⌘

The next morning Boaz sat at a small wooden table that was scarred with the many years of cutting various foods and meats. The cramped kitchen overflowed with unwashed dishes left on the counter. He had searched for wine and

Blizzard

found none. He rested his pounding head in one hand, and in the other he held a stylus, poised as if in midthought. Boaz put his feelings into words on the wax tablet in front of him as instructed. He was not sure how this would help his hangover.

What have my beginnings become? What am I now, compared to when I was young?

Boaz moaned and rocked back and forth. "Aaggggh!" He scraped the words clean as he would scrape the scarred edges of an ulcer with a curette. Despite his reluctance, his thoughts poured out. He etched them on the wax tablet:

Once full of joy,
Now lacking spirit.
Once sober in what I think,
Now a prisoner to the drink.
A perfect relationship.
Now . . . so confused.
Once tender and caring,
Now cynical and abused.

The man who stopped Boaz from cliff diving placed breakfast in front of him, then sat down at the table with his own plate of fruit and boiled eggs. He held a highly crafted silver cup. Around its sides were bas-reliefs of physicians treating patients. An honorable cup for certain. He spoke in the same local Greek dialect in which he had addressed Boaz on the mountain. "You must eat, or you will never grow old."

Boaz pushed the breakfast aside. "I'm too young to be old and too old to be young; too fearful to be bold and too bold to be fearful," Boaz said in Greek.

"Ah, but you *are* poetic this morning."

Boaz winced. Scraped the tablet clean again. With the stylus, he cut a deep chasm-like groove into the wax and dropped it and the pen to the table.

"Tahdah took my brother, Jachin, and me to a place like that cliff. No, not like that. It was a cavernous cave. We were almost there, but he became angry—I don't know about what—and we left. Never even saw the mouth of the cavity. As we returned to town, he pulled the chariot up to a tavern. He wanted us to come in with him. Reluctantly, we did. We ate, fearful of the loud patrons. We felt ashamed for being there. The bar maid thought we were cute and fawned all over us, but the other patrons made the sign against evil and looked the other way. I sometimes think that it would have been worse if we had gone into the cave."

"Who is this 'we' you speak of?"

"My brother and I."

"How old were you then?" the man asked, his mouth full of egg.

"Six, maybe seven summers old."

"Why did the men make the sign against evil?"

"My brother and I are Comghans."

"I do not know this word 'Comghan.'"

"'Twins.' We were identical."

"Were?"

"He is dead"

"Do you feel responsible in some way?"

Boaz had never thought of it that way. He was responsible. Responsible for *everything* that had happened to him. All the time. He especially felt responsible for the death of his brother, Jachin. He pushed the tablet aside, and it fell to the floor.

"I sought you out because I need a responsible man."

Boaz bent over and retrieved the tablet. His head pounded. "You have the wrong person."

"I need your help. You are the physician everyone talks about, are you not?"

"I probably am. That should have been your first clue that I am not your man."

"You do a hundred positive things, but only allow the few mistakes you've made reside in your considerations."

Boaz picked up the stylus and began to poke at the shell of his egg. "Maybe so." In that awkward moment, Boaz rehearsed everything he had ever done wrong. The thoughts so much on the surface.

"The need for a physician in Ephesus is excessive. It is too much for one doctor. My need is great as well. I require help at the surgery."

The way Boaz felt, he thought he wasn't worthy enough

to be alive, let alone to help others to remain so. He glanced up at the man. "I will do as much nothing as possible."

The man laughed. "I do not believe so, my most excellent friend."

Boaz dropped the stylus and picked up his fork. "What did you say your name was?"

"I am Loukas of Antioch. When you finish, call for me, and I will show you the *klinein* where we see the patients." He got up from the table and placed his dishes precariously on top of the others on the counter. "Not as nice as the Temple at Men-Karou, but we endure."

Loukas. His name is Loukas. No wonder he spoke Greek.

CHAPTER 39

Investigation

*Knowledge is a refuge in adversity
on the path of duty.*

— Scribonius. Largus

Days grew into weeks. Boaz kept away from the wine and ale, but it was not painless. Every day he wanted to escape his mental anguish. Loukas helped with that. Held him accountable. At first, all he could think of was where he could find alcohol. The cravings were strong but weakened as time passed. Loukas made sure he ate three healthy meals a day.

Whenever Boaz tried to rationalize his drinking, Loukas reminded him of his responsibility and the effects of consumption. They took walks together, as the physician said he needed the fresh air and exercise as much as he needed the nourishment. Because of that, Boaz began to be whole. Loukas told him that only he alone could change, but that he couldn't do it alone. It was not easy, but it was doable. They often talked into the night or during breakfast about deep things—Greek and Roman law, philosophy, and the newest medical approach to pharmacology and therapeutics.

This day began as any morning in the new city of Ephesus. Boaz ate a light breakfast of fruit and figs with Loukas. Sometimes they ate eggs, but that was rare.

"Of all physicians, he will succeed laudable in the cure if he understands requisite their first cause," Loukas lectured, drinking water and lemon juice from his silver cup.

"I disagree. Through experiment and reasoning, one can determine the remedy by observing the outcome, regardless of the cause," Boaz said.

"The infirmary will declare the treatment. Remove the cause, you cure the disease."

"What you are saying is interesting, and I must agree, important, but I am an Empiricist," Boaz said.

"Rather *Empiricist*, *Methodist*, or *Dogmatist*, the cure is in the patient. He alone can change. We are but the vessels of God in assisting this transformation," Loukus said.

"Some say, 'A chance to cut is a chance to cure.' I say, 'A chance to care is a chance to cure.'"

"I like that, my most excellent friend. I know you care, Boaz. I have seen it."

"I bind the wounds and hide the scars."

"A wounded healer. Tragic is this love of yours, Boaz. Time will take away the pain from the memories that remain."

"Loukas, there is an emptiness inside me that I tried to fill with drugs and drink. I still feel hollow."

"God can remove the hurt and fill that void."

"My mother used to say that too."

"She was a Jew, was she not?"

"Yes. I miss her exceedingly."

"I know you do." Loukas laid a hand on Boaz's shoulder. Boaz sighed.

"Growing up in a Jewish home, are you familiar with the Passover?"

"Somewhat. I still remember the things to say at the Seder meal. But they mean nothing now. Jewish teachings are nothing but myth. No different than the accounts of gods or goddesses."

"*Mythos* means 'word' or 'tale' or 'true narrative,' referring to facts rooted in truth. Mythos is story told from person to person. Does it make the Passover story and others like it any less true? Is that not how you learned the art of medicine?"

Boaz nodded his head. Yes, Loukas made a good point. For the most part, Boaz accepted only *epistími* and empirical evidence, but he still wondered who taught a spider how to build his web.

Loukas was a writer like Boaz. He wrote lengthy treatises on the life of one certain man. A history of sorts. He spent all his free time gathering information, reading letters from someone named Marcus, and spending time with a teacher in the synagogue. This seemed odd since Loukas was Greek and not a Jew.

"Who is this man you visit at the synagogue?" Boaz asked.

"Paulus—he is a friend. I attend to the teacher's physical discomforts. He writes large like you do," Loukas said.

"Maybe he needs some of my Phrygian powder for his eyes."

"I will take him some if you will compound it for me."

"I'd be glad to if I have any free time."

They finished their meal, and Loukas left to make his morning visits.

Boaz studied daily before he went to the clinic. He read anything he could find. Ephesus had a wonderful library, and Loukas, although meager in his household amenities, had a shelfful of scrolls—classic poets such as Aristotle and Plato's dialogues on his teacher, Socrates. He thoroughly enjoyed the epic poems of Homer, *The Iliad* and *The Odyssey*, reading them over and over. Inspired by the heroes, Boaz imagined himself a champion of the righteous like he and his brother did as children in the wheat fields of Albion. Perhaps a physician is a hero in a way. He hoped he could

Investigation

be, even if it meant improving someone's life by degrees—to make them better than they were.

In this flourishing city by the coast, Boaz began to get a glimpse of who he could be and what he might accomplish. He had overheard about the need for doctors at the gladiator school in Rome. The excitement of the arena would be like watching one of Homer's epics first hand. Boaz could see himself in that setting. Most of all, this might be a way for him to start over. Another beginning.

Fear of slipping back into the bottle kept him where he was for now. He vowed to not be like his father, but he kept seeing himself fall short despite his goal to always do good.

For now he practiced the medical arts every day until worn out. In the evenings, he processed the day's endeavors with Loukas.

When he finished his reading, he left to attend to patients with Loukas. Dressed in his white tunic and a set of new solea that Loukas gave him, he ambled to the clinic, where a perpetual protracted line of patients waited. He thought he recognized a lady in the line, but when she turned around, a purple shawl partially covered her face, so he wasn't sure. Patients often returned for the same ailments if cures did not happen overnight.

"Are you the owner of the clinic?" a man with a shabby looking bandage on his hand asked. "They said I was to come to Boaz's clinic." People saw Boaz—not as a young boy but as *the* physician.

Boaz pointed the man to the line that formed outside the building and smiled.

He liked the city well enough, yet he had a challenging time feeling at home. Because of the sizable port at Ephesus and the excellent roads, the harbor was always busy and full of ships carrying goods back and forth from Italia to Greece. A monumental gateway near the public baths welcomed the weary travelers. Boaz could see the immense theater from where he stood and beyond that, the city's temple honoring the goddess Diana, known as *Artemis Ephesia* to the local Greeks. Its pillars and massive all-marble roof were a marvel to behold. Boaz preferred a much quieter environ.

He did not forget about Lais. He longed to find her. He sometimes found himself walking the streets—poking around corners, standing outside the brothels, and looking at strangers, wondering if they might be Lais. At times he ventured the audacity of asking if a customer of the brothel knew Lais. Of course, they did not. Back in Carura, Didymus told him that she was a hetaera. He didn't know where else to look. He saw her in crowds she wasn't even in.

Oftentimes he would go to the cliffs around Ephesus and sit. Not to think about his work, but to disappear and enjoy the quiet. It was there he could reflect on his life and hear his own beliefs, unencumbered by responsibilities. Many times he brought his papers and wrote about the remedies he learned from Loukas. He wanted to compile his vast knowledge of herbs that he learned from Sophronios and other teachers. Much of it he discovered on his own. He included elaborate drawings of the plants, and one day he hoped others would benefit from his information.

"Good morning, Master," said Phoebe the *Latreousa*. This nurse assisted the physicians, as she always said it was a "sacred service to others." Caring for the affairs of another and aiding them with her resources was her mission in life. She referred to herself as a *diakonon* or deaconess—a title Paulus gave her as she followed his teachings.

"I am not your master. You know that, Phoebe."

"Yes, Master."

Boaz repeatedly corrected others that called him Master or Teacher. But it didn't do any good. Yes, he was a physician, although technically he was still a slave. They still insisted on calling him Master. Finally, he just gave up trying to amend them.

He greeted curly headed Rufus, the *therapeutes* sitting at the table gathering the patients' information. The young man aspired to be a physician himself. Assisting in the clinic was a good chance for him to check the pulse of what medicine entailed—to be exposed to the sights, sounds, and smells that accompany the profession. Rufus wrote down on his wax tablet the patients' names and their complaint. Those who could afford it brought a votive for the Temple of Asklepios across town. The small offerings stacked up like

Investigation

Loukas's dishes and filled the courtyard like amputated limbs waiting to be discarded.

This clinic was like what he was accustomed to in Carura—remarkably simple. Not exactly a temple, but not a gymnasium either. It was a separate building next door to Loukas's house, purposed for treating the ill. Not only was Phoebe the Latreousa but she was also rumored to be the *prostatis* to the clinic. As patron, she financed the various needs of treating the many destitute patients, but Boaz suspected Loukas paid rent from his own purse.

Most of the physical complaints were the same—headache, cough, and neck pain. These were common ailments related to the arduous work and poor conditions of the workers and slaves. Boaz prescribed the same recipes to everyone: exercise, lots of clean water, and a diet rich in vegetables. To a few, he prescribed herbs. Occasionally, a complex patient would come in who would challenge his skill. Although he liked solving mysteries, he enjoyed the surgical patients, as he was able to assess the problem and fix it without much thinking. The work was long and at times tedious. Boaz received nothing for his ministrations. At least he had a place to sleep and meals provided. Loukas was a terrible cook, but one will eat anything if it is *gratis*.

For the last several days, Loukas worked closely by Boaz's side, except when teaching at the synagogue or making house calls. Most of the time the physicians worked quietly.

The man who asked if Boaz was the owner of the clinic waited his turn in line. He was careless in using his sword to chop weeds around his fence. When Boaz finally removed the wrappings on his hand one at a time—an old shirt, gauze, muslin, wool, felt, and olive leaves—he revealed a large gaping wound. Not a bad bandage, and probably would have healed on its own, but the injury would do better if the ends of the wound were brought together with the new braided silk sutures Loukas had received from the Far East. It was far superior to the gut suture made from the twisted intestines of sheep.

Loukas approached Boaz as he sewed.

"Nice work. Do you understand the Latin word *ligare*?"

The Golden Cord

Boaz tied a two-handed knot. "Yes, it means 'to bind.'"

"Very good. It is where we get our term ligature, or ligament, which binds muscle to bone. It is used to describe whatever is used to bind something tightly together."

"As in the *fasces lictor* that the Roman soldiers carry?"

"Yes, the bound rods that show a Roman's rank. Excellent! That is the same root word. Now that we have established that your knowledge is still intact, let me ask you another question. What is the greatest *ligari*?"

Boaz cut the suture and threaded another into the curved silver needle. "You mean to use in *chirurgia*?"

"Not exactly. I am talking about life, not surgery. For instance, the cord that binds soldiers to duty. What do you suppose that cord is?"

"Fear, money, or perhaps purpose?"

"I have seen a man do all he can on the battlefield for those reasons and more. Yet he returns home to his wife and child and hands them the bounty, keeping none for himself."

Boaz finished with his patient by applying a bandage of clean linen. "You will be better now. You may go," he told the man, who held his arm as if a miracle had occurred. He bowed to Boaz.

After the man left, before another came, Boaz poured vinegar on his instruments and wiped them clean. He laid them beside the table. "Well, then we are talking of love."

A man carrying a young woman hurriedly entered the room.

"We were robbed!" the man said. "My wife is hurt."

He placed the woman on the table. A young boy, no more than ten summers old, raced over and put his head down on her chest. Blood oozed from her stomach.

Easing the boy aside, Boaz examined the wound. Knife? Sword? No, this was not a clean cut. A rusty rod perhaps?

"I chased 'em off, I did," the man said. He proceeded to recount the incident, as if rehearsed. He repeated himself and stumbled over the details. The story changed with each telling. Boaz noticed fresh scratch marks on the man's face. When asked, he said he ran into a tree limb. Boaz examined the woman's fingernails.

Investigation

The boy paced close to the woman. He rocked on one foot to the other. He bit his lip so hard that a trickle of blood snaked down his chin.

Boaz looked to Loukas and said, "Experience, emotion, or truth?" Loukas would know he referred to their talks of diagnosing the problem, yet this didn't seem an appropriate time to discuss philosophy. It was Boaz's way of letting Loukas know he saw more to this than what was presented.

Phoebe recognized the situation and silently left the room. She returned with several Roman guards.

Boaz attempted to assuage the gushing wound as Loukas handed him instruments and cloths. The violent attack had pierced the spleen and tore the bowel.

The boy screamed when the woman began to convulse. Loukas embraced him as he struggled to reach his mother.

Then she exhaled and didn't take another breath.

"We have done all we can," Boaz said.

"No!" the boy cried as he broke free and hugged his mother. "No!" He seized a scalpel from the table and rushed the man who brought her in, yelling, "Father did it!"

The guards snatched the boy, but not before he sliced his father's arm.

Then the boy tried to cut his own wrist with the scalpel, resulting in only a scratch. The guard wrapped his arms around the boy's chest from behind, and the other guard wrestled the scalpel from the boy's hand.

"I want to be with her. Let me be with my mother! Let me go!"

Loukas attended to the child to assure his safety.

The husband cursed the boy. Cursed the woman. He stepped up to Boaz and got in his face. "You killed my wife!" he said. "Look at this!" He thrust his lacerated arm in Boaz's face. It bled profusely.

Boaz hesitated a second, moved the dead woman's legs to the side, and motioned the man to sit on the bloody table next to his dead wife. Boaz poured vinegar on the man's wound. The man screamed. Wiping the arm dry of blood and liquid, he attempted to stitch the man's laceration. He was not gentle. All the while the man complained and kept moving his arm.

Boaz had enough. He seized the man's wrist and held it against the thin mattress. With suture and needle in hand, he fastened the man's hand to the table, putting a stitch through the web between his thumb and first finger. Any attempt at moving now was wrought with pain. The man finally held still.

The guards watched and waited. When Boaz finished, he cut the suture, letting the man loose and ushered him into the hands of the guards.

CHAPTER 40

Aftermath

We must become the person of the moment and throw off other's expectations and yesterday's tormented identities.

— Scribonius Largus

The rest of the day was uneventful. Finally, they saw the last patient. Phoebe and Rufus left, and the sun descended into the west. Boaz and Loukas finished cleaning up the mess of the day.

Boaz sat on a divan in the back of the room. "I wanted to hurt him."

"That is not who you are," Loukas said as he joined him. "There were no thieves."

"Things are not so black and white. All is not what it seems. I am not so set that I do not look at all the evidence," Loukas said.

"You know he was the one that assaulted his wife."

Loukas set his ever-present silver cup on the table. "Yes, I discerned that as well."

"Your philosophy is insufficient to explain the actions of the body or the man who rules his frame. We need rules for this method of abuse. Otherwise how will we know what to do? There should be laws," Boaz said.

"You don't need more protocols. They are but maps to help us as physicians to better treat people who are imperfect. Man's answer is to do this and to do that—to follow the rules. If one accepts the protocols without protest, will they be blameless if they make an error in treatment, yet they followed the rules? These things are not so easy to deal with, Boaz."

"I don't know, Loukas. I just want to do what's right."

"The rules will only guarantee failure, and your heart will still hurt. You can do it on your own—many do, but you'll always come to brokenness. All we can do is care until we cannot care any longer."

"Even for those that are evil?"

"Even to that man who stabbed his wife in front of his son."

"She shouldn't have died. I could have saved her. I should have tried harder."

"Do you think I have never felt that I could have done more? Do I feel responsible? Yes. I always wonder what I could have done different or if I could have done more, or if I was guilty of a death due to sins of commission or omission, but after I examine my role, I bury it and move on. Unfortunately, people die. Earlier in my career it bothered me more, especially with preventable deaths such as suicide. You can't hold a blade to someone's throat, and you can't keep them from holding a knife to their own neck. I do my best with the skills I have. You did your best with the skills and knowledge you had. Responsible or not, move on. For every diagnosis I have missed or life I didn't save, there are

Aftermath

hundreds, if not thousands, that I did make a difference to. Boaz, you will do the same."

"If only."

"It deeply hurts me to hear you talk like this, Boaz. You don't realize it, but no one in Ephesus cares as much as you."

"No one cares . . ."

"That's not what I mean. Boaz, you care more than anyone. You avoid the pain and look away from your own injuries, thinking all is okay, while your own wounds fester. Healing hurts. An honest look at yourself bears more pain than the original hurt. I know this. We don't want to feel like that ever again."

These words sounded similar to what Sophronios said to him. "How then do I heal?"

"A wound must be washed, or it will worsen, and you will die. Boaz, one can never change what happened. There will always be scars. It is the brokenness inside that must be mended."

"So you are saying I am broken. I knew this. Can one as broken as me be made whole?"

"I have seen others try to make themselves whole. You can assert yourself. Create boundaries. Structure your own reality. Do what you think is right. But you will still die having only lived for yourself. That is loneliness. I have seen you with your patients. You care."

Boaz glanced at Loukas. A tear formed in the corner of his eye. He didn't know why.

"A doctor must give himself to others, Boaz, and lose himself in their hurts, not deny or avoid their own pain, but enter into it as well. He must heal himself. Neglecting your own soul and beating yourself up with 'shoulds' will only leave you bruised and alone. Establishing your own worth on what others think about you is like filling a cup with bitter water. The cup may be full and quench your thirst, but it will leave you wanting something much more different and more pleasant."

Boaz fumbled with the surgeon's knife. "My vessel is damaged beyond repair."

Loukas gently took the knife from Boaz's hand and put his arm around him. "You are skilled at suturing a wound and lancing a boil, but that doesn't make you a physician. My excellent friend, you are honest and kind. You tell your patients truths and not what they want to hear. Your predictions of outcome are precise and exacting, even when the illness portends death. This is what makes you a good physician and not a charlatan."

Boaz studied Loukas. The man cared. The man accepted him. He somehow understood. Like Sophronios. Like Lais. Like Jachin.

"Loukas?"

"Yes?"

"The boy wanted to be with his mother."

Loukas nodded and picked up a length of leather strapping used to restrain reluctant patients to the table.

Great. Where was that when I needed it?

"Boaz, think once more, my friend, about what we were discussing in the clinic. Beyond death there is only one cord that will bind you to the one you love."

"Yes, the soldier. He did what he did for love. I get that."

Loukas continued, "Boaz, what if that same soldier came home to an empty house and graves in the yard? His duty, fear, purpose, and love would be meaningless if the bond he had with his loved ones ended there."

"I understand that emptiness. I saw that chasm in the boy's eyes today." Boaz pulled his knees closer to his chest as he sat on the divan. "I searched for Matrona when they told me she was gone. I couldn't comprehend that we were separated forever. I reached out to her with my mind, but only grasped memories."

"What bond do you have with your mother that will not just connect you in this life, but connect you upon death? In other words, is there a bond that death cannot break?"

"I lay in her lap. I heard her stories. I was her child."

"No, I'm afraid that is not a bond that will take you to her in the afterlife."

"She bound my wounds. She kept me alive when Tahdah beat me."

Aftermath

"No, that is still not sufficient."

Boaz turned his back on Loukas and viewed the table where the woman died. He didn't know what Loukas was implying. "I am trying to understand. You know I love to figure out a puzzle, and mysteries intrigue me, but you talk in riddles."

"Think once more, my friend. Beyond death there is only one cord that will bind you to the one you love."

Boaz had not thought about such deep questions for many years, if at all. Not entertaining memories lead to not experiencing feelings. No guilt. No shame. No hurt. To not think about the past means it didn't happen. It didn't exist, yet brutal memories long repressed hounded the back of his mind. He was tired. "These are questions for temple priests . . . or my mother. Matrona was Jewish. I don't know what I am."

"Boaz, when I first met you, this is who I saw: a troubled young man who was numb, distorted, whose senses were greatly altered. You observed things outside your body as a bad dream. You were indifferent, detached, passive. You walked as if a man dead. By intellectualizing your pain, you thought without feeling. Drank to not think."

"I drank without thinking."

"Yes, to remove the sensation of pain. Did you use opiates too? I would not be surprised. And worst of all, you separated from others."

Boaz stood and walked to the table with his belongings. "I thought that if I crawled into the carafe of wine, I would be safe."

"Safe from feeling?"

"Yes." Boaz returned his medical instruments to the leather pouch.

"Boaz don't shut me out. You feared and distrusted me at first. That was prudent. However, once you felt safe and began to confide in me, you established your identity as a doctor. You began to come alive." Loukas joined him at the table. "I see before me a man of uncommon skill and a sense of caring. I believe we have become friends. That is why I talk with you about these profound issues."

"I have no friends. Others are happy. Not me. I expect I'll die young and alone. Everyone looks at me, and all they see is a half-breed Jew who can't do anything right."

"Everyone? Like I said before, Boaz, people care one thousand times less than you do. They don't care. You do."

"Who am I? I was forced to face tragedy. I watched my mother die. My father killed her. Just like the drama played out before us today!" Boaz started to cry. He couldn't hold it back any more. He told Loukas about things he had never told anyone. Not even Lais. It all came out so fast. He told him about the raven his father killed and fed to the pig, the drunk Roman on the road that he was forced to strike with the sword, and the death of Primus . . . Boaz paused for breath and wiped his eyes. "The earthquake where all those people died, and those who didn't lost everything." He gestured with his hands, palms up, looking around the room. "And now all these patients who need so much more than I am able to do for them."

Loukas stood silently letting Boaz experience feelings.

"The beatings. I never thought to escape. To do nothing, to think nothing. Just to survive was my only goal. Just to make it another terrible day." He turned to face Loukas. "I didn't care if I lived or died."

"You were not totally passive when you were beaten, were you? Did you fight back?"

"My brother did that, and in the end, so did my mother. Not me. To fight back meant more beatings. At times I felt I deserved them. I gave in. I gave up. And yet, they continue, even by my own hand. Now, as you say, I am already dead. A walking corpse."

"Don't die by your own hand, Boaz."

"Oh, so now you are going to help me?"

"That is not what I mean. You are not on the edge of the cliff now. To take your own life is an act of anger, not an act of giving in or giving up."

Boaz clenched his fist.

"Who are you angry at, Boaz?"

Boaz was exhausted. He wished to go to bed—to sleep and not think. But in some way, he felt bound to a table as if this sacrifice was necessary. He couldn't move. Thoughts

Aftermath

flooded over him. Thoughts of past horrors and future failures. He remembered the constant dread. Door slam, constant fear of doom. To think of what was farther down the road for him gave only a sterile hope and expected disappointment. The future for him was what was next to him. He couldn't think of any answers for Loukas. What is the greatest bond that holds beyond death? Who was he angry with? He didn't know. And thinking brought desire for that which was lost. He wanted a drink. He wanted Sophronios. He wanted Lais. He wanted Jachin. He turned to leave.

"Where are you going?"

"Does it matter? I am nobody now. Even God forsook me. My father killed him."

"Where is this coming from? You were almost there. Where are you going?"

"To the cliff."

Loukas touched his arm and beckoned Boaz to sit down. "My most excellent friend, can you please stay and talk for a moment longer?"

Boaz felt like his father breathed down his back. He ducked as if from a blow when Loukas reached for him.

"Why do you insist on beating yourself?"

"I'm used to it. Self-flagellation is the flag I fly."

"Please, Boaz. You must not suffer now what you suffered then. When young, you coped the best you could. You had no defense. You had no choice. As an adult, you get to choose how to respond to suffering."

"I am always the chosen sacrifice. My depravity is the cause."

Loukas didn't respond. Boaz expected him to counter and say, "Yes, you are bad." But he didn't.

"I'm saddened by your pain, my friend. Would you tell someone with a stab-wound, or loss of a limb, to bear their infirmity without remorse since there are many who have also lost a limb? Would that stop their pain? Or lessen their loss?"

Boaz shook his head. "Tell me the answer, Loukas. What is the greatest bond to others after they die?"

"Truly, you are a friend of God. I know in my heart that you will discover the answer."

Boaz stood again and gathered his pouch of instruments. "I need certainty; I need evidence."

"Let me ask you one last question before you leave, Boaz: What about your brother? What is it that connected you to your brother? What is it that bound you two together? Love? Shared adventures? Shared trauma? Will those things bind you in the afterlife?"

"No, it will not," Boaz said, and he walked out.

CHAPTER 41

History

Listening is a greater way of learning than assuming you possess knowledge.

— Scribonius Largus

Days of work and study improved Boaz's mind and heart. There wasn't a minute that passed that he didn't think of Lais. The grief of losing his mentor affected him as well. So much loss all at once would be hard for anyone to take, let alone a young man whose early life was so tragic. But things were better. He felt alone most of the time, even though he had friends and coworkers. It wasn't the same. Most of the time he kept his thoughts to himself. He didn't have much time to think as the days were busy, but in the evenings, he always let the thoughts roll in like a thick fog.

Boaz joined the older physician in front of the fire. "Loukas, I have a question. And please, no more riddles."

"What is your question?"

"Why do you believe what you do?'

"*Christianus sum*—I am Christian," he said. "I came to it slowly, Boaz."

"Well, then tell me slowly."

"So wonderful to hear your humor reestablished, my friend. For your sake, I will speak slowly." Loukus smiled, took a sip of his cider and after a while continued. "My father was a mathematician and philosopher. He insisted I acquire knowledge and understanding. As such, I have an interest in all intellectual matters, as you know."

"Your curiosity far exceeds mine, and that says a lot," Boaz said.

"I did not like dogmatism. Accepting one view alone did not appeal to me. As I traveled in my younger days, I examined each and every one of the philosophies I encountered. I made attempts to connect those beliefs with my understanding of the world of *epistimi*. I wrote commentaries and treatises on medicine and philosophy.

"Ultimately, my studies of anatomy and medicine led me to the arts of Hippocrates. I began to care for the injured and ill. I enjoyed the work, and before long I was asked to practice here in Ephesus." He pursed his lips as if his mouth was dry and took another drink.

Boaz sat quietly listening to the story of this gracious man.

"A few years ago, I became acquainted with Paulus. We debated regularly at the library about a multitude of issues. Paulus is knowledgeable and scholarly. That is what drew me to him at first. Well-studied and trained in all things, yes, but he is of a weak demeanor and unimpressive. I first met him when he came to the clinic regarding an eye ailment. He stooped, and at times his speech lisped. I first thought he was a Jewish philosopher.

"I considered all philosophers as salesmen trying to convince another to accept or buy whatever they were selling—whether it be goods, or ideas. I won't be sold anything, Boaz," he said, "If I desire something, I will search it out and buy it if it suits me. I won't choose something because everyone believes it or because the teachings of someone I admired made me feel important. Was it false, or was it true? I needed empirical evidence."

Boaz listened. He had told his own life story to Loukas but knew little of this man of such marvelous reputation and character. He wondered what brought him to be a man of integrity and honor. Boaz wished he could aspire to such repute after all the terrible things he'd done while drinking.

"The Way," Loukus continued, "as they call their beliefs, is accepted solely by faith. That did not appeal to me. But I listened to the Christiani—not about what they believed, but in *whom* they believed. They didn't profess a creed, but a Christus. A messiah. A deliverer.

"The Christiani belief and actions are reality to them. It is hard to convince them otherwise."

"Scared people will follow anything if they believe it will save them from what they fear," Boaz said.

"Not so. From the moment of believing, these people stand strong in their denial of all names and existence of other gods. They worship God. Not gods, but the only God."

"It would be easier to not believe anything," Boaz said.

"Perhaps, but my friend, I cannot believe without thinking out its reasons. The procurator Pontius Pilate put Christus to death during the reign of Tiberius. This is an established fact. But these Christiani serve a *risen* God. Men once crucified do not rise again! I needed evidence."

Boaz nodded. "Dead is dead is dead."

"Cynics say the Christiani speak to dull minds—that only slaves and children follow Christus. They dismiss the tales as fictitious stories of a secret association. Insurrection is their purpose, the skeptics say. They insist in conspiracies propagated by misanthropes."

"I heard these things about the sect myself. How can one discern the truth?"

"Ah, that is the question of a clever man. I found that the teachings of the Christiani speak to those who reason. Should eyewitnesses that agree in their telling all be suspect? Should those who follow the teachings not be deemed true? These things I asked myself. I heard many observations of the same events, and they rang true every time. Observation is evidence. You cannot doubt those who walked with this man.

"My father told me that one can learn much from the study of honorable men's lives. So I listened. I examined all things and considered their merits. Yet this man, this Christus, was not a philosopher, nor a salesman. But a god? It didn't make sense. Either he was who he said he was, or he was the source of the greatest lie ever propagated. His perfect life frustrated me."

"How so?"

"Live a moral life? I thought I could do that. But then again, I knew I could not."

"No man can live in perfection. You have told me as much," Boaz acknowledged.

"At that point in my life, I felt entangled by the errors of my past life and wished to be freed from the constant turning to immorality. This God offered something unique from everything I had studied."

"What is that?"

"I have not had a moral life, Boaz. To have the stains of my life washed away fascinated me. Paulus talked of power. Not miracles, but of a power to change a life. Not power of Paulus or some leader, but the power of Christus crucified, and God's loving forgiveness.

"Once I accepted the Christiani beliefs and God's forgiveness, matters I could not see opened up to me as if a lamp was lit in the darkest corner of my soul. Immediately my doubts became clear. Why did I convert? I tested the empirical evidence."

Boaz found it difficult to believe this man was ever anything than what he appeared. "Interesting testimony. One day you must write in order those things you speak of and what these Christiani most assuredly believe," he said.

"I think I will."

42
CHAPTER

Liberation

Buy freedom and sell it not.

— Scribonius Largus

The moon waxed and waned three times before Boaz got up the nerve to show Loukas the letter from Sophronios. Boaz felt healthier—both physically and mentally, but it was as if the letter weighed more than the Temple of Diana in his mind. So he decided to show Loukas the letter. His friend didn't say much, only that Sophronios must have been very astute to recognize the raw talent in a young boy. "Well done" the note said. Boaz smiled.

Being here in Ephesus with Loukas was good for him, and he enjoyed his work in the clinic. Occasionally the team took time off to enjoy the amenities of the city. Today they were going to the theater. Boaz danced with joy, then

The Golden Cord

looked to make sure no one had seen him look so foolish. He laughed out loud and danced some more.

It was a free day, as the clinic was closed for the holiday to celebrate the Ephesian *Artemisia* festival. The activities began at sunrise each day and included games, contests, and theatrical performances—all held in the goddess's name.

The citizens gathered to watch her procession through the streets. Maidens danced around a statue of the goddess as men carried it through town. They tossed flowers and sang songs. It was a day that many young people sought out each other looking for a suitable marriage partner. Boaz searched the crowds for Lais, knowing it was futile.

Boaz joined Loukas, Rufus, and Phoebe at the majestic theater located on the slope of *Panayir Hill*, opposite the street that ran down to the harbor. Over twenty-five thousand spectators would be there in the open-air theater to watch the drama. Boaz enjoyed the crowds, as there was as much drama going on in the seats as there was on the stage.

"Our seats are this way," said Loukas.

The troop entered from the upper *cavea* then eased their way down the *diazoma,* surrounded by other families looking for their places. The lower section seats were made of marble and had backs on them. Usually reserved for important people, Boaz wondered how Loukas was able to retain such marvelous seating.

The stage building was three-stories high and adorned with beautiful carved reliefs, marble columns with niches, windows and statues. Everything one would need for a play to take place. A man dressed as a chicken tossed sweets and nuts to the crowd. Deafening music blared from the orchestra pit to the right of the substantial stage rivaling the boisterous throng.

"Today is the fifth day of the festival. A comedy play will be presented to cheer the audiences who endured tragic plays the last few days. Expect a lot of drinking and vulgar rude jests. The actors mock everyone of power, from politicians to the gods," Loukas explained, trying his best to be heard over the audience.

Liberation

"So which play is this going to be?" Rufus asked.

"Satyrs—half human, half beast—are slated to mock the tale of Odysseus," Phoebe said.

"I know Homer's story of Odysseus," Boaz said. "It is about a warrior going home after the war with Troy. He reaches an island and ends up a captive in a cave by a giant with only one eye."

Rufus couldn't sit still. "The cyclops! I love this story!"

"In this play, the satyrs escape by luring sailors into the cyclops's cave to take their place as the monster's slaves."

Rufus caught a bag of nuts and shared them with the others. "Odysseus deceived? I find that hard to believe."

"Satyrs always complicate the lives of others," Loukas said.

"Oh, so that is the reason my life has been so complicated?"

"Your life isn't any more complicated than anyone else, Boaz."

With the sound of a trumpet and cheers from the crowd, the play began.

Boaz and the others were having a good time, laughing and shouting with the rest of the audience at the raucous display before them. The dancing and display on the stage of gaiety from drinking the wine that Odysseus brought made him think briefly about his own drinking, but it was just a thought. He no longer had the desire to numb his senses. He thought of Lais and fantasized finding her again when the cyclops spoke of Helena of Troy.

When asked his name, Odysseus replied, "Nobody."

The satyrs got the cyclops drunk, and then Odysseus blinded the giant with a sharpened log hardened in the fire. The actor turned, revealing his blackened eye, stunning the crowd.

Satrys: Ah! How ugly you look! Did you fall into the fire?

Cyclops: No, no! It was Nobody! Nobody has blinded me!

Satyrs: Yeah? Nobody has blinded you? So . . . so that means nobody has caused you any harm?

Cyclops: No, no, no! Nobody plucked my eyeball out! It was Nobody!

Satyrs: So you're not blind, then, Cyclops, are you?

Cyclops: Ah! The pain! The horrible pain! Stop making fun of me! Tell me where this Nobody is!

Satrys: Who? Nobody? Nobody is nowhere, Cyclops.

Cyclops: It was my visitor who did this to me. That horrible visitor who got me so drunk with that wine of his!

Satyrs: Oh yes! The wine! Wine is a very dangerous thing.

Boaz and Loukas shared a knowing look. When the play ended, they all clapped.

"Odysseus got away!" Boaz stood and cheered. "Ah-ha! He is free! He tells them his *real* name!" He laughed like he hadn't laughed in a very long time. "'*Nobody poked out my eye.*' He said his name was Nobody! He bought his freedom with a pun! So funny!"

Phoebe and Rufus joined in the laughter.

"But they left out the hiding under the sheep scene. Very funny anyway. Very funny."

"At last Odysseus will travel home," Loukas said.

The crowd erupted in applause as the actors took the stage again and bowed. The satyrs chased the cyclops off the stage as he made bombastic noises with his mouth.

Boaz and his friends joked with each other as they pushed through the crowd, laughing all the way to the exit.

"What do you call a blind cyclops? Greeks have no word for zero. A No-eyed clops?"

"Ha! Here is a good one I heard the other day: A man is dreaming that he is selling a pig, and he is asking one hundred denarii for it. Someone offered fifty, but he won't take it. At that point he wakes up. Then, keeping his eyes shut, he holds out his hands and says, 'Okay, give me the fifty.'"

Boaz laughed. "A person went to a doctor and said, 'Doctor, whenever I get up from sleeping, I'm groggy for a half an hour afterward and only after that am I all right.' To which the doctor replied, 'Get up half an hour later.'"

"I once had a woman come to the clinic and said her slave had no pillow, so she gave him an earthen jar to place under his head. The slave said that the jug was hard. 'What shall I do?' she asked me. I told her to fill the jar with feathers," said Loukas.

Once outside the theater, Loukas pulled Boaz to the side. "Have you bought your freedom?"

Liberation

"That isn't funny, Loukas."
"I'm serious, my excellent friend."
"No, I do not know how."
"Well, we must do it right away!"

⌘ ⌘ ⌘

The next morning Boaz upended his leather satchel onto the kitchen table. "Will this be enough?"
"Oh, most definitely. If not, I will help you," Loukas said.
Boaz's face warmed. "Thank you."
"What are these pieces of clay mixed in with the coins?"
"Those are the remnants of the vase in which Sophronios saved and kept all of this money. I made the vase. It was one of my first attempts at pottery. It was atrocious! Just throw them out."
Loukas selected two shards and fit the pieces together. "May I have these?"
"I guess."
"Perfect! I love puzzles."
They separated the coins and the fragments of clay.
"Now let's get your *freedom*!" Loukas exclaimed.
The two traveled to the city council, and Loukas asked the clerk for the Book of Manumission. They paid the fee, although Boaz thought the price was excessive. He had more than enough.
"Now we need a name."
"A name?"
"Yes, to be free you have to have a new name. Most take on the *nomen* of their master."
"I don't know. I don't think of Sophronios as my master. He was more of a father to me. Like you." Boaz smiled. "Why don't *you* give me a name."
"All right, how about *Theophilus* for *Praenomen*. The *most excellent* Theophilus, 'Friend of God.' I will scribe it in large letters like you write. Now the other two. *Nomen* and *cognomen*. What was Sophronios's full name?"
"Sophronios Demetrios Alkimopoulos."
"Demetrios. That is Greek. We need a Roman name. Latin."

The Golden Cord

Loukas showed him the new names as he wrote them in the book of *libertas*. "Since you are not keen on taking his name, how about this?"

"Perfect!"

The clerk finished writing the decree and closed the book.

"Now you are a freedman, what will you do?"

"There was a line in the play by Homer that plagues my heart, Loukas. The cyclops asked Odysseus why he was there. He said he traveled back to his wife. The cyclops said, 'Sail all that way for the sake of a woman? Disgraceful expedition! All that bother going to Phrygia! Disgraceful!'"

"You sound just like the cyclops!"

Boaz didn't laugh. "I wish to find Lais."

"Why?"

"Because before you, only Sophronios, Jachin, and Lais believed in me."

"I pray that you will find her in the first place you look."

"In all probability, I'll find her in the *last* place I look!"

They both laughed.

⌘ ⌘ ⌘

A fortnight later, when they sat down for the meal, Loukas brought out a package wrapped in plain wrappings.

"As we walked back from the theater a while back, I'm sure you saw the many signs on the shops in that area that had the word *sincere* on them. There are many pottery shops in Ephesus. Do you understand the meaning of the word *sincere*?"

"Is this a test?"

"No, it is just my way of making a point I wish to make."

"*Cere* is a word for wax; *sin* is a word for without."

"You see, my friend, there once was a problem in Ephesus. Potters created pots that were not perfect. They were cracked. No one would buy them. So the potters would fill the cracks with wax, and they then appeared brand new and flawless. When the customer got home and put the pottery on the flame to cook their meals, the wax melted. The pot fell apart. Therefore potters put up signs to let their

Liberation

customers know that they sold pots that were not cracked. *Sincere.* Without wax. They did this to show integrity of their product saying that there were no hidden flaws.

"Boaz, if anything, in our friendship, I have learned you are a sincere man. I know you will find what you're looking for. I sensed for a long time that you were ready to leave. That is your longing and desire. I wish to give you a parting gift."

Loukas handed the package to Boaz.

"I've taken the concept of the sincere pots and applied it to something I learned from a traveler I once healed of the gout. I made this for you."

Boaz carefully unwrapped it, not knowing what to expect. There on his lap was a vase.

"You put my vase back together!" No longer did it look hideous. Veins of shining silver laced throughout the vase where Loukas had pieced the shards together. "It's beautiful!"

"It is now a vessel fit for use. I described to Paulus what I was doing, and he said, 'Shall the thing formed say to him that formed it, why hast thou made me thus?' He quoted from the Holy Scriptures, where it equates God as the master potter. Treasure is found in earthen vessels, my friend. But sometimes the vessel must be broken to reveal what is inside. God puts our life back together, much like how the master potter repairs a vase.

"The silver beautifies the breakage and treats it as an important part of the vase's history. The broken vessel transforms into something more precious than it was before. Thus, the form draws attention to the *life* rather than the *look* of the vase."

"But where did you get the silver?"

Loukas looked toward the kitchen shelf, where his silver cup always set.

"Your beloved cup?" Boaz set the vase on the table and hugged Loukas. "You have been so good to me. How can I ever thank you?"

"Do not forsake what you learned about yourself. Write to me often."

⌘ ⌘ ⌘

The next morning, just as the sun first came over the mountains in the east, Boaz left. He sat tall on the bench of his wagon packed with all his earthly goods, herbs, medical instruments and supplies. Loukas insisted he take plenty of bread and honey with him.

The harbor of Ephesus provided ample anchorage for ships carrying goods to *Italia* and beyond. He would arrange passage and sail from Ephesus to *Aquileia*. It would take ten days if the weather was agreeable. The rest of the trip he would travel with his wagon over the Alps via a well-traveled road that led to the Rhenus River. From there, he'd secure a barge to take him north to Batavia. He would be careful to journey with others to assure safety as he traveled the western border of the Roman Empire.

Loukas prayed he would find Lais in the first place he looked. If he stayed here, he'd never find her. And if he never found her, any future would be lonely and incomplete.

43
CHAPTER

Battle

*The closer you are to power,
the harder it is to survive.*

— Scribonius Largus

BONNIA, NORTHERN SHORES OF GAUL

Gaius abandoned his plan to spend the winter at Gallia Lugdunensis. Instead, the Roman army approached the northern shore of Gaul near the town of Bonnia. Legio X, II Augusta, the IX Hispania, and XX Valerio consisted of more than two hundred thousand men. Arranged in battle array, they had marched almost a month from Mongontiacum in the cold muddy snow.

Jachin fumed the entire way.

Before that he waited impatiently for a month while Gaius paced around the castrum at Mongontiacum like a

The Golden Cord

mother duck followed by her ducklings, constantly complaining about family matters as attendants fawned over him. One trailing him carried a bundle of rods that symbolized Gaius's office and power, called the *fasces lictor*. Another lugged two bulky books, one under each arm. The books were named. One was called *Dagger*, the other was called *Sword*. Jachin assumed the books contained the names of those Gaius didn't like. It was a compelling impetus to remain in his favor. Jachin didn't want his name in either book.

The family matters involved more than the usual drama of most families. Apparently, a plot to assassinate the imperator surfaced. When Gaius discovered the conspiracy, he removed the consuls involved and broke their *fasces,* thus symbolically breaking their power. They were summarily executed.

It appeared that Lentulus Gaetulicus sought revenge because Galba replaced him and took command of training the legions. Gaetulicus conspired with Gaius's sisters. Some of the senators supported the subversion. It was important—Jachin supposed—that Gaius spent his time dealing with these family matters. It must be hard to live each day looking behind your back. Then again, at least he *had* a family.

Jachin was sure the name of Lentulus Gaetulicus was in one of those books. "Honorably fell on his sword," Gaius told him. Agrippina and Livilla were exiled to the Pontine Islands after first having to carry their coconspirator's ashes to Rome.

What did that matter to Jachin? He grew tired of waiting on Gaius. He'd wasted two summers imprisoned on the trireme, now he spent boring days marching on an empty stomach. And to what end? Gaius didn't seem to understand the urgency of the situation.

His own family matters needed attending. Amminus opted out of the battle, and apparently went to Rome to talk to the Senate, leaving him alone again. Amminus was all words and no show.

What mattered was that Jachin's passion to kill his father was about to be realized, and he fed on that idea

Battle

until it consumed him. Jachin often imagined the encounter. Caradoc would fall to his knees and beg for mercy at the point of Jachin's pugio. Of course, none would be given. *Would he honorably fall on his own sword? He's not an honorable man.* If the warrior fought, Jachin envisioned himself stronger and faster. He was younger than the old man. The daydreams all ended the same. His dream delivered—his father, dead.

As Jachin trudged over the snow-covered hills, sweat ran down the back of his neck and soaked his tunic. Frost formed on his five-day beard. He wore the same clothes every day. The chill of winter bit this far north, so today he wore his woolen brown cloak over his *Lorica Hamata*. Despite the cold, marching in line with the legionnaires in this heavy chainmail shirt exhausted him. The tunic identified him as different from the soldiers as chalk and cheese. His plaid pants marked him as foreign. His shield was borrowed from the Batavii. He painted a raven on the front like the shield he chose so long ago in Albion. He was not a legionnaire . . . yet.

His head pounded as his helmet flopped loosely with every footstep. He gained in strength what he had lost in weight. His muscles and sinews were hard and well defined.

Jachin's stomach rumbled. He had not eaten all day. Like the other soldiers, he frequently drank from a flask of vinegar mixed with myrrh. It deadened the pain of the march and the gnawing of his gut; however, the rumblings of his stomach were no match for the relentless thoughts of hunger centered more on the moment his pugio would meet its mark in Caradoc's heart.

What if someone else killed Caradoc? He chewed on that morsel as he clinched his jaw. *Good. Just tell me where he is, so I can desecrate the body.*

The trek was long, the day tiring, but Jachin put his chin forward and breathed deeply the anticipated victory. *One foot in front of the other. One step closer to my goal.*

Men from sixteen to forty-six summers old moved as one as they marched in a threefold line as far as he could see in either direction. He regarded none of them as friends. Why attach yourself to something temporary? Their length of service was twenty years, but Jachin didn't know anyone who had lived that long. The life of a legionnaire was brutal and dangerous. He didn't care.

He considered enrolling if it meant he could kill his father. The pay was decent. Conscripts were paid ten *assari* per day and their allotted share of the proceeds from stripped enemy goods, so at the end of their term of service, they could retire well and get married.

As a legionnaire, you were not permitted to marry. Yet there were plenty of camp followers eager to be with the soldiers. He couldn't say he wasn't tempted, but he had only ever had true love for just one girl. A kiss debt danced through the wheat field of his mind many times. He smiled for the first time that day. The visions always included Raena. His childhood friend drew amorous feelings from deep within him, ever since the day they first met in Albion.

Before the march, Jachin helped the men gather their gear. Soldiers put all they owned on their shoulders—shield, tents, everything. Baggage poles weighed more than 140 *librae*. Jachin didn't know how they could carry them on such long marches, but he found out when given his own kit to carry.

In contrast, centurions carried nothing but a vine-wood rod to beat laggards. Other than bawdy songs to keep cadence, thrashings from the vine staff was the only encouragement legionnaires got.

Finally, the army headed down from the hills. The air warmed and the going was easier. The trees thinned, and the ground was firmer.

Jachin wondered what the others thought about while marching. Did they run through their drills and commands? Recite poetry or sonnets? Pray? More likely they thought about their next drink or visit to the tabernas and brothels. *When would they arrive?*

Suddenly Jachin tasted the tang of salt water in the air. The smell was immediately recognizable to him. They had reached the sea. As the legions rounded the hill, the beach and ocean lay before them. Briny blue with splashes of white crests of constant crashing waves. This was *Bonnia*. Julius Caesar embarked on his expedition to Albion from this same beach over one hundred years ago. Now Gaius would finish the first Caesar's quest. He glanced around at the others. *Wouldn't standing in the open on the beach make them vulnerable to attack?* Jachin faltered in his step on the loose pebbles and sand.

Spread out before him, the majority of the Roman fleet was beached and pulled up above their tidal mark, ready to leave at high tide. Jachin would have to wait even longer for the troops to load before they crossed the sea and he stepped on the shore of his homeland to fulfill his desire. Most likely *Oceanus* was cleared of enemy ships and the path opened for the conquest on the farther shores.

Artillery was yet to be loaded. *Ballistae*, arranged in a straight line ready for inspection, stood like race horses eager to begin. These light ballistae, called "scorpions" for their sting, were mounted on carts. They would be used at the beginning of the fight to shoot shield-penetrating bolts. Shields stopped most arrows, but not these mighty stingers.

The larger ballistae flung stone balls that would take off limbs or heads but were more difficult to control. They were called "kicking mules" for that reason.

As the men marched to the beach, the call was made for battle array. The legionnaires arranged into nine lines deep all along the beach as though they were going to battle and not as if they were boarding the transport ships. Perhaps the imperator would have them set up camp for the night and wait to embark during the morning high tide. But for now they waited for his orders.

"I hope I come home with all my limbs," a soldier said. He was one of the zealots who preferred the front line. These men were Batavii. Others called them barbarians or *Bracati* for the braccae trousers they wore underneath their tunics. Jachin emulated these warriors by wearing the same chain-mail, but he did not put his hair in a Suebian topknot like they did when not wearing a helmet. It was like the style he wore as a child in the wheat field. To show themselves brave, these men cut themselves with their swords. It was with these men who Jachin marched and acquired his kit.

"Why do the devotees cut their arms?" Jachin asked one of the men.

"They sacrifice themselves to their god," was the reply.

Jachin learned that troops, like the sailors he lived with, were governed by their desires. He guessed these zealots' enthusiasm toward the gods was no different. He admired their bravery to covet the front of battle. Some said it was valiant. Others said it was because they were expendable. But the Batavii didn't look or act that way. They appeared fearless and able.

"Why do you fight for the Romans?" Jachin asked.

"Ha! I do it for the bragging rights. No one has conquered Britannia. One can dine off this victory for a long time."

"I'd rather dine off the fare at a brothel!" another soldier chimed in, and the men all laughed.

Jachin didn't find it amusing. "Regardless of how you honor the victory, it demands respect."

Jachin adjusted his cloak as the sun blazed on the beach. He wished the order would come to board the ships. While he waited, he was surprised that the men did not complain about the coming fight, with its certain wounds and pain. They complained about boredom, not battle.

"I go because I will not let my teammates down. We are part of a whole. I will die with my *contubernalae*."

"You go to die?" Jachin asked.

"All die someday. At least I get to choose how. I want my death to amount to something. For glory. For family. Honor—"

"For plunder!" another said.

The soldier turned to Jachin. "What is your reason, outsider?"

Without hesitation, Jachin said, "To kill my father."

⌘ ⌘ ⌘

"Hail, Caesar!"

Gaius galloped his white horse toward the line of soldiers. He'd named the horse, *Incitatus*. It was an excellent name. It meant "swift" or "at full gallop." Jachin called him "Speedy."

Gaius halted. Incitatus reared. The imperator appeared regal in his shiny helmet and golden breastplate armor. His

Battle

masked helm now sported bright-red plumage that matched the flowing cape draped behind him.

He lifted the mask and reviewed the troops. The imperator nodded and moved on a bit, looking the soldiers over with a careful eye. All were quiet. Only the crash of the waves and the cry of seagulls overhead broke the silence. Hoofprints washed away with the surf after each pause, as if he had never been there.

A centurion stood on the front left corner of each legion. His bright red horse-hair crest was positioned transversely on his *galea* helmet in order to direct the men as he led them into battle. On the left rear rank stood the *Tesserarius*. He kept the *tessera* tablet with the day's watchword written in the wax. It changed daily, and all legionnaires had to know it. If not, immediate death was their punishment.

On the extreme right in the columns' rear rank, the *Optio* dealt extreme consequences to prevent deserters. That is where Jachin was *supposed* to post. However, not being a legionnaire and always somewhat rebellious, he stood in the front with the brave Batavii.

"There should be drums and horns," Jachin said.

"We don't do drums, outsider. Drums are for dancing."

"Silence!" said another.

When he reached the end of the legions, Gaius lowered the mask and shaded his eyes like a salute. Then Incitatus pranced back along the beach. The imperator had not spoken a single word, but the men swelled their chests in pride and banged their spears and swords on their shields. It was as if he had honored them personally and individually before the gods.

Gaius galloped his steed to a rocky prominence to the right of the army. There he removed his galea and addressed his men. The words carried with the wind, and his speech was heard by all from this natural podium.

"We stand on the northern shore of Gaul. It is from here we embark to squelch tyranny. It is from this beach we make history."

The men all cheered.

"The high king of Britannia's army stands beyond the sea to greet us. He thinks Britannia controls the waters, yet the waves go back and forth on both shores. The high king is afraid to venture to our shores to fight. Therefore we go to him."

More cheers.

"Even so, the high king will wet his feet."

Laughter erupted from the legions.

"We will pluck him from his position, and he shall bow before me in Rome. Britannia will fall. There will be no constraint against our might!"

The army shouted as one, "*Romana victor!*"

Jachin stood quiet, keeping his questions to himself. He saw the pieces on only one side of the Latrunculi board of this battle. All he could think about was his goal. Caradoc may be ready for them, but the high king would not win this game. Jachin was certain of it.

Gaius dismounted, and several men accompanied him to a shallow flat-bottomed skiff. His general, Galba, in full armor, boarded the boat first. It appeared that Gaius would be rowed to a quintreme stationed on the horizon and wait there for the tide to bring all the legions with him to war. Perhaps more ships were beyond the horizon. Julius Caesar used eight hundred transports when he went to Albion.

After delivering the command, the men dismissed to set up camp. Jachin made his way through the ranks as the legionnaires, for the first time since they began the day's march, removed their packs, and ate a belated cold lunch, the *prandium*. To assuage his angst, Jachin walked along the beach by himself. Other soldiers were not as excited as he was. To them, it was just another battle. They had less to gain.

The late afternoon sky darkened. A fog drew in from the west.

Unable to ease his apprehension, Jachin joined the soldiers and ate with his fingers as did everyone else. He cut dried meat with his pugio and placed it on a hard bun—after checking for weevils. Water with honey for sweetener washed the small meal down. *How can an army fight with so little in their bellies?*

He sat by the *aquilifer*, who, even while eating, carried the legion's symbolic eagle standard. It was a death sen-

Battle

tence to lower the *Aquila*. If fallen in battle, another would pick up the eagle and hold it high for inspiration.

"This is not the time for campaign," he told Jachin. "Up to the tenth night of *Martius*, the seas are closed. It's way before that. Rumor has it that Britannia's king has amassed an immense army on the coast, ready to meet us if we survive the seas. Despite the bad timing, we will go, rough seas or not. Mark my word."

Jachin doubted Caradoc would set up the fight on the south coast. He was ruthless, not witless.

The trireme carrying the imperator disappeared over the horizon as the sun descended in the west. Jachin would be on a ship again, only this time he was very willing to do so. Last time he was a slave. Now he was a freedman.

"Aren't you the one who fares from Britannia?"

"Yes, I am eager to join the fight."

"You will fight against your own countrymen?"

Jachin took another bite. He didn't owe them an answer to his reasons.

"Sometimes ships don't make the crossing and have to turn back." The aquilifer said.

"I know the Great Green," Jachin said. "I will rally the troops. I will lead if it comes to that."

"You lead? Ha! You have no alliances, boy. No one will follow you."

Jachin raised his pugio. "They will fear my blade."

"We fear Caesar's penknife more."

Jachin lifted his chin. "Gaius *will* align with me."

CHAPTER 44

Betrayal

We spend our lives trying to lessen the dreaded disparities of living with unfulfilled desires.

— Scribonius Largus

The next morning couldn't come soon enough for Jachin. All night long he tossed and turned as he obsessed about his desires. He never dreamed about his hope at night, but it was his constant yearning. Every minute. Every thought. I will kill my father, even if it takes the whole Roman army to do so. They would board the ships today, sail across the Great Green, and attack his father's armies. Soon he would experience the exaltation when his pugio pierced the heart of the high king of Albion.

Jachin wanted to lead the charge, but Galba once again consigned him to the back of the legions by the Optio. Next to the man who would kill him if he deserted.

He expected the days' activities would begin just before dawn, as the tide was set for early morning. Soldiers dressed, packed their gear, and busily cooked breakfast.

Jachin plunged his hands into lukewarm water in an iron pot over the campfire and splashed the liquid on his face. He drew his fingers through his hair and tied it back with a leather thong. He squatted and warmed himself by the fire as dawn awoke. A gray storm rolled in from the north from Albion. Dark whirling clouds and a distinct rain curtain lay just beyond the horizon.

Silhouetted against the coming storm, a Roman quintreme sailed tight hauled on a reach. Then another. A trireme. Two ships. Only two. Perhaps others waited beyond. There were many on the beach, ready for the legions to load. At high tide, they would be on their way.

Jachin did all he could to maintain his composure. He felt like his sickened heart would burst out of his chest and race across Oceanus to defeat Caradoc by itself.

A trumpet sounded the men to arms. To muster? Not to board the transports? They claimed their gear and assembled into lines.

Not a legionnaire, Jachin had no line to join. Disregarding yet again where he was supposed to stand, he left his kit at the tent and struggled through the massive assemblage of legionnaires' closely knit shields. Their duty prevented access.

"What's going on? I can't see a thing!"

"Shush. *Tace fatue!*"

Working his way to the flank, Jachin pushed through to Vespasian. *Titus Flavius Vespasianus*, a big man, stood a head taller than the other soldiers. Strong. His alternately colored black and natural tan horse hair crest, running front to back of his galea, signified his position as *praetor*, commanding the army in the field. Aligned to command a legion someday, many held him in veneration. Information, rumors, and speculation passed through the ranks and always seemed to find its way to Vespasian. He would know what ensued.

Eagerly, Jachin approached the man.

Vespasian's heavy black eyebrows almost touched as if deep in thought.

"Why aren't we boarding the ships? Is it because of the storm on the sea?" Jachin implored the praetor.

"Gaius touches the sand," Vespasian said.

"Its high tide. The men are ready. What are we waiting for?" Jachin's voice pitched and cracked as his anxiety grew. "I can't see!"

"What do you want me to do about it? Put you on my shoulders like a child?"

"Just tell me what is going on!"

"They're building a platform on the beach, putting it together like a puzzle box."

"They must have planned this ahead of time. He's going to encourage us before we get on the transports! We sail today!" Jachin shouted.

"A group of soldiers carried a throne-like bench and positioned the chair before the troops on the platform and now, Imperator Gaius is climbing the steps. So I perceive you may be correct in your presumption of encouragement."

Immeasurable moments passed.

"What's taking so long?" If Galba heard him speaking this way, he would beat him for breaking ranks and talking. Jachin didn't care. He'd been flogged before.

"Another boat, smaller, pulled up on the beach. A chained man dressed in leggings—Britannii."

"What?!" That was all Jachin needed. They had a prisoner from Albion. "Who is it?" He pressed forward, pushed his way past Vespasian to the front. He drew his Pugio.

The legions remained unmoving and deathly quiet in their respective positions.

Gaius sat on an elaborate golden throne on the makeshift platform. A hooded man knelt on the platform before the elevated seat.

The hooded man spoke loudly in Jachin's home language.

"Most noble and excellent *Gaius Julius Caesar Augus-*

Betrayal

tus Germanicus and distinguished senators. Most gracious people of Rome," a translator shouted.

Jachin held his pugio to his chest, straining to hear the man.

". . . I surrender Albion."

"What?!"

The guards forced the man to stand and face the legions, his lowered head remained covered, his hands bound behind him. He has betrayed Albion? Without a fight? *Could this possibly be my father?*

The interpreter announced, "I give you the son of Cunobelinos, king of the Britons—the true king of Albion!"

A cheering wave rustled through the ranks.

Jachin raced ahead. "Murderer!"

Five legionnaires pounced and dragged Jachin to the ground.

Jachin's flailing pugio rang out, striking lorica segmentata.

The men shoved his arms to the sand. Held him there.

Straining against their hold, Jachin gripped his blade.

"My honorable, most valiant legions." The imperator stood and raised his hand. "As this beach connects to the shore of Britannia, it is as if you were there. Like a lake with two shores, he who owns the lake owns the sandy borders. I come before you to announce that your advance across the Oceanus ceases where you stand. This king of Britannia met us upon the troubled sea. Once aboard my ship, he crawled on his weak knees to surrender."

They dragged the captive from the platform.

"*No!*" Jachin screamed.

A soldier pushed his knee harder against his back.

"I drafted a dispatch extolling our victory to Rome, commanding the couriers to ride all the way to the Forum and the Senate with due haste. I directed them not to deliver the decree to anyone except the consuls in the temple of Mars. Before a full meeting of the Senate they will announce my triumph." Gaius paused.

The men roared.

"And to commemorate our success, I will build a monumental tower on this beachhead to aid the return of ships transporting men and supplies to our conquered land. This mighty *Pharos* will be lit nightly to direct our men and remind them of your victory!"

Again, a shout arose from the assembled army praising the planned lighthouse.

Jachin fiercely struggled to no avail.

Gaius pointed to the ships. "My quintreme and the surrendered Britannii vessel will go before us to Rome. We will bear these seashells in our victory triumph parade.

"And for your efforts and courage, I promise a donative of a hundred denarii for each man on this beach today. Go your ways," he said, "and be happy! Go. You are now wealthy men."

What have I just heard? Jachin stopped struggling in time to notice that several soldiers removed their helmets and placed shells in them.

"Did he say 'shells'? Are we supposed to pick up shells?" said the man with his knee in the small of Jachin's back.

"No, *morus*! You misunderstood him. He obviously meant for us to pick up our tents—those mollusk shells we live in—and go home."

Vespasian walked up to the men holding Jachin down. "You idiots, he meant the boats. *Concae. Seashells.* Didn't you see him point to the ships? We are to carry them back to Rome to commemorate our conquering—something even Julius Caesar could not accomplish. It is customary."

"Release me," Jachin said.

Vespasian leveled his gladius against Jachin's throat.

Jachin tightened. *Will they enslave me as well?*

"Put your blade away, Praetor," Gaius commanded. "We will return to Mongontiacum to celebrate. Thenceforth, on to Rome." Gaius reached out to Jachin and pulled him to his feet. Brushing sand off him, the imperator leaned in to Jachin, "Apologies, my contubernalis, but you will have to wait to get your revenge. Stay with me, and we will finish your *long-aimed blow*."

Gaius marched down the beach in the direction they had taken the prisoner. "Let the boy go. He can do no harm."

The legionnaires tore down the platform as rain pelleted

them. Thunder boomed overhead. Transports floated in the tide, anchored fast, not going anywhere.

The legions packed up and left.

Alone on the beach, Jachin seethed with rage, he rushed the waves, attacking the sea with his pugio.

45
CHAPTER

Reaction

Kindness without caution can lead to hurt.

— Scribonius Largus

"How can I be a brother-in-arms without combat?" Jachin said.

The trip back to Mongontiacum was tedious. The march made the thunder in the distance sound like a nagging echoing whisper.

Jachin adjusted his helmet. His head throbbed. It had rained ever since they left the beach a week ago. Jachin's tunic under his lorica hamata stayed constantly damp and smelled of mildew. They would march like this for another month before they arrived back to the castrum at Mongontiacum.

While marching, Jachin ruminated on what had occurred. It didn't seem to make any sense. The vinegar and myrrh he drank numbed his body to the march but couldn't numb his mind. Why hadn't Gaius told him about

Reaction

Caradoc beforehand? Surrendered? What would lead his father to do that if there was not something in it for him? Caradoc never yielded. Ever.

Gaius planned to kill the leader of Albion. In that Jachin more than agreed. Of course, the imperator would make an example of him first. That, Jachin didn't like. A waste of time. And how in Bel's name did they capture Caradoc? It all seemed odd. Jachin shook the rain from his helmet.

Although proud to have met this "Little Boots" man who commanded all of Rome, Jachin struggled over the significance of the day's events. Gaius was more than imperator— he was Jachin's friend.

Questioning the actions of his friend bothered him. It seemed like betrayal. *Why didn't he let me in on what was going down?* He trusted the imperator. Gaius was very intent in telling Jachin his life story. Why did he do that if not to gain friendship and trust? This man was very wise. Astute in controlling things his way. He had much to inventory in his bag of wiles.

Gaius knew the land. He grew up here with his father. *He is not a fool.* His childhood playground wasn't a battle zone, yet, Gaius had learned much about warfare. He walked among the legions as a child. He observed the soldiers and saw what worked and what didn't. Whereas Gaius hated the name Caligula, it showed fondness and gained him access to the secrets of the soldiers and their leaders. So it confused Jachin as to why they had spent so much time preparing for invasion, only to pick up shells and go back home.

Jachin contrasted his own life to that of the imperator's. There was much to compare. Except this one thing: everyone *loved* Gaius. But did they follow him out of love, or respect? Or fear? "They all loved Germanicus," he had said. Gaius's father was an ideal father, but just like Jachin when his mother was killed, the perfect life of Gaius was ripped out from under him when his father died. He said the whole world cried.

Both men dealt with harm in their own way. *Even a future Imperator can be abused. He's my friend!*

Jachin grimaced.

When together, Gaius and he shared many stories of their pain. No one else was privy to Gaius's private horrors. And only Gaius knew Jachin's anguish. He never shared the trauma of his family with anyone else. He never revealed the physical abuse he endured and overcame while a slave on the ship for two years—not even to his uncle Amminus. There were things as a child that only Boaz knew. Experiences they shared. But there were things he had never even let Boaz in on. Regrets and secret sins.

Sometimes he wondered if anyone would find resonance with him if these memories and thoughts were spoken aloud. He once imagined Gaius might be that person.

"Show no emotion at all. That is what you learn," Gaius told him. Gaius could remain cold and uncaring even when he poisoned his brother and his sister. In that Jachin connected with Gaius. But to show no emotion? That was not for Jachin. He was furious, and, lately, he didn't care who saw it.

For the last two days along the road, people tossed flowers and accolades at the soldiers as they passed their village. Had they heard of the victory? Generous Gaius tossed coins in return. They would have been happy with just a wave from the imperator.

Jachin knew Gaius's gifts were with purpose. Gaius planned every act. The coins had slogans on them. This is how he published his image—like a farmer would brand his livestock. Jachin saw this as good. On the other hand, Gaius humiliated these peasants by flaunting his power in their face. Once Gaius said, "One day I will wear pearl slippers." That was not the goal of a giving man.

One more step. Another after another. Jachin plodded away from the end of his journey. Wagons trailed the prodigious parade. One of the closed wagons held his target: his father.

The legionnaire in front of him chucked mud-clods back at Jachin from his muck covered caligae as they marched. Jachin suspected he did so on purpose. Each step of the man in front of him revealed hobnails in the shape of a stick figure of a man. "How creative," Jachin said through clinched teeth. "Every step he takes is on the back of his enemy." The constant muck flinging did not help his disposition, and the last thing he wanted to do was to waste his pent-up anger on some hobnailed lackey who only marched to the tune of duty. For now, he let it slide.

Jachin slogged slower until a Batavii horse guard cantered up alongside him. He paid the man five assari to ride one of the empty horses.

Once on the mare, Jachin's anger turned inward. *I should've killed him when in Albion. But I was too young. Now I am at the whim of others' purposes.* His angst struggled to stay buried. It seeped out like salty stinging sweat from every pore.

Gaius said he'd have his chance. What did he call it? A long-aimed blow? It was a promise made between contubernales. It couldn't come soon enough. Kill his father. Then what? He hadn't thought that far ahead. That soldier had asked him about fighting his own countrymen. What if others died? If his goal was achieved, it didn't matter. Afterward, he guessed he'd go back to Albion with his uncle, Amminus. Somehow it didn't seem like home anymore and he wasn't sure he would even be welcomed. All he loved about the land was gone. Raena? A girl like her was most likely betrothed to another long ago. No future there.

Jachin spurred his mount on.

As they rode, Jachin conversed with the Batavii auxiliary soldiers. They knew of a place close by where someone had built a hothouse by a cool stream. Jachin liked the idea of a dry sauna, so when the group swerved off the road to a path leading south, he followed. What could the Optio do to him if he joined them? Didn't matter.

Expecting this bath to be a short distance, he soon became discouraged as the shadows lengthened and the sun sank slowly below the horizon.

Beside the road, sat a man. He was not dressed like a beggar, yet the soldiers one by one steered their horses to the other side of the path to avoid him and kept going.

Jachin slowed and when the man imploringly held his hand out to him, Jachin grabbed the man's arm, and pulled him up behind him on the saddle. If he headed down the same road, why not help?

The man was no sooner on the horse when Jachin smelled the sickening smell of barley brew. The man was drunk.

"I's Mogurix. Can youse take mesh ta ma homes?"

What could Jachin do? Push him off?

Mogurix pointed into the woods. "It's only a short way off the path that-a-ways."

Not wanting to cause trouble in front of his new friends, Jachin chose to take the man to his home and then gallop back to the path to catch up with the troop headed to the bath-house in the woods. Jachin turned right.

He was truthful. His farm was not far from the path. And a meager farm it was. Only a pig and an emaciated cow stood in a muddy makeshift pen next to a ramshackle mud-brick and straw house.

Dismounting, Mogurix pulled on Jachin's leg. "Youse must come in, and I will give you something for your trouble."

Jachin rolled his eyes, took off his helmet, and followed to the doorway of a small uneven and pitiable cabin.

"Youse can meet my loverly wife."

Jachin doubted he had a wife, or that she was lovely.

They entered the small two-room hut, and in the gray light stood a table. Two chairs—one with a shorted leg leaned absurdly to one side.

A petite woman, dark tangled hair, retrieved a flask of the same putrid ale the man reeked of and swigged a swallow down. She offered the flask to Jachin.

Jachin smiled and put it to his lips, planning not to taste the awful grog, but make a show at politeness.

The farmer pushed the flask up. "Drink!" A gob slithered down Jachin's throat. He gagged and coughed.

Mogurix laughed the loud chortle of a drunkard.

"Sit."

Jachin flopped into the wobbly chair.

Sitting across from Jachin, Mogurix immediately began reciting stories of battle. His tale was nauseating as he described a hideous event of his own making. The man had worked for the Romans to clear the Teutonburg forest of the enemy Germanii. Only he wandered from the battle and came upon the place where the enemy's children and their mothers were kept safe while their fathers fought. He told Jachin of the cries of the women and children as he had slit their throats. All of them.

Mogurix sobbed. "I have been such a bad man. I have done horrors."

Jachin didn't know how to respond. He glanced to the wife who smiled a two-tooth grin.

"Thank you for your hospitality. I must take my leave and return to my unit," Jachin said.

The man laid his hand on Jachin's shoulder and urged him to sit again.

"I have to get something," the man stammered and left to the other room. Perhaps their sleeping quarters?

A chicken flew from the room.

Jachin asked Mogurix' wife, "Is he always like this?"

"Oh yes. He is a terrible man."

"How do you stay with a horrible man like that?"

She took another drink from the flask. "I stay to remain alive is all."

Somehow, deep in the recesses of his mind, that made sense to Jachin. His Matrona could have said the same words. He felt sorry for this woman. Perhaps he should help her.

At that moment the drunken man returned carrying a nocked bow. He pointed the arrow at Jachin and said, "Ah-ha! I finally caught you. You are the one who has been sleeping with my wife!"

Jachin reached for his pugio, and Mogurix rushed him, knocking him to the floor. The wobbly chair fell to pieces. The man aimed the arrow at Jachin's chest.

"Tell him I didn't do anything. I didn't do anything."

The woman kept quiet, holding the chicken.

Jachin ran his hand through his locks and closed his eyes. Was the man reliving the massacre in the Teutonburg forest? He waited for his chance to counter this attack.

Mogurix relaxed the arrow and slumped to the floor. Passed out limp like a dead goose.

This man was nothing but a drunk. Jachin picked up his pugio. He thought about killing the man but hesitated when the wife dropped the chicken and ran to her husband.

Jachin wasted no time and scurried out the hut. He jumped on to his horse and raced down the path to rejoin his troop—sputtering and spitting—the fowl taste of the ale lingering on his tongue. "That was *not* my father."

He didn't slow down until he reached the Batavii warriors. They were inside the makeshift bathhouse. It was like the roundhouses back in Albion. Tightly thatched roof. Smoke spewed from the top. Only a small leather flap of a door faced a slow flowing stream. It appeared about a stone's throw to the cool water. Jachin reveled in the idea of the hot sauna and invigorating quick plunge into the creek.

A man stopped him. He did not have a *Suebian* topknot on his head like the Batavii soldiers.

"You have to wait until the group finishes," he said in a thick accent.

Jachin sat on a stump. Several such seats scattered about the clearing like standing stones. Apparently placed for waiting guests.

"Woo-hoo!"

Jachin's head jerked up.

The doorway flap flew aside. Men *and* women fled from the heated hut. Steam rose from their bodies as they ran naked to the cool waters below.

Jachin felt his cheeks heat up as he turned his head. He had never seen a woman without clothing.

Once again he felt like he was in a place he didn't belong.

⌘ ⌘ ⌘

Once back in Mongontiacum, Jachin ate with the Batavii soldiers at their tents outside the fort. He regretted opting out of the steam bath but felt too embarrassed to join the men. They were mostly a bunch of simple farmers and cattle herders known for their excellent horsemanship. A trivial tribe who learned the hard way that it is better to join your enemy than be destroyed by them. In that they survived. Like the woman at the drunk's house. Just like him.

They were more than that, Jachin conceded. These warriors were not fainthearted lads who jested their way off a bully's fence like he did.

Robust men, they wore simple braccae and plaid tunics. Some donned the lorica hamata like Jachin wore. A customary armor for horsemen or auxiliary. Not as heavy, and the chain like rings were easy to maneuver in. He felt somewhat conspicuous with his long dark hair. All the Batavii were either red or golden haired with long locks emanating from the base of their helmets and flowing down their backs.

A friendly group. They appeared to have no fear and celebrated in the fact that they did not have to pay taxes to Mother Rome. They owed no man anything, but honor and loyalty, and they did not confer that easily. Apparently, a talent most valued was that these men could cross rivers in full armor on horseback. They had mastered the arduous skill growing up along the Rhenus River.

Jachin felt comfortable with this group and grew to know some of them well as they traveled together along the road the last few days. Seeing one in their altogether nakedness makes for easy company. At ease in their midst, he concealed his obsession to kill his father. He even found that he could laugh. The only thing he didn't like about them was their penchant for water. Jachin still feared the water. He never learned to swim.

CHAPTER 46

Raena

Focus all the scattered rays of your thoughts upon one place or thing and you will shine the brightest.

— Scribonius Largus

GLESTINGA—WEST COAST OF ALBION

"It hardly rains anymore."

"Your showers of complaint come often enough."

"Do I really need to learn this stuff? Manners. Deportment. Poise. Languages."

"You don't take to learning easily, do you, Raena?" Joseph said.

Dressed in an Eastern-style robe and large blue belt, this bearded Jewish man was the one her mother said was a friend. Originally from Arimathea, he now made his home here in the west of Albion. It was perhaps due to his influence that the town of Glestinga prospered. Still a tin merchant, he was a stringent teacher in his spare time.

"How will this help me fight in the coming battles?"

"Depends on which battle you are fighting," said Mara.

It had been two years since Raena arrived in the west. Not long after her arrival, Mara showed up with her infant daughter, seeking asylum. She said she was Caradoc's wife, but Raena wasn't sure it was official. Gladys was now over two summers old and a pain in the neck—always in the way and quick to say no to anything and everything asked of her. Things with Caradoc grew worse, and the people suffered for it—even here on the west coast of Albion.

Raena constantly fumed that she was away from the fight. For some reason, she thought she could make a difference if she was in the middle of things, instead of out here on the edge of nowhere.

Joseph gathered the study scrolls.

"Gladys loves to learn," Mara said, taking the scrolls from Joseph. She placed them on the shelf.

Raena stood.

"Where are you going, my dear?" Joseph asked.

Picking up her sword and strapping it around her waist, Raena said, "I am not a child like Gladys. I'm going to practice. Someone around here has to defend against evil."

"You see evil everywhere." With a look of disgust, Mara grabbed her daughter's hand. "Come, Gladys. We can play outside by the large oak tree."

You people don't know anything, Raena thought. She would be critical of evil no matter who it was or how impossible it might seem to oppose. Although she had learned much in her time here, her studies bored her. She pulled her green tunic down and adjusted the sword belt. Her braccae and heavy boots made her look more like a young man than a princess in training.

"Sit down. You are not finished for the day," Joseph said.

"I've learned enough."

"It is *not* enough. It's like a fishing net with holes so large that the fish slip through. You must tighten the chords to grasp the game."

"Hmmph." Raena sat with a huff. "I'm tired of this game."

"You are correct. Sometimes you have to change games. Every learning is not from teachers. I have a task for you. I

The Golden Cord

want you to go with me into the small village of Godney by the Mendip Hills. It's a small hamlet situated on the river Brue, five leagues northwest of Glestinga."

"I know where Godney is."

"We will travel there today and walk through the town. I want you to observe."

"Famine and pestilence is all there would be to look upon. The people are vile."

"Are you the judge of evil now?"

Raena glared at Joseph.

"Yes, you hate evil. I see it in your eyes all the time. But what makes a man evil? Is Caradoc evil? Am I evil? Are you evil? Your heart has grown cold, my dear. It needs broken. This town is not evil, Raena. The people there are not evil. Caradoc cut off supplies and aid because the West has not joined him. Disease and hunger are the result. I want you to bring food to the poor there."

"Why me?"

"You must learn heart service."

"I don't want to do it."

"You must work out your education, my young warrior child—my *bachur*. You will go, want to or not, or your mother will hear of it."

⌘ ⌘ ⌘

"Hey, I saw it first!" a ragamuffin boy wearing torn and muddy braccae yelled. Probably four or five summer's old, his hair was crowded with lice. He grabbed at the piece of bread Raena offered.

Joseph held back and let Raena work.

"Haven't eaten in three days," a toothless woman with the same louse infested and matted hair said. Raena handed her the loaf of bread and an apple.

"How will she eat it with no teeth?" Raena asked the Tinman.

He didn't answer.

The woman sat in the mud of the alley with the boy and tore the morsel, giving the largest part to her child. She cupped water from a pool in the mud next to her and gave her son a drink.

"Left over rain water?"

"More likely it came from someone throwing out their dishwater. The boy doesn't seem to mind," Joseph said.

Raena gave the woman more bread. "When I was younger, I played in the rain and splashed in the puddles."

"Rain seldom comes here," Joseph said.

"Do you think this child ever plays?"

"I doubt it. It's probably a full time task to find food."

"What is your name?" Raena asked the woman.

"Why do you want to know?"

"I wish to talk to you."

"Her name is Kennocha, and I'm Brann."

Raena saw the stress in their faces and felt a chill. They had no cloaks and the barefoot boy didn't even have a shirt. "Where do you live? Do you have a home?"

"Our troubles started in the vineyard," Kennocha said with a mouth full of bread. "My husband yelled at the wine god Bacchus because the grapes withered and stank. When the vile odor crept into the house, I did all I could to clean and wash it away." There was bitterness in her voice. "Then came disease."

Raena saw the pustules and scabs on the woman's face and hands. The boy was sweating, even in the cool alley. He had a faint rash on his chest. Brann had the malady also.

"It was just past two weeks later that my husband died. We took to the streets to live—thrown out of our home by the chieftain who confiscated our possessions."

"I don't like the dark," the boy said.

"Why is that, Brann?"

"It's cold!"

"Don't you have a cloak?" The boy just glared at her. *Apparently not.*

A loud cry came from the street. "The land is ruined! The city is fallen!"

Brann dropped his bread. He quickly retrieved the morsel, brushed dirt off and took another bite. An old man passed them calling out his declaration of doom. Soiled with what appeared to be dirt and mud, the completely bald man rubbed at the tell-tale scars on his face.

"We call him Ancient One. He's the oldest of our elders and the only one still living."

Children chased the man, mocking him by calling him names. Some threw small rocks and sticks at him.

"Your tongues provoke the gods' eyes!" the Ancient One said to his pursuers. The children stopped, stood quietly for a moment, and laughed scornfully at him.

The Ancient One continued on his way with the mob of children chasing behind.

"He's not the only one affected by the disease in this town, but he is one of the few who has survived."

Raena shivered as she stepped into the causeway, into the sun. "The city is full of odd sorts."

Brann and his mother followed.

There was a man in the square with a placard on his shoulders that read "Woe to my soul" in big red Latin letters. Raena was amazed at how far Rome's influence had traveled. His face was painted white, perhaps to hide the pustules and scabs, or maybe it was some sort of salve to ease the discomfort of his sores. The sight of this man declaring his woe was comical.

In her musings, Raena giggled.

"You laughin' at the gods, little one?" the Ancient One said as he walked up to her.

"No, sir. I'd never speak ill of the gods." She stepped back a few paces, afraid she would catch the disease these people carried.

The man stared, then reached out and with an almost sane touch brushed back a tangled lock of dark hair from her face. It was like a touch of tender mercy, strange coming from such a crazy old man. He then closed his eyes tightly and gritted his teeth. Transfixed by the scars on his face, she overlooked the filthiness of his body.

"May the gods bless you. It shall be well with you, child. You shall eat the fruit of your doings," he declared, face all contorted and flushed as if in great pain. She wondered if he meant the fruit on her cart. She gave him an apple and a piece of bread.

He had called her "child." She didn't think of herself as a child. She was more than that. She stretched herself taller and put her shoulders back proudly.

"Thank you for your blessing, sir," she said. It seemed like the right thing to say.

He nodded and walked on.

Raena shaded her eyes from the brightness of the sun as she viewed the evil all around her, all the illness, all the wickedness that had come to this town. People walked with no intent to go anywhere; carts abandoned in the street, wheels stolen to sell the metal rims to get food.

She grimaced as she saw a man with no hands go by.

"Look, Mother, a thief!" said the little boy now standing behind her.

"Be quiet, boy," Kennocha said. "We're *all* thieves."

"I'm not." He began to cry as they walked. Little Brann was innocent—in his own eyes, anyway.

The town walls were mostly rubble.

"The valley beyond was once lush green with trees and golden fields ripe for the harvest," Joseph said.

She pictured men cutting wheat and bundling it on wagons. A memory of her mother's vineyard with its dark leaves and fragrant fruit filled her with a brief sense of peace. These fields had been that way here at one time. Not now.

Ahead was another group of children throwing rocks at the ancient man.

Joseph pulled Raena back into the shadows to observe like she was instructed.

Over to the left, three men stood watching the abuse. One slender man slouched near a broken down fence.

"He's the chieftain of this town. Or once was," Joseph said, referring to the slender man. "Nels is his name. He led fifty men. Now he hasn't even one man of war to his charge. The only thing left to him is his mantle of sackcloth and a *crisping* pin to fasten it. It declares his rank, which was probably why no one has taken it from him, or why he's not yet traded it."

Raena nodded. She wondered how Joseph was so knowledgeable about the people in the village.

The Golden Cord

"The man standing next to Nels is the town druid," Joseph said.

"It seems ironic that he would watch such sport and not chase the children away." Raena put her hand to her mouth. She had not moved to help him either.

"The third man leaning against the post had once been an honorable man. A strong warrior."

Honorable or not, he was now gaunt. A torn red girdle held up his now oversized trousers. Sores marked his face. *He must have the disease.* She winced.

They left the cart and moved on. People rushed to grab what was left of the food.

Their stench nauseated her. Raena wanted to get away. She followed Joseph as they journeyed to the crumbling town wall. Finding footing to walk through the rubble's rocks made a tinkling sound as they scattered in front of her.

"The sound reminds me of my mother. Oh, beautiful mother. She wears the prettiest of ornaments, chains and bracelets. Her jewelry clinked together when she would dance around the house in such joy. At times she'd ask me to dance, too, and gave me a headband and earrings to wear. The sound was wonderful."

Behind her huffed the little boy as if the climb was too much for him. He was so frail.

"You don't need to follow me. We are out of bread," Raena said as she pulled him up to where she was.

The boy smiled and picked up a stick. "Take that!"

He pretended to fight an unseen enemy. She saw him as if he was now no longer a small child. He was a mighty man, fighting the great enemy with his sword. You could almost see the glory that should have, would have, been his one day as a great warrior of Albion.

The boy turned in a mock feint, lunged forward, stabbed the air, and then lost his footing on the wall. Before Raena could scarce gasp air in dismay, he fell over the wall to the ground below.

His cries now silent, Raena carefully made her way down to where he lay and gently picked little Brann into her arms. He cried out in pain. He had several abrasions

Raena

on his knees and arms. Raena gave him to his mother who came running when she heard her son's cries. The woman's sunken eyes communicated hurt, not gratitude. They ambled off together, the mother scolding her son for being so careless.

Picking up the stick Brann had used as a sword, Raena walked along the wall, stopping at the place where the gate once stood. There she sat and wept.

Joseph sat quietly next to her.

It began to rain.

"I understand what you mean by not judging. Who in this town was evil? The pestilence and disease? The little boy, Brann? His mother? The Ancient One? The boys who chased him? Those who stood and didn't help—including me?"

"I think you have seen enough, Raena. Let us depart."

Quietly, head lowered, Raena left the town behind her. She wept out her sorrows as she made her way back to Glestinga. Joseph walked with her, his arm around her shoulders.

With her head on his chest, she sobbed. "What can we do?"

Joseph set her at arm's length and looked into her eyes. "Dear, you may beat down the fruit from an evil tree until you are exhausted. Yet the root remains. If that is not tended, the tree will only produce more bad fruit. You will never progress in your endeavor to rid the world of evil unless you get to the bottom of it."

Intending to break her heart and make it tender, this experience only hardened her toward Caradoc. She felt ashamed she had stood while the children attacked the Ancient One. Raena determined she would stand still no longer. She left Glestinga for the east the next day.

That spring Caradoc burned the entire town of Godney.

CHAPTER 47

Employ

Begin where you are and go on from there.

— Scribonius Largus

NOVAESIUM, GAUL

"Theophilus," Boaz said. "Call me Theophilus."
It was the name he used to remain incognito on his travels. No one accepted a Jewish doctor from Albion.

A soldier of the Nineteenth Legion, who currently occupied the castrum, arrived with a bellyache. Boaz palpated the man's abdomen, searching for clues as to his discomfort. So far, all he could ascertain was that the soldier didn't like marching.

Over the last year or so, Boaz amassed a huge following and developed a successful medical practice at the *valetudinarian* in Novaesium. He continued free of the drink and no longer thought much about it. As he considered the

Employ

past, he couldn't believe that was him. He was thankful that someone cared enough about him to help him. Loukus was a faithful friend.

The Roman hospital was the first and largest of its kind in the empire's eastern border. Initially intended for the treatment of sick slaves and soldiers, it allowed Boaz to provide medical and surgical care to the Batavii villagers and travelers as well. Boaz flourished in the land of Lais's people on the west side of the Rhenus. Wealth, and a retinue of paid servants who attended to him, allowed Boaz a life of ease. He had things he had never pursued.

Built on a natural terrace, the castrum was protected in the South by the *Erft* River. The fort lay along that minor river and the village north of the castrum. Boaz loved to listen to the water as it flowed slowly on its way to the Rhenus and eventually to the sea. Despite all the soldiers, or maybe because of them, the area was at peace. He never felt afraid, either in the village, the castrum, or when he traveled.

"Here. Take one teaspoon of this tonic three times a day until you are relieved of your discomfort." Boaz handed the man a potent purgative, knowing that he would not soon be back with more complaints.

The hospital, situated southwest of the *principia*, was initially made of wood, but recently was rebuilt in stone and marble. It consisted of dozens of small rooms, divided by hallways and in the center, a magnificent open herb garden. Many medicinal herbs like *henbane* and *centaury* could be found there. Other herbs were ones he had brought with him in Sophronios's old wagon or collected in his travels north through Gaul.

He loved helping others. Rome rewarded his challenging work by bidding him to apply his trade in the *caserma dei gladiatori* in the capitol city. He liked the idea of working with gladiators, but he wasn't ready to leave the valetudinarian yet. He still had not located Lais.

She had told him she was of the Batavii near the mouth of the Rhenus River. Boaz had traveled to *Agrippinensis* searching for her, and there heard of the need for a medicus at the valetudinarian downstream at Novaesium in the fertile valley of the Lippe on the west bank of the Rhenus.

He didn't get much time off, but when he did, he searched for his lost love. She said, "Come find me." So that's what he tried to do. He met many from nearby villages that knew her but hadn't seen her since she left so long ago. They described her as gregarious and a stranger to no one. Yes, that was Lais. The fires that sparked her to come home, were long out and the villages rebuilt in other locations. Her father was dead and her mother's whereabouts was unknown.

Boaz washed his hands and decided his own stomach needed attention. He gathered his hat, a pocket-sized scroll, and headed toward the center of town to find something to eat. The sun at the horizon projected colors of gold, salmon, and violet on the marble colonnades of the buildings. In the middle of the castrum was the forum, behind it, the *praetorium*, where the general resided and next to that, the *quaestorium* for the supply officer. Boaz had seen both in the valetudinarian for various heat-related illnesses.

Tonight, the weather was cool, and the officer's quarters were dark. They must all be at the taberna. There was a time that Boaz might have joined them, but he no longer had any desire to drink. He walked past the baths that were under repair with wooden scaffolding surrounding three sides of the building. The smell of the incense and herbs reminded him of Carura and their natural steam baths. Sophronios liked the calamine, but Boaz preferred the lavender. He missed his former master.

He finally arrived at his destination. A restaurant of no consequence. He liked the food there, and it was always quiet. Less likely to run into a patient. He chose his usual table in the back and ordered some lemon water and a meat pie.

Loukus said he'd pray for him. Boaz prayed, "God, I am tired. I have looked so long. I have done all on my own. Help me. Bring Lais and I together again."

"Are you the medicus looking for the young lady?"

Boaz choked on his pie. He looked up to see a gray-haired elderly lady. Stooped over with a twisted back, she held a cane in her right hand that quaked in rhythm to her shaking head.

"I know where she is."

CHAPTER 48

Bridge

*Love's pure bond is always unexpected,
but never a surprise.*

— Scribonius Largus

Lais strummed the lyre and placed it on the shelf with the others. She moved the Phrygian pipes higher so that the children could not reach them. For some reason, they loved to blow into the pipes and make as much noise as possible. She appreciated their enthusiasm but not their disordered notes. The dogs in town howled their dissent as well.

During the mornings she taught singing and lyre-playing to the older children of her rich patrons. In the afternoon, the ten-year-olds arrived to learn grammar and rhetoric. Most of the time she felt more like a baby sitter than a *grammat-*

icus trying to extract moral behavior out of restless and privileged boys.

Only a few girls came to the *Scholae*. Lais had some private tutoring jobs in their homes. She barely made enough money to pay rent on her classroom and feed herself. She lived with her grandmother, a little old lady who worked baking meat pies and pastries for a local pub. Lais helped her at home and loved the company. In the evenings, they worked together on a tapestry they were weaving. She never went out and had no social life to speak of.

One night a week she taught music to the legionnaires of merit who achieved the privilege to use the education center during their leisure time. Many of them worked on fight training in the open hall. Those who either enjoyed music or hoped for a career as an officer took her classes. Men sought her out due to her ability to speak the local language as well as Latin and Greek. The way they ogled her she thought that her language and musical skills was not the only reason they came to her class. When they became bored or rowdy, she would have one of the better students play the lyre and she would teach the men to dance. She had never seen a more clumsy and dull class as the one tonight. She was glad they had fun but felt relieved when they departed.

She tucked a wisp of blonde hair back up under the braid that wrapped around her head like a crown. She wore it up like that because she thought it made her look more matronly and therefore due more respect. She never took any gruff from the students. Her wit and sternness tempered with her easy smile would always disarm the aggressor.

Lais sang softly an old tune. "It would be good to have a bear for a friend . . ."

". . . to be able to walk silent in the forest with him," a voice finished.

Lais jumped and turned to see a man silhouetted in the doorway. He stepped into the candle-lit room.

They stood unmoving and looked at each other for what seemed forever.

"*Boaz*!" Lais ran to him and fell into his arms. They

Bridge

kissed. When they finally came up for air she said, "You found me!"

"I have been looking for you forever. I nearly gave up. Loukas said I would find you the first place I looked, and you were right here under my nose the entire time."

"Sit. Tell me what you have been up to."

"I have been practicing at the valetudinarian here in Novaesium."

"No way!" She punched him on the arm. "Really? Why haven't I heard about you?"

"I have been using the name Theophilus."

"I heard of Theophilus. I didn't know it was you."

"I searched everywhere for you. No one knew where you were. I even checked the brothels. I never thought to look here at the School of the Arts."

"The brothels? Why on earth would you look there?"

Boaz bowed his head and blushed. "Didymus said that you were a hetaera."

Lais laughed.

"You never said anything to me about what you did in Carura or where you lived. I never knew. It's all right. I don't mind."

"I am not, nor have I ever been a hetaera." She sat back on her chair. "I was only a maid at the brothel. When it collapsed during the earthquake, I was out buying eggs. Sadly, they all died, but I survived."

"So you are not a hetaera?"

She leaned in to him and smiled. "Are you disappointed?"

"There is nothing you could say or do, either now or in the past, that would cause me disappointment. Except for maybe leaving again."

"I'm so sorry about that, Boaz. I was scared."

"Scared?"

"Yes, scared of what happened to my family in Batavia. But mostly scared of my feelings for you."

"How would that make you afraid?"

"I was afraid that if I loved you, I would lose you."

"So you left? That doesn't make any sense."

"I was just tidying up. Will you be so kind as to walk me

home? It isn't far. I would like for you to meet my grandmother, Diona Granni."

"I think I met her."

They walked lightheartedly down the cobblestoned street, hand in hand, singing a song of love.

⌘ ⌘ ⌘

Two days later, Boaz, wearing his petasos, waited by the pier on the river Rhenus. He bartered with a patient to rent a small sail boat. The old man showed him how to raise the sail and to work the rudder. He offered advice on how to tack and catch the wind, but Boaz wasn't listening. How hard could it be?

"Don't forget my gout medicine," the old fisherman said.

"I have something much better. I will bring the black torpedo sting-ray first thing tomorrow morning."

"What will I do with a fish? Do I eat it?"

"You place your foot on the live ray and the repeated shocks will numb the pain."

"*Torpere?*"

"Yes, numb. You'll like it!"

Lais arrived carrying a basket and a blanket. "I brought some dried fish and bread for our lunch."

The two men laughed. "What did I say?" she asked.

"Nothing, we were just talking about fish." The fisherman waved goodbye and hobbled up to his shack.

Lais scrunched up her nose when she saw the old wooden boat on the sandbar. "Is this where we will picnic?"

"No, now that spring is in the air, we are going sailing to a place up river where there is a beautiful copse of trees and wild flowers that remind me of you. It is just beyond the bend."

"Boaz, I cannot swim."

"It'll be all right. Get in."

Boaz held the boat steady as Lais stepped into the small craft. She set the basket in the center and took a seat up front. Boaz grasped the sail line and pushed the craft into the widest part of the slow-moving river, so it would be easy for him to board. When ankle deep he leapt into the boat

Bridge

and started on an easy reach across the water. The sun warmed his back.

Lais relaxed and looked to the sky, closed her eyes and let her hair blow in the breeze.

Boaz turned the rudder to catch the wind. "This is the life."

Lais screamed when the boat lurched with a gust of wind, and Boaz laughed. He was happy. He was with Lais. His practice at the valetudinarian prospered. Soldiers and villagers alike respected him. Soon he would be appointed *Primum sane medicorum esse*. As hospital manager he would be able to make a real difference in the health of those he served.

He planned to take Lais to the copse for a meal and sit under the long bridge across the river. The man who rented him the boat told him that when the carts left the city after the long day at the market they passed along the bridge. The way it was built with gaps in the planking caused the wheels of the traveling carts to thump. Under the bridge, he said, it sounded like a heartbeat coming louder with each beat as the vehicle came closer. He said it was a splendid place to kiss a girl. Boaz planned to not only kiss Lais, he intended to ask for her hand in marriage.

The wind was perfect and pushed the boat at a pleasant speed upwind. When they reached the bend in the river, the wind shifted direction and came from upriver. Boaz tacked hard to control the canvas sheet as the wind flipped the sail around. The line raced through his fingers and burnt his palms. He held on, but the sail jibed again. He shifted his position to the other side of the boat. The craft heeled till the mast almost touched the water as the boat leaned and pirouetted before the wind, dumping them into the water. The boat turned upside down.

Boaz scissor-kicked his legs. The red lateen sail obstructed his path to the surface. Trapped. The current pushed against him, pressing him into the submerged sail. The more he kicked and struggled, the more he became entangled in the sheet and lines. He didn't know which way was up, so he let himself float. Grabbing the sheet, he strained to drag himself out of the enfolded canvas. Eventually finding an opening, he emerged, gasping for air. He reached for the edge of the upturned boat.

His first thought was for Lais. Panting, he searched the water around the boat. All he saw was the lunch basket and its contents floating haphazardly downstream.

"Bo—"

Boaz swam around the boat to find Lais reaching for the edge of the craft. Suddenly she slipped under the water. Boaz grabbed a line and dove. He grasped her hand and swam to the top of the water with her in tow.

She coughed.

"Are you . . . are you all right?"

She nodded.

Barely recovered himself, he made sure she was safe. He handed her the line and placed his heels against the upturned hull of the craft and clutched the mainsail line that lay over the hull from the other side. He pulled and felt the line tighten. The boat dipped toward him. He tugged again with all his might until his muscles ached, hauling the rope close to his chest. As the boat began to right itself, he walked up the side. When the sail and mast drew free of the water across from him, the boat slapped hard into position. Jumping into the boat, he wrenched the boom and turned it into the wind until the sail luffed. He tied the boom to the rail and pulled the rudder up. It was just luck, but it worked.

Lais latched on to the line, treading water.

"Hold tight! I'll haul you in!" He reached over the rail, grasped her hand, and pulled her into the boat. She flopped on top of him like a landed fish, shivering and cold. They lay there breathing hard and holding on to each other.

"When did you learn to sail?"

"This morning."

"Did you learn what to do if it turns over?"

"No."

"Well, you did a splendid job. You are truly a prince of ingenuity!" She hugged him again. "Thank you for saving us."

He blushed.

"Sit up. I have something for you," Lais said. She reached

Bridge

around Boaz where he lay. He thought she attempted to hug him. Instead, she lifted her hand and planted Boaz's soaked hat on his head. She tied the leather thongs under his chin.

"Now all you need is a flower in your bonnet."

Boaz laughed. "Well, all is not lost!"

"What happened?" she asked. "How did you save us?"

"At first I could only think of you. I was afraid you would drown."

"Well, I didn't."

"I got mad because no one saw us in trouble or came to help. My arms hurt so bad and were so tired, but I couldn't let us die. I set my mind to it, and knew I had to get on that boat. I put all my strength into the effort, and I'm not sure where it came from, but I pulled myself up. My relief of getting in the boat mixed with exhaustion and fear for you was a feeling I will not soon forget. I thought I'd lost you! And there you were—still hanging on the line."

She hugged him.

"Do you think you can get us to shore now without dumping us into the river again?

"I will do my best. Look, there's the bridge!" Boaz sailed the boat to the shore under the sturdy bridge that spanned the river. He lowered the sail and helped Lais out of the boat. They pulled it up on the shore until it was secure. To make sure, he tied a line around a tree.

"We are soaked to the bone!" Her loose green chiton clung to her body, held at the waist with a braided red cord. She lifted her long skirt and wrung water from it. "I wish we still had the blanket and the basket with our lunch. I guess it is out of the question to expect you to make a fire."

"I do have my flint, so consider it done." He gathered some driftwood and soon had a decent fire going on the beach under the bridge. They sat together on the sand, leaning against a log and warmed themselves.

"There sure is a lot of traffic on the bridge."

Boaz put a finger to her lips. "Listen."

Quietly sitting together under the bridge, they heard it. *Thump-thump*. Then again, *Thump-thump*. It grew louder and closer.

Lais wrapped her arms around Boaz. "What is it?"

He gazed into her eyes. "It is my heart."

He brushed a string of her wet hair behind her ear then cradled her face in his hands. He lightly kissed her soft lips.

"Will you become my wife?"

She squeezed him. "I thought you'd never ask! Yes. A thousand times YES!"

Lais curled up against him and laid her head on his chest. "You're right. I can hear your heart. It sounds happy."

After a long while, she fell asleep in his arms. Boaz smiled. In his mind he could hear Sophronios saying, "Well done."

49
CHAPTER

Reputation

Take one more step. You never know what future lies beyond the bend.

— Scribonius Largus

AD 41—Mongontiacum

Unexpectedly, Boaz received a summons to meet with the imperator at the castrum in Mongontiacum, thirty leagues south of Novaesium. For some reason, they encouraged him to bring his wagon and his implements of surgery. There must be a profound need since they bade him to make haste. Maybe it had something to do with Gaius's gladiator school in Rome.

"I want you to come with me."
"Of course." Lais placed the plate of Diona Granni's

The Golden Cord

meat pies in front of him and kissed him on the forehead. "Will we be gone long?"

"I hope not. I have my writing to do, and there are the patients at the valetudinarian."

"I think they can make do until you return. It will be fun!" She sat down to join Boaz for breakfast. Her grandmother baked pies in the kitchen.

"We need a Covenant of Engagement," Boaz said, talking quickly as if the wedding would take place tomorrow. "And I need a dowry to give to your family. Then the washing . . . uh, not in the river. Do we have to give offerings for fertility at a temple somewhere? When is the next full moon? Gifts. Got to get gifts for the guests. Songs. Music. Is there a bard connected to the school? What will we say during the ceremony? Does it have to last three days? What about the feast afterward? Isn't it supposed to last a week? Where will we live? At the hospital? No, I will have a new house built. It will be magnificent!" Boaz took a breath and a bite of his pie.

"We don't need all that," Lais said. "A simple hand-fasting will do. Just as long as I can wear a garland of wild flowers."

Diona Granni entered the room with some more food. She started to sit down but stopped as if she forgot something. "Wait here, you two. I'll be right back."

Boaz looked at Lais.

She shrugged.

The lively old woman brought out a tapestry and handed it to her granddaughter.

Lais held it up. "It's lovely!"

Boaz could only see the backside of the tapestry. "Looks kinda confusing . . . and twisted to me."

"Silly, you are looking at your past." She turned it around and showed the beautiful stitching. Boaz immediately recognized it. A scene with trees, the deer, and a nightingale. A man, and a woman with golden hair, reclined on a blanket. Beautiful yellow flowers grew around them. It was the scene from their encounter long ago in Carura.

He sighed. "Perfect."

⌘ ⌘ ⌘

Boaz brushed the dirt of travel from his tunic and stepped politely into the imposing tent of the imperator in Mongontiacum

He removed his petasos and bowed to the imperator, who sat in front of a game board. Chin in hand. Elbow on one knee.

He repeated his often-told salutation. "I am called Theophilus."

"So, Theophilus, you must be the famous medicus who trained in Phrygia, but now plies his trade at our legionary station north of here. You come well recommended."

Boaz stroked his beard and nodded. "Thank you, Imperator. I do what I can—saving lives and stamping out disease."

The imperator laughed. "Please, call me Gaius. I think we shall be friends."

Boaz nodded again. He would find out what the man needed and be on his way never to cross paths with him again. He had more important tasks to do than to entertain royalty. He would have to rescue Lais from the market or she might buy more flower seedlings for the new house he promised her. He observed the imperator for signs of sickness, disease or hurt. None.

"I see you have a game board. I know that game," Boaz said.

"Excellent! Let's play."

Boaz hesitated.

"Please, join me."

He took the seat offered him across from Gaius at the white stone table to play Latrunculi. Immediately a servant offered him a cup filled with cool water.

"Should I win or lose to an Imperator?" he asked.

"I always play to win. I suggest you do the same."

Gaius positioned the pieces on the checkered table and sat back as if sizing up his opponent. "I generally play with a master at this game. Perhaps you would rather play him."

Gaius called a guard over to him. "Rescue my contubernalis from his training and bring him here."

Boaz picked up two stones and put one in each hand

behind his back. "Choose a side. White stone chooses color and goes first."

Gaius chose the right.

Boaz produced the hand and opened his fist. The stone was white.

"Excellent! I shall be white."

Boaz replaced the stones, careful to not reveal that he had a white stone in each hand. Gaius could not have lost.

The imperator made the first move. Boaz counter-moved in such a way as to make it look like the game could go either way to a victor. Yet, he found himself not willing to provoke this important man. He was not here to play a game. Boaz hoped he would get to the point of this called meeting.

"Tell you what, Medicus, if I win, you will join me for a gladiator show I am arranging."

Was this the purpose of his visit? There must be more to it than just a contest. This man was a master at using others and would trap him into attending a spectacle that he had no desire to see. It was like being caught between two Latrunculi pieces. He would lose. If he won, surely this man would take what he wanted anyway. If he lost. He lost more than a game. His patients depended upon him. He needed to get back to the valetudinarian. More importantly, he would lose several days of precious preparation for his marriage to his love, Lais. He didn't trust this man.

Gaius leaned in and the game turned to the imperator's advantage.

"Ha! I win. Now I will proclaim a show for the day after tomorrow. We will have oration contests and cut out the tongue of the losers. We will have feats of skill. And animals. Yes, many animal acts in the theater would be delightful. The people will like that. And the main attraction? A gladiatorial combat!" Gaius stood.

"Apologies, your greatness. No occasion to wait for your Latrunculi expert?"

"Oh no. Definitely no more time. Need to prepare for the games. You will be there sitting next to me."

Boaz shrugged his shoulders and bowed. "I will be pleased to attend your celebration, although I know not what you are celebrating. Nor why you summoned me here."

"I need a true physician to verify an important death."

"Don't you have your own physicians?"

He embraced Boaz's face with his hands and examined him. "None like *you*."

After Gaius dismissed him, a somewhat confused Boaz made his way to the market.

CHAPTER 50

Battle Lines

Confidence is an herb of slow growth,
yet carries much potency.

— Scribonius Largus

"You sent for me?"

"Yes, contubernalis."

Jachin pushed the hair from his eyes. "What may I do for you, Gaius?"

"I intended for you to play against a Latrunculi master extraordinaire from Phrygia. A medicus at the valatudinarium in Novaesium. He reminded me of *you*—only different."

Since he had returned to Mongontiacum, Jachin was suspicious of anything Gaius said. He was done with cordial behavior. The imperator controlled all the game pieces and Jachin didn't care for his ambiguity. It sometimes seemed Gaius was playing *him*. With a sideways grin, Jachin said, "I don't see any experts here."

"Have a seat, boy. We shall see who's an *expert*."

Battle Lines

Something about the position of the winning pieces seemed familiar. He couldn't put his finger on it. Jachin sat at the table and moved the objects on the board to begin the game. He arranged the glass pieces like a centurion setting up two sides of a battle. He distributed the troops evenly on the edges of the world. The battlefield was white. Squares showed the sections to be conquered. His confidence was high. He had learned there was no fear in this battle. And he was skilled at this clash of stones. Some might call him the best.

This was different than when he and his brother played the game—there were two kings now. Each had their armies. Each ready for conquest of the lands that separated them. They would move throughout the squares without fear of injury.

Moving a stone forward, Jachin took the first advance into the game. He had not always grasped the skill of this game—he moved more by what felt right—what his gut told him to do. He moved without thinking. Boaz was the only one who could beat him, though. His brother always thought too much. It would take him forever to move.

However, by observation and practice, trying out new moves and tactics, Jachin learned the strategy without knowing it. Over time he learned the name of the actions, but just like learning Latin, he didn't like to let on that he knew. It worked to his advantage to play dumb. By doing so, others underestimated his skill in this game of soldiers.

The pieces moved in this first phase were called *Ordinarius*. The glass stones, or *calculi*, were moved in a fixed order depending on the tactics of the player. Jachin preferred to move more at random. Or so he liked the opponent to think so. Gaius called Jachin's moves *vagus*. With a simple ploy, he attempted to draw Jachin into a trap. He would not fall for it.

The goal was to attack and surround the enemy king or at best remove all his opponents' pieces and win. Jachin changed up his tactics every game he played just to throw his enemy off.

Troops were moved on all sides around him. No captures were made.

Attempting to outdo Gaius's defense, Jachin recognized that the imperator used it to set up the final attack. An assault that Jachin would foil.

Imagination filled his thoughts. They fought on the plains, the mountains, and once Jachin pictured them warring in a wheat field. Playing Latrunculi always took him to good places where he didn't have to think. He only needed to outdo his enemy. Anticipate his moves, and counter with skill.

Jachin surprised Gaius with two pieces surrounding one of his. How had he not seen it coming? The imperator was visionless, despite his vanity. "*Alligatus*," Jachin called out, referring to the trapped piece. He removed it from the gameboard. "Your soldier is dead and with that pitiful move of the stone, the game is over."

He rose to leave, but Gaius moved another piece to an empty square. Jachin stood looking at the board. He moved another stone to surround that piece knowing Gaius could not counter.

At no time did Gaius show fear. Jachin liked that. He moved in for another capture. "As I said before, the game is as good as finished," Jachin said, meaning every move would be countered till none were left but his. He could see ahead that far.

The imperator smiled. Moved again.

Jachin feigned that he did not see the attempted set up. He moved an unnecessary piece to a square that made it unconquerable. Stones in such a position are powerless—unable to be moved. They call them *incites*. Gaius often talked of the people of Rome who were beggars as *incite*—those for whom there remains no hope of advancing farther. And it was what Gaius named those who could not enhance his own progress. He had no use for them.

"Only give honor to those who can give you honor," Gaius said.

Another stone was placed by Jachin between two of Gaius's pieces.

"Suicide, huh?" Gaius moved again.

Jachin's next move was a multiple capture. He had Gaius running in all directions. Jachin shook his hand, rattling the horde of pieces he had taken. *I have held the wolf by the ears.*

"You play like a child," Jachin taunted. He pulled the ear again.

"Yes, but what soldier has not retreated before me in the real world?"

"I retreat only to seize and swindle my pursuer." Jachin returned to his seat.

"The spoils go to the victor," Gaius said.

"Why do you hold pieces back? Surrender them to my might. If not, I will divide your forces and encircle your king."

Gaius reclined with his arms behind his head. "You can if you will, but you will never defeat me."

"I already have."

Gaius's king fled to the back row as Jachin chased him ruthlessly. To make him suffer, he attacked the other pieces until only the king was left. Then he trapped him and made him *incite*.

"The battle of the brigands is complete," Jachin said.

Leaning on his fist, Gaius studied the board. "What piece is not lost when *you* are its player?" he asked, as he picked up Jachin's king and studied it.

"The king."

Gaius held the game piece in front of Jachin's face. "Do you want to fight the king of Albion in the gladiator ring?"

"You're playing with me."

"Indeed I am not. Your blade will taste blood if you choose to do so."

"I do so choose."

"You played your game well, my loyal contubernalis." The imperator waved his hand in dismissal. "Sleep well tonight, for two days from now is recompense for all your sorrow."

Proud of his victory, Jachin bowed before his Imperator and apparently still a friend. Gaius never gave up a game on purpose. Jachin turned to leave the tent, knowing he had bested a better man. He smiled. Two more days he would do it again.

A moment later, a legionnaire stood in the doorway

blocking Jachin's exit. With him, stood a thin man wearing an oversized white toga. He shuffled a rolled papyrus in his hands.

"Yes, yes. What is it?"

Jachin stepped to the side to let the man in.

"I am sent from the Senate."

"The Consuls give me nothing but headache." Gaius took the parchment from him. "Just tell me what the dispatch says, *morus*."

The messenger bowed. "Rome requires the illustrious Imperator Gaius to come without delay. You are to receive special honors and distinctions."

"Special honors or something else?" Gaius said. He doubled his fist around the Latrunculi king, and his breath quickened. He paced. "I will return home only to those who love me. To the equestrians and my people. Not to the senators. They will name me *precepts divine*. I will be a god!"

He tossed the parchment across the room. "This subpoena disappoints me. Tell them I'm on my way—and so is this." Gaius slapped his sword at his belt—behavior not exhibited by his friend before.

Gaius studied the board morosely, then smiled as he set the king piece on the board. He looked at the messenger and then to Jachin. "You are all *Incite*, my friend. You are all *Incite*."

Shoving the table over, Gaius stormed out of the tent.

CHAPTER 51

Gladiators

Death of a guide never shortens the journey.

— Scribonius Largus

AD 41—Theater at Mongontiacum

Jachin sat on the central dais with those of importance. Gaius must truly think highly of him as a friend. His chair was to the right of the imperator.

The amphitheater in Mongontiacum had a diameter of 300 *pes* by 141 *pes*. The grandest Roman theater north of the Alps. Jachin smiled at the idea of over ten thousand eyewitnesses to his long-aimed blow. That is what Gaius called his journey's quest. It was accurate. It fit. The tyrant would finally pay for his wrongs.

Gaius planned other contests to occur throughout the day. Chariots, acrobats, and who cared what else. Jachin focused his thoughts on the fight ahead. He approached it like a Latrunculi game. He would not lose. He never lost.

The Golden Cord

Servants handed each attendee a basket of fruit as they entered the stands. Where it all came from, Jachin had no idea.

Once the crowd filled the seats, Gaius came into the area on a golden chariot wearing his gilded helm and face mask. He threw gifts of bread and bundles of expensive cloth into the theater seats. During the feasting, Gaius gave his share of the ceremonial dinner to a man in the stands opposite him, making a big show of the gesture as the imperator carried the meal to the villager, who ate like a starved hog. The crowd loved the benevolence of their leader.

To the left of Gaius was another empty seat. *Reserved for some dignitary?*

The shows began in the early morning hours and lasted until well past sundown. Gaius would light up the whole city for the main show. He introduced exotic animals that Jachin had never seen before—ostriches, horned gazelles, and panthers. Condemned men entered the arena to slay the beasts. The crowd delighted in the panthers, as the criminals didn't stand a chance. The more blood, the merrier the mob grew. They threw their leftover meals at the animals to provoke their rage.

After the panthers consumed their fill, a line of legionnaires entered the ring with their shields and herded the beasts to a waiting cage. While slaves cleared the sand of body parts and raked it smooth, Jachin begged his departure and went to the holding area to prepare for his time in the theater.

⌘ ⌘ ⌘

"Here, put this on!" Galba said as Jachin entered the back rooms of the theater.

"I thought I was supposed to fight as a fisherman."

"Gaius wants you to look like a Roman legionnaire."

Rather than the usual costume of the *retiarius*, who wore only a loincloth, no armor, and carried a trident and net, Jachin wore a leather cuirass over his red tunic. Galba helped him fasten the breastplate and backplate together. "Not too tight, I have to be able to move quickly."

Gladiators

Galba tightened the straps even more. "You don't want it so relaxed that it lets in a blade to your ribs now do you?"

Jachin grumbled.

As the leader of Gaius's legions helped fasten the apron straps and pendants showing below his belt, he coached Jachin on the correct things to say when he took the field of battle.

"I know, I know. I practiced the lines all night!"

"You did not sleep?"

Jachin gave Galba a mean look, strapped his pugio in its worn rabbit-skin sheath on his belt, and arranged the *Paenula* cloak about his shoulders. "Stop lecturing me and hand me my shield." He chose his own round shield that he acquired from the Batavii instead of the usual *scutum*. Green with a black raven on the front, it felt comfortable on his arm.

Galba handed him a trident and placed a helmet on his head. "You're on your own, boy." He left Jachin alone. "Don't mess this up."

Once readied, Jachin stood by the chariots to view the extravaganza until he could settle his heart's aim in battle.

While *Procurators dromi* smoothed blood-soaked sand, impromptu oratorical competitions were held on a dais erected in front of the imperator, who would choose the winner and the punishment for those who failed. The loser might have to erase his writings in the wax tablet with his tongue, or perhaps be beaten with heated rods. They carried one unfortunate orator off the field on a one-wheeled cart. Evidently, he did not do well.

The seat next to Gaius on his left was now occupied by a man in a white stola. He looked familiar. But with the dark beard, and at this distance, he couldn't place where he knew him from.

"Throw him in the Rhenus! Even my horse writes better poetry," Gaius said to rousing laughter from the crowd.

Gaius introduced a pair of dark-skinned *pugiles*. Boxing didn't concern Jachin, although he loved to see a good brawl.

Into the sand strode a strikingly vigorous man who towered over the others. Jachin had only met one other man that impressive—back in the Nemeton in Albion when a giant brought Jachin's dead mother for cremation. That was a long time ago. They introduced the big man as *hippomania*. Horse-madness? That was odd.

Most Gladiators were huge heavy-set men with powerful forearms and shoulders. This man's stature made others appear as children. He was doubtless a soldier condemned for insubordination. Jachin would bet on him if he had the denarii to do so. He fought well—his practiced and refined technique showed years of training. Maybe he wasn't a soldier after all.

Next, an effeminate class of gladiators in yellow tunics, fought as *retiarius tunicatus*. They put on an exhibition fight where there were no injuries. Their flamboyant and exaggerated manor reminded Jachin of a mummer's show he once saw when the *Morta Columbarium* docked at a port in northern Hispania. Those masked and silent actors staged a grand performance like this one.

Jachin's forehead beaded with sweat. He stepped back from the sunshine and positioned himself within spitting distance of the Faction supporting the chariot team waiting their turn in the arena. They were to race after his climactic fight against Caradoc. The *Aurigatores* all seemed relaxed, jesting with each other and making bets on the outcome of the demonstrations.

Jachin wished he wasn't so anxious. He thought it was due to his restless night of little sleep. Curious, and perhaps to ease his tension, he asked the men next to him what their jobs were.

"*Sparsores,*" said the head charioteer assistant. "I clean the chariots while *Armentari* groom the matched teams of horses after the race."

"You don't participate in the race?" Jachin asked.

"No, brave master, that is for the *aurigae*—the drivers."

"And the men greasing the wheels? What are they called?"

"*Conditores.*"

They also told him of the *Moratores* who sat back and gambled as they drank sour wine and ate biscuits full of

Gladiators

what smelled like leaks and garlic. These Moratores held the most dangerous job of all—grabbing the horses at the end of the race. To Jachin their name sounded like the Latin word for "death." Perhaps fitting to their occupation. Jachin guessed many of them did not live long lives.

Other soldiers who attended to riots in the stands also paced in the dark waiting area, eager to get in a few of their own licks. It was a beehive of activity behind the scenes.

Jachin stood with his back against the wall, one caligae up behind him to balance. He set the trident against the wall and fingered the hilt of his pugio.

The crowd booed as a group of Germanii prisoners-of-war armed with short javelins entered the arena. Trick riding archers cut them down one at a time. Death was an amusement.

Jachin listened to the cheering crowd. He delighted in the idea of hearing accolades when he cut Caradoc's throat. The people would not understand how much this meant to him.

"Five to three odds," a charioteer said.

Were they betting on his fight? There were no odds. Jachin was certain he would be victorious. If the pugilist seemed skilled, wait until the audience saw Jachin's moves. He had trained his whole life for this moment. *I will kill my father. If I kill him, he will no longer hurt me or anyone else. He will no longer control my life. I will be myself again. And I can do whatever I please with no fear of penalty.*

Pushing against the doorframe, Jachin stretched his legs. *With every ounce of my flesh I hate him. I am ready. I will make him suffer. No, I will just end it. But if I prolong his death, I will have more joy. And give him more chances to stop me.*

He stood, feet shoulder width apart. *Yes, just go straight out and do the things Gaius requested me to say and kill him straightway.*

He bent down to touch one foot and then the other. *No mercy. Ha, he never showed any. A man must pay for his crimes. His hurt. His evil. I cannot believe they captured him without a fight.*

Lifting his hands above his head, he clasped them and stretched again. *Doesn't matter. Today, my father will be no more, and I will be free.*

Torches were lit all around the theater's edges as the sun began its decline. The flickering flames sent shadows into the holding area. He paced like a caged lion waiting to be released to his prey.

The fanfare began. Gaius promised a gallant ending to his celebration today. Britannia now belonged to Rome. The imperator would milk this moment to solidify his role as the person responsible for Britannia's surrender. Jachin would give him that—as long as it achieved his goal.

Jachin could not hear Gaius give the rest of the pronouncement because of the thundering crowd's cheers. Didn't matter. Jachin adjusted his helmet, grabbed the trident, and stepped into the arena.

CHAPTER 52

Accomplishment

*Success is not measured by achievement,
but by the overwhelming opposition
you have encountered and prevailed.*

— Scribonius Largus

"If one of them should fall, I want you—what was your name again?"

"Theophilus."
"Hmm, I thought it might be something else. Very well, Theophilus, I want you to run to the arena and care for the injured gladiator. If the man is dead, you are to proclaim it."
Boaz took his leave from the imperator and made his way to the stalls where the gladiators waited. *He brought me all this way for this? Is he testing me, or using me?*

⌘ ⌘ ⌘

The high king of Albion stood in the center of the arena, facing the imperator. His helm covered his entire face except for two small eyeholes.

Jachin eyed his opponent standing in the middle of the battlefield. Unlike the *secutor*, whose helmet was smooth and round on top, a figure of a fish adorned this dome, giving the king of Albion the look of a Gaul. A loincloth—held up with a thick leather belt—right arm guard, and right leg gaiter were his only other protection. Once a slave on a ship, where they called him "Little Fish," it humored Jachin to think that they would dress Caradoc this way.

"Kill the cowardly king of Britannia!" Gaius proclaimed.

"Kill him!" The crowd echoed the imperator.

The horns sounded.

Then quiet.

That was Jachin's cue.

He gripped the trident in his right hand, his shield in the other. He bowed his head, tapped the trident to his chest, and jogged into the arena.

His opponent stood still.

The full-face mask bothered Jachin. He wanted to see his father's fearful eyes. Blood dropped from the man's chin. Had he already been beaten?

As he faced Caradoc, Jachin raised the trident and pointed it to the man's face.

"I seek not you, I seek a fish," Jachin shouted so that the crowd heard every word.

A gladius in the man's motionless hand dropped to the sand.

Jachin thrusted the three-pronged spear and his opponent stepped back. "You are the fish plucked from the sea. Why do you run from me, oh Britannia?"

It was another line Gaius had commanded. Jachin had other things he *wanted* to say.

Another attack. This blow glanced off the shoulder guard as the man turned away.

Why doesn't he defend himself?

A blow to the helmet from Jachin's trident again provoked no counter punch.

Accomplishment

"Fight me, Fish!" Jachin roared. Furiously, he knocked the man to the ground with his shield.

The crowd held their breath.

Jachin tossed his shield to the sand and pressed forward. Played with him. Pricking him with the tips of the three-pronged trident, Jachin cursed Britannia, per Gaius's directive. As he did, two legionnaires advanced. Why? He didn't need them.

They took the trident from him and gave Jachin a net that he adroitly tossed over his enemy.

Caught in the web, the fish turned away from his attacker to face the imperator.

"I'll not stab you in the back. Turn and look me in the eye!" Jachin vowed to shove the pugio into his father's gut as he had forced Jachin to do to his mother. He stepped around the man to get in place, drew the pugio and raised it for the crowd to see.

The other gladiator squirmed out of the net like a fish escaping the fisherman.

Cheers erupted from the grandstand seats.

Not waiting a moment longer, Jachin lunged for the blow. "*This is for Matrona and Boaz!*"

Suddenly the guards yanked Jachin back.

Gaius stood and nocked an arrow into a proffered bow.

"No!" Jachin screamed.

An arrow struck the king of Albion in the left shoulder.

"Our imperator, the magnificent conqueror!" the crowd screamed.

Another arrow.

The arrow hit its mark, and the man staggered to his knees.

"He's mine!" Jachin wrenched from his restraint and raced forward. Ducked. A third arrow flew past him, barely missing him but hitting the fish.

The man collapsed into the bloody sand.

Falling to his knees next to the man, Jachin removed the fish-masked helm of his enemy. Jachin faltered.

Bloodlust screams came from the crowd around him. Flower petals drifted down from above.

Horns blared.

Chariots with banners circled Jachin as he stood. Arms limp at his side.

The imperator betrayed me!

"Uncle Amminus?"

"Do you have anything else to say, Fisherman?" Gaius yelled.

Gaius commanded Jachin to say that the imperator alone was to be given the credit for the kill . . . and for conquering Britannia. *Gaius paraded an imposter as Caradoc? He fooled everyone. He fooled* me.

The chariots rounded in front of him.

He only told me of his pain—of his childhood—to pull me into his web of deceit. To use me in this charade. Jachin sheathed the pugio and recovered his trident and shield.

A cruel laugh from Gaius in the stands sounded just like his father's disdainful laughter.

"Amminus, what have I done?" Jachin waited for the next chariot to pass. Through the cloud of dust, he flung the trident. Gaius ducked as a guard lunged forward and caught the three-pronged spear in his shield. He tossed it aside, drew his sword, and attacked Jachin.

Twisting low, and with a sudden thrust, Jachin stabbed the man in the stomach with his pugio while more guards advanced.

"You want my life too?" Jachin raised his blade countering the attack.

Cheers and praise for Gaius echoed from the crowd.

While the battle in the blood-sand raged, the big pugilist ran to the field. Pushing through the gladiators and the guards, he easily knocked them aside.

The crowd immediately hushed—waiting to see what would happen when the large man lifted Amminus, daring anyone to stop him. Then he carried Amminus's body, walking through astonished guards to the holding cells.

Savage cries, entwined with merciless epitaphs and cackling laughter, filled the arena.

Amid dust and din, Jachin darted through the distracted guards for the exit.

53
CHAPTER

Surgery

Bitterness is a prolonged piercing arrow.
Removal can kill or heal.

— Scribonius Largus

"Quick! Move him to the board. No. Not here. Into the shadows. Careful! No one must see. Gaius wants him dead. I do not." Whoever this man was, Boaz would do what he could to give him longer days.

The gigantic pugilist carried Amminus to the wooden table in the back room of the long *postscaenium* where the gladiators dressed, and where Boaz waited reluctantly to pronounce the man's demise. Boaz immediately recognized his uncle, despite his bruised and battered face. He never in a *mille* years expected that. *Can't react. Must respond.*

The Golden Cord

The physician held a lighted lamp to examine his patient. The man barely breathed. Quick gasps followed by a period of quietness. Three arrows pierced the body. One shallow. Left side. Just above the heart in his thick chest muscles. Another pierced his gut through his belt. The extent of that wound not readily obvious. The last projectile deep into the upper right thigh near the bend of his leg. Boaz wasn't certain he would live.

"Arrows can't kill. They only wound," the pugilist said.

"You are mistaken, my friend. Arrows kill in many various ways and will keep killing long after the barb is removed."

Boaz unrolled Sophronios's satchel and arranged the instruments on the table. He chose a vial from another leather pouch on his belt and poured a portion of the contents slowly into the unconscious man's mouth. "This will ease your pain," he said.

The breathing calmed.

Slowly, Boaz examined each wound. His teacher's voice echoed in his head telling him the anatomy and proper measures to ensure success. Over and over, Sophronios made him repeat the medical procedures for arrow removal, first by rote, then by practice on a pig's hindquarters obtained from the butcher. Afterward, they roasted the pork for their supper.

"Think of an arrow like a long-distance punch." Boaz realized now it was his voice, his advice, and not his former master's words. "An arrow is narrow in its effect, but if it were to strike a major blood vessel or vital organ, it could initiate fatal hemorrhage within moments before you even realize you have been hit. A projectile to the heart leads to sudden demise of the victim."

"They wear me down, but do not take me out of the fight," the large man said. "An annoyance to be sure, I have been hit many times and kept going. I don't think they are significant in battle. So many arrows fly from so many bows that hit so many useless targets. It is a waste of arrows. It is as if they are trying to kill the ground around you.

"You keep moving or be mowed down. Standing still,

Surgery

hiding or running. Either way, you might get hit. Better to keep moving."

"Do you always talk this much?"

"Not always."

"How do you fight with arrows poking out of you?"

"I'd pull it out and fight till I'm dead."

"And dead you may well be. Here hold this." Boaz handed the fighter a wad of bandages. "You must keep in mind that being wounded is not inconsequential. Hold still, this is going to hurt." He took the arrow extractor and inserted it into the wound of Aminius's chest. He grasped the arrow point and pulled it out. There was a rush of air, which meant the lung underneath the muscle was compromised. Amminus groaned.

Boaz threw the arrow across the room where it smacked against the stone wall. He briskly rubbed the wound and surrounding skin with a vinegar solution.

Amminus coughed up blood. Bright pink foaming blood oozed from the wound and a sucking sound emanated from the opening as he tried to breathe.

"I need something to seal the wound." Boaz took his scalpel and incised one of the hanging leather *baltea* from the pugilist's *cingulum militare*. The giant jumped back but Boaz was too quick. The wide leather belt with unadorned baltea protected the gladiator's waistline from being injured in the games.

Boaz poured vinegar on the leather piece and placed it over the wound. The hissing stopped and Amminus immediately breathed deeper. Amminus's face went from pale white to pink.

"Next time warn me if you plan to come after me with that knife again."

"There was no time. I needed to seal the wound," Boaz said. "Quick, put the gauze on top of this leather patch and hold it while I bind it. We have other wounds to attend."

"I did not expect that to happen. You plugged the hole and stopped the air from escaping!"

"If left in place, an arrowhead may result in substantial disability. A wound that is easily dismissed might lead to certain death at a time when you are celebrating your bravery." Boaz wiped his forehead. "If you remove the arrow, one might cause even more problems as you witnessed."

"Then why remove it? Just break off the shaft."

"A lodged projectile of any kind exacerbates the wound when you move, lacerating the tissues adjacent to the foreign body. Even if you have the strength and fortitude to keep fighting, any movement on your part that involves the area of the arrow would bring not only more pain, but further laceration and harm. And, my new friend, if the arrow hit you anywhere besides a useless target like your big butt, then you will have difficulty continuing the battle. Can't swing, stab, run or ride, I would presume." He pulled the second arrow from Amminus's leather belt. The tip broke off in the hard-tanned hide and thankfully did not pierce through to Amminus's vital organs.

Then to the last. "Here, I need another hand. Hold this shaft steady."

The pugilist held the lamp up with one massive hand and grasped the third arrow shaft with his other like Boaz showed him.

Boaz looked closely at the last wound and then to Amminus's face. Although somewhat ashen in color, there was no grimace. "Hang in there—one more to go."

"He must survive."

"I'll do what I can, but he is badly injured," Boaz said. "First you want to ascertain the location, depth, and whether it caused an exit wound." Boaz didn't know why he schooled this man other than it helped him keep his composure. After all, the man he worked on was his uncle.

"As a rule, limb wounds heal well, but major wounds will leave lasting effects on the body."

"Scars?"

"More than physical evidence of battle, emotional harm as well. This one is deep—a lot of blood. His color is worsening. The injury is significant." He carefully straightened Amminus's leg.

"Why is that?"

"The projectile is lodged in his upper thigh where his leg joins the body. This diminishes my options. Generally,

Surgery

I would incise the skin and remove the projectile. Not so with this case. If I remove the arrowhead, it may slice the artery—if it hasn't already done so—and he will die. If left in, he is at risk for it to sever the femoral nerve, and he would lose use of his leg. If it moves, it may cut the vessels further and he will die. He already has lost a substantial amount of blood. There is no answer to this puzzle that is agreeable to me."

"Remain," Amminus said. He must have awakened enough to overhear Boaz telling of the risks.

"Thank God, you are alive!" Boaz's helper said as though he and the man were great friends. "And I'll pray against infection."

"The danger is not yet abated. Amminus, this wound is most grave. Even if I am successful in removal of the arrow, you may not be able to use your leg for any kind of running. And maybe not even for walking. The wound is too high, such that amputation is fruitless. The scar tissue that would form throughout the arrow wound would impact any muscles in that area. Despite all that, I recommend removal."

Amminus's words slurred as he tried to speak.

"Thankfully, it will not be outright paralysis. It could be. There may be intense, lingering pain regardless of the action we take this moment. To remove the arrowhead is your best chance of survival."

"Pain."

"I am aware of your pain, Amminus. Do you know who I am?" Boaz asked.

"Jachin?" he scrunched his eyes tightly. "No . . . Boaz."

"Yes, Uncle. I am that and much more. Now rest. I will take care of you." Boaz gave his patient another draught of the *Morpheus* and waited until he was asleep again before continuing.

The noise of the crowd going wild with the chariot race permeated through the hall and drowned out Amminus's moans.

Boaz passed the limb to the gladiator who let go of the arrow and held Amminus's leg with one arm. The smoke of the lamp made his face appear shadowed and surreal.

His features so coarse he reminded Boaz of a horse. With a small saw, he cut the shaft of the arrow close to the skin, throwing the shaft against the wall where it landed with the others. He chose a round bellied scalpel and incised around the shaft of the arrow, careful to move with measured strokes.

Amminus flinched, but the fighter held his leg still. Boaz began the delicate surgery. He hoped that his hands would not falter or shake.

The arrowhead rested in the confluence of three important structures. The femoral vein, artery, and nerve. "If big blue or big red is lacerated, he may bleed to death before I can repair them. If the nerve is severed, he may never walk again—if he survives."

Boaz ligated the smaller bleeding vessels and then cautiously removed the arrowhead. So far so good. He set the barb on the table and closed the wound in layers using both cat gut and silk sutures.

"Why are his arms and legs so blue?"

Boaz put an ear to his patient's chest. He was not breathing. His neck vessels bulged.

"Let him go, Physician. He is dead . . ."

"He has a tension pneumothorax—a buildup of air in his chest. Help me turn him on his side."

They turned Amminus to the side. Boaz lifted the bandages and the leather seal. Air rushed out in a whoosh. He replaced the seal and lay his uncle on his back. For what seemed a lifetime, he lay still, not breathing, like Sophronios.

"It did not help. His soul has succumbed. My friend is gone."

Boaz pounded on the man's chest with his fists. "No! Not again!" Nothing. He pushed on the chest several times trying to encourage the lungs and heart to work. Time stood still.

Amminus sighed and began to breathe shallowly. He groaned.

Realizing he had also been holding *his* breath, Boaz sighed.

"We need to watch him closely. I may need to release pressure if his chest again fills with air." The slow and deep-

Surgery

ening breaths of his uncle and improving skin tone encouraged him.

"That is a good sign. Good breathing. Once he is stable, we must secret him to my wagon, though I fear for his life. We must leave this cesspool of a place as soon as possible."

When Boaz thought it safe, they carried Amminus and hid him in his wagon. Remembering the arrowhead on the table. Boaz raced back to retrieve it and the arrows, so that Gaius would not know their deeds.

Gaius met him on his way back to the wagon.

Boaz quickly hid the arrows behind his back.

"Looks like you were not needed. Did you dispose of the body?"

"We placed the remains in my wagon to drop off on our way to Batavia for proper burial."

"Batavia? Oh, did I not tell you? You're not going there. I need you immediately in Rome to prepare for my return. There will be many games to celebrate my victory. The gladiators will need your expertise. And I intend to display the body as evidence of the surrender."

"It's going to take twenty days at least to get to Rome. You can use any body, and it would look the same. No one knows that man's visage. And as far as veracity, thousands witnessed the surrender and subsequent death of the high king," Boaz lied.

"Did you not recognize the man?"

"I did not," Boaz lied again.

"Hmm, I am surprised. You are certain of the high king's death?

"Most certain."

"Very well. You must take him to Rome, even so." Gaius shoved Boaz. "Now away with you," and then in a sarcastic voice, "*Theophilus.*"

Boaz looked at Sophronios's wagon—*his* wagon now. Lais sat on the bench. She wanted nothing to do with the gladiator games. Instead, she had walked into town to view the varied flora and fauna of the area. How she happened to be there now was a mystery to Boaz, but he was glad she was here. He sighed and moved up next to her. She had not seen them put Amminus in the wagon. But Boaz was certain she saw the bloodstains on his tunic and hands. The pugilist sat in the back with the injured man.

"What are we doing?" Lais asked.

"I will explain later. It appears we are going to Rome."

54
CHAPTER

Healing

There are those who respond well to remedy from physicians or priests and those who are too conflicted for cures."

— Scribonius Largus

CISALPINE, GAUL

The path to Rome was a long one. Riddled with bumps and frequent stops. The imperator and his retinue were going to continue south along the Rhenus, while Boaz and his wagon would take the road through Gaul toward Divodurum Mediomatricum. Boaz gave the excuse that he needed to replenish his supply of herbs and painkillers that he would not be able to get south of the Alps. He wasn't sure why Gaius granted him the deviation. He seemed distracted. Boaz also knew that he and Lais would be hunted down and killed if they did not meet up with him in Rome as promised with the body of Amminus. He didn't know what he would do if his uncle survived. He'd figure something out. For now, his thoughts were only to save a life.

At a stop to rest the donkeys, Boaz crushed herbs in his palms letting the leaves fall into the small caldron in front of him. He had gathered the remedy last spring in the forests near Novaesium. Since leaving there he often worried about the patients he left behind. He took a pestle and mortar and crushed a dried mushroom, adding that to the broth as well. Bringing the concoction to a boil, he placed it off to the side to steep and cool. He then tended to his patient.

Amminus's skin appeared ashen. His lips dry, cracked, and blue. Breathing slowed at times so quietly Boaz shook his uncle to ensure he was still with them. Most of the day and night Amminus slept or remained unconscious.

Searching each wound for infection, Boaz found the leg wound swollen, red, and hot to the touch. *Tumor, rubor,* and *calor*. What Sophronios called *angry*. Something must be aggravating the wound.

"If something is in there, I need to remove it."

Lais sat next to him and quietly watched as the pugilist waited outside the wagon.

Lancing the swelling produced a profusion of yellow pus. Boaz followed the pus pocket with a metal probe, exploring the wound for other pockets of pus. He snagged a foreign body deep in the wound. Using small forceps, he gently removed the infecting intruder—a retained dirty piece of leather that the arrow had pushed in.

He matched it to the torn area of Amminus's belt. Satisfied he had pulled out what he searched for, he poured vinegar on the open wound. He packed the abscess, and rebandaged Amminus's leg. Remarkably, Amminus hadn't

Healing

made a sound. Boaz took the warm solution and spooned as much as he could down his uncle's throat.

"Will he make it?" Lais asked.

"I don't know."

While Boaz cleaned his instruments and put them away, Lais sang softly.

Boaz smiled, which was difficult knowing that his uncle might die at any moment. The song was more healing than the herb broth.

When the herbal infusion cooled, Boaz set it on the fire again to warm it. He continued his vigil for most of the night, taking a break to check on Lais. He would do the same again tomorrow and the next day until his uncle woke from the sorrowful sleep of near-death.

It rained the day Amminus opened his eyes.

"Thank you for your song," he said, and passed out again.

After several weeks, he was able to sit up and eat more than herb broth. Too weak to speak, Amminus nodded his head or waved his hands to communicate. Then when Boaz thought the worst was behind him, Amminus relapsed. His fever returned. His chills so severe that Boaz was afraid he was having a seizure. Lais helped place hot compresses on his leg to draw out the poison.

The pugilist prayed, "Great Physician, please heal my friend." The fever finally broke, bringing with it a deluge of sweat. Boaz placed cool rags on Amminus's forehead.

Boaz decided to travel on. Afraid of the risk, he insisted his uncle remain unseen in the wagon, and when improved, only to come outside at night. The pugilist stayed with Amminus or walked alongside the wagon. He cared for him constantly, refusing to leave his side. Boaz tried not to think about the fact that he had not only lied to the imperator but had stolen one of his fighters.

When they stopped at a crossroads on the road, Boaz brought lunch. Amminus being more awake, asked to be in the sun. The travelers sat on the side of the road to partake of the nourishment.

Amminus took the broth readily and took a sip. "This is awful!"

"It is a broth made from the herb *centaury* named after the mythical centaur *Chironia*, who cured a poison arrow wound with the herb."

"It is very bitter."

"That is why the Romans call it *fel terraae*. Now drink it all."

Amminus took a deep breath and finished the broth in one big swallow. His cheeks ruddier and his eyes less dark. "This is truly the *bile of the earth*." He handed the bowl to the giant.

"If it makes you well, then it is worth the bite," said the pugilist.

"Wait! Don't I know you? What are you doing here?"

"I brought you to the medicus from the arena."

"Thank you, friend for being there for me. But that is not exactly what I meant. How did you get *here*?" Amminus said.

"I joined a troop of aged gladiators like me who were seeking employment. We found work in the arena. Now I guess I'm traveling to Rome. My steps are ordered by the Lord."

"Have you met Epos?"

Boaz changed his uncle's dressings. "Yes, he is a good fighter."

"He is more than that. He was a friend of your mother's."

Boaz dropped his scissors. "Really?"

"Yes," Epos said. "I knew you and your brother when you were but babes-in-arms."

Boaz stared at him, his mouth half open.

Epos picked up the scissors and handed them back to Boaz.

Amminus sat up.

"I was not as I am now," Epos said. "My true name is long forgotten. Caradoc himself gave me the name *Epos*."

"What?"

"I was bound to a tree in the Druid Nemeton. The holy men planned a big sacrifice, and I was the offering. Don't ask how I ended up in Albion or in that sacred grove. A lengthy story to tell another time."

"The Ne-me-t-ton?" Boaz stammered, his mouth dry.

Healing

Amminus touched his nephew's arm.

Boaz flinched.

"Do you know the place, Boaz?"

"I heard of a druid holy place in the Andreadsweld when I was a child. Adults spoke of this woodland in whispers. Said that is where the great fire began."

"Then, this may be difficult for you to hear."

"Go on."

Lais opened the wagon door and stepped out, carrying clean rags she had laundered in a nearby creek.

"Come over, child. You need to hear this story as well, although I warn you it is a story of the greatest brutality and abuse," said Amminus.

She set the linen down and joined Boaz on the blanket. She slipped her hand into his.

"Caradoc brought two newborn babies to the Nemeton to sacrifice," Epos said.

"Babies?!" Lais cried.

"Yes, there wasn't time for introductions. I learned many years later that it was Boaz and his twin brother, Jachin. Flames ignited. I was able to escape my bonds. I rescued the twins, and returned them to their mother, unharmed."

Boaz stared in awe at the man before him. "That would explain the burn scarring you possess on your extremities."

Epos nodded.

Boaz could not wrap his head around this. The Nemeton? Druids? Sacrifice?

A tear fell to his cheek. "I never knew." He wiped the tear away. "Thank you for saving our lives, Epos. Thank you."

Epos bowed. "The Lord delivered you, I was just His instrument."

Later, Boaz had questions. "What was that gladiator stunt all about?"

"It was not part of my plan," Amminus said.

"Was getting killed in the arena part of your plan?" Lais asked.

"No, of course not. My plan was to surrender. To make it public. To save lives. The troops were not ready. Morale was low. They needed encouragement. At the same time, Gaius was being pressed by Rome to do something. Rumors were going around that the imperator was only in Gaul to raise a bodyguard and get money from the people. He partied instead of doing his job as the imperator. Beset by numerous conspiracies, Gaius needed to come up with a way to win Rome to him. I provided the means for him to do that."

"You conspired with the imperator?"

"I wouldn't use that word. I spent two years in Gaul before I went to Gaius. But I was not idle. I communicated regularly with Gaius during that time. I considered our prospects for success and one option had to be; what if Gaius doesn't go to Albion at all? Not an option I would choose, but an option nonetheless. How could we take Caradoc down and win back Albion? My plan was to surrender, which is what Cunobelinos had made plans to do—that's why Caradoc poisoned his own father. Your great-grandfather, Tasciovaunus, attempted a truce when he gave Alexenah to Caradoc in a bargain with Rome regarding their offspring. Caradoc broke that contract. Now Rome is already occupying Albion: one merchant, citizen, and warrior at a time. The south is, for the most part, Romanized."

"Why did you surrender, Uncle?"

"Caradoc is self-destructing. His boasting of saving the land is a barren promise. The people want to be Romans. So to concede was my plan. To make a truce with Rome and be recognized as the high king of Albion. I believed this would not only save the land but protect the people from attack. Gaius came up with the idea of taking troops to the beach and making a big show of it. He could claim he had conquered Britain without a fight and win Rome's accolades."

"Seems the imperator loved preforming roles rather than actually doing something brave," said Epos.

Amminus took in a long breath. "Gaius is only in it for Gaius even though he will say otherwise. The imperator double crossed me after the surrender. He had his own plans. At this point it doesn't matter for me—or anyone—to be a client king of Albion. It would be impossible to rule in peaceful unity with Rome."

"Why?" Lais asked.

"Because Gaius wants to be a god over all," Boaz said.

Healing

"This is beginning to make sense. How could you have not known he was feigning friendship?" Amminus said.

Boaz rose to check his uncle's bandages. "I suspected sedition in Gaius. Why did he send for me in the first place? I sat next to him at the games to only have him reference that he needed a physician—not from among his own retinue to record the death of a gladiator, which was—let me guess—announced as the king of Britain. But it was you, Uncle."

"How could you have known? Gaius did not recognize you?"

"I don't think so, but now I wonder . . ."

"He must have known you were my nephew. I believe his plan was to humiliate you with my death, and then to murder you as well."

Removing the leg bandages, Boaz smiled. Gathering new cloth, he bound it again. "Why would he do that?"

"Because you and Jachin are the only heirs to Caradoc."

"So he would rid himself of two enemies at once."

"Three."

"What do you mean three?" Boaz said sitting next to Lais again.

Lais hugged his arm and leaned into him.

"Your brother," Epos said.

Boaz rested his head against Lais. "Jachin is dead."

"Oh, he's very much alive. At least he was," Amminus said.

Boaz sat up, wide-eyed in disbelief. "*Was?*"

"Yes."

"This is the first I had even a morsel of hope for that. Tell me! Where is he?"

"Jachin fought me in the sand of the arena, believing that I was your father, Caradoc. That's why I say Gaius planned *three* deaths."

Epos nodded. "Three arrows. Three deaths."

In complete shock, Boaz didn't know what to say.

"You could have found your brother if Gaius hadn't demanded that you come work for him in Rome," Lais said.

"I took you both from the Nemeton." Epos bowed his head. "I could not steal your brother from the theater."

Boaz touched Epos on his scarred arm. "You rescued my uncle. I am grateful."

"In regard to my plan, there would be no bloodshed. No fighting. No more deaths. I wanted to do good. And . . . to save Jachin. And by 'save,' I mean more than just his life. I mean save *who* he is. Who he *was*. From what he was *becoming*. If by stopping the battle before it started so Jachin couldn't kill his father helped save him, then I would do it. I would do anything for him. I could not reveal the plan to Jachin because I felt he would sabotage it. My plan contradicted his vow. So I told Jachin I was traveling to Rome."

"Jachin didn't know?"

"I can only assume that Gaius led him, and all involved to believe that your father was the man who had surrendered. When I saw him in the arena, I knew he thought I was Caradoc."

"The crowd only cheered the death of the king of Albion. There was no other pronouncement," Epos said.

"Gaius didn't know you were still clinging to life when I told him I put your body into my wagon. I wonder what he thought when I told him I didn't know you? I showed no emotion at your supposed death."

"After me, Jachin was next in line as high king," Amminus said. "I cannot see how Gaius would have allowed him to survive. But then why would he let you go if he knew who you were and planned your death as well?"

"We were pushed down the road to Rome. Why?" Lais asked.

"Who can know the schemes of a madman? Perhaps, Jachin was caught and taken to Rome in chains?" Epos said.

"Jachin can take care of himself," Amminus said. "But if that is true, that he has your brother captive, I fear he plans to do the same to you, Boaz—when *you* arrive in Rome."

55
CHAPTER

Passages

Extraordinary opportunities are found within a man. Therefore, seize common occasions, and make them great."

— Scribonius Largus

DIVODURUM MEDIOMATRICUM, SOUTHERN GAUL

Uncertainty filled the road ahead. They journeyed several weeks more, and as Boaz tended to his uncle's injuries, his uncle relayed stories about Jachin's misfortunes and misadventures. He also heard tales of his brother's feats of bravery.

Boaz was delighted with the news about Jachin, but at the same time worried for his safety. Amminus told him all he knew, up to the gladiator ruse staged by Gaius. Boaz learned more about the giant, Epos, and found him not only jovial but gifted in intelligence and insight. He heard

The Golden Cord

of Joseph from Arimathea, also known as Tinman, and of his mother's faith. Epos claimed the Christianii religion and enjoyed talking of his encounter with the Messiah—meeting him face-to-face.

Amminus improved. He was able to eat, sit up, and at night would limp around the wagon with Lais holding on to his arm. He slowly gained strength but stayed to the shadows for fear of discovery.

They eventually stopped outside a small town by the *Blesam* River where a *menhir* stone stood. It looked like a giant *colus* that her grandmother used with weaving, except this distaff along the road was four times as tall as a man. The standing stone was a good place to stop for the night on the way to *Divodurum Mediomatricum*. The capital of the *Mediomatrici* tribe of Gaul was located on the banks of the *Mosella* and the *Salia* rivers. They would reach the city soon.

"This looks like as good a place as any to have a wedding," Amminus said.

"What do you mean?"

"I can perform the ceremony. We are at a sacred site, the menhir. The sun and moon are in the same sky. You are engaged to be married. I know the words to say. Epos will bear witness. What more do you need?"

"Ah . . . a . . ." Boaz faltered.

"We do need something of importance in which to bind our hands," Lais said.

"I have just the thing!" Boaz ran to the back of the wagon and under a secret slate on the floor of the vehicle, he found what he needed.

"Will this suffice?"

"The golden cord!" Epos exclaimed.

"You know what this is?"

"Yes, where did you get it?"

"I found it in the dust of our home in Albion after Tahdah beat me."

"That is the cord that was around you and your brother in the Nemeton. The druid said it would bind you together," Epos said.

"Is it magical?" Lais asked.

"It is precious, but I am not sure it holds any power."

"Can you use this, Uncle Amminus?"

"Most certainly so."

"What do we do?" asked Lais.

"Stand near the stone. The sun sets, and a full moon rises higher in the heavens."

Epos placed a garland of wild flowers on her head. "Where did you get this?"

"I just made it," said Epos.

"You are a man of many talents." She kissed Epos on the cheek. "I don't have a wedding dress."

"Is that a necessity?"

"You are beautiful the way you are, Lais," Boaz said.

"Take her hand in yours, Boaz."

They faced each other in the shadow of the stone. Boaz clasped her right hand and gently kissed it. Amminus took the golden cord and wrapped it tenderly around their hands, binding them together. "This ritual has been done for ages without end. It is the same as when I first wed. This cord symbolizes your lives. Bound together. Each strand an aspect of each other's being. All things separate—yet shared equally, whether happiness or heartache. Your hopes and desires are now bound together. All things become one. As this cord is made of gold, it symbolizes your love, which becomes your commitment to each other. It is pure. It is precious. Genuine.

"Now, Boaz, make your vow, and, Lais, you make your vow to Boaz."

Boaz swallowed hard as he stared into Lais's blue eyes. "I have loved you since the first time I saw you in Carura. I will love you until the end of time."

"I will love you until the stars fall," she said.

"This completes your binding and the commitment it portends. May all that is good bless your lives together," Amminus said.

The couple's kiss sealed the bond.

The next morning they gathered around a fire for breaking fast. Boaz and Lais held hands and smiled. They ate very little, if at all.

Amminus broke the silence of the meal. "I have spent many days in deep thought. I can no longer hope to rule

Albion, Boaz. I cannot stop Caradoc. Fate will find a way. Either Rome will lose interest, or they will conquer. It is up to God now. I am only a man who has overshot his purpose. With your permission, good Physician, I will take my leave."

"Amminus, where will you go? What will you do?" Lais said.

"But we just got back together." Boaz noticed Amminus's stern jawline. "However, if you must go, you must leave before we reach Divodurum. You must become *incognito*," Boaz said.

"The *Treveri* live near here. They will take you in until you are strong again," Epos said.

"I can never claim the throne. Not sure I would want to after all that has happened. Perhaps I'll disappear into the dark to settle down and have a wife and children in my old age."

"You mean find another to love?" Lais said.

"Perhaps, or perhaps not. I shall never be able to love as I did with my wife or feel the love I had for Boaz's mother, Alexenah, but perchance I will find some toothless old woman who will take me in. Love at my age and in my condition is nonsense."

"Aw, Uncle, may I call you that now?" Lais said as she hugged his arm. He smiled at her. "There is more to love than what old men call nonsense. There are long walks, and dinners at sunset, and appreciating a beautiful view while holding hands, and a look into each other's eyes."

"What would you know about love?" Amminus winked at Boaz and smiled a half grin.

"I learned it from a young man in a shady grove where even the deer came to witness our pledge of love."

"The memory of that day lingers on the touch of my fingers, and no other day feels the same," Boaz said as he put his arms around his wife's waist.

As they finished breaking fast, Lais played on a small lute, and Boaz sang her bear song to while away the time. It seemed a sad and forlorn sound, not the joyful and bright ditty they sang before. "What's wrong," Boaz said.

"I am happy to be with you, but sad that we were not able to plan the wedding where I could wear a dress fit for a celebration lasting a week. I am also sad that we are going to have to say goodbye to Amminus. I have grown to like him and think of him as a second father," she said.

After the song, silence reigned around the campfire, broken only by the crackling of the burning oak logs.

Suddenly they heard a sweet, soft, sound like a musical note. Like the quavering trill of a songbird.

"Surely no bird can be singing out here in the middle of nowhere this time of day," Boaz said.

Again, it came. Faint. Sweet. Melodious, yet mysterious enough to provoke wonder.

"It comes from the log on the fire!" Epos exclaimed.

"'Tis true enough!" Amminus said. "The flame has let loose the music imprisoned there many years ago in the ancient oak. It comes from the oak's inner heart." He mused a bit then softly continued as if the words came from a very deep place. "Perhaps one day long ago birds sat on the limb of this tree that now makes our fire." He paused. Deep in thought.

"Once days were happy and worry free and the bird warbled a beautiful song. But over time, the oak grew old and wrapped around that little bird's song, ring after ring. It lived through storms, cold blasts, and . . . terrible fires." He clutched his tunic at his chest. "The oak grew hard. Callous. Each painful day made the knotty bark stronger until it sealed up the long-forgotten strain." He looked to Boaz. "The flames have wrung from it once again the beautiful melody of long ago. Yes. This heated hearth of a passionate blaze has bestowed upon us that sweet, sweet song once again." Amminus placed his hand on Boaz's shoulder. "Until the fires of our circumstances burn us deeply, perhaps we are like this old oak. Insensible to the beauty that lies within us. Were it not for the fire kindled upon us, we would never have remembered the harmony hidden in our apathetic heart."

The fire sang on.

Epos looked at the scars on his arms.

"Boaz? I know you have been hurt. I bear that hurt, also. And . . . I carry your hurt, and your brother's hurt, and Albion's hurt as well. It hangs heavy about my neck like an anchor stone." Amminus sighed. "I made a declaration to Fergus long ago." He bowed his head as if in prayer. "There are souls who call out to my passions. Those who are oppressed and exploited, I must release those who are enslaved and used. I must free those who don't have a voice."

"All these bad things happened to me while I have spent my life trying to do the right thing. Some travesties were my fault, either by action or complacency. I accept responsibility for those times and blame no one, not even God. I feel that this decision I have made is as if I have lost an arm in battle, leaving it on the field as I run away. Sometimes it is best to let things go. I must live in peace with myself and not harbor bitterness. I must let go of things that have weighed me down—responsibility, regret, and remembrance. I do not seek revenge, I seek peace. I have determined to stop trying to be what I think everyone wants me to be. A leader. A father. A husband. A friend. A warrior." Amminus stood. "Once, my passions listened to the calls of the oppressed and exploited. I felt the need to rescue the enslaved. I wanted to be their voice in a dark world. But now I am afraid I must pass my passions on to others who will accomplish those dreams that I have failed to fulfill in my life. Perhaps I will find happiness when I stop looking for it. Not being responsible for everything and everyone. Just being. Not being irresponsible, but by being kind. Maybe I will seek out followers of the teachings of the Messiah, and humbly give myself to others."

Amminus gathered his food satchel and some supplies. Handing an old leather pouch attached to a leather cord to Boaz he said, "I want you to have these. They are to remember your mother . . . and to remember me."

Limping into the darkness toward the direction of the town, he stopped and picked up a long stick to use as a cane. He turned back to the three sitting by the fire. "Thank you for your friendship, Epos. Thank you for your song, my new niece. And—thank you for saving my life—Medici Boaz."

Boaz opened the leather pouch to find two stones. One a blue bead of the Brigantes, the other gray and plain. It sparkled when he held it up to the light of the fire. "Matrona's precious jewel," he whispered.

CHAPTER 56

Descent

Quae ascendit deveniatur.

— Scribonius Largus

ROME

When Boaz, Lais, and Epos finally crossed the mountains and traveled to the grand city of Rome, the landscape didn't look right. He had seen the largest cities of Greece and Gaul, but nothing like this marvelous city of Rome. Shops, granaries, warehouses, towering apartments and every street paved and adorned with statues and flowers. Townhouses, bathhouses, palatial homes, and places of amusement, including theaters, abounded.

Epos commented continuously as if he was a hired tourist guide pointing out not only the landmarks, but the alleyways and streets to avoid. He led them to a townhome where the newlyweds would live.

Although he had never been to Rome, Boaz noticed statues of Gaius lying on the ground—toppled and destroyed. Graffiti on the walls declared the imperator *persona non grata*. Gaius was not welcome. That seemed strange.

After settling himself and Lais in their new home, Boaz stopped at a local bread merchant before his interview for a job attending the Gladiators at the *Ludus Aemilius Lepidus*. This gave him time to enjoy the morning and to think about his commission to work at the school. The travel had been uneventful and enjoyable with his new wife. Epos was a splendid companion and filled their evenings with many long tales of his life. He had acquired employment at the Ludus to train new gladiators. He was well suited for the position.

The land of Italia was ripe with agriculture and commerce, which pleased Lais. The people welcomed and dotted on the newlyweds wherever they rested.

"I have been traveling an extended time. Can you tell me about the graffiti and the ruined statues of the imperator?" He asked the proprietor of the cafe. The man was happy to share the news.

"Before Gaius returned from Gaul, he built a monstrous temple to himself on the Palatine. It was gawdy and, in my mind, atrocious. The pandering citizens paid a lot of money for the honor to be one of his phony priests. The weasel planned on returning to the temple and be declared a god. Can you believe that man?"

"Yes, I can believe that. Did he?"

"When he finally arrived, he stopped just outside of town. Perhaps fearing assassination, as well he should—the man thought much more of himself than others did. But maybe he wanted to wait for the ships to arrive for his ovation and triumph for conquering Britannia—so I was told. In the meantime, Gaius impersonated the gods by dressing lavishly and parading about forcing others to bow before him. It is said he had his servants dissolve pearls in vinegar for him to drink. He often invited the moon to his bed and talked to the god Jupiter as an equal. At times he expressed anger to the gods as though he presided over them as well as ruling Rome. He ordered his own statue to be placed in the temple in Jerusalem to replace the Hebrew God."

"Sounds like the man was unhinged."

The proprietor handed Boaz more hot bread and a fruit jam to spread on it. "Oh yes! In my opinion, he was several slices short of a full loaf."

Boaz laughed. "Did that happen? I mean the statue in Jerusalem?" Boaz couldn't imagine the sacrilege of that act.

"No, another conspiracy was discovered, and senators were executed right and left."

"I thought him deeply suspicious. Did he ever enter the city?"

"He slipped into the city silently under cover of darkness in the month of Augustus. There was no triumph. No ovation."

The man excused himself. "Need to check on the bread. Be right back."

A mouthwatering aroma wafted out of the bake room. Boaz sighed and told himself to remember to take some home to Lais.

When the man returned, Boaz resumed his investigation. "No talk of his conquest of Britannia?"

"Nah, unless you count the jests about sea-shells. He took to entertaining and loved attending the theater. Evidently, he thought if he won the populace, then he was safe from harm from the Senate. Dressed in woman's silks, he showered gold and silver on the people from the roof of the palace for several days. Some people were crushed in the push for gold. They counted thirty-two men, two hundred forty-seven women, and one eunuch who died."

"Oh my, he must have felt very insecure," Boaz exclaimed. All this happened while they were going over the alpine mountains. So much in such a short time. He wondered what happened to Jachin, but he didn't ask the man. How would he know about his brother anyway?

"Then officers of the pretorian guard and their commander, Regulus—used to be a slave trader—drew up a plan, so they say, with Clemens to kill the beast. In the month of Janus, the imperator attended the Palatine games. On the last day of the games, it all came down."

"How is it you know all this?" Boaz took a bite of the bread and jam. It reminded him of the *treacle* they used at the medical school in Carura.

"Gossip is a frequent visitor to my establishment. The imperator Gaius usually took a bath and lunch and then went back to the theater for the afternoon. Their plan was to get him as he left the theater, so I've been told. Gaius traveled down the narrow passageway out of the theater and stopped to watch some boys practice a song to be performed later. It was there that Choera snuck up behind and slashed the imperator's neck. Another man, Sabinus, stabbed him in the gut as he turned around. As he lay there, begging for his life, others rushed him. They said he had been stabbed more than thirty times." The shop keeper gave Boaz a cup filled with a most delightful smelling hot liquid. "Someone claimed they had chopped his head off, but that man was a known chinwag, so I don't believe it."

Boaz took a swig of hot liquid. "Mmm, this is good. What is it?"

"From Aethiopia. Anyway, they found the self-styled god's uncle Claudius hiding behind a curtain in the palace. The guard took him before the Senate, and they declared him the new imperator. And that is what happened." He held out his hand to receive coin for the story.

Boaz gave him a gold denarius.

CHAPTER 57

Transitions

*We never realize all of our losses
until we lose ourselves.*

— Scribonius Largus

AD—42 Calleva, Albion

The sun sank below the walls of Calleva as Caradoc walked the streets alone. The central thoroughfares of the city were awash with activity; however, he kept to the shadows and back alleys. A light easterly wind blew clouds around like horses' tails on a run. Rain must be coming.

According to his spies, someone assassinated Rome's imperator, Gaius. Romans often killed each other to advance whichever cause or candidate for office they promoted. A new imperator took his place. Amminus gave Albion to Rome, and they killed him for it.

Transitions

I am the king of Albion! How could these people be so naïve? Did they think that by consenting to the rape of our home that they would enjoy the desecration? That Rome would pretend Albion was a prized possession and not take from us everything we are? They saw it as victory; Caradoc saw it as vandalism.

He passed by the inn. No more favors. No more free wine. He missed Camulodunon and the Boar's Head Inn. Was Fetch still the proprietor? *That barkeep understood my position.*

A spear flew from the shadows. It slammed into a door over his shoulder. Caradoc cursed. Footsteps and laughter as the perpetrators scrambled. Perhaps he needed to rethink procuring bodyguards. He couldn't see both directions at once anymore.

A woman sweeping her porch spat and gave Caradoc a vulgar gesture.

Simpletons.

The cobblestones beneath his feet felt uneven. In their haste to Romanize, the people of Calleva had forgotten to add sewer paths. Filth lined the alleys. He had to watch his step.

Two men sat in a cart by a closed pottery workshop. Caradoc listened to their talk.

"Is it true? Does that make us all Romans? What about the high king?"

"Yes, finally we will get all we ever wanted."

Caradoc rested his hand on the pommel of his sword. *I have given my countrymen all they have, and they praise an imperator in Rome they have never met.* He walked to the other side of the street. Normally any opposition to his position would evoke the deepest rage in him. Now he questioned his schemes. Not his motives, but the results he now observed. *Who will take responsibility for Albion if not me? Has everything I've done for these people been in vain?*

He cut through a narrow alleyway to his intended destination. A homeless man sat in the dark and made slobbering ruminations while holding his hand out for alms. Caradoc ignored him. *Fool.*

He kicked over a Roman urinal pot and stepped into

The Golden Cord

another new cobblestone street. Rome was not even on his shores, yet the merchants had frequented Calleva for quite some time. No matter how hard he tried, he could not hold back the deluge of change.

Become a client king of Albion? Why not just do that? These thoughts had never entered his mind before. He never lost. By the gods, he believed he was still going to win.

He turned on to an empty back street. Horses stood hitched to a post at the back door to another inn ahead of him. But instead of going to the public house, he turned off another side street toward the western gate that led to the forest.

The only man on this street was a carpenter working on a broken chariot.

"You're not fixing that correctly. It will fall apart down the road," he said to the carpenter. Caradoc could repair anything. Why couldn't he mend Albion?

The man waved his hand and cursed him along.

Caradoc marched through the unguarded gate and closed it behind him.

This part of the forest was familiar. It was through these woods that he and Epaticus came to take the city of Calleva. That last black night spent with his traitorous uncle he remembered well.

"Where were you the night Tasciovaunus disappeared?" his uncle had asked.

I was in an awful place. That is where I was. No one asked about how he felt, only about where he was and what he did.

About a furlong into the woodland was a small clearing. He saw the campfire long before he arrived at his proposed meeting. The man he was to converse with served him faithfully for several years; infiltrating and eavesdropping on the Romans. He hoped that he held information that would be amiable to his desires.

Sitting close to the flames was a man of small stature. This was not an old man, yet his bald head shone in the light. Dark tufts and strands that remained flowed over his ears and down to his shoulders.

Caradoc stood in silence as the man ate from a tin bowl.

The man licked the dish and drank from a flask that Caradoc recognized. He looked up and smiled.

Caradoc knelt across from the fire and warmed his hands. "What do you bring me, Toenin?"

"Look around you, My King. Reality surrounds you."

"What do you mean?"

"I bring reality. Gaius assassinated. 'Bout time. There is no more Albion. Belongs to the Romans now. No concern of succession needed here." He pointed at Caradoc. "At some point, another will take your place. You are not long for this land anymore, in my opinion."

Caradoc scoffed. "I like your honesty, but who would dare assassinate me to gain the throne?"

"Amminus is dead. Togodumnus—well, what would he care? Jachin has joined the military. Aligned with Rome. Perhaps he has designs of his own with the new imperator."

"What is Imperator Claudius's plan for Albion?"

"He named his son *Britanicus*. Claudius wants us all in togas."

"What do they need from us? We are nothing."

"Cash-flow problems." Toenin retrieved a knife and picked at his fingernails. "Lead mines of the *Mendip* hills was mentioned more than once. And even though we surrendered, they have yet to receive taxes. Free trade of goods would bring financial help as well. Yup, Gaius's legions *were* prepared. They remain supplied. I wouldn't count them out yet."

"Claudius means to use them?"

"Perhaps."

"Will he set up Verica as king?"

"Verica would like that. But he fled Albion, and Rome sees him as weak. No. Tiberius Claudius Cogidubnus."

"A Roman? Who is that?"

Toenin shrugged. "Some young relative of Verica."

"Sending an insignificant force to install a king? Claudius will fail. We are eighty thousand strong. The Romans fear me. They will not come."

"An invasion force is prepared. I saw it; they will come." He grabbed an apple from a leather sack at his belt and took a few chomps. "Rome has a food shortage. Claudius has designs to improve the harbor at Osios. He needs more grain."

Caradoc took all this in. "The idea of Rome still invading, even though the imposter Amminus had surrendered, bothers me. Why? Is it for show? Must be. A prideful man has poor judgement."

"Don't underestimate Claudius."

"Tell me about the imperator."

"Tiberius Claudius Caesar Augustus Germanicus. Born in Lugdunum."

"A Gaul?"

"Yes. And mocked for it."

"What of his upbringing?"

"Claudius is invalid. Hidden from public out of shame to the family, so much so that some didn't even know he'd been born for many years. 'A monstrosity of a human being that nature began but never finished,' his mother said. Took no part in public life, and others had to speak for him." He held his hand up and moved it back and forth. "Claudius's head shakes. And hands too. The veritable butt of jests."

"Palsy?"

"Right hand is limp. Drags his right leg when he walks. Looks like a puppet with a bungling puppet master. Hardly anyone can understand his fractured speech. Better when he reads a script or seated."

Toenin put his knife away and took another drink. "Stammers, he does. Can't tell what language he speaks. Latin, Greek, or something altogether different. He slobbers, his nose runs, and at times you hear uncontrollable laughter. I understand that he has frequent outbursts when frustrated."

"You have seen this?"

Toenin took several scrolls of old parchment from his tunic. "Homer's poetry is a favorite of his. Has tried to write poetry himself. So I hear."

"So he studies the arts." Caradoc held the paper up to the waning light of the fire as the sun now passed the horizon. He separated out one page and took a twig from the fire. Using the burnt end of the stick, he scribbled some words on the parchment and folded it.

"This broken clay pot that is Claudius. Is he educated?"

"He is not mentally weak. He studies history, philosophy, and medicine—and keeps medici around him at all times."

Caradoc tossed the parchments into the flames—all but the one page. "When you are a man, you should know what is best for your health."

"He employs a doctor named Callistus. An expert in poisons and treating wounds. Some implicate him in Gaius's assassination."

"How do you know this, Toenin?"

"I know all, hear all, see all—if there is money in it. I walked their alleyways and halls at night. No one notices a mouse."

"We can take advantage of his weakness. Rome will not hate him or shake in trepidation as they feared Gaius. Like you said, he will most probably be a puppet of the Senate. He is not a threat. He cannot command men."

"Yes, but he has paid a *donative* to the soldiers. They will fight for money, if not loyalty to Rome."

Caradoc stood. "He sounds like an incapable fool."

Toenin poured the remaining liquid over the fire and rose to leave. "No more a fool than you paying warriors to follow you."

Caradoc would kill others for such an insult, but he needed Toenin. "One more question. Is he *seen* as a leader of men?"

"He is a gambler. He drinks to excess. A womanizer. Most see him as a joke."

Caradoc reached over the extinguished flames and gave Toenin the remaining folded parchment. "Take this message to him."

"Yes, My King."

As Caradoc walked back to the city of Calleva, a thunderstorm arose. Temperature dropped. The wind changed to a westerly gale. Rain pelted through the trees above.

If Gaius was not a threat, and the new imperator isn't either, does that mean there is a reprieve? That Rome thinks they already won? That they won't come? Won't fight?

They will come.

The Golden Cord

A lightning bolt slashed the sky. The roar of thunder quick behind.

Rome seeks control of the world. All I desire is Albion.

"Great Borrum's beard. No! Definitely *no!*" he yelled. "They won't get away with this takeover. They are cowards!"

Stepping through the gate, he took a cloak from the man hiding under the unfixed cart. He wrapped himself with the cloak and marched back to his home. As he walked through his doorway into the cold empty room, he had a strange thought.

I miss Mara.

CHAPTER 58

Scholae

Confidence is a vision reflected from the surface of experience.

— Scribonius Largus

AD 42—ROME

"*O bon deus! Medius fidius!*" Martianus cried as two other gladiators carried him into the room. His chariot had overturned on him, and the fighter's scalped hair lay in a flap pulled back over his shiny skull.

"Pour the vinegar over the scalp. Don't be stingy," Boaz ordered.

Since coming to Rome, Boaz practiced at the Ludus Aemilius Lepidus bordering the bronze workshops. The air of the gladiator school reeked with the odor of the smelters and ovens as well as the sweat and blood of the men.

The Golden Cord

Boaz lifted the gladiator's eyelids to look at his pupils. "Martianus, don't you have a girlfriend who works at the palace of the imperator?"

Martianus nodded.

"I must preserve your good looks, then."

Claudius retained twenty thousand gladiators in his private ludus. There were only two who never blinked in the presence of a threat, and because of this they remained unbeaten. Martianus wasn't one of those two. His pupils looked fine.

"Smile, Martianus. Show me your teeth."

Once a prisoner of war, Martianus now learned the life-or-death, hand-to-hand combat style of the gladiator. He led with his chin by the look of his teeth. His mouth was like an abandoned cave with a few stalactites on top.

One of Boaz's jobs as the medicus was to try and repair the damage caused *cum ad dentem pervenit pugnus*. He recoiled at the man's breath. Like the other gladiators, he did not eat meat, but ate barley, boiled beans, oatmeal, and dried fruit. This man obviously infused it all with garlic and stale cheese.

This gladiator before him represented a significant asset for the *lanista*, so they treated him well. That included regular massages and, of course, high-quality medical care.

Suturing his hairy scalp back in place, Boaz carefully matched up the premature receding hairline. "Hold still so I can make you pretty again."

Martianus grunted. "That assumes I was pretty before."

The giant came in to see how the medicus progressed. He stood quietly behind Boaz.

"Can you move to the side, Epos? Your shadow blocks the light."

Epos was now the head trainer of the gladiators. It didn't take him long to rise to the top. As a former slave and gladiator, he identified with the others and was respected by all. Boaz enjoyed working with him and was appreciative of his friendship and knowledge of the arena.

"Martianus, my friend, I must finish so I can keep my appointment with Callistus—thanks to you for setting it up. Now you do your best to keep me from it."

"I didn't mean to lose my mind."

"You did not lose your mind, just your scalp. Besides, losing your mind would mean you had one in the first place."

Martianus laughed. "Ow, that hurts."

"Sorry. The vinegar will help you heal. Now sit up and let me look at you."

"He looks better than ever," Epos said.

"*Nymphidia* is the daughter of Callistus. How is it that you came to be her lover?" Boaz asked.

"My dashing good looks?"

Boaz wrapped a bandage around his head. "Looks can be deceiving. More likely because you are a famous gladiator."

"Yes, that too."

"Tell me about Callistus. I sent him samples of my writing as he asked."

"You will like him—everyone does. He was once a slave, sold for being of no use. He rose to be rich and powerful not only being the personal physician of the last imperator, Gaius, but he was close to his ear as a counselor."

"Do you think he had anything to do with Gaius's death?"

The gladiator held his head. "Oh no, not him. He now has the favor of Claudius. Strange man, that Claudius. Why would the senators choose a man like him as imperator?"

"Don't let his disability fool you; Claudius is an intelligent man who leads well."

"Have you met him?"

"Not yet. But I do know others with the palsy such as he, and believe me, he knows a lot more than he is given credit for. The mind and the body do not always agree in health, nor do they always work in tandem. Claudius may look the fool, but I assure you, he is no buffoon."

Martianus thanked the physician, and Epos escorted him out. Boaz continued to treat patients till the afternoon.

⌘ ⌘ ⌘

A line of people stood at the front gate of the huge home of Callistus when Boaz finally arrived that evening. Does he hold clinic at his home? No, these didn't look like patients,

The Golden Cord

at least not like any he was used to. They all wore togas of various stripes that signified them as senatorial or upper class. They must be in line waiting for an audience with Callistus. Was he that important?

Boaz walked up to the gate and introduced himself to the guard. He thought he would have to go to the back of the line and was surprised when a servant ushered him to a side door that opened into the dining room of the stately home.

There were thirty tall black onyx columns in the room with a massive marble table in the center, surrounded by ornate chairs and servants. It was indeed a change of fortune for a "slave once sold by his master as being of no use."

Sitting at the table were two men, deep in conversation—one quiet and dignified in speech, and the other loud with a voice that varied in tempo and volume. It was what Boaz would describe as "singsongy." He couldn't catch what they were talking about. After waiting a while, one of the men looked to him and smiled. He stood and waved Boaz over.

"I am Gaius Julius Callistus." He turned to the man at the table. "This is the imperator, Tiberius Claudius Caesar Augustus Germanicus."

Boaz swallowed.

"This is the young physician I told you about," Callistus said.

"I am Theophilus."

"I am PLEASED to ME-eet you THeoPHilus. I read YOUR paper and m-my WIFE loves the TOOTHpaste you see-e-ent He-eer," Claudius said, his speech very exact but difficult to understand. His movements were jerky and uncoordinated. A drop of spittle ran down his chin. He wiped it with a cloth.

Boaz bowed. "Thank you, *deus noster Caesar*. I am pleased to meet you. If your wife needs more dentifrice, let me know."

"The imperator wants to employ your services and attend to him exclusively," Callistus said.

"What about the gladiator school?" Boaz asked.

"Let them hire one of the bone-cutting hacks," Callistus said. "Your skill is needed in the palace."

"Come work for me," Claudius said.

Boaz bowed respectfully. "Thank you, Imperator. I shall honor your request. When shall I begin?"

"Tomorrow," said Callistus.

"Very well, then. I shall arrive at the palace at sunrise . . . for each morning is a beginning."

CHAPTER 59

Revelation

The saddest journey is when a friend walks down one street and I walk down another.

— Scribonius Largus

ROME—IMPERATOR CLAUDIUS'S PALACE

"Others go to battle," Galba once said about the Batavii, "these men go to war." In the last few months, Jachin found the old trainer to be correct. Every activity of the Batavii auxiliary was warlike, whether it be drinking, gambling, chasing women, or snoring in their tents. Jachin proudly accepted his place among these warriors. His escape from the arena led him back to his new friends. The Batavii shielded him from discovery until Gaius moved south. After that, the warriors took any mercenary job available. Numerous skirmishes *allowed Jachin to prove his worth. And now that the imperator was dead, Jachin could move about freely without fear of running into assassins sent by Gaius.*

Improved in stature but, according to some, declined in moral fiber, Jachin grew hardier—his mind more vigorous than those of the dim-witted legionnaires who only followed commands and marched without thought. Perhaps due to his own single-mindedness and purpose, he prospered among his peers.

This life was much different from his days as a galley slave. These men accepted him as one of their own. They brought him into their fold eagerly and with much celebration. At first Jachin didn't know what to think about it, but he got to where he liked the notoriety and the companionship of the other men.

In times of war, these long-haired men did not trim their beards until they had slain an enemy. On the field of battle, in the midst of the fight, they would signal their victory by grasping their lengthy chin hair and slicing it free with their blade. Only cowardly and lazy warriors remained unshorn. A peculiar habit was to cut the hair from their fallen comrades and attach it to their helms in tribute to their departed fellow warrior's bravery in battle.

Jachin excelled at defeating his foes. Since there was much opportunity for battle with these mercenaries, he stayed clean-shaven most of the time. His long dark locks cropped short.

Symbolically wearing an iron torc, he vowed to wear it around his neck until his enemy breathed their last breath and replace it with Caradoc's torc.

The Batavii were quite fond of their fish and the various ways of making it palatable. The warriors bragged about their skill in fishing and spoke often of their Island at the mouth of the Rhenus in the north. He found a liking to seafood, which surprised him after spending so much time on the Great Green. They excelled in cooking eggs from various

The Golden Cord

fowl and kept hens in cages that they carried with them when they traveled.

Some auxiliary provided short-term support for the legion's campaigns. Recruits were taken as needed. Jachin's soldier friends were in it for more than the few skirmishes. They were men of honor. Not necessarily of good character, but they had their principles. Amminus once said he acted on the principle of doing what was right and good. These warriors were not of the same ilk. They acted upon what they considered right and good for *them*. Jachin could identify with that sentiment. It was their hope to one day have a long-term partnership with a specific legion and it seemed this was to finally happen. The new imperator, Claudius, invited the Batavii to Rome to join his legions in preparation to invade Albion.

The road to Rome had been long and fraught with perils and much opportunity to sharpen his fighting skills. He was somehow constantly getting into trouble, and his anger was always barely beneath the surface. To travel this far to only turn around and go back to the mouth of the Rhenus was foolish. However, the opportunity to go back to Albion with an army at his back is what he lived for. He figured the Batavii nominated him as their negotiator, not only because of his language skills but because he was born and raised in the land they were planning to conquer.

Eight full Batavii units were already in Rome's employ, and each unit numbered over five hundred warriors. The units were further divided into contubernales of eight men. Jachin reckoned that his group of warriors were sought after because of their unique abilities. One of the most storied skills of the Batavii was how they crossed wide bodies of water as a unit in full armor.

Finally learning to swim, Jachin still hated being in water. However, if he visualized the approaching shore, he assured himself of safety.

Claudius bade the Batavii to send a spokesperson to his palace to discuss their association. Fluent in Latin, and able to mimic the proper accent needed for mediation, Jachin took on the role of bargainer for the auxiliary unit.

Revelation

Notorious for his haggling skills, he could negotiate a bear out of his skin.

Taken into the palace by a centurion of the palace guard, a Praetorian introduced him to the noble imperator of Rome. "May I present the freedman Sallustius Amminus Lucullus"

"That is a very impressive knife you wear," Claudius said.

The way his tongue stumbled and tumbled around the words made it difficult to understand him. Jachin looked around. No evidence of ale or wine. He got the jist of what the imperator wanted when Claudius pointed at Jachin's pugio.

Jachin drew the pugio. "On the hilt are figures of wings and fighting men—" he turned it over— "and on the other side, a dog with two children." He offered the blade to the imperator.

Claudius reached with a jerky halting movement and took the pugio. He carefully examined it, holding it up to the light. "Not a dog—a wolf. Its length is more than that of a legionnaire's pugio. Much like the difference between a *gladius* and a *spatha*. Unique."

"There is an inscription on the blade. There." Jachin pointed to the words etched in the metal. "*Memento mori*."

"Memento Mori—remember that you, too, will die?" Claudius repeated. "Who told you that it said this?"

"My Matrona, sir."

"She was mistaken. It never said 'memento mori' on the blade. Most of the letters are worn off. She must have assumed that is what was written since it is a common Latin phrase."

Jachin looked at the runes again.

"What it does say is MOR. There should be an *S* on the end. MORS. *Crocea Mors* to be exact. *The Yellow Death*!" The imperator called out enthusiastically. He wobbled on his skinny legs and waved the pugio excitedly, nearly losing his balance. When he stopped, he bowed and handed Jachin the pugio.

Jachin didn't understand all Claudius said, but the

imperator seemed thrilled and amazed by his pronouncement of the inscription.

"Come with me." Claudius led him through a maze of long hallways until he came to a velvet curtain against the wall. He smiled at Jachin and pulled the curtain aside to reveal an imposing marble statue. The figure was larger than life, nearly twice the height of a man. The sculpture portrayed a man sitting naked, except for a cloth over one arm, which draped over the figure's thigh. A sword held in his hand, and his foot treading on a helm. A Roman shield leaned against his muscular leg. His eyes were stern and full of wisdom. A laurel crown sat on his balding head.

"Gaius Julius Caesar." Claudius pointed to the sculpted marble sword held by the first Imperator across his knee. "The only statue of Caesar with a weapon. Fashioned as if he were Mars, the god of war. He was not fond of this look, so I've been told."

"Thus the curtain?"

Claudius stepped to the side. "Yes. Look closer, young warrior."

Jachin held his blade up next to the statue's magnificent blade. "Is it the same?" he asked.

"It is the same. You have in your hand the lost sword of Julius Caesar," Claudius said.

Jachin noticed the marble sheath carved in the stone. The same as the one his mother showed him back in Albion; the one that he dropped when he aimed for his father with the pugio. Jachin clenched his jaw.

"You hold the *Crocea Mors*. Fascinating. I must hear your story."

Taken to another room, women served wine and steaming meat with bread to a grateful Jachin. He told the imperator how he had come by the pugio. He left out some of the story, but told him about the barrow and the skeleton, and that his mother had the blade hidden in their stables. When finished, the imperator spoke.

"Your Batavii soldiers will be attached to the XIIII *Gemina*."

Jachin chuckled. "The twin unit?"

"You find that amusing?"

Jachin rose from the camp chair. "No, sir. It is amusing only to me."

"Sit down. We need your help, soldier. You hail from Britannia, correct?"

"Yes, sir."

"I need a guide. I need someone who can communicate and assist in planning strategy. Most of all, I need someone I can trust to be on the front lines. Can you do that?"

"Yes, and more. The auxiliaries, as you know, will be at your command. They are prepared to fight."

"Is it true that they can cross a river in full armor?"

Jachin nodded.

"Superb." Gaius clapped his hands. "I need you to lead a group of men to Albion."

Jachin started to push his hair back out of his eyes, then stopped, remembering it was cut short now. "Me? Lead a battalion? I don't know. I am not a leader."

"We meet to plan in three days. By the way, your name precedes you, my young man. The men you have allied with don't fear your blade, though they should."

"What do you mean?"

"They fear *you.*"

60
CHAPTER

Ligare

Brittle are the bonds of forgotten companions.

— Scribonius Largus

Jachin and Claudius talked until the purple dawn turned red then orange through the slotted windows. His new friend suddenly said he needed to leave, as if the sun's rays would burn his skin. They said their farewells and promised to meet in three days to plan the invasion.

Jachin felt pleased about the interaction and gladly said he would attend.

Needing to wash his face and wake for the day, Jachin made his way to the *triclinium*. Peering into the basin he saw the reflection of Boaz. He swatted the water aside, splashing it out of the fountain to the floor. Another look, and hatred filled his heart. He stared at his reflection until the room appeared to grow dark around him.

Toenin had once been the one to ridicule him. When Jachin was a captive on the ship, he suffered relentless derision and scorn. Two full years of men making fun of him. Incompetence filled his mind with his father's voice as Caradoc threw dirt clods at his head or spilled out a torrent of epithets and mockery. Now he constantly heard the derision in his ears, in his own voice now.

The trierarchus always said he couldn't trust a boy from Albion. Jachin had never been untrustworthy . . . just rambunctious. He seldom looked at life as an adventure anymore. It was more like a nightmare. He wished to rid himself of any target of ridicule. Anything others found different in another was a reason for jest. He couldn't even go to the bathhouse with his fellow soldiers for fear of teasing. *There's a new medicus attending the imperator. I wonder if he does circumcision reversals?*

Perhaps he would do that later in the day. He normally went to the baker to procure fresh bread for his comrades for the evening meal. The Batavii ate one meal a day. The baker made bread in the morning and again late in the afternoon. *I'll go get bread and then seek out the physician.*

The *Panis Perfugium* was not far and easy to find if you followed your nose.

There were tables set outside for patrons and an extensive counter covered with plates of dates, and sweetbreads for morning guests. The sign at the counter said, "*ad locum configere a refugium.*" Jachin translated: "In our place, take refuge." He liked that.

An older man wearing an odd hat sat at one of the tables, drinking a hot beverage and eating sweetbread and figs.

"*Salve,*" Jachin said to the baker behind the counter.

"*Salve. Perfugium et praesidium salutis,*" said the man. "You came early this day. Can I get you anything?"

"Fresh panis as usual, and," he looked to the man at the table, who had taken out a gameboard from his satchel, "I'll try whatever the old man is drinking."

"Ah, a new blend from *Aethiopia*. Don't think it will catch on. More bitter than full-strength *Vinum Operarium*. Your friend over there enjoys the taste, as he doesn't drink wine at all. Not even *posca*."

"I don't care much for the cheap Roman wine either, unless it is mixed with honey or gall, like the soldiers do when marching. Even then it is bitter."

The *panifex* poured Jachin a steamy cup of the dark aromatic liquid.

"And a slice of your course *emmer* bread with honey and a bite of cheese if you don't mind."

"Careful," said the man at the table, "Roman bread will wear down your teeth."

Jachin laughed. He liked the graininess of the Roman bread.

As the baker went to gather bread from the ovens, Jachin sat down at the second table, his back to the other customer. In the back of the shop, the rotary mill ground more grain. Jachin reached into a side pouch and pulled out salt to sprinkle on the bread.

As he ate, he heard the old man setting up the game board. It called to his competitive spirit. Perhaps this was a new victim to beat down in excruciating pain of loss to his proficiency as a player.

"Do you play?" the man asked in a harsh Greek accent.

Jachin turned to look at the man. The hat shaded the man's face—that is, all except a long dark beard flowing to his chest. Maybe he wasn't as old as he first thought. Dressed in a white toga with red *clavi* stripes down each side, he must be one of the *equites* or from the look of his hat, a land-owning farmer. He appeared harmless enough.

With his dish and cup in hand, Jachin moved to join him.

"Latrunculi?"

"*Iacto.*"

Toss off? Jachin had never heard it called that except by himself and ...

"Your move," the man said.

Jachin took a sip of the drink and made the first move.

The man positioned his stone with measured authority. His fingernails were well-manicured. Not the hands of an old man or a farmer. Maybe he had misjudged his opponent. He played as if he knew Jachin's next move. As if he read his mind.

Ligare

Jachin resolved to win this game quickly, get his bread, and head back to the Batavii camp and get some sleep. Jachin grew frustrated because this man played well. He moved his piece, placing it roughly on the board.

The man leaned back and crossed his arms. "I will not play with an angry man."

Jachin drew back his arm to clear the table of the stones. The man caught him by the wrist and held his arm. "Where did you get this blue marking on your arm?"

Snatching his arm away, Jachin abrupty stood. "None of your business, old man!"

The man stood to face Jachin. He pushed his hat back and smiled. "Other than a slightly crooked nose, your appearance hasn't changed much."

Not old as he first appeared. This person before him stood taller than Jachin by a finger's width.

"I also noticed you still prefer to wear green. Once more, you have forgotten your hat."

An insult? Jachin placed his hand on his pugio and prepared to fight.

"Put your blade away." The man laughed. "Always acting without thinking. Remember the time when that bull came after you in the pasture when you ended up on a road without your pants? And that girl who owed you your first kiss in the wheat field?"

"What?" How could this man know these things? "Did my contubernales put you up to this?"

"I thought you were dead. Why didn't you let me know?"

Jachin drew the pugio. "Look, I don't know who you are, and I don't like you making fun of me."

"Matrona's pugio!" the man said. "You still have it!" He reached into his satchel and pulled out something enfolded in a scarf. He held it out to Jachin.

Confused and curious, Jachin took the object, holding his pugio ready. The man before him seemed eager. His eyes twinkled.

"Open it."

Jachin placed the package on the table. He carefully unwrapped the scarf. "Where did you get this?"

"It was on the floor when I awoke so long ago."

The Golden Cord

"Awoke?"

"After our father beat me in the roundhouse."

"Wha—"

In the depths of the scarf was a scabbard—a pugio scabbard. Jachin lifted the case and sat down with a sigh. He smoothly sheathed the pugio into the scabbard.

"Look at me, brother."

With tears in his eyes, Jachin beheld the face that looked back at him from the water fountain. "Boaz?"

"Do you not know your own twin?" Boaz beamed.

Jachin leaped from his chair and embraced his brother. Finally, Jachin stepped back and hit his brother on the arm. "You were playing with me." He cocked his head and examined the man's face. "Your appearance *has* changed, *old man*," he said. "I can't believe it's really you!"

"I was real the last time I checked."

"What on earth are you doing here? What have you been doing?" The questions poured out faster than Boaz could answer them.

The next few hours they talked. Going back and forth. Reminiscing about their childhood and catching up on events in their lives. Not interrupting each other, as if their thoughts were interwoven. Their tales entwined and weaved a tapestry of story and adventure.

They laughed about the two-headed Bel-tene Beast and how they fooled everyone. They talked of unfinished debates and wrestling matches in the fields that would end with them giggling hysterically. They talked of hunting frogs with arrows and chasing cats. And of the sign people made against evil when they saw them together.

"They were jealous of our friendship," Jachin said.

"And of my good looks," Boaz added.

Jachin hadn't laughed that much in ages. He reminded Boaz of the game he stole and brought him when he was hurt.

"You mean this one?"

Jachin looked at the Latrunculi board. It *was* the same.

They would cheer each other up whenever times were tough and when their father was on a drunken rampage. They reminisced about the time when they stood up for each

Ligare

other in a fight or got beaten. They were always together. It was never "I did this." It was always "we."

Conversation moved to what they liked to eat. And who they used to hate. They talked about the wheat field, and Boaz told him that their hillfort home was no longer there due to the fire.

"That is sad," said Jachin.

"Life was so much simpler then."

"So you are a physician?"

Boaz nodded. "And you will lead the auxiliaries in the fight against our father?"

"That's what Claudius promised."

"When do you leave?"

"Soon."

"Are you married yet?"

Jachin put his shoulders back. "No."

"Well, here's something you don't know. I *am* married."

Jachin swallowed. "Married? You *have* changed!"

"She's very nice. Lais is from the Batavii in northern Gaul. You will like her."

"The Batavii? I'm a member of their unit!"

"That is how I learned you were in Rome. Lais and I visited the warriors yesterday. One of the men said I looked like one of their contubernalis. I thought that strange until he said your name. They told me you always come here in the mornings for fresh bread."

"Lais—beautiful name. Congratulations! Got a child on the way yet?"

"Uh . . ." Boaz blushed.

"Bread is ready!" the baker called several times.

"I forgot I ordered something!" Jachin laughed.

He waved the baker to bring it to him.

"I have made three batches of bread; you boys talk so much! Here, take it and go. I have customers waiting."

Boaz opened his coin purse. "Let me pay for that."

"No, I've got it. Besides, the Batavii pay me back. I always inflate the amount I paid when I tell them."

"Jachin . . ."

"What? I have to make a living too."

"What are you doing tomorrow?"

The Golden Cord

"No plans yet. Though I did talk to the baker about helping him in an important short-term employment opportunity. I have a meeting with the imperator in a couple of days. Other than that, I'm going to see the new physician this afternoon at the palace about a personal matter."

"Me too! Well, not a personal matter, but an appointment with Imperator Claudius. I'm his new physician," Boaz said.

"Uh . . ."

"Maybe we can get together later, and I can introduce you to Lais."

"Sounds terrific. Oh, the time. I have to take bread to the troop!"

"We will get together later."

"Where do I find you?"

"You just did."

"No, later today."

"Meet here at sunset. Bring Lais, and we can go get some dinner."

The baker offered Jachin the basket. "I put a few extra loaves in for a blessing. Watching you two reunite has brought me great joy."

He handed an envelope to Jachin who looked at it briefly then quickly placed it under his belt. "I've got a great idea for tomorrow. Let's go to the circus!"

The twins clasped hands, smiled, and then embraced. Jachin couldn't believe how this day had turned out. How could it possibly get any better than this?

CHAPTER 61

Ententainment

Friendship can be an unstable anchorage, but life's wind blows wildly on the sails of a rudderless vessel.

— Scribonius Largus

ROME—CIRCUS MAXIMUS

Early the next day, Jachin and Boaz entered the magnificent Circus Maximus. Men, women, and children by the thousands filed into the racetrack arena through the atrium. Some had begun before daylight and traveled far to arrive early enough to get seats. It was first come, first served. Women could sit with the men in this stadium, but with Jachin having only two tickets, Boaz had left his new wife at home. When Jachin voiced his apologies, Lais told him that she had herbs to plant anyway and didn't mind.

The Golden Cord

Dressed in his usual white tunic with red *cavea* and Jachin wearing a green plaid tunic with light brown *braccae*, the twins made their way past wine merchants under open arcades, pastry cooks, and a booth set up by the *Panis Perfugium Bakery*. Jachin and Boaz waved to the baker. Astrologers and prostitutes also practiced their trade in the numerous booths. It was like a small city had sprung up overnight.

"Where'd you get these tickets?" Boaz asked.

"From the baker."

The twins pushed through the crowd to find their seats.

"The racetrack is six hundred paces long, two hundred paces wide," Boaz read from a placard on one of the many gateways under the tiers of seats.

"This stadium holds two hundred fifty thousand spectators, but I think they could get more, if people stood instead of sat on benches."

"I, for one, am glad we have benches."

"Who's racing today?"

Boaz continued reading, "The *factio albata*, who are the whites, the green *factio prasina*, the blue *factio veneta*, and the red *factio russata*."

The drivers, called *aurigae* on the placard, were also named. Someone had written in charcoal something nasty about one of the drivers. Jachin laughed.

Positioned between the Palatine Hill on the north and the Aventine Hill on the south, the *Ludi Circenses* spread out in a depression of the *Vallis Murica*, giving it a natural incline for the seats in the stadium. Built during the reign of Augustus, the circus was the Roman version of the Greek *hippodrome* with a long, narrow U-shaped design, which was perfect for chariot races.

"Perfumes, perils, and prowess. Beauty of the stallions. Agility's perfection. Decorated toilets. I love this place!" Jachin said.

"Not a single surgeon to attend the crowd?"

"You're here Boaz. Who else do they need?"

"I'm here to watch the races, not patch up the reckless participants."

Many patrons sat on the free wooden seats as the pricey stone seats, called *cavea*, were reserved for dignitaries, sen-

Entertainment

ators, and those who could afford them. Jachin and Boaz sat on the cavea.

It was so much fun being with his brother again. It was as if a vital part had been restored.

Before them lay the elliptical racecourse. Marble statues lined the two ends of the colossal race path. Covered with a bed of sand, the track sparkled like wet grain in the sun.

Two gilded bronze posts stood tall at each end of the field where the charioteers would turn. "Do you think that the columns we were named after at Solomon's Temple look anything like that?" Jachin asked.

"I picture them to be much larger . . . like your ego, Jachin."

"Hey . . . for your information, those posts are called *metae*."

"How do you know that, soldier man?"

"I attended the races in Mongontiacum, doctor man. The westerly one where the horse stalls face is the *meta prima*. The westerly post facing the horse stalls is the meta prima." He pointed to the seven wooden dolphins.

"What are the dolphins for?"

"They are moved to indicate which lap the racers are on. That way they know how to pace themselves and when to pour on the speed to the finish."

"Nice. And those statues must be Hermes and Mars holding a golden cord between them." Boaz pointed to where a rope stretched between the statues of the god of speed and war.

In the distance, music could be heard as the parade began. First came the trumpets and the drums followed by the incense bearers. After that, the imperator arrived riding in a magnificent golden chariot pulled by two perfectly matched white horses with elaborate plumes of gold on their heads. Their manes were braided with many colored ribbons that flowed from them like rainbows in the breeze. Claudius, appearing like a living statue, wore a scarlet tunic and gold embroidered white toga that wrapped around him. He carried an ivory baton topped with a golden eagle in flight. On his head rested a wreath of golden leaves. Cheers greeted the imperator as he waved to the crowds.

The Golden Cord

Following the imperator, the aurigae with their two wheeled chariots entered to even louder cheers. Four magnificent horses, manes and tails knotted and decorated in the team colors, pulled each chariot. Snorting and stomping in the sand, the horses were eager to compete.

These four teams, owned by contractors, separated themselves as red, green, white and blue. A whip in hand, each aurigae wore a short tunic and a tight-fitting colored cap, corresponding to which *factio* they represented. They wore leather leggings, and the horse reins were bound around their body so that they would not lose them. In their belts were shiny daggers meant to sever those reins in case of an accident.

"Boaz, they will do seven laps around the end post. A heat is called a *missus*. There will be at least ten *missii* or more today."

"That seems like a lot! Do we have to watch them all in the sun?'

"Seven laps. Six Roman miles. It goes pretty fast."

With the parade concluded and the imperator seated, the aurigae took their places. Patrons waited for an official waving a white handkerchief to reach the middle of the track.

"What is that man doing?" asked Boaz.

"Just watch."

The official dropped the handkerchief, and the race commenced. Dust flew from horses' hooves and chariot wheels as the official barely got out of the way.

"They race straight toward the far post. Watch them turn, Boaz."

The racers hugged the post closely. They all tried to secure the inside of the turn.

"It's a wonder they don't topple over," Boaz said.

"The strength of the turn is on the two outside horses."

One trying to pass crashed into another chariot that turned too close and grazed the post. The chariot flipped, and the crowd exclaimed their joy. Men rushed out to carry off the fallen and remove the debris.

"The horses!" Jachin stood and hollered.

The horses, now free of their chariots, continued the

Entertainment

race. One *aurigae* could not cut the reins, which dragged him roughly behind the fleeing animals.

"Is this usual?" Boaz said.

"Oh yes, happens all the time. They will improve pace on the long tracks. It is my favorite part!"

"I would wager it's not the favorite part of the poor man being dragged behind the horses."

A lady behind them laughed.

"I didn't think it was *that* funny," said Jachin.

Boaz pulled on his sleeve. "Did you purchase any raffle tickets? They are going to give away a *domus*! Lais and I could really use a home like that. Much nicer than the *insulae* we are renting now."

"No, but I bet on Diacles of the green team. Better odds."

"Advice from the baker?"

"Maybe . . ."

After five races and six calamitous wrecks, one of which resulted in a wrestling match between the fallen, Jachin said, "I'm hungry."

They bought meat on a stick and a small loaf of bread, filled with sliced apples. The sixth race ended with a mix of applause for the winner and enthusiastic disdain for the same man. Going back to their seats they watched the seventh race. This is the one that Jachin was most concerned about as he had bet on one of the chariots. He was thrilled when his man rounded around the pole in the lead. An easy win.

"The green team won!"

"Let's fetch my winnings."

Jachin walked up to the window.

"*Felicter* Jachin, I happily wish you well," the man said as if they were old friends. "Will you bet on the *Luca bos* race?" He handed Jachin a *Quinarius Aureus*.

Jachin gave back the coin and said, "Put it all on the blue team in the *Luca bos* event."

"Jachin, that's worth twelve denarii."

Jachin grinned. "I know."

"They race *Lucanian* cattle?" Boaz asked.

"Yes, more commonly known as *elephantus*," Jachin said.

"I have never seen such an animal, but I have heard of them. We must watch that race, Jachin."

"Would you like to see one close up?"

⌘ ⌘ ⌘

While slaves cleared the course and raked the sand for the upcoming premier event, Jachin directed Boaz to the stables. In the interim, the *venator* performed tricks with animals. He placed his arm in a lion's mouth while a clown rode a camel. And at the last, he made an elephant walk a tightrope.

They passed chariots waiting repair and numerous horse stables until they finally came to an enormous malodorous room.

"Remember that time at the taberna when we rode Tahdah's chariot into the ditch?" Boaz said.

"Yes, it was all your fault."

"No, it wasn't. You were the one who was acting stupid, not me."

"Let me show you how a soldier man does it."

"You're not going to drive a chariot, are you?"

"Nope, we are riding an elephant!"

CHAPTER 62

Competition

*Brotherhood binds the brave
to conquer the impossible.*

— Scribonius Largus

"We?"

"Of course, brother. The two riders were badly injured two days ago when they were tossed from their beast in practice. I said we would take their place."

Boaz took a step back. "What?"

"How do you think I got the tickets?"

"I thought it was because you gave so much business to the baker."

"He's not *that* generous."

They approached four large gray beasts, and Jachin went over to where one stood with its trainer. Its head swayed, brandishing huge ivory tusks tipped with gilded iron. Large ears flapped as the trainer checked his straps. The tail snapped like a whip causing Boaz to duck. Decorated with huge tinkling bells around its massive neck and an iron plate on its forehead, the elephant's headdress included an extravagant plume of blue peacock feathers, which added to the effect of majesty. No other heavy armor encumbered the beast except iron spikes attached to leather straps on the animal's hips. On its back, a beautiful blue tapestry was fastened tightly with a plaited leather strap under the neck and behind its floppy ears, and another strap was placed under the small tail and up over its back. Below this saddle-like rug draped an enormous blue cloth draped over its massive sides. It hung almost to the ground. On this banner blazed a name written in large yellow letters above the baker's emblem.

"*Panis Perfugium*," Jachin read. "*Ad locum configere a refugium*. In our place, take refuge."

"Advertising on an elephant?" Boaz said. "That thing must be over twenty hands tall. Twenty paces long. Almost a ton in weight! How fast can something that big race?"

"Faster than you think."

"And we have to ride it in exchange for free tickets?"

"Exactly."

"You were going to tell me about this . . . when?"

"I'm telling you about it now."

"This has got to be the dumbest idea ever, Jachin. We could get killed!"

"Rarely happens with trained riders."

"Oh, that's reassuring . . ."

"Listen, if something happens to me, Boaz, and I die on the sand, will you fulfill my vow and kill Tahdah?"

"I will not kill or give poison to any man. I, too, have made a vow." He looked at the elephant's tusks. "Besides, nothing will happen. Together we are invincible."

"Only when on your shoulders, Boaz. Here, help me up."

Boaz bent down, and his brother climbed on his shoulders.

Jachin clambered on to the beast and reached his hand out to Boaz to pull him aboard.

"No way. I'm not getting up there."

"They're tame and gentle."

Competition

"They're big and smelly. And you said they almost killed the last riders."

"Come on, it's all part of the adventure."

Jachin grabbed his brother and yanked him on to the beast in front of him. "Put your legs on either side under the ears. Watch out for them, though. They are sensitive."

The elephant shook his head, and his large ears flapped. "Woo! Now you tell me!"

Jachin sat on the back of the elephant facing the tail with his back to his brother. He loosened the leather cords and wrapped them around his hand several times. The other riders climbed on to their mounts. The trainer gave Jachin a whip and handed Boaz a long stick with a curved point.

"What do I do with this?"

"It's to guide the beast—makes him turn. Just touch him on the side you want him to turn from."

"Tell me you have done this before."

"I've seen it done . . . does that count?"

"No."

"Ready?"

Boaz started to say "no" when the trainer nudged the elephant forward. All the beasts walked out to the field.

"Jachin, I believe these things were not built for speed or comfort."

"Just watch the others and do as they do, only faster. We need to win."

The animals swayed, waiting to begin. Trunks touched the ground. Drums and foreign dancers entertained an excited crowd while they waited. Stomping its foot, the red team's animal to their right raised its trunk and made an awful trumpeting sound in defiance. The twins' beast reared up in reply. Boaz held on with all his might.

"Hoo-ha!" Jachin called.

A squealing pig behind the elephants frightened the beasts, starting the race. Men chased behind the charging elephants yelling encouragement.

Terrified, Boaz held on as the beast trotted out on the track.

One elephant bumped into them right out of the gate

flinging Jachin off the elephant's backside. Flapping wildly, Jachin hung onto the strap. Pulling himself back aboard like he used to pull sailing rope, Jachin yelled, "Whew, it stinks at this end!"

The dancers still on the course scrambled out of the way, narrowly avoiding being trampled by the stampeding beasts.

The crowd cheered.

Lumbering, more than racing like the chariots, the animals headed down the stretch toward the first turn. The red rider used his reins and swung off the side of his beast to snatch an admirer's handkerchief from the ground. The crowd applauded and waved their red scarfs.

At the first turn it was red who had the favorable inside track. The blue team, with the twins, close behind. The other two held back as if the elephants resisted the lash.

After the turn, Jachin stood and used the whip, urging the elephant ahead.

The white team's elephant hesitated, then lay down in the middle of the track, almost crushing the riders.

With the Baker's banner flapping wildly, Boaz nudged the beast alongside the red team's racer as they came to the *meta prima*. Bumping against them, the red beast's iron spike cut into their elephant's flank. Trumpeting loudly, the elephant swung his tusks and bumped the brut.

The twins raced ahead.

Tapping the elephant with his stick to keep it moving, Boaz called out, "He didn't like that at all! He wants to get away from the pain."

"Let's use that then," Jachin shouted. Standing firmly, Jachin whipped the animal on the gashed flank. The elephant roared and sped faster.

Rounding the first lap assuredly ahead of the others, Boaz used his stick to dodge the elephant on the ground.

"Look out!" Jachin hollered to the green team. Veering sharply to avoid the resting elephant, the green team crashed into the iron bars around the arena erected to protect spectators. Men and women scrambled. The fence buckled under the elephant's impact. Several spectators were speared by tusks before the driver could turn the rat-

Competition

tled beast back to the field. The audience reveled in the turn of events while others moved to help the injured.

The elephants turned the post flanking each other. Jachin and Boaz had the inside track. Another sprint down the straightaway, followed close by the red. The teams dashed to the finish at the *meta prima*. This two-lap race was enough for Boaz. He kicked the elephant and urged it to move faster while Jachin, sitting now, whipped the elephant's backside.

A man with a bag full of chalk rushed down to the *meta prima* and drew a line across the track signifying the finish line.

The red team gained ground, while the twin's elephant seemed exhausted. The two teams were now tusk to tusk. If nothing changed, the red team would pass them and win. Boaz looked at Jachin who pointed to his ear and showed his teeth. Boaz shrugged. Jachin did it again. Ear and teeth.

Boaz leaned forward just as the red team started pulling ahead and bit down hard on the elephant's ear. The beast shrieked and butted his head into the red team's elephant, stabbing it in the side with his mighty tusk.

Their beast abruptly stopped. The riders on the red team's elephant flew off their seats. The foremost rider scrambled to roll out of the way, but the beast reared his tree-sized legs and trampled the man. The maddened monster stood in front of him trumpeting and stomping its feet.

Boaz and Jachin dashed across the finish line.

They were rushed by a crowd of spectators who pulled them down and carried them to the stand where the imperator applauded excitedly. Claudius gave each a wreath of leaves to put on their heads, while others wrapped a fine robe on their shoulders and gave each of them a gold figurine in the shape of an elephant.

Jachin danced around. "I won big on that bet!"

Boaz stood with a concerned look on his face. He shoved the trophy into Jachin's hand and shrugged off the robe. He ran to the injured man from the red team who had almost defeated them.

Jachin didn't know what got in to his brother, but he followed.

"Let me die," the man said to Boaz.

Boaz examined the man's injuries. "I can fix you; I am a surgeon," he said.

"I am dying. Kill me."

"He's been disgraced, Boaz."

"By his injuries?"

"No, by losing."

"He didn't fail."

"Boaz, can't you see? He begs to die with honor," Jachin said.

The man looked at the twins. "A soldier and a surgeon?" the man said. He sat up and coughed up blood. "One heals. The other hurts. Seems like you cancel each other out." He turned to Jachin. "Kill me, Contuberinis."

Jachin moved behind the dying man and placed one hand under his chin and the other on his head.

"Please."

Jachin twisted the man's head with a jerk.

The man's neck snapped.

CHAPTER 63

Preparation

*Does uncertainty surround the brave
when adventure leads the way
and ambitions guide your plans?*

— Scribonius Largus

Rome—Imperator's Palace

The planning committee met that next afternoon. Boaz whistled as he strolled to the palace. Everything seemed to be going his way. Not only was he the imperator's head physician, with a salary he never dreamed he would make, but he also married the love of his life, who supported him in ways he never thought possible. She waited happily for him at home.

Their comfortable insulae included space in the back with plenty of sunshine for her garden. Too bad he didn't

The Golden Cord

win the raffle for the domus. Lais would have made the place a happy home. She planned on growing and selling cut flowers. Most of all, Boaz was grateful for the return of Jachin. However, he admitted to himself that seeing his brother take a life nagged at the depths of his soul.

The imperator's palace, located on the Palatine Hill, looked out on a stunning view of the sprawling city of Rome.

Men escorted Boaz to a patio in the center of the garden. A massive marble table, replete with maps and replicas of Roman Quintremes arranged like a game about to be played, were the center of attention.

Around the table stood men he knew—the other players in this game. Drinks in hand. A table of fruit and cakes off to the side.

He met Verica once as a child. The derogatory things his father said about the man's mother was all Boaz knew about him. He was a chieftain in Albion once. Next to him stood Toenin. That was a shock to Boaz. He wondered what in the world his childhood friend was doing there. He looked healthy but hadn't grown any taller than the last time he saw him. He hadn't grown any hair on top of his head either. He was bald!

The trierarch, Caelus, dressed in finest breastplate and helmet, didn't surprise him as the former captain of the *Morta Columbarium* had been promoted to commander of the Roman navy due to his extensive experience sailing and fighting pirates. Jachin confided that he was not at all pleased with the appointment, but he understood its merit. Next to him stood General Aulus Plautius, the *Consul Militaris*. His arms were crossed as he studied the table. And there was another man he had seen around, named Narcissus.

Callistus waved to him from across the room. He insisted that Boaz attend. His friend and fellow physician had the nerve to bring his dog with him. A miniature mixed breed that barked way too much. Other than to see to the medical needs of Claudius, Boaz was uncertain why he was called to this meeting. Nonetheless, a chance to be with his brother was all that mattered.

Everyone stood at attention as Claudius, his guards,

Preparation

and servants all entered the room. Jachin entered with the imperator, dressed in his best military garb.

Claudius motioned to begin, and the players stepped up to the board.

"The potential risks involved in taking and holding Britannia are considerable," Narcissus read from a prepared script. A freed slave, he often accompanied Claudius interpreting for the imperator when he had difficulty being understood because of his speech—which was all the time. Narcissus was like a doting mother who explained to others what her babbling child said.

"We will have to establish a significant presence along a new boundary of the Roman Empire in Britannia. In the event we succeed, this could prove a major source of trouble for years to come," Narcissus said.

"It'd be easier to get tribute money from them," Claudius added in his dissonant speech.

Verica stepped forward and pounded his fist on the map. "Caradoc stopped sending tribute! I doubt he would ever agree to renew a bond with Rome. What you call Britannia is increasingly unstable. The clan relationships are falling apart. Caradoc destroys everything."

"We need grain from Britannia for the legions stationed north of the Rhenus. The only way we're going to get that is not through tribute money, but through control of the sources of supply. My men cannot eat money," Aulus Plautius said.

Verica continued, "My lands have been pro-Roman for years. We have traded with Rome without hindrance until recently. Caradoc controls those resources, now."

"Berika." The Romans could not pronounce the letter *V*. "We're talking about at least thirty thousand men who will need to be fed during the campaign. Can you guarantee not only a steady supply of grain, but a safe passage for Claudius?" Aulus said.

"And the elephants," said Claudius, dabbing slobber from a huge grin.

"No ship with a single fore and aft sail can have accurate directional stability on all points sailing this sea. We would have limits of wind resistance. We would have to sail close

The Golden Cord

to the wind, which is harsh on both my ships and my sailors. I believe going south to Berika's land presents a very low chance of success," Caelus said.

"All we need is a favorable wind," Jachin said. "If the fleet departed when the tidal stream still flowed southeast, the wind would become favorable at about three in the morning. If we use leather sail material, our ships could withstand the weight of the harsh weather conditions."

"We use hides for tents, not for sails. They are too heavy," Caelus said.

"You and I have both seen sails ripped in the wind, Caelus. Hear me out. The total distance covered by the fleet must be made in two stretches, leaving two hours before the high-water tide streams in. Winds normally run between North and Northeast at that time. They would carry the fleet toward, rather than away from, Albion's coast. Six hours later or at four hours after high water, the tides begin to run favorably again. After only a total elapsed time of ten hours, the faster fleet would arrive at an agreeable position just as the tide turns foul." Jachin moved the ships on the map to show the others his approach. "We need two and a half days from boarding to landing. Any slower and the changing tides will weaken, if not totally defeat our plan," Jachin said.

"Agreed. If we delay for any reason, we could find the tide against us," Trierarch Caelus said. "My old navigator is trustworthy in his assessment; however, a beam wind from the south would be downright dangerous."

"We may have to allow considerably more time," Claudius said.

"Caelus and I have sailed it before. I am confident of the timing," Jachin said.

"Greater caution should be shown when the Army takes to the sea for battle. And keep in mind, these are not simple Pirates we will fight against, but hardened warriors," Aulus said.

Boaz spoke up. "We can't chance rough seas and sick soldiers."

"I am glad you are on board with us, Theophilus," Claudius said.

Preparation

"We should wait until the spring equinox is past and then make our way up to the east coast of the Cantii and create a landing spot for Claudius. A fortified beachhead through which necessary supplies would be transferred, could be prepared quickly," Aulus said.

"You may encounter resistance that far north," said Verica.

"There is a sufficient place there for waging war," Aulus said.

"The area east is sufficient for fighting; however, Caradoc will be there waiting. In the South, there is shelter available in the harbor," Jachin said. "We have established friendships there."

"It depends largely on the friendly cooperation of the local tribes from the coast all the way to the Tamesa River," Verica said. "I can guarantee the Atrebates will align with us."

Aulus paced. "If we go first to Rutupiae on the east coast, we could go ahead of the legions and fortify the beachhead immediately."

"It would depend on the security or friendliness of the local tribes, as Berika has stated," Claudius said.

"The Catuvellauni are aligned with Caradoc," Verica interrupted.

Claudius gave him a stern look and turned to Aulus. "What if we meet with stubborn resistance on the eastern coast? Is it not plausible to land in the south first and make our way to Rutipiae in the east to prepare for my landing?"

"The layout of the land and the disposition of the enemy is important. The distances between places. The quality of the roads, any shortcuts, any mountains, any rivers," Aulus said.

"Most importantly, Sallustius," Caelus looked to Jachin, "we need to have a sailor pilot who has knowledge of the area and sailing experience in the harbor. He'd have to be familiar with where we're going to disembark."

"Who's Sallistus?" Boaz asked.

"That would be me," Jachin said. "I've spent two years navigating that area. I know the tides, the winds, the harbor. Verica knows the roads to the Tamesa."

"I understand that Theophilus knows the area as well," Claudius said.

"Who's Theophilus?" Jachin asked.

"That would be me," said Boaz.

"How can we know that our informants and sources are reliable?" Aulus said.

"Verica knows the latest political situation. And his shadow, Toenin, is a spy for Caradoc," Jachin said.

Toenin had been focused on eating cakes but lifted his head when Jachin said "shadow." When he said "spy"—Toenin choked.

"Is this true, Toenin?" Claudius asked.

"Only on the surface, Your Majesty. I work for you alone and feed the enemy false tales to enable me to get the information you need," Toenin said.

It was grand seeing Toenin again. He was just a diminutive man trying to be big and yet, underneath, Boaz knew he had a goodness about him. Boaz believed him.

"We must treat this information with caution. For all we know, Caracticus is feeding you misinformation," Claudius said.

Verica pointed along one of the maps. "Yes, I know well the cross-country routes from the harbor to the Tamesa."

"Splendid," said Claudius. "And Theophilus has walked the hillsides gathering herbs for his teacher."

"One more thing," Aulus said. "We need an adequate supply of grain, fodder, and other provisions. We need more than what can be smuggled. Our supply will not last. We will need places to forage."

It is a fine commander who is always mindful of the troop's needs, thought Boaz. He hoped they would be as mindful of the men's health as well.

"The road will be paved before you with kindness," Verica said.

"Then it is a go," Claudius said. "Two landing parties in the south will make their way on land to Rutupiae and set up a beachhead for the third wave, which I will command. Callistus will attend me. Since Theophilus knows the area, he will be with Sallustius and his troops."

He was glad Claudius enlisted their advice, but Boaz

Preparation

was uncertain of this whole adventure and his role in it. The twins played in the fields many times when young. They knew their way around Caradoc and how to hide from him. The princes where headed home, but not in the manner Boaz had hoped. This was Jachin's long-aimed blow—not his.

"We are destined to overcome Caradoc. Together, Jachin and I will do our best to be of service to you," Boaz said.

"Then it is settled. I accept this plan. Sallustius, bring *Crocea Mors* for luck," Claudius said.

At that moment a guard, followed by Lais, entered the room. She trotted up to Boaz and put her arm in his.

The soldier handed Claudius a roll of parchment. "From Caracticus," he announced.

Claudius took the parchment from the messenger and, after reading, handed it to Narcissus to read aloud.

"This is addressed to the imperator. '*You, why are you so afraid of war and slaughter? Even if all the rest drop and die around you, grappling for the ships, you'd run no risk of death: you lack the heart to last it out in combat—coward!*'"

"It is a challenge," Toenin said.

"That is a quote from the *Iliad*," Boaz said. "I know it well."

"Excellent! I will accept his challenge. Odysseus's homeward trip will inspire us as we journey together to Britannia," Claudius said.

The men around the table cheered.

Boaz drew his arm around Lais. "I thought you were at home."

Lais leaned close and whispered to him, "I was, but I wanted to be with you."

"That's nice, but . . ."

She held his chin with both hands and looked into his eyes. "Boaz, I am with child."

Boaz looked at her dumbfounded. When it finally sunk in, a tear fell from his eyes. He embraced his wife, pulling her deeply into his gladdened heart.

"Wait, there is more in the note. He has taken a hostage. Someone named Raena? He says: '*Come and get her, Jachin ap Caradoc!*'"

CHAPTER 64

Contentment

*How quickly we sever the golden cord,
when anger masters our lives.*

— Scribonius Largus

Jachin wasn't certain another chance to invade his homeland wouldn't be just like the last time on that dreaded beach with Gaius. A total fiasco and charade. But, after months of fighting someone else's battles, he would grasp any foothold to climb the cliff of revenge. The letter from his father did more than anger him. The challenge gave him resolve. Yes—he would come. He would come to set things right.

That evening the imperator allowed Jachin to bathe in his heated hypocaust pool and gave him a *cubiculum* for his stay in the palace for the night.

Contentment

Relaxed after his long soak in the pools, Jachin followed a male attendant past a living tree that grew from a perforation in the highly polished tile floor. The green foliage exited through the ceiling's aperture. The servant showed him to a lush garden, complete with fountains of scented water, and then he left Jachin alone.

The cubiculum was big enough to house a herd of elephants. Painted murals of daily Roman life covered the walls. The marbled mosaic floor composed of a multitude of small black, white, and colored squares, sparkled in the light of scores of wax *candelae* on the raised metal candelabras. The *opus tessellatum* appeared fashioned as fresh cobblestone paths weaving their way through the city, decorated with scenes of joyful children playing. Stationed about the room stood busts of honored men along with large vases of flowers and green plants with elephant-ear-sized leaves. At the end of the room underneath a blue lace-curtained window, much like a waterfall, sat an inviting double-armed settee bed with a gray pillowed divan. A flowing water fountain containing lilac petals added to the effect and soothed the senses.

Jachin descended into the yielding pillows of the bed, allowing the cool breeze that swept through the light curtains to revive his tired body. In the quiet, he thought about adventures he'd have down the road to Albion. The prospects and opportunities he faced encouraged him. He and Boaz were together again. It seemed only yesterday that he said he would kill his father, and now the whole Roman army was with him. Not only that, he had received an imperial command and would lead the Batavii auxiliaries. This time it could happen. Would happen. Jachin envisioned the final blow. He smiled.

Claudius seemed wiser than Gaius. Not so scatterbrained, going from one thing to another, but more directed and focused. Much more practical than his predecessor, even if his arm movements were like a storm with sudden bursts of lighting and wind, his speech coming in squalls. It seemed so strange for such a learned man to speak with such difficulty.

Jachin lay his head on the feathered pillow. "This imperator really knows how to treat a guest," he sighed. *Fortunus* smiled on him. He marveled at his luck. He was privileged to sleep in the palace while his contubernales slept in smelly barracks on the outskirts of the city.

Tucking his pugio under the pillow, he drifted into a deep sleep.

Outside a raven called.

Jachin woke and looked around the room. The moon shone through the fluttering curtains, creating shadows on the floor. The unmovable statues stood guard over his bedchamber. Nothing but the cool breeze coming through the window. He felt no alarm. Comforted, he eased under the covers and promptly fell back asleep.

Cold steel lifted his chin.

His eyes opened. A shadow stood above him.

"Don't move."

The assassin's breathing fluttered. *He's uncertain,* Jachin thought. His hand inched toward the blade under his pillow, careful not to reveal his movement.

The hooded man slammed his knee into Jachin's chest. The knife bit harder into his throat.

"Don't go there, my friend," the voice warned. He reached under the pillow and took out the pugio. "Hmm, a pig-sticker. Must be worth a lot." The assassin flung the pugio across the room and pressed his own blade tighter against Jachin's windpipe until a tiny trickle of blood formed.

Jachin smiled as though he was about to laugh. "What're you waiting for? Do it!"

The End of Book Two